ABOUT THE AL

The author was born in Cambridge in Anns area of Nottingham until he was then moved to the Clifton Estate wher ...ʊɪ was a pupil at Whitegate Junior School before he graduated to Fairham Comprehensive School in 1960. He left school in 1965 with no qualifications whatsoever and a damning report as to his chances of a successful career in any walk of life in the future. He worked in the construction industry as a heating pipefitter and plumber before retiring in 2013 He is a first time author with no previous experience in writing anything apart from the occasional betting slip. The enforced solitude of Covid 19 gave him the opportunity of his first attempt at writing a novel with this subsequent conclusion. He would dearly like to thank Marilyn for the countless cups of tea and coffee and the occasional biscuit that she provided for him during the many long hours of isolation he suffered struggling for renewed inspiration to continue to finish this novel. He is very gratified in the knowledge that this novel will undoubtably be a best seller within his own household.

i

Dedications.

My very patient wife Marilyn.

My wonderful sons Daniel and David.

My gorgeous daughter's in law Lindsay and Marie-Anthea.

My beautiful grandchildren Emilia, Harriet, and James.

Pipefitters and Plumbers of the World.

Landlords and bar staff everywhere.

Roberto Duran

A P McCoy

Acknowledgements.

Mr David Waddington for his very patient and much valued assistance in proof-reading.

Mr Anthony Ginn for his considerable help and advice.

Mrs Marilyn Hardy

Mr Daniel Hardy

Mr David Hardy

CHAPTERS

OPPORTUNITY

"Well, that's the easy bit, now comes the hard part," Duncan thought as he finished the letter. It had confirmed he had been successful in his application for the post of Senior Production Manager at a new faculty in a large pharmaceutical company in Nottingham, and could he confirm acceptance of the post by Monday 10th June? The salary on offer was £12.5k per annum, which in 1985 was well above average and almost double the wage he was currently earning. Yet how would the rest of the family feel about moving three hundred miles to Nottingham? Convincing his wife was going to be extremely hard, he knew that for certain. It was Tuesday evening, and Elizabeth would be home soon from the golf club so he would find out one way or another. Both their children were out.

When Elizabeth arrived home, he inquired, "How did the golf go today, Lizzie?" There was silence, and the sadness etched on her face told him more than mere words could say. "Is everything okay? Whatever's the matter?"

Elizabeth sat down and sighed heavily, as if to collect her composure before speaking. "It's Maggie," she replied. "She was taken ill and collapsed as we came off the last green. She was rushed into hospital. It's so unfair. Maggie is the last person on Earth who deserves that, especially with everything else she has gone through already. I'm so sorry for her."

Elizabeth had tears tumbling down her cheeks. She had always said that Maggie was a real comedienne; she had a string of anecdotes and jokes, and a rapier wit. Occasionally, she would make the air turn blue with her earthy language and she could make fun out of the most mundane of happenings. Elizabeth had a strong friendship with all her golfing partners, especially her very best friend Sylvia. Duncan knew instinctively that tonight was not the time to have a discussion about leaving Kirkcaldy and the job offer, it would have to wait.

The following morning, Duncan arrived at work and his mind was certainly not on his job. He spent the entire day planning what he would say to Elizabeth to convince her that a move would benefit the whole family. The order of service was rehearsed over and over in his head until he felt that he had conquered all the angles and pitfalls.

When he arrived home, he was quietly confident that he could easily respond to any questions that would be thrown at him and convince his wife to agree to the move. As he entered the kitchen to say hello to Elizabeth, he was pleasantly surprised by the aroma of a cooked dinner, unusual in such hot weather.

"Hello Duncan," she said, "You've just got time to go up for a quick shower. I've made a shepherd's pie and it will be ready in fifteen minutes. After you've had your dinner, let's go for a walk along the waterfront and go down to Williamson's Quay. I've got some fantastic news to tell you."

Duncan went for a shower quite relieved to see that Elizabeth appeared to be over the subdued melancholy of the previous night. He came bounding back downstairs ready for his dinner. Shepherd's pie was his favourite. As she served the meal, a pensive Duncan wondered what the fuss was about, as he had hoped that he would have the opportunity to discuss his job offer.

"Surely, she is not pregnant again," he thought, his mind racing overtime.

After Duncan had wolfed down his dinner, they set off for the waterfront. Elizabeth could hardly contain herself, and she started to tell Duncan her exciting news as they were closing the front door. "We've received a letter today from Mr Quigley of the Scotland Swimming Association. He is one of the coaches. They asked us to ring their office between 9.00 am and 5.00 pm, so I rang them this morning because I knew you would not be home in time. Mr Quigley said that Alexander has enormous potential to make an international swimmer. Apparently, about two weeks ago he raced in Edinburgh at the Royal Commonwealth Pool in a school county regatta between Fife and Lothian. We know that he represented Fife, and that he won easily, because he told us that when he came home. What he did not say (or maybe he didn't even know) was that he smashed the Scottish Junior record time for the one hundred metres freestyle."

"He then said that Alexander is doing the old-fashioned touch turn at halfway which is far too slow, and he needs to learn the modern way, something called a tumble turn. He said that if he learns how to do that it will make him much faster and then he could be one of the fastest swimmers in his distance in the whole of Scotland. The coaches want to ask him to attend training every two weeks in Edinburgh. They have not spoken to Alexander about any of this yet as they are aware of his age and school commitments, so they wanted to speak to us first."

"Mr Quigley also said that potentially there's no reason why Alexander shouldn't definitely make the Scottish team at next year's Commonwealth Games that are in Edinburgh. The Games are only about thirteen months away from now, but they reckon that he has the potential to get even faster as he continues growing, and with some fine tuning of his technique and the tumble turn, he could even make the British team for the Seoul Olympic Games in 1988. That's only three years away."

"Mr Quigley has asked that you speak to him tomorrow, Duncan, before we both speak to Alexander. He said that we would both have to commit parental support to his training schedule to assist with travelling to Edinburgh and back because of his age. Obviously, his school has been organising travel to the Junior regattas, but this special training will be at weekends, so it doesn't interfere with his schoolwork. Oh, I'm so proud of him, what do you think Duncan?"

"That's fantastic. I knew Alexander was good, but I didn't realize he was that good. To represent Scotland at any age would be great, but by next year's Commonwealth Games he will only be sixteen. I will ring Mr Quigley tomorrow from work during my lunch break and ask for a bit more information about the training. Lizzie, I'm absolutely delighted, but this has come as a bit of a shock, and we need a bit more information to see how things are going to affect us all. Obviously, we will do everything we can to help Alexander, but we must take into consideration his education as he has very important exams coming up in the next year. We need to know how long this training malarkey will take and how many weeks, or even months, that it's likely to go on. But one thing is for sure, we'll do our level best to help him."

They were approaching Williamson's Quay, and, as it was still quite early in the evening, they sat for a while watching the boats mooring for the night and the gulls hovering to see if there were any scraps or spoils to scavenge. They could also see the ruins of

Ravenscraig Castle where memories of the many idyllic family days on the beach in the castle's shadow were captured in photographs, safely stored behind cellophane in photo albums. The shrieking noise of the seagulls was at fever pitch and the jukebox in the bar across the road from the Quay added to the noise as it was playing a song by Frankie Goes to Hollywood.

Duncan said, "Look, there's a table, let's have a drink."

Duncan sat at the table while Elizabeth went to the bar, and his thoughts turned to the letter and the employment that was on offer. It was too late now for a conversation about selling up and moving to Nottingham, as the news about Alexander and the possibility of his representing Scotland had taken over the whole evening and he didn't want to dampen the mood. Tomorrow would have to do.

They arrived home just as Beatrice Cormack arrived to collect Charlotte's friends Kerry and Rebecca. The girls had originally told their parents that they would meet up on weekday evenings to help each other with their homework and take turns in hosting. The reality was that they gathered to play their favourite music and talk about which boys they fancied at school. The homework was only a minor consideration. Their parents were aware of proceedings but were happy enough that their children were not out on the streets.

That night Duncan slept like a log and the following morning he awoke feeling as happy as at any other time in his life.

As Duncan was driving to work, he was reminiscing about his life to date. He couldn't remember his real birth parents; he had been fostered by a wonderful couple in Dysart, and he had a very happy childhood. He called Jack and Alice McKinlay "mam" and "dad" like all the other children, and didn't know he was fostered until he was almost eight years old. He never did find out what happened to his real parents other than they died in an accident, although the actual truth would have been hard for him to bear. When he was fifteen months old, his mother was strangled by his father after he caught her in bed with another man. His father took the baby to his own mother's house in Falkirk and left him there to go on the run. He was eventually arrested, tried and hanged for murder. The widowed grandmother had his surname changed to Baker, which was her married name. Thus, he became Duncan Stanley Baker. She put him into care when he was barely three years old as she left for a new life in Northern Ireland with a welder from Belfast.

Duncan was upset when he first knew that his real parents were deceased, but he could not have had better parents than Jack and Alice. They taught him right from wrong, and Jack always instilled in him that if you have a problem of your own making, then face it head on and don't try to avoid it, as it will only make things worse. Alice always made sure he was well dressed, and he fondly remembered the great meals she would serve.

He prospered at school and secured a place at St Andrews University where he studied medicine. It was there he met Elizabeth. He fondly remembered seeing her for the first time on the university campus. She had long black hair and she was wearing a mini skirt that revealed her long beautiful legs. He could recollect being stood frozen like a statue, watching her walking towards the library, and feeling an incredible urge just to be with her. He was overjoyed when she agreed to go on a date with him, and they soon became besotted with each other eventually deciding to get married in May 1966. They had enjoyed nineteen years of marital harmony and they had two children born fourteen months apart. Alexander was the eldest, although they often called him "Sandy". He was at a critical time in his education with important exams due the following year. He had just turned fifteen in April and was incredibly happy and content at home with a highly active sporting and social life.

Charlotte, whom they called "Lottie," was almost fourteen and growing up rapidly. She had recently become a vegetarian, and she was hoping to become a veterinary surgeon eventually.

Duncan dropped out of university temporarily, after completing his second year, to acquire work so they could afford to rent a flat. After Elizabeth attained her degree, they moved to Kirkcaldy where they had lived happily for nineteen years. He completed his degree at night school while playing football as a part-time professional for Raith Rovers.

Suddenly, he was alarmed as he heard a low grinding noise coming from beneath the car. He was on the bridge going over the River Forth heading towards Queensferry when he realized the handling of the car had suddenly become very awkward, and the grinding noise was getting considerably worse. He slowly crawled on to the edge of Craigcrook on the outskirts of Edinburgh where a loud metallic clunk from beneath the car brought him to a complete standstill. He trudged down the road towards Edinburgh cursing the fact that against all advice he had bought the wretched Morris Marina.

After he stumbled across a garage, he explained to the owner what had happened and was told, "It sounds bad, I'm afraid it looks like trouble. We'll have to get it towed in and get it up on the ramp for inspection. It'll cost twenty-five pounds for the pickup and tow in and then there'll be a labour cost on top for the inspection. Here's a card with the garage phone number on. Ring me back this afternoon and hopefully I'll have done an inspection by then."

"Well, I'll be grateful if you can get it shifted as soon as possible as it's parked on double yellow lines. I've left a note on the windscreen saying it's broken down. By the way, the MOT is due in a few weeks, so while you have the car here under inspection can you give it a once-over and see if anything needs doing. It makes sense to get it done at the same time?"

"Sir, if we have to get parts in from the main distributors, we may not be able to start work until next week, but I'll certainly have some answers for you and if there's not much wrong with it, hopefully, I can give you an acceptable quotation."

Duncan completed his journey by bus and arrived at work an hour late. As he was clocking in, he met his good friend Robbo, one of the loading bay labourers. "Hi, Duncan, you need to watch your back this morning. Creeping Jesus is on the warpath. He ripped me a new arsehole this morning and I was only five minutes late. You've only just turned up, he'll go ballistic. I would keep out his way if I were you," warned Robbo.

"Hi, Robbo. Why do you lads all call him Creeping Jesus? I've often wondered where that came from." Duncan inquired.

"It was way back about twenty years ago when he used to come to work every morning wearing his sandals before changing into his work shoes. He's always had that shoulder length hair with his curly locks, and he looks like a throwback to the sixties. It's as though he's stuck in a time warp. One of the lads reckons he looks like a refugee

6

from Woodstock. Mind you, some of the lads and the girls on the assembly line call him Buffalo Breath."

"What do they call me then, Robbo? I suppose that with me being his assistant, there's some very unflattering nicknames directed at me," asked Duncan.

"No, I've never heard any of the lads slagging you off. In fact, you're very popular especially with the girls in the admin and wages department, and the girls on the assembly line. They all call you "Dunk the Hunk", so you ought to be chuffed about that."

Duncan was pleasantly surprised at hearing his nickname with the ladies. However, he still had to face up to his boss, so he reluctantly decided to look for him and get it over and done with. When he was a young lad, his former foster parent Jack McKinlay drummed into him time and again that he should never run away from a problem of his own making. With the distant words of wisdom prominent in his thoughts, he set off to find his boss.

Bernard Savage was an uncouth brute. He was a devoted company man, and although he wasn't the brightest of employees, he was hard working, punctual, ambitious and, according to the writing on the gent's toilet wall in the production area, he was blessed with an extremely brown nose. His parental heritage was dubious and in serious doubt too.

Quite by accident the two almost collided in a doorway leading through to the offices, and Bernard, who was suddenly taken aback, barked out harshly, *"Baker! My office. Now!"*

One minute later, the two men were facing each other across the desk in Bernard's office. Duncan was standing while Bernard was sitting in his leather swivel chair.

"Well, Baker. I suppose you've got a reason for traipsing in at whatever time you like. Most of us manage to get here on time by 8.30, what's your excuse?"

"Well, for a start, Mr Savage. I never call anyone by just their surname. You are out of order shouting "Baker" like that and belittling me in front of the staff. Anyway, if you are remotely interested, my car has broken down outside Edinburgh. I had to walk a long way to a garage to find someone to tow it in, *and* it's on double yellow lines. I've got to call the garage this afternoon to find out the damage."

"I don't give a shit if your offended by how I speak to you. You're all the same the lot of you. There's three of you come in late today and not one of you showing any remorse. I've been running round like a blue-arsed fly wondering where you are and covering your back for you. I'd have thought that the last person to come in late would be my understudy. I mean, what will the staff be doing when I'm on my holidays and you're in charge, when they all know full well you don't give a shit what time you arrive? It's not good enough. I'm telling you now, if you can't get here on time, you'd better start looking for another job. Shut the door on the way out."

"That's not fair, Mr Savage, I've been here over ten years, and I can only remember being late twice before today. On both those occasions there had been an accident on the A90, and the traffic was horrendous getting into Edinburgh. As you know, I'm usually here early about 8.15 as and when you arrive."

"I said shut the door on your way out. One more word and it's going on your record." Said a raging Bernard.

"You can put it on my record, or you can shove it up your arse." Scoffed a belligerent Duncan.

Bernard Savage rose from his chair incandescent with rage. A stream of uncouth expletives and spittle came pouring from his mouth, and he was shaking violently. His shoulder length hair was unkempt, and his curly locks were dancing a lively fandango over his shoulders. He came round the desk to come face-to-face with Duncan and his eyes were glazed. Duncan immediately knew it was time to back off and leave the office hastily or there would be no chance of making up or redress. Anyway, Bernard's halitosis was particularly bad that morning, and as Duncan left the office, he was more than relieved the confrontation didn't get any closer. He was certainly ecstatic at not having to smell his awful breath anymore.

An hour later, a notably becalmed Bernard approached Duncan carrying a pile of invoices and delivery notes. "Mr Baker, I want you to check these delivery notes that all the materials are accounted for, and the invoices can then be paid. Could you sign them off, then take them down to the accounts office please?"

"Yes, Mr Savage, I'll do them right away;" Said Duncan, both relieved and pleased that normality and manners had now been restored. With so much on his mind, and worrying about his car, his thoughts were anywhere bar the task in hand.

At the dinner break, his thoughts turned to the phone calls he had planned to make. First, he rang the swimming coach Mr Quigley. It appeared that Elizabeth had acquired most of the information in her previous phone call, but several important factors were not discussed or confirmed. The pool was hired every two weeks for eight months. Nothing had been totally finalised, but it was thought that the sessions would start about ten o' clock in the morning and go on until mid-afternoon. They also had to consider that several of the coaching staff were volunteers and as such were giving their time freely, so they had to be taken into consideration. They were due to have a final meeting on Friday to finalize the schedule and would send out the details and the programme by post a few days later. However, with Alexander being the only swimmer still at school, they needed parental approval before approaching him, and a promise of parental support especially with travelling. He was adamant that Alexander had enormous potential: his speed over the water was as fast, if not indeed faster, than any other swimmer in the Scottish team. The only things letting him down were his slightly slow start, which could be rectified easily, and his turn at halfway. If he could master the tumble turn, he would shave between one and two seconds off his time and he will definitely make the team, even with a great chance of winning a medal. In another twelve months he would be taller with a longer reach, he would be physically stronger and with good coaching, there would be no reason why he shouldn't get on the podium. "If you're happy for us to invite your son, I'll inform Mr Burkett who is the head coach and in charge of recruitment. He'll be mightily pleased. Mr Burkett is the coach who first noticed how good Alexander is and what potential he has. You must be very proud of him." Said Mr Quigley.

"Yes, we certainly are. Go ahead and send us all the details." Duncan replied.

Duncan now felt confident about talking to his son to see Alexander's reactions regarding the offer of coaching. He felt sure that his son would be excited and thrilled, so that was something he had to look forward to when he got home from work that evening. It was time to call the garage. As he picked up the phone and dialled the number,

9

Duncan had a sense of foreboding that all would not be well, and his premonition was correct.

"Hi, it's Mr Baker, I'm ringing you to see if there's any news on my car? The Morris Marina. It broke down this morning and you were towing it in."

"Yes, sir. We've towed it in, and we've done a full inspection. I'm afraid it's very bad news. The main problems are that the suspension has gone completely, front and back, and needs replacing. Unfortunately the differential has burnt out and needs replacing. The gearbox selector is seriously worn and looks on its way out. The suspension and the differential needs doing before the car can be moved. You asked about an MOT inspection, well it's more bad news I'm afraid. There is some corrosion on the sub-frame that needs some plate welding doing. The exhaust manifold has begun to break away from the exhaust pipe, and that needs replacing. All four tyres would need to be replaced as they are right on the limit. You also need new front brake pads and discs and new rear brake pads and new windscreen wiper blades."

There was silence on the line for about twenty seconds.

"Are you still there, sir?"

"I'm a bit taken aback; I didn't expect it to be that bad. What would an estimate be to put it all right and pass the MOT test?"

"We haven't got that far, sir; I never turn away trade or business, but I think it's not worth starting to chase prices for the parts and put a tender together. The cost of all those repairs will be a damn sight higher than the actual worth of the car."

"What do you suggest." Pleaded a desperate Duncan.

"It's up to you, sir. I know a car breaker over in Grangemouth who buys cars like yours for spare parts. I'll give him a call and see what he says."

"So it's a write-off. It was just my luck that I only filled it up with petrol last night and the tank is nearly full." Duncan moaned.

"Give me a couple of hours and then give me a ring back. I'll see if I can get it sorted for you."

Later in the afternoon, Duncan finished his paperwork and set off for the accounts office to drop the invoices off. He was looking forward to seeing if he could catch any of the ladies giving him an admiring glance after hearing of his nickname with the ladies of "Dunk the Hunk." On the few occasions he had entered the accounts office, he had always noticed the pleasant aroma of the ladies perfume, not too heavy, just enough to titillate the nostrils. It was a far cry from the stench of the works canteen on the loading bay that usually emanated a stink of body odour, bad feet, stale breath, and flatulence. As he left the office, Duncan was a trifle miffed not to catch any of the ladies giving him a lecherous glance or even a pleasant smile. "I reckon Robbo was pulling my leg," he thought disappointingly.

When he returned to his desk Bernard was waiting for him, "Duncan, tomorrow morning I want you to be in my office at nine o' clock. I want you to see the serious side of being in management, the worst side, so then you might realize it's not all beer and skittles. Then you might understand how lonely and depressing a manager's job can be at times and you'll learn how to show me a little more respect. Unfortunately, I will be dismissing an employee in the morning. He has been a persistent offender in timekeeping and has received several warnings regarding smoking. I want you to be present and learn what it's like to be involved in a dismissal. Any questions?"

"No, I'll have to get the two big deliveries to Newton's and Barnwell's sorted this afternoon so the drivers can get away early in the morning. I won't be late."

Duncan felt that Bernard was trying hard to befriend him and get him onside, perhaps as a result of their little *tete-a-tete* earlier in the day.

Later in the afternoon, Duncan called the garage to be told that the car breaker from Grangemouth was interested in buying the Marina. He would be in Edinburgh on Saturday morning in his tow truck and would call at the garage to have a look at it. If Duncan could be there about ten o' clock, they could meet up and possibly do a deal. He also had to settle his bill at the garage for the towing in, the labour on the inspection and the failed MOT.

As the time ticked round to five thirty, and the working day was over, Duncan gathered his jacket and his lunch box and set off towards the time clock where he was always amused to see the mad scramble of the men clocking out and racing out the door, some towards the car park and others towards the bus stop. As he clocked out, the familiar voice and bad breath of Bernard Savage caught his attention.

"Look at them, they can't get away quick enough. You'd think the klaxon has just sounded for a nuclear attack and they're all rushing to the pub for one last drink or rushing home for one last quickie with the missus. They're like rats deserting a sinking ship." Complained Bernard.

"I feel like rushing off to the pub myself, Bernard after the day I've had. I've been told my car's a total write-off. I have to catch a bus to Waverley Station and get a train home. I haven't got a clue what time the trains are. I'll just have to see when I get to the station."

"If you fancy a quick pint, I'll have one with you. There's a pub just up the road. it's only about a minute's walk."

"Perhaps another night, Bernard. I don't know what time the trains are, I'd hate to miss one by a few minutes and then have to wait an hour for the next one, just for the sake of a quick pint. I'll see what the timetable is like and maybe have a drink another evening, okay?"

"Yes, okay. See you in the morning. Goodnight, Duncan."

"Goodnight, Bernard. By the way, who is getting the chop in the morning?"

"Robertson, Samuel Robertson. He works on the loading bay."

As he was boarding the bus, Duncan thought about all the day's events, the highs and the lows, the car being written off, a resounding rollocking off "Buffalo Breath" and then the final act that Bernard had suddenly morphed into "Creeping Jesus" and had tried to become very friendly with him. It bothered him tremendously. He didn't want to be seen as a confidant of the boss or as an accomplice in a sacking. Nor did he want the men to think he and Bernard were bosom pals, and he certainly didn't want to go to the pub with him for a drink. He shuddered at the thought. Twenty minutes later, he was at the ticket office at Waverley Train Station buying a single ticket to Kirkcaldy.

Duncan had twenty-five minutes to wait for the train to leave, so he made a quick phone call to Elizabeth to say he'd be home about 7.30 and he bought a local evening newspaper. On the journey home, he looked at the prices of cars in the advertising section but there was nothing of interest. He was still hoping for a talk with Elizabeth about the job offer when he got home, but he knew it was likely to have to wait until the weekend. He had noted with a sense of disappointment that he would need to catch the 6.50 am train in the morning to get to work on time, which would mean leaving home much earlier than usual. He would have to get up at 5.30 and he was not looking forward to such an early start.

He was also dreading being involved in a sacking. He wondered which poor unfortunate soul was getting his notice. Who was it that Bernard had said, Samuel Robertson? And then the penny dropped. He had not linked the name at first, probably because he had too much on his mind at the time. Samuel Robertson. It must be him; it must be Robbo. He couldn't think of anyone else it could be. It was Robbo. His best friend at work.

MEMORIES

Robbo and Duncan always sat together at lunchtime in the canteen, and had grown a mutual friendship based mainly on football, and in particular their love of Scottish football. Robbo supported Hearts FC, and he would wear the distinctive maroon and white coloured scarf. They usually had a daily compilation of football conversations littered with past stories, legends, great games, going to Hampden Park, travelling to London to see Scotland at Wembley Stadium and generally putting the world to rights where Scottish football was concerned.

Duncan had once told Robbo that in 1968 he nearly got the chance of playing for Hearts arch-enemies Hibernian who played just across the city. The trial, in a hastily arranged practice match did not go very well. He was rejected by Hibernian and stayed on as a part-time professional at Raith Rovers. His career at Stark's Park, where he became something of a cult hero, lasted eight years. A cruel knee injury in a freak accident in a pre-season friendly match finished his playing career prematurely. His anterior cruciate ligament was badly torn, and the specialist advice was to not play again as further damage on the knee could possibly leave him permanently crippled.

The accident happened just as a big money transfer to England or one of the big Glasgow clubs was imminent. Several of the English first division clubs had taken notice of the prolific goal scorer north of the border and inquiries for his signature came pouring in. Raith Rovers wanted to sign him on professional terms because if they had signed him to a professional contract, they would then be able to sell him for a sizeable amount and make a healthy profit. Unfortunately, the injury occurred before a contract was formally agreed and at 28 years and 7 months his career was finished, probably while he was at the peak of his career. Duncan never tired of listening to Robbo telling his many tales (some of them may even have been true) of following Scotland, especially the trips to Wembley in the 1960s. He had his first trip to Wembley in 1963 when Robbo and seven mates who were all Hearts supporters, travelled to London early on the Thursday morning. By late afternoon, they had found a cheap B&B on the Caledonian

14

Road just a mile up from King's Cross Station. They had to pay in advance for the four nights as they planned to go home on the Monday morning. Despite paying for four nights at the B&B, Robbo only managed to sleep there once on the Sunday night before going home on the Monday. On the Thursday night they were all drunk and finished up somewhere in Camden Town at a party. Six of the lads headed off back to the B&B around midnight, but Robbo and Kenny McKenzie stayed on until the booze ran out. The party eventually broke up and they headed back to King's Cross, although they didn't have a clue where they were. They were so drunk they couldn't find their way back to the B&B, nor even remember the name or address of it, so they finished up sleeping in the waiting room at Saint Pancras Station. After a mere three hours sleep, they were forcibly awoken and thrown out of the waiting room by four British Rail police officers who gave them a harsh rebuke. Kenny had been sick on the waiting room floor and Robbo remembered a sour faced cleaner dragging a hose pipe and a bucket and mop into the room as they were leaving.

Later Robbo faintly recalled that on the previous night the other lads were talking about a big get-together in Paddington at a pub called The Charles Dickens. They headed to Paddington and were delighted to see many Scotland supporters all heading in one direction. As luck would have it, the rest of the crew came in just twenty minutes after them. When the laughter had died down, Robbo asked one of the boys for the name and address of their accommodation and could someone write it down on a piece of paper to help him find it in future? There were about three hundred supporters all clamouring for a drink, and it was hard work getting to the bar. The landlord had to close the pub in the afternoon as the pub was virtually devoid of anything alcoholic left to sell. The bar staff were exhausted, and the pub floor was littered with broken glass, so the mob then headed off to Soho, howling like banshees and singing their hearts out.

They all headed into Soho looking for the nearest bar that unfortunately happened to be totally unprepared for the tidal wave that was about to engulf it. It was a tsunami of tartan-clad drunken revellers all trying to get served at the same time. A dozen more supporters were outside urinating on the pavement, and at least two more were being sick in the gutter before all entering and resuming their quest to pickle their livers. The bar staff didn't stand a chance, and it was going to take ages to get a drink so the eight lads decided to move on to another pub where it might be easier to get served. After yet another heavy night's drinking, they were paralytic and became embroiled in a mass brawl in a kebab shop. They all got arrested for being drunk and disorderly and spent the night in a police station bridewell somewhere on the Old Kent Road. There was only one wooden bench and an old enamel chamber pot on the floor in the middle of the cell. If things couldn't get any worse, a giant of a man built like a silverback gorilla was snoring his head off on the bench. He had already told the police that if anyone woke him up, he would thrash the living daylights out of them. Robbo was gutted. He spent the night sat up against the wall. The police had taken his cigarettes, he was starving and extremely tired from lack of sleep over the two nights. He didn't get a kebab either.

The next morning, they were released early without charge. Robbo was delighted to see that as they were leaving the cell the silverback was still fast asleep, and furthermore he had a big wet patch in the crotch area where he had obviously had a little accident in the night. Robbo put his finger on his lips and pointed it out to Kenny who nearly burst his sides trying not to laugh until they were outside.

A few hours later they were in a pub in Willesden when Robbo had the most incredible piece of luck. He was coming back from the gent's toilet when he passed an old one armed bandit. He had three sixpences in his change, so he thought, "Why not?" After he inserted the second coin, he turned away expecting another failure. The resounding noise of the bell ringing and klaxon blaring startled him so much, that his first reaction was to run away as if he had done something wrong and broken the machine. The bell wouldn't stop ringing, and then finally Robbo noticed an avalanche of sixpences pouring into the tray under the tumblers. The avalanche lasted for about ten seconds, by which time half of the drinkers in the pub were swarming over to see the outcome. Robbo had won the jackpot, and he looked down at the unexpected windfall and then to the tumblers where the display was reading "TIC-TAC-TOE." The landlord changed the coins for banknotes, so Robbo's worries were over. He bought the next round of eight pints of beer and eight shots of whisky plus a drink for the landlord. It was the most expensive round he had ever bought, but the two pounds and two shillings and ninepence for the whole round was not a concern now that he was flush.

After the dinnertime session, they walked to Wembley Stadium and were delighted to see Scotland win. Robbo was ecstatic, his first ever trip out of Scotland and he saw his team win at Wembley, his massive win on the one-armed bandit was more than a week's wages. Life could not get any better.

The eight lads made their way back by tube train to Soho, a Soho that belonged to Scotland that Saturday night. The streets were packed with singing and dancing supporters, many soaked in beer and deliriously happy. It wasn't too long before the heavy day's drinking started having a marked effect on them. Colin Davenport and Gary Chapman could hardly stand up and they staggered off to find a taxi. It seemed to have a marked effect on the six that were left. It wasn't too long after that the Gray brothers decided to call it a day. Without saying goodbye, they disappeared, leaving four of them who were all on their last legs. Nobody wanted the ignominy of suggesting they finish for the night and head back to the lodgings, so they carried on drinking, albeit at a lesser pace. Larry Burns was quite upset with the brothers for sloping off without warning. He was sure that one of them had not bought a round of drinks all day. "The tight bastards" he moaned, and he promised to have words with the brothers the following morning. Larry was one man it paid not to upset. They were all shattered and exceedingly drunk. Robbo even said he was too tired to go to a strip club. Terry Lloyd was virtually comatose by a quarter to eleven, so they all mutually decided to call it a day.

They made their way to Covent Garden tube station to get a train back to King's Cross, all of them eating a fish and chip takeaway. While on the platform waiting for the tube train, Robbo and Kenny began chatting up two Scottish girls from Cumbernauld who had also been to the match and were very drunk and willing. They ended up going back to Paddington with the girls who were staying in a cheap hotel in Sussex Gardens.

The lads were full of hope that they would have a perfect end to the day by sharing a bed with the girls. It was a far from perfect end to the day for Robbo. His conquest fell on the bed with most of her clothes on, and she was snoring immediately. She was laying in the foetal position and her bulbous arse was taking up three quarters of the single bed. Robbo lay at her side with his own backside having to hang over the side of the bed in the same position. He was waiting and hoping that later in the night she might wake up and then he might be able to cajole her into performing some carnal gymnastics, but there was very little chance of that happening. After half an hour he gave up hope, but he was delighted that for the first time in three nights he was sleeping in a proper bed, so he gladly dozed off as any thoughts of passion were well and truly past him. What had made it seem worse for Robbo was listening to Kenny and his trollop in the act, although within ten minutes they too were both snoring.

The next morning, Robbo and Kenny crept out of the fleapit at 7.30 and went back to the B&B for the very first time. Breakfast was served at 9.30 on a Sunday morning, to allow the landlady to have a lie-in, so Robbo decided he needed a quick bath as there was ample time before breakfast. It was the first time since Wednesday he had seen soap and water and it was well overdue. When he returned to his room, he suggested to Kenny to, "go and jump in, I've left the water for you." After drying himself, he was delighted to put on clean socks and pants as well as a clean t-shirt. He was horrified at the stench of his dirty clothes, and when Kenny returned from the bathroom it was their main topic of conversation.

When they went down for breakfast and met the rest of the lads, he joked that his socks were howling so much that he reckoned they could walk back to Edinburgh by themselves. They were all belching and farting after breakfast pondering where to go, when suddenly the landlady burst into the dining room.

"Which one of you arseholes has had a bath and used all the hot water? Can't you read the notice on the bathroom door? It clearly says no baths until after 7.00pm. How can I wash the breakfast pots and pans now with no hot water? Who can't bloody read? Which one of you has left a dirty tide mark round the bath? Eh, speak up."

Robbo kept a straight face, but Kenny was caught totally off guard. His face was blushing as red as beetroot, and he looked as guilty as the village parson caught creeping out of the back door of a brothel. He spluttered. "Sorry, it was me."

"Well, shift your fat Scottish arse back up those stairs and clean the bath, and you can pay me an extra shilling because I need to put the immersion heater on now and it costs a bloody fortune during the daytime to heat up the water," she bellowed.

The lads were howling with laughter, and it was a splendid way to start the day off. However, the Sunday turned out to be something of a damp squib and they all regretted not going home after breakfast. Their train tickets for the journey home on Monday were bought and paid for in advance, so they had to stay, and reluctantly they had to endure another day in London. The pubs did not open until twelve o' clock, and they didn't know where to go or what to do. Somebody suggested a visit to Madame Tussauds to see the waxworks, but after a brief discussion Larry Burns ended the argument by saying that he had "seen enough dummies yesterday wearing England shirts to last him a lifetime." When the laughter died down, they decided to go sightseeing in the city centre until the pubs opened, and then in the afternoon when the pubs were closed, they would go to the Tower of London. Sundays were bland, abject days in the 1960s when the clocks seemed to take forever to eventually tick round to seven o' clock for the night-time drinking session.

During the afternoon, Kenny had all the lads laughing at Robbo's expense regarding the previous night with the girls from Cumbernauld. He boasted of his own success and thought it hilarious that Robbo spent the night choking on the farts of the girl with the enormous arse.

Robbo was happy that night to sleep in a proper bed by himself, and felt the better for it the following morning when they went home. It had been a great trip.

By the Thursday, Kenny noticed he was itching constantly around his testicles, and it was driving him mad. When the itching got worse, he had to see a doctor, who informed him, after a close inspection with a magnifying glass, that he had contracted pubic lice. He was given a prescription for some cream with a name he couldn't even pronounce. He told Robbo all about it in strictest confidence when they met for a pre-match pint on the following Saturday lunchtime. It was a mistake. Robbo couldn't wait to tell the rest of the lads at the match.

19

When they were in the pub on the Saturday evening, the lads were all in buoyant mood as Hearts had won and they were all singing to the tune of London bridge is falling down. *"Kenny McKenzie's got the crabs, got the crabs, got the crabs, Kenny McKenzie's got the crabs, poor old Kenny."*

Kenny always swore that if he had enough money and could do anything he liked with impunity, he would drop a nuclear bomb on Cumbernauld. Duncan loved hearing these stories, and he was amazed by the fact that however many times Robbo told them he was nearly always word perfect, so he wondered if indeed they may be true.

Robbo had a similar tale to tell on their trip in 1965 which resulted in his divorce. He had been married for four months, and his wife bought him the ticket for the match as his birthday present. She was aware that he was leaving by train on the Thursday and returning on the Monday so that wasn't the problem. What she didn't know, was that he would leave without saying goodbye, he would leave with all the housekeeping money, he would leave with all the shillings from the tin that they kept for the electric and gas meters and the sixpences for the television meter. She was left without a penny, no coins for the meters and hardly a crust of bread in the house. That was the end of his first marriage as his wife went home to her parents and never returned. Fortunately, there were no children involved.

Robbo told another funny story of their trip to Wembley in 1967. He had once said to Duncan that he couldn't fathom out how Scotland could play like world beaters against the English, and yet they could be so ordinary and sometimes hopeless against other teams. He thought they ought to employ the services of a hypnotist to put the players in a trance before the game and convince them that they were playing against England every time they donned the Scotland shirt. Duncan agreed and thought it a capital idea.

The train rolled into Kirkcaldy station and Duncan set off on the twenty-minute walk after what he could only describe as the strangest day he had had in years, or maybe in his whole life. He was hoping to be able to have an hour or so on his own with Elizabeth to discuss the job offer so that he could give an answer the following morning, but this day was turning out to be like no other. When he arrived home

Elizabeth had a dinner waiting for him which he was looking forward to as he was ravenous.

It was while he was eating his dinner that Elizabeth quietly whispered to him, "Charlotte has brought a boy home with her and announced him as her boyfriend. She is in her bedroom with him now and they are playing records while he is helping her with her homework. He seems like a lovely lad and his name is Fraser. I told them that he will have to go by ten o' clock. I hope you don't mind, but I didn't know what else to say or do when she just brought him in like that unannounced. What do you think?"

Duncan nearly choked on his pork chop. He was trying to speak while spluttering and spitting little pieces of undigested meat all over the table. "*Are you serious?* You mean he's up there with her now and they're in her bedroom where we can't keep an eye on them. They could be up to anything. Are you crazy?"

"Duncan, I'm very disappointed with you. Let's give her credit for being honest and bringing him home. At least we know where they are. We should respect the fact that she feels comfortable enough to bring a lad home and we should have trust in her and let her show us how responsible she can be. She will never show us trust if we don't show trust in her."

"*Trust!*" bellowed Duncan. "She's only thirteen, I can't believe you've let them go up there on their own, doing God knows what. I'm very disappointed in you. She's too young."

"Duncan, she'll be fourteen in two weeks' time, and we can't hide from the fact that she is growing up fast, and having boyfriends is part and parcel of being a teenager. If we can't trust her now, we'll never be able to trust her. If we tell her not to have a boyfriend until she's older then as sure as night follows day, she will damn well have a boyfriend. We've got to trust her; yes, we can't keep a close watch on her, but I have spoken to her on many occasions about boys and respecting her own body, and until she proves to us that she cannot be trusted, we have to let her have the responsibility of caring for her own body and her own welfare. Well, anything else?"

"It looks like it's a waste of time me even saying anything, as *you* seem to have made up your mind that's it's okay for them to be up there," he moaned.

"What's up with you tonight, Duncan? You're like a bear with a sore head."

"I've had a day from Hell. First the car broke down and it needs scrapping, then I got a right rollocking for being late, then later the boss was all over me like a rash. And just when you think it couldn't get any worse, the gaffer wants to sack my best friend at work tomorrow morning, and can you believe it, the snipe-nosed bastard wants me to be there in the office as his back-up when he gives Robbo his notice. Oh, and I've got to get up even earlier tomorrow morning as the train leaves at 6.50 am, so I need to be gone for about 6.25am as it's a twenty minute walk."

"I'll get up early with you and give you a lift to the station in Cuthbert if you like."

Cuthbert was Elizabeth's pride and joy. She had named the car Cuthbert in tribute to Virginia Hall[1], her favourite heroine of the Second World War. Her parents had given her the car as a present on her 21st birthday seventeen years earlier in 1968. It was a black Morris 8 with the old-fashioned trafficators used for signalling when turning or overtaking, not that the car ever overtook anything except the occasional cyclist. Originally her father bought the car in 1949, and after 19 years sterling service he decided to give it to Elizabeth as a coming-of-age birthday present. It was also a reward for passing her degree with honours at university. She generally only used it to go to the golf club and to do her local shopping. With Cuthbert now thirty-six years old, the engine was in a decrepit state, although the car's bodywork was still in a passable condition. Duncan usually bought a gallon can of oil every month to top the engine up and keep it going, but Elizabeth would never part with it. She loved all the admiring glances and comments made when she arrived at the golf club, and it was always a favourite starter for the ladies' conversations. She would often flick the trafficators on both sides several times to make the ladies giggle.

Duncan had no intentions of asking to use Cuthbert for his daily trip to Leith and back, as he knew it wouldn't bear the workload of

[1] Virginia Hall, a remarkable SOE agent in WW2. Read 'A Woman of No Importance' by Sonia Purnell.

sixty miles daily travel. He was pleased that Elizabeth would give him a lift to the station in the morning as it meant another quarter of an hour in bed. However, he was beginning to feel insignificant in his own home, a feeling he had never experienced before. He would normally have had the final word in discussions regarding the welfare of the children, but tonight he had been put firmly in his place, and he didn't like it one bit.

He sat quietly reading his evening newspaper with his ears strained for any little noise or sign of wrongdoing from upstairs. However, his tortured night was totally unnecessary. Charlotte and Fraser had kissed each other several times and on one occasion Fraser had surreptitiously brought up his right hand to fondle Charlotte's left breast, but she knocked his arm away while still engaged in a passionate kiss. He did try again a few minutes later with the same result and with discretion being the better part of valour, he gave it up as a bad job.

Duncan didn't have the opportunity to speak to Elizabeth regarding the job offer on that Thursday evening. He did tell her that he was getting fed up with work, and that he wished he didn't have to play second fiddle to Bernard Savage, but that was as much as he thought he ought to say, so he left it at that.

As soon as Charlotte bade her goodnight to Fraser, Duncan made his way up to bed. He was not exactly in the mood for small talk. He was feeling very ill-tempered, and he was dreading going to work in the morning. Elizabeth waited up until Alexander arrived home before she came up to bed. Duncan was still wide awake. He couldn't get to sleep at all. His mind was racing overtime and he had a thumping headache. Neither of them managed to get much sleep that night and Elizabeth detected a distinct feeling of hostility emanating from her disgruntled husband.

In the morning Duncan apologized to Elizabeth, "I'm sorry about last night, I'm dreading this morning when I get to work, and I shouldn't bring my problems home with me. Am I forgiven?"

"Of course you are, you big dope," she said.

Duncan recognised that his family was all that mattered, and work came a distant second in his list of priorities. Duncan was at the train station early and had ten minutes to wait for the train even after buying his ticket. While standing on the platform, he heard a small conversation between a passenger and a railway guard. He was sure that it was a voice that he recognized from his youth. There was a slight European accent mixed in with the usual Scottish brogue. It sounded like Karel, one of his friends from his years as a schoolboy when they were both at primary school together. He had not seen Karel for more than twenty years, but he was sure it was him.

"Excuse me, is your name Karel?" Duncan gingerly inquired.

"Yes, I'm sorry, who are you?"

"I'm Duncan, can you remember? from school. You all used to call me Dunk."

They fell in each other's arms, hugging and handshaking as they were delighted to meet up again after all these years. Karel was also going to Edinburgh and explained to Duncan that he caught the same train every morning. In the evening he would catch the 5.45pm and had been doing so for nine years. As the train arrived, they boarded together and talked during the whole journey to Waverley Station in Edinburgh.

"Do you ever see any of the other lads from our gang? I often wonder what happened to Libber and Stig and Wasser?" inquired an excited Duncan.

Karel replied. "I did hear that Libber joined the Navy about the same time you went off to university. I saw his mother about five years ago and asked about him but all she said was he's okay and he now lives somewhere near Plymouth, but she hardly sees him. I felt no end of a fool as I couldn't remember his proper name. I've only ever known him as Libber. Why did all the boys call him Libber?"

"Crikey, years ago when we were about seven or eight years old, he had a lousy cold one winter. I can remember that his nose was always running. One day we were on the park and the snot hanging from his nose made him look like a walrus. Two older men saw us playing and one of them said to the other, 'Look at that snot hanging from that kid's nose; they look like Liberace's candles.' "We thought he had said Libber Archie, as none of us had ever heard of that bloke who played the piano, so we called him Libber Archie at first, but it got shortened down to Libber after a while." Explained Duncan as Karel was in fits of laughter. "I can't even remember what his name was either. I remember Wasser, he was always seeing how high he could pee, and what with his name being Wallace I think that it just fell into place, Wasser Wallace we called him," continued Duncan.

"What about Stig?" inquired Karel.

" I can't remember why we called him Stig. He was a nice lad; I think his name was Steve or something like that." Said Duncan.

"It was Steve," agreed Karel. "He used to be a steel fixer working on big building sites. I heard he had a very bad accident when a crane jib got caught by a massive gust of wind and swung round out of control and knocked him off a ladder. I think that he suffered a broken back or something like that. Anyway, he is disabled and in a wheelchair now. It's very sad."

Duncan wanted to change the subject as quickly as possible, so he came up with the first thing in his mind from their childhood days. "Can you remember when we used to go down to the railway lines, and we used to lay old halfpennies on the track so that when the trains went over the halfpennies, they would flatten the coins out and make them bigger? Then we used to try and put them into penny bubble gum machines, but it never worked. We were daft in those days."

"Yes, I remember that." Continued Karel. "I can also remember when we used to go to Den Burn and we used to pick May Bells and Pussy Willow. We used to knock on houses on the way home selling little bunches at threepence a bunch. Some of the miserable sods used to haggle and try to make us accept a penny a bunch. We always used to call at the corner shop on the way home and spend all the money on sweets and chocolate, and make sure we ate them all before going home. Old Mrs Hodge who owned the shop must have loved it when we came in with a pocket full of threepenny bits and pennies."

Duncan was doubled up with laughter, as the memories and stories came flooding back and continued all the way to Waverley Station. In Duncan's life, he could never remember an hour passing so quickly.

"Will you be on the train next week, Duncan?" inquired Karel.

"Probably. We are starting to look for a new car this weekend, but I don't think we'll get one straight away. I hope to see you again next week. Have you got far to go now?" asked Duncan.

"No, just a two-minute walk to Saint Andrews Square. My office is just round the corner. What about you?" Karel asked.

"Just a ten-minute bus ride down into Leith. Hey Karel, I've just remembered why we called him Stig. His name is Steven Trevor Ian Grummitt. That's his initials, S-T-I-G. I remember now he once carved his initials on a tree with his penknife, that's how it became his nickname. See you on Monday, have a nice weekend." Said Duncan.

"And you. Cheers, mate."

Duncan set off to catch his bus feeling much happier than when he left home. It was great to see Karel again after all those years. It was his voice that Duncan had initially recognized, it had a slight European slant mixed within his own Scottish brogue, probably formed because his father was from Czechoslovakia and his mother was Scottish. He had learnt his father's national language as a child and spoke it fluently.

Duncan arrived at work with plenty of time for a quick coffee out of the loading bay canteen vending machine. It was guaranteed to bring on a further frantic visit to the ablutions, but Duncan was very thirsty after all the talking and laughing on the train journey, so he drank it anyway. It wasn't until Bernard Savage caught his attention that he remembered what was on the agenda at nine o'clock. He was dreading it. "How can you sit there under duress while a man you do not like forces you to be in attendance as he sacks a man that you consider a friend?" His thoughts on the matter were supposedly immaterial, so why should he be there in attendance? Was Bernard frightened of Robbo? and did he want someone there in case he was attacked?

"Mister Baker, please come to my office before Robertson arrives, I don't want you coming in after him," said Bernard.

"Yes, I'll make sure I'm on time," stuttered Duncan.

The clock in Bernard's office ticked over to nine o'clock and Duncan was already seated next to Bernard waiting for the arrival of Robbo. He felt his stomach churning over and he had a terrible feeling of nausea that had nothing to do with the vending machine coffee.

"I see Robertson is late. He can't even get here on time to be sacked," scoffed a petulant Bernard as the clock ticked over a further two minutes.

26

Half a minute later there was a timid knock on the door. Robbo meekly apologised, saying "Sorry I'm a bit late, Mister Savage. We've just had a very big delivery in from Webbs."

"Sit down, Robertson. Right, well, I don't know if you are aware, but the company invested in a new computer system two years ago. During those two years, all the data for each employee has been rigorously stored on record and can be brought up at the touch of a button. During the last board meeting, the main item on the agenda was the increased level of apathy regarding bad timekeeping, and I have been instructed that it must cease, immediately. While going through your files we have noticed that every week in the past two years you are five minutes late at least once a week, and on odd occasions you are late twice a week. As you know, the company has always been very lax and tolerant with the odd slight timekeeping discretion and would normally pay a full salary ignoring the fact. It has also been noted that every single working day in these last two years you have always been the employee who clocks out first at exactly five thirty. How do you manage that? Are you there early hanging about waiting for the clock to tick over? It would appear so. We suspect that this has been going on for the entire duration of your employment. Unfortunately, our records only go back for the last two years so we cannot actually confirm it."

Bernard's rant came to a temporary pause while he regained his breath and composure. Duncan looked across at his friend, Robbo. His shoulders were slumped forward as he slouched awkwardly in the chair. He looked like a man who had just been found guilty of murder, looking across at the judge as he donned his black cap.

"Robbo," Duncan thought, "straighten your back, sit up straight, take that guilt-ridden look off your face. It's so obvious that you are guilty as charged."

Bernard continued, "Your timekeeping, Robertson is totally unacceptable. We also have here a brief report from Mr Taylor. He is the agency manager who was here covering the loading bay for two weeks when Mr Baker was on holiday and I was in hospital. It was two years ago. Can you remember him? He certainly remembers you. Here's what he said on his report:" 'Generally, everything ran smoothly for the two weeks as most of the men on the loading bay were competent, diligent, and fulfilled their duties with the minimum of fuss. There was one exception. I found the attitude of Samuel Robertson to be slovenly and surly. When lorries arrived and needed to be unloaded, he was always at the back of the queue. He would often disappear, presumably to the toilet block, and then return smelling heavily of cigarette smoke. When all the lorries were loaded for the following day's deliveries, the other operatives would generally pass the time by sweeping up the loading bay and stacking up the pallets, but Robertson would disappear again and would not do anything unless instructed, I recommend that disciplinary action is the only way forward with this operative.'

"Well," barked Bernard, "What have you got to say for yourself, Robertson?"

"He never liked me from the start because he's a Hibernian supporter and I support Hearts. He had it in for me from day one. As for timekeeping, I admit that sometimes I'm a bit late when I miss my normal bus, but usually I'm here at 8.20, so I'm early most of the time."

"Yes, you may be here at 8.20 on occasions, but then you go straight to the canteen, and you never start work until after 8.30. The amount of time you have swindled over the years must add up to quite a considerable total. You know what you are doing, and you have taken advantage of the company's laxity. Furthermore, while we're talking about the canteen, it's strongly suspected that it was you who defaced the vending machine. You might think it very funny writing, 'The tea in this vending machine tastes like ferret piss,' "but the management take a very dim view on defacing company property. I have had a rollicking from above because of this as they said that the discipline at ground level is too lax and needs to be addressed. Also, Robertson, we have it here on record that you have received two verbal warnings and one written warning for being caught smoking in prohibited areas. That probably explains why you have frequent visits to the toilets and always come back with breath like an ash tray. You have been very fortunate in the past that your discretions have been overlooked but I'm afraid we've come to the end of the line and there is no alternative but to terminate your employment. Have you anything to say?"

"I can't help being late occasionally. My wife and my two daughters monopolize the bathroom in the morning, and I struggle to get in, that's why I sometimes miss my bus. Give me another chance and I promise I won't be late again" spluttered a desperate Robbo.

"I'm afraid it's too late for that, Robertson. It's been going on too long now so I'm afraid that I have no alternative, it's time to terminate your employment. You will receive two weeks' notice starting from today, what do you think Mister Baker?"

Duncan swallowed heavily and felt a sudden chill sweep over him. His brain was working overtime thinking what to say. He didn't want to agree with Bernard, but also he did not want to disagree with him and fall out over the issue. Eventually he said. "Well, as I see it, Mr Savage, this is something that should have been addressed well before now. It's patently obvious that a firm word and a reprimand should have been implemented years ago. The company must accept at least some fault for letting this go on until we arrive at this situation where it would appear to be too late. Has Mr Robertson had warnings placed on record regarding his timekeeping? If not, it sounds like he should have been reproached before now. I can only suggest that he is given a final written warning, and he is put on some sort of a probationary period regarding his timekeeping and working attitude. Perhaps a twelve-month probation, when, if he persists with his bad timekeeping it would leave us with no alternative." Duncan put his hands on the desk and relaxed waiting for Bernard's reaction and decision.

Bernard concluded. "Robertson, you are a very fortunate man, I *was* prepared to let you go, but after Mr Baker has spoken, I must concur with his comments. You will receive a *final* written warning and enter a probationary period. An account of this meeting will be recorded in the company files. That is all Robertson. You can go."

Robbo left the office moving more briskly than at any time in his employment. As the door closed, Bernard swivelled in his chair to speak face-to-face with Duncan. Surprisingly, he had a smile on his face and appeared pleased with himself. "Well, we handled that superbly. He'll soon change his ways and he will not give us any trouble in the future. Well done, Duncan. We make a good team."

Duncan was mortified. He was aghast at the idea that Bernard thought that they were a team and were possibly becoming bosom friends. Duncan didn't hate Bernard, but by the same token he didn't really like him either. He certainly didn't want to be bracketed as his sidekick. His breath stank like an open drain and Duncan was relieved to leave Bernard's office to resume his duties.

At lunchtime, Duncan went to the canteen as normal but was surprised to see Robbo sitting at a table with three other loading bay labourers. Normally, he would be sitting at a table alone waiting for Duncan to join him. The atmosphere in the canteen was eerie. The men were giving Duncan the occasional furtive glance and then looking away as though it may have been an accident. Nobody said a word to him, nor even acknowledged his presence. He knew from that moment that the men had been talking about Robbo's disciplinary meeting and were standing together with their colleague. Duncan felt vexed that although he had ultimately saved Robbo from getting the sack, the men were obviously wary of him and were treating him like a leper.

As he finished work for the day, Duncan felt that he just wanted to get home as quickly as possible for the weekend.

After he clocked out, he went to the bus stop just as it had started drizzling with rain. "Bloody rain, no damn umbrella," he was thinking to himself when he received a tap on the shoulder. It was Robbo. "I see Buffalo Breath is your new best mate now then," he said sneeringly, "It's a wonder you both haven't gone to the pub to make plans for who gets sacked next."

Duncan was appalled at the vitriolic tone in his voice. He replied, "Robbo, you can think what you like, but I can tell you now that Savage was hell-bent on sacking you. He'd already told me that earlier. I was instructed to be there although I didn't want to be in attendance. It's lucky for you that I *was* there. If I hadn't come up with that idea right at the last moment you would have had your notice already."

They boarded the bus together and Duncan continued. "Look, Robbo. It's up to you. You either accept the fact that you've had a rollocking and make sure you arrive on time, don't get caught smoking and liven yourself up a bit, or you carry on in the same manner and lose your job. At least you still have a job, which you would not have had if it wasn't for me sticking up for you."

There was silence for about five minutes. The bus was only two stops away from Waverley Station when Robbo grudgingly muttered. "Aye well, I suppose I ought to thank you. Sorry, Duncan, no hard feelings?"

"No, all water under the bridge. It's my stop in a minute. Have a good weekend. By the way, was it really you who wrote on the vending machine that funny quote? What was it that it said?" 'The tea in this vending machine tastes like ferret piss.'

"What do you think?" sniggered a smiling Robbo.

"Couldn't agree more. The bloody coffee does as well." Duncan agreed.

FRUSTRATION

Duncan was certainly glad that the week was over as he had found the last three days at work among the most stressful times of his whole career. At least he managed to spare Robbo from getting fired, so it wasn't all bad. But when, oh when, would he get the opportunity to speak to Elizabeth about the job offer? He'd already missed the chance to give an answer by Friday, so Monday it had to be. On Saturday morning, he had to be up early again to go to the garage in Craigcrook to settle the bill for his car. Perhaps there would be time to look for a new car while he was in Edinburgh, something a bit more reliable than the last heap of junk. All these thoughts were racing through his scrambled mind as he trudged warily home.

"Have you had a nice day, Duncan?" inquired Elizabeth.

"Awful, that boss of mine is really getting on my nerves. He thinks we are a team now, a sort of good-cop and bad-cop double act. Nobody likes him. His breath is appalling, and the lads all call him "Buffalo Breath," and much worse behind his back! He tried to get me on his side today while he implemented a sacking, but I managed to avert it by the skin of my teeth. What's more, the man is a good friend of mine so that made it worse. I feel like packing up and getting a new job. The travelling is wearing me down. I fell fast asleep on the train tonight, and luckily for me the guard woke me up just before the train arrived in Kirkcaldy Station. If it wasn't for him, I might have ended up in Aberdeen."

Without realizing it, Duncan's little rant had set the ball rolling: he had sowed the seeds for the imminent conversation that would determine whether he accepted the job offer or not.

Elizabeth giggled, "Aberdeen? You're such a drama queen, Duncan. Do you fancy going for a walk after dinner? I love going down to the quay at this time of the year."

"Yes, okay. I could murder a nice cool pint of lager," he replied as he thought " I'll never have a better chance, just the two of us on the seafront. Now's the time."

As they arrived at the quay, Duncan accepted his optimism had been totally misplaced. As soon as he had broached the subject of leaving his employment in Leith and accepting the job offer in Nottingham, he was met by a wall of silence. The silence lasted fully for three minutes. Elizabeth was piecing together the events of the last few days. She was not as gullible as he thought.

"So, that's why you said you want to leave your present employment. You've already had a job offer which I knew nothing about. When did you get the offer? Why didn't you tell me?"

"It came in the post on Tuesday when you were out playing golf. I was shocked at first as I never thought for one minute that I'd get the job, but It's a great opportunity. The salary is massive compared to what I get now. Five thousand five hundred pounds more. There is a good pension scheme and twenty-five days holiday, plus another eight bank holidays, and there is scope for further promotion. It's just a pity it's in England. Nottingham is about three hundred miles away, so it would mean selling up and moving house. There's lots of very good housing within ten minutes of the location in Beeston, and Nottingham seems to be a lovely city. There's lots of cinemas, swimming pools, golf clubs and a nature reserve right on the doorstep. Wouldn't it be great to be home from work within five minutes and not to have almost four hours travel every day? What do you think Lizzie?"

The basilisk stare that Elizabeth directed towards him said more than words could say. Eventually she said, "What do I think? I think you're On Cloud Cuckoo Land. *If you think* that we ought to sell up and move three hundred bloody miles to Timbuctoo or some other place you're sadly mistaken. It's taken us seventeen years to make that house into our home, and I for one don't want to move to another country. What do you think Sandy and Lottie will think of that idea? Sandy has important exams next year. Oh, and if you've forgotten, he has the chance of representing Scotland in the Commonwealth Games next year, so how will he feel about that? And what about Lottie? She will certainly not want to go anywhere now that she has a boyfriend. Even if things don't work out with Fraser, she will still have all her friends here in Kirkcaldy. So will Sandy. You know how much he loves playing football with his mates for the local team. He would be mortified to have to leave. I certainly don't want to go anyway. I can't ever imagine losing contact with Sylvia. She's been my best friend for over twenty years and since she lost her husband, she looks forward to meeting up with me at the golf club and I don't want to ruin that for her. Our life is too settled here, Duncan to have such an upheaval. I seriously don't think you have thought it through. As far as I'm concerned, you can forget it."

Duncan was totally deflated. There was nothing to be said for the moment. He understood she was probably right, although he was surprised that she used her friendship with Sylvia while stressing her point. They had been very close friends since they first met at St Andrews University in 1965 and they had become inseparable for over twenty years. They had shared a room together at university. They studied and socialized together. When Elizabeth and Duncan married in 1966, Sylvia was her only bridesmaid. Elizabeth would often speak to Duncan about how wonderful Sylvia was and how she was always smiling and happy, and was, "the best friend anyone could ever have." She had pink chubby cheeks, a radiant smile and a twinkle in her beautiful green eyes. She had an extraordinary gift of managing to make everyone smile and lighten up a room just by appearing through a door. Sylvia had also been a rock for Elizabeth when she lost both her parents, and two years later Elizabeth had to be there to comfort and console her best friend as Sylvia received the awful news that her husband had been tragically killed in May 1982 over eight thousand miles away at Goose Green in the South Atlantic Ocean.

"What do you want to drink?" The words came out in a feeble croak as a blushing Duncan swiftly changed the subject, accepting he was on the losing end of the argument. They chose an outside table at the quayside bar, and when Duncan brought the drinks out, Elizabeth, was sitting stony-faced staring out to the horizon. Although it was a warm evening, the atmosphere was icy cold and positively resentful. They were like two gargoyles set in stone with barely a facial tic or muscle movement between them.

"Are you going to sit there sulking and moping all night?" scoffed a belligerent Elizabeth.

"Er no, I was thinking about how I am getting to Edinburgh in the morning. I could possibly risk a trip in Cuthbert if that's okay with you. I could make a day of it, and look round the car showrooms in Edinburgh to get some idea of the cost of cars nowadays. Do you want to come with me tomorrow?" he asked.

"I may as well, but I want to be home no later than 5.45. Charlotte is going to an under-sixteen disco at the community centre with Fraser. I want to be there at 6.00 when the disco finishes to pick her up and get her home to make sure she isn't off somewhere to get up to no good. I think if we take our time, we should be okay in Cuthbert," she replied.

It was a slow frosty walk back home. Elizabeth made herself a hot drink and went to bed leaving Duncan scouring through the evening paper looking at the situations vacant and the used car section. Then he sat in deep thought wondering how and why it had all gone wrong this evening, but he was not about to give up hope however.

The next morning, they were on their way to Edinburgh chugging along in Cuthbert, when Duncan noticed there was much less traffic than on weekdays, and although Cuthbert only had a top speed of about forty-five miles an hour, they made reasonable time to the garage in Craigcrook. Duncan received twelve pounds for scrapping the Morris Marina, but he had to pay the garage a bill of forty pounds for the car being towed in and the failed MOT test and inspection. The garage owner had generously deducted seven pounds off the bill as he had syphoned off all the petrol into one of his own vehicles. He also gave Duncan the road tax disc which still had six months left to run. After they had left, Elizabeth told Duncan that she saw the garage owner and the scrap man wink at each other when Duncan's back was turned, which left a bitter taste in Duncan's mouth. Was he ripped off? He would never know for certain, but the doubt was there.

They visited several car showrooms in Edinburgh, and both were appalled at how much the car prices had risen over the last few years. It was obvious that they would need a sizeable loan to purchase a decent car. Even when viewing the second-hand cars that were on sale, there was nothing that was in their price range that was worth further investigation. By mid-afternoon they were on their way home to Kirkcaldy when Elizabeth surprisingly resumed the conversation from the previous evening.

"Duncan, nothing would please me more than to see you get a job like the one you have been offered. You deserve a promotion and a position in management like the one on offer. I agree the extra

35

money would be fantastic. I know that you have been unhappy with all the daily travelling, and I sympathize enormously. However, just think what the consequences would be if we sold our house in Kirkcaldy and made the move to Nottingham and your job didn't work out. What would we do if you were unemployed there for any reason? We would be like castaways on a dessert island, strangers in a foreign land, isolated with no income and probably saddled with a big mortgage. All our friends would be three hundred miles away in Scotland. It's too much of a gamble. It's not just us, we must think of the children's future. I know that we've had to tighten our belts recently. Our savings have dwindled enormously and it's costing a fortune to keep Lottie and Sandy in clothes and trainers. I spend twice as much on Lottie as the rest of us put together. She forever needs the latest crop top or T shirt, jeans, make up and the list goes on. Sandy gets through trainers every three or four months. He takes size eleven now and he's only just fifteen. It's not that long ago he was taking a size six. The woman in the shoe shop who served us last week said that he'll be wearing two canoes on his feet by the time he's twenty-one. There's not a lot I can add to that. I just wish that the job was a damn sight nearer to home than three hundred miles."

"Yes, I understand. I suppose it was only a pipe dream after all. Still, the money would have been very nice." said a crestfallen Duncan, appreciating that his wife was correct.

"I know it's extremely hard for us, I could try and get a job myself, or maybe I could start writing again," said Elizabeth.

"Will you be Doris this time?" sniggered Duncan, bringing Elizabeth out in a big smile as they both remembered the time when she chose her pen name nine years earlier. Elizabeth had written her first novel and taken it to a literary agent to see if it was worthy of printing and release. The publishers agreed and a contract was produced, giving Elizabeth a percentage of the royalties and profits of the sales. A polite enquiry was made as to the name she would use as an author. She was advised to use a pseudonym, or a name that rolled off the tongue. As the publisher said, female authors like Catherine Cookson and Daphne Du Maurier have instantly recognizable names that roll off the tongue.

On the Saturday night they had bought a large bottle of wine and started writing down names that Elizabeth could use as a pen name. After two hours and with the wine bottle empty, the evening turned into a complete farce. It then became a contest to see who could come up with the silliest name. Duncan suggested Doris Dumpling and then Penelope Pancake and many more ridiculous names. They fell about laughing at the sheer absurdity of the matter and eventually went to bed with the subject unresolved. Duncan recalled how they made very passionate love on that Saturday night, and in the morning, he made a note of the label on the empty wine bottle so that he could get the same brand the next time they were having wine.

It was on the Sunday morning at breakfast that Elizabeth eventually came up with the name Ophelia O'Neill, and it was under that pen name that her first novel was published.

Her initial offering was a relative success, selling nearly three thousand copies in the first six months, eventually reaching three and a half thousand after two years. Her second book released ten months later was only a moderate success and sold less than two thousand copies. Her third novel was published but failed miserably and was destined to gather dust on bookstore shelves. Elizabeth did write another novel which, when presented to the publisher, was turned down flat. She was advised that there are only so many novels one can write about a seventeenth century Scottish heroine with long flowing jet-black hair, riding a big white stallion, brandishing a claymore and smiting down her despotic English foes. Perhaps a different theme or topic would be advisable.

The royalties that Elizabeth received for the first two novels contributed most of the money that they paid out for the brand-new Morris Marina. But after two years the payments slowed down to a trickle and ultimately dried up completely. Elizabeth had also enjoyed writing poetry, mainly for her own pleasure and satisfaction, and it was not unreasonable to think that she could resume her literary career. Elizabeth recalled how Duncan had always jokingly favoured the name Doris Dumpling. He was continually sneaking up behind her when she was unaware, fondling her breasts from behind and whispering in her ear, "Come here, Doris. Let me squeeze your dumplings." After the umpteenth time in three days, Elizabeth lost her temper and a sharp elbow into his midriff brought his annoying habit to an abrupt end. Yet, she had been flattered, and was very happy with the knowledge that her husband still had a lustful streak for her body.

Duncan had always been happy for Elizabeth not to have full-time employment. When the children were born within fourteen months of each other, Elizabeth's daily routine centred around them continually for many years, until they were both old enough to be able to walk to and from school unescorted.

Duncan accepted that it was now patently obvious a move to Nottingham was never going to happen. Elizabeth had brought up something he had never even thought of: If the job didn't work out for the best and he became unemployed, they really would have been isolated and would regret the move and wish they had stayed in Kirkcaldy. After the tiring day they had endured, they were both happy to get home. Alarmingly, when Duncan unlocked the front door, he could hear muffled noises coming from upstairs. His first thoughts were that they had burglars.

"Wait in the car, Lizzie and lock yourself in." He shouted as he bounded up the stairs. The noise seemed to be coming from Alexander's bedroom, so he burst through the door with his fists clenched expecting a confrontation. It was a nightmare situation for everyone. Alexander and his latest girlfriend were frantically trying to get dressed before they were discovered. Alexander had managed to get his pants on, but the girlfriend was still gathering her clothes and she was totally naked. Duncan fled downstairs in a state of complete shock. He was speechless, and when Elizabeth opened the car window and called out, "Is everything all right, is it burglars?" Duncan just gave her the thumbs up, so Elizabeth locked the car before coming in the house at the exact same time as Alexander and his embarrassed girlfriend were leaving.

"Just taking Emma home, mam" said Alexander.

A mortified father was sitting in his favourite chair, staring blankly into space. He could not believe what his own eyes had just witnessed. "Alexander, for Christ's sake! He was only just fifteen, how old was she? How long had that been going on?" he thought. His eyes were glazed, and the shock had completely overwhelmed him. His mind was in turmoil. Should he tell Elizabeth what he had seen? Should he confront Alexander about having sex at just fifteen years and two months of age? Should he tell his son about the responsibility of having safe sex, and being aware of sexually transmitted diseases? It seemed that he would be far too late to give his son advice on most of these matters as the deed was already done. Elizabeth surely had a right to know! He decided to wait until Alexander came back home, and hopefully they could speak of the events and get things settled before Charlotte arrived home. Duncan was fidgety and couldn't sit still, getting up out of the chair and walking to the garden in deep thought.

As the evening approached, Elizabeth said, "It's time I went to pick up Lottie from the disco."

Elizabeth arrived at the Community Hall five minutes before the disco finished and she was fascinated to see so many parents waiting for their offspring. It was an amazing sight when the doors opened, and all the teenagers came spilling out. All the girls were dressed in the same style of crop top and jeans, with the same hairstyle, and most of them had a boyfriend swinging on their arms and Charlotte was no exception, as she and Fraser trooped out holding hands. Elizabeth realized that as she and Duncan had been out all day, she had not been present when Charlotte got herself ready for the disco.

"Say cheerio sweetheart. It's time to go," said Elizabeth.

Charlotte and Fraser were glued at the lips like a couple of leeches, and when Fraser eventually broke away gasping for breath, Charlotte bade him farewell for the night.

On the way home, Elizabeth asked Charlotte to explain, "why are all the girls dressed identically and all with the same hairstyle?"

"Mum, you are so old-fashioned. Have you not heard anything about Madonna? All the girls dress like this now, and all the girls have Madonna's hairstyle. That's the latest trend."

"Oh okay. We're having a takeaway tonight. Can you decide what you want when we get home," said a red-faced, embarrassed Elizabeth, as she quickly changed the subject. When they arrived home and went into the living room, Duncan was aghast at the sight of his daughter. He had never seen her dressed like that and wearing so much make up. For the second time in less than two hours he had been shocked by his own children. Charlotte went upstairs to get changed and Duncan immediately began an angry tirade at his startled wife.

"Who gave her permission to go out dressed like that? she looks like a two-shilling tart. She's not even fourteen yet and she looks like she could be out there selling her wares. Did you know she was going out like that?"

"No, I gave her some money to buy clothes as it's her birthday in less than two weeks, but she has obviously bought the latest fashion which we know nothing about." replied Elizabeth.

"Fashion!" bellowed Duncan. "She looks like a prostitute, and who paid for that bloody hairdo? Another early birthday present I presume. We're not made of money."

"All the girls were dressed the same, Duncan; Don't be so old-fashioned! We must let her grow up and be part of the crowd. The last thing we want is Charlotte feeling left out and isolated with the rest of the girls taking the mickey out of her for not keeping up with the latest fashion. This craze will die out eventually and then she'll be wearing something completely different. You'll see."

"Eventually ... Old Fashioned." He roared. "So, she'll be walking round dressed like a backstreet whore in the meantime, I'm not happy about this.. It's not right."

"Is everything okay?" It was Charlotte, she had changed into casual clothes and come back downstairs without her parents hearing the creaking of her footsteps on the staircase. "I could hear shouting; I hope you're not arguing. It's not about Fraser and me, is it?"

"No, everything's fine. Your dad's just a bit upset because we had to scrap his car this morning and he's just letting off a bit of steam. Weren't you, Duncan?" Explained Elizabeth.

"Er yeah. Bloody car, useless pile of scrap, I wish I'd never clapped eyes on it."

"That's odd, I thought I heard dad shout 'fashion.' What did he mean?" Charlotte asked.

"Oh, it was the car, it had an overhead camshaft that was the latest fashion and all the rage when we bought it. It's just a useless pile of scrap metal now. I'm starving. What takeaway are we having for tea?" Said a red-faced father.

Duncan had wriggled his way out of an embarrassing situation with a little white lie. After all, the car was a useless pile of scrap metal. There was no sign of Alexander and they settled on a Chinese takeaway and Duncan poured himself a can of lager from the fridge while Elizabeth fetched the food. He was feeling as downcast as at any point in his life. Elizabeth was permanently gaining the upper hand in arguments concerning the family, and she was continually putting him in his place. His son Alexander had evidently matured into a lusty carefree adult without Duncan giving him any fatherly advice or guidance. His daughter Charlotte was now dressing like a Parisian whore, yet her mother couldn't see any problems with the way she dressed. She had a boyfriend, whom they knew nothing about. He felt out of control, and he was still smarting from Elizabeth gaining the upper hand in the discussion regarding the job offer.

Duncan was halfway through his second can of lager when the food arrived. It was strange that for the first time that he could remember, there was hardly any conversation between them during the rest of the evening. Charlotte went up to her room to play music, leaving her parents alone. Normally on a midsummer Saturday night, Duncan and Elizabeth would go for a walk in the evening sunshine down to the coast, but tonight Duncan was not in the mood. He finished the four cans of lager that were in the fridge and then set about making a large dent in a bottle of brandy. He didn't even notice Elizabeth slip out of the living room and go upstairs to bed, alone, with a face like thunder and a temper to match.

Drink and tiredness held him in a vice-like grip. He fell asleep in the chair, snoring like a warthog until he was awoken by his son just before midnight. "Are you okay, dad? You ought to go to bed, I've turned the telly off. See you in the morning."

Alexander disappeared up the stairs leaving a groggy Duncan feeling no end of a fool. He had wanted to have harsh words with his son, but in his drowsiness he had missed the opportunity. Duncan crept upstairs, quietly slipped into bed and was soundly asleep within two minutes. He eventually woke up quite late on the Sunday morning. His hangover was giving him a severe headache and he felt sick. Elizabeth had not one iota of sympathy for him. Alexander and Charlotte had already had their breakfast and gone out with friends.

"Is there anything for breakfast?" Duncan meekly asked.

"Bacon in the fridge, eggs in the larder, cereals and bread in the cupboard, milk in the fridge and pots and pans in the cupboard, get it yourself," snarled Elizabeth.

He knew from the acidic tone of her voice that all was not well. She had never spoken to him like that before, and he was shocked.

"What's the matter Lizzie?" he meekly inquired.

"You come crawling down here at this time with the day half gone and ask what's the matter? Have you forgotten that we were supposed to be going out for the day and having a walk on the Fife coastal path? It's glorious weather and I've been ready since 8.00 listening to your snoring rattling the floorboards. Well, it's too late now, it's not worth it by the time you will be ready. Get your own breakfast. I'm going out in the garden."

Duncan was not happy to see how his heavy night's drinking had affected his relationship with Elizabeth. He loved his wife very dearly, but he was not going to go begging for her forgiveness. "If she wants to play the wounded martyr, let her get on with it," he thought. Fifteen minutes later, after two slices of toast and a mug of tea with two paracetamols, Duncan went out not knowing where he was going, or even why, but he was not staying at home to incur the wrath of his wife until he had cleared his head and recovered his composure. He was more than a trifle miffed that she had attained the upper hand and the high ground in all their arguments over the last few days.

He set off walking towards the town centre, and within fifteen minutes was looking admiringly at a gleaming new Ford Escort in a showroom window. The royal blue colour was an added attraction, matching the car to the colours of the Scotland football kit. The price of the car was £4,949.00 which was less than the extra salary he could earn by taking the job in Nottingham. He entered the showroom more out of curiosity than anything else as he knew they could not afford a new car, not without having a sizeable bank loan or possibly a finance agreement.

An overenthusiastic salesman sauntered towards him asking, "Can I help you sir?"

"Possibly, I'm just getting some idea of the costs of a new car," said Duncan.

"Are you looking at anything in particular, sir?"

"I was wondering what these Ford Escorts are like, I've never even been inside one, let alone driven one. Do you recommend the Ford Escort?" Duncan replied.

"Yes sir. They are state-of-the-art in modern technology and development, more reliable than any of the previous Ford cars that are sold in the UK. I'm sorry, but excuse me ,sir. I'm sure that I know you. Your face is very familiar. Are you Duncan Baker?"

"Yes, why?" confirmed Duncan.

"I remember you well. You used to play centre forward for the Rovers. I'm a season ticket holder and I have been supporting them for over twenty-five years, and I reckon that you were by far the best centre forward we've ever had. It was a sorry day when you had to retire. It was a pre-season friendly if my memory's right, wasn't it?"

"Yes, please don't remind me. They were about to offer me professional terms as there were quite a few enquiries from the top English clubs, and I think they would have sold me anyway. I did hear on the grapevine that one of the scouts who came to watch me had said his club were willing to pay around seventy-five thousand pounds for me, and that Rangers, Celtic, Hearts and Dundee United were also showing interest and in the process of tabling a bid. That would have suited me best, staying in Scotland. Still, it's all in the past. Life goes on," reminisced Duncan.

"It's a pity you weren't here when we opened up this morning, you could have met our boss. He always comes in on Sunday morning to open the showroom, but he usually only stays for half an hour. Our boss is on the board at the Rovers, and he's been going to the games longer than me. He was the chairman years ago. He has said to me on numerous occasions that Jim Baxter and Duncan Baker are the best two players ever to play for the Rovers. He will be gutted to have missed you, but I'm sure he will be very delighted to know you are interested in one of our cars.

"Sir, I've just had a thought: all the Rovers players come here to buy their cars, and I'm pretty sure that they all get a decent discount on the price. The players all ask for him when they come in. He usually takes them into his office, and he deals with them exclusively. Anyway, I know he thought the sun shone out your backside when you played

43

for the Rovers, and it's possible he might look after you as well if you come back when he's here. He's always in on weekdays and Saturday mornings."

"Yes, thank you I will. I'll speak to my wife about the finances and see what she has to say and what she thinks of the new Ford Escort. We have a joint bank account, so we would have to decide together. We'll probably both come in later in the week if that's okay," said Duncan.

"Just one thing, sir. Before you go, here's my card. My name is Stuart, Stuart Bowyer. It would be nice if you mention my name to the gaffer if you do buy a car from here. Please tell him that after our meeting you were very impressed, and you became interested in buying a Ford. Oh, and another thing, it would be cheaper for you to get a bank loan as the interest rates at the bank would be much lower than our finance. I'm not supposed to tell you that, so please keep it to yourself."

"Okay, Stuart. Hopefully see you later in the week."

Duncan cast one more longing, admiring glance at the brand-new blue Ford Escort and left the showroom in a much better mood than he had felt all weekend. It was pleasing to hear that his football abilities were so well admired and appreciated, certainly better than his parenting skills if the last couple of days were anything to go by.

There was a slight spring in his step as he was feeling much better, so he decided to go home. It was no good making things any worse than they already were with Elizabeth. He felt sure that she would have calmed down a bit by now, and although he wasn't expecting the red carpet when he got home, he was hopeful that her anger would have dissipated. As Jack McKinlay had always said, 'if you have a problem of your own making, face up to the consequences.'

He was passing the corner shop on his way home, and decided to go in and get a bar of chocolate, anything to soak up the alcohol and take the taste out of his mouth. By sheer chance, as he opened the door, Elizabeth was about to leave the shop.

"Hi, I'm just on my way home. If you wait a minute, I'll come with you," said Duncan. He was mightily relieved that Elizabeth waited for him outside the shop, although she was still not in the best of moods.

44

"Where have you been?" she asked.

"I've been to the car showrooms to have a look and see if there's anything interesting that we can afford. The second-hand cars are nearly as expensive as the new ones, so I don't know what we are going to do. But I do know one thing: I'm not working the rest of my life, getting paid a salary for eight hours work and then being out of the house for over twelve hours. At least with a car I can get home for about half past six. Do you know how much money we have altogether in both accounts?"

"Not enough for a decent car. There's about five hundred in the current account and just over one thousand two hundred in the savings account. We were supposed to be having a holiday in July although nothing's booked yet. I don't think we can afford to go anywhere nice. Two years ago, we had nearly five thousand in the savings account, Lord knows where it's all gone! It's not as if we have had a proper holiday for the last two years. We are spending more than you earn I'm afraid. That's why I've just been here to see Mrs Hodge. I've asked her if she needs any part-time assistance, at any time of the morning or afternoon. She wished I asked her years ago but it's too late now. She is on the verge of retiring, and she has had an estate agent in on Friday to value the shop. The whole business is going up for sale. Two or three years ago she would have welcomed me with open arms she said."

"Never mind. Thanks for trying. I'm sorry about last night, and this morning Don't worry. We'll think of something."

Half an hour later they were at home working out what to do for the best regarding their finances. Primarily, a decent car was a priority. It wasn't going to be long before they would be taking Alexander to Edinburgh and back for swimming training. Without doubt, Cuthbert wasn't up to the regular sixty-mile return journey. Additionally, there was Duncan's necessity for transport to work and back. They would have to be putting funds to one side for Alexander if he acquired a place at university. Then, a year later, it would be the same for Charlotte.

Elizabeth spoke first. "We must accept the fact that Lottie is now growing up fast, probably faster than Sandy, and it costs a fortune to buy her clothes and make-up. I've spoken to her about it, and she has offered to try and get a job on Saturdays so she can pay her way. Mind you, that was before she met Fraser, so I don't know how she'll feel about it now. She has spoken to me about getting a paper round, but I know you would be against that as you didn't want Sandy to have one. I will go to the job centre tomorrow morning. At the very worst I can look for some barmaid work. I will start writing again, as Elizabeth Baker this time. That is my name. I'm proud to be Elizabeth Baker, and while I still have breath in my body, I will always be Elizabeth Baker. What do you think, Duncan?"

"I think I have the most beautiful, considerate, kind and wonderful wife in the whole wide world." said a misty-eyed Duncan, fighting back a tear that was in danger of slaloming down his cheek. "I don't deserve you."

"No, you bloody don't, but what do you think about me getting a job?" she asked.

"I'm happy for you to get a part-time, or even a full-time job if you could manage it. I don't want Lottie out on the street taking newspapers. If anything nasty happened to her, I would never forgive myself. I think we need to keep at least a thousand in reserve in the bank for when Sandy goes to university. As I see it, we could do with about five thousand straight away. The only way we can do that is to go cap in hand to the bank for a loan. I know it doesn't matter now, as I'm not taking it, but that job in Nottingham would pay an extra five and a half thousand per annum. It's such a pity there's nothing local round here in the pharmaceutical industry that I could go for. If I got a decent job here in Kirkcaldy, we could get away without borrowing any money for a car. I could then walk or even cycle to work. But there's absolutely nothing suitable."

"Duncan, we are going to need a car for when we take Sandy to Edinburgh on Saturdays. I will go to the bank in the morning and make an appointment to see about getting a loan, then I'll go to the job centre afterwards and see what's on offer."

"Lizzie, try to get an appointment at the bank as early in the morning as possible on Wednesday or Thursday. That way I can head off to work after the appointment, and I'll only lose a morning and not a full day's pay."

When they arrived home, Elizabeth brought him back down to earth with a resounding bump. "Duncan, go and have a shower, I can still smell the brandy coming out of you. It must be in your sweat. I'm sorry darling, but you absolutely reek."

A red-faced, embarrassed husband sloped upstairs to the bathroom, while he was thinking, " Ah well, never mind, at least she's talking to me now."

HOPE

The new week dawned, and Duncan was at the train station early. He was delighted to see his former schoolmate Karel on the platform, and they boarded the train together, to find an empty carriage where they could reminisce in private about their childhood. A few minutes into the journey Duncan asked Karel how his family were getting on as he could remember his mother being a lovely lady. She always asked them to come in when they called at his house for Karel to come out and play, and she would always give them a biscuit each. They called for Karel often in those days. Duncan remembered Karel's father being seated in the same armchair. He always had a smile on his face when he saw Karel's friends, yet he never took him to the park to play football, or go swimming with him. He didn't join in any other activities as most fathers would occasionally do.

"My mother is fine; she still lives in the same house in Dysart. I get to see her most weekends because she loves to see her grandchildren and we all go over together. I have one girl and two boys. I'm afraid my father passed away thirteen years ago." Karel explained.

"I'm so sorry to hear that, he wouldn't have been that old, would he?" Duncan asked.

"No, he had just had his fiftieth birthday, we had a party for him on his birthday and he looked awful, his lungs were packing up and he could hardly breath. I found out more about his life on the day of his funeral, than I ever knew before. Unbelievably there were two Czechoslovakian men at the funeral. They were pilots who had served with my father and fought with him in the Battle of Britain. He was in the 310 Fighter Squadron that was made up of Czechoslovakian pilots and they were based at RAF Duxford in England. Apparently, when he applied to join the regiment, he was under suspicion by the authorities of being a German spy. I didn't know that the Gestapo went to such lengths. One pilot was called Bohdan, and the other Marek. It was Bohdan that told me that my father was under surveillance for months, until he had shot down his first two Messerschmitt's and the kills had been confirmed. It was only then that he was trusted. My father finished up with eleven confirmed kills before he was shot down. His Hurricane suffered severe damage, and he was forced into an emergency crash landing in a potato field somewhere in Kent. The undercarriage and landing gear had been shot to pieces and the plane burst into flames upon landing. It was the fumes that nearly killed him there and then as apparently they are as dangerous as the flames. They didn't expect my father to last as long as he did, he lived for another thirty years after the crash."

Duncan noticed the tears welling up in Karel's eyes, yet there was a hint of pride in his voice. He asked Karel how his father came to live in Dysart.

After three months in hospital, the burns on his hands and scalp had virtually healed but he was told he could never fly again because his lungs were so severely damaged. He was transferred to a training camp where he helped to train new recruits. The camp was in the Borders, at Charterhall. That's where he met my mother, she was a WAAF, and they became engaged and married in 1944. One year later, after the war had finished, they moved to Edinburgh. The first winter in Edinburgh nearly killed my father as the smog and the smoke from coal fires was destroying what was left of his lungs. So, they moved away from Edinburgh to Dysart. The fresh air coming off the North Sea was much easier for my father to cope with, although his movements were severely restricted. He had a very long journey from his original home in Czechoslovakia. He lived with his parents in a town called Lidice, but he was lucky enough to escape to England before the German invasion. His parents and his sister were not so lucky. He never saw them again and he never wanted to go back home to his motherland. My mother said he hated Germany for what they did to his family and his country. There was one occasion he fell out with a neighbour because the neighbour had bought a German car."

Duncan decided to change the subject, "How are your sisters going on these days? I remember your eldest sister was called Jana, but what was your younger sister called?" Inquired Duncan.

"Eliska. They're both married and doing fine. Eliska lives here in Kirkcaldy with her husband and their one son. She's now Eliska Stone. Her husband Roy is a lawyer." Explained Karel.

"What about Jana?" Duncan asked.

"Jana now lives in a suburb of Edinburgh, a place called Broomhouse. She's married, but they don't have any children yet, although they have not given up hope that one day it might happen. They both work at Edinburgh Airport full time. Ian, her husband, works for a cargo-handling company and Jana works in the booking office for British Midlands Airways. It's very handy for them as they only live four miles from the airport. With Jana working in the booking office, she knows how to get massive discounts on flights from the company. They often fly down to the Channel Islands for long weekends and then straight back to work at the airport. Good luck to them I say. Anyway, that's enough about my family. What about your family?"

"My ex foster parents still live in Dysart. I occasionally visit them. The last time was about four or five months ago. I'm married now to Elizabeth; we have one son who is fifteen and a daughter who is almost fourteen. Her birthday is on the twenty-first of June. I suppose we are just a normal family, scraping by as best as we can."

"What sort of work have you had, Duncan?" Asked Karel.

"Where do I start? I dropped out of university after two years because I got married and needed to earn a wage so we could rent our own flat, in St Andrews. That's where Elizabeth was still finishing her degree at the university. I worked as a brickie's labourer on building sites for two years. Mainly housing developments. It was hard work, carrying bricks and mortar in a brickie's hod, especially when I had to carry the bricks up the ladder onto the scaffold. It was good because I used to get paid cash-in-hand. In the winter, we had lots of weeks when it was too cold to lay bricks so I did a bit of work in a hotel. A waiter during the day and a barman in the evening. I made more in tips than wages. I was a postman once for a brief period, until a massive Alsatian acquired a particular taste for my arse. When the weather improved, I packed it in and went back to the labouring. I enjoyed the labouring in summer. It kept me fit and built my strength up."

"When I was twenty-one, we bought the house in Kirkcaldy. My father-in-law got me a job at his engineering company as they needed a storeman and general labourer. I was quite happy with that as I was earning a reasonable wage and because I was settled in a regular job. I was also playing football as a part-time professional for Raith Rovers. I was in the junior team at first, but I soon got into the first team. However, I was still only paid as a part time professional, and in the summer, I once worked for three months as a waiter again at weekends. With my regular wage at the factory and money coming in for playing football we were comfortable, and I managed to finish my degree at night school. That took me two years.

It was only when my playing career finished at twenty-eight that I seriously looked for a job in medicine or anything similar in the pharmaceutical industry. After all, that's what I went to university for and won my degree with honours. Currently, I am the undermanager in the manufacture and transport department at a company in Leith. We make cough sweets and medicines. I hate it, but I started there about eleven years ago when I finished playing football, and I've never got round to leaving, although I think about it all the time. It's the travelling apart from anything else, and the salary is *woeful*."

"Why did you finish playing football?" Karel asked.

"I had a very bad knee injury; I was only one more bad tackle away from being crippled, so I called it a day after taking specialist advice. I used to love playing football. I think it's the only vocation I've ever been truly happy doing. It didn't matter to me whether we won or lost, I just enjoyed the game. To think I got paid for doing it as well made it even more enjoyable."

"How much did you get paid for playing football?"

"Not much to begin with. In 1969 I was in the Junior team for half a season before I got in the first team. When I was in the first team, I got paid twenty pounds a week, but that was only during the football season when I was playing regularly. I didn't get a penny in the summer months as I wasn't a full-time professional. Mind you, there were quite a few times when I got a bit of bonus on the quiet. I once scored a hat-trick in a cup game and one of the directors slipped twenty pounds into my hand in the car park. I remember him saying, 'Keep it to yourself, laddie, you've earned it' I reckon I received as much in backhanders as I got paid in real wages. They were happy days. I wish I could do it all over again. Anyway, what do you do for a living? You've never mentioned it." Duncan asked.

"I work for Her Majesty's Government. I work in the Lothian and District tax assessment office. I am an income tax inspector," said Karel, and they both fell about howling with laughter at the sheer absurdity of the conversation. When he had regained his composure, Duncan made a gesture with his forefinger of zipping his mouth shut, which made Karel laugh even more.

"I don't think I could stay somewhere where I'm not happy. If you're not happy at work, you should leave. Something will always turn up, eventually. A person with your qualifications will always find a job." Said Karel, with a voice of authority.

"It's bloody ironic that I've recently had the chance of a new job. Unfortunately, it's three hundred miles away in Nottingham. They are expecting a decision today. I have spoken to my wife about it, but she doesn't want to sell up and move all that way. She has a point: if the job fell through, we would be up the creek without a paddle and we would regret it for the rest of our lives. It's five and a half thousand a year more than I earn now, but Elizabeth is right: it's far too risky to move now we are so settled." explained Duncan.

"Have you thought about commuting?" Inquired Karel. "You don't need to sell your house and move to Nottingham. Why not consider travelling and coming back at weekends? If I were offered an extra five and a half thousand, I'd be off like a shot."

Duncan had never even thought about the possibility of commuting to work. The idea hit him like a sledgehammer, and he was momentarily stunned into silence.

Karel continued. "You can drive there. There's the train, there's also an airport just outside the city. What's the problem? There's lots of ways you could do it. I know that I would for that sort of money. You would be silly not to."

"Yes, but they need a decision today, and if I was going to commute, I would need to speak to Elizabeth first to gauge her reaction. I can't make a decision just like that."

"Well, stall for time then. Ring them up today and tell them yes, you would like to take the job, but to be fair to your current employers you would like to give a month's notice. You could always throw in that you have booked a holiday for two weeks in July, so could you start after your holiday? See what they say. It's worth a try. If you then decide to take the job, you will have lots of time to hand in your notice. If you decide to stay where you are, then you can ring them up in Nottingham and say you've changed your mind. What can they do?"

"Did they teach you all this skulduggery when you were training to be a tax inspector?" Inquired Duncan, much to Karel's amusement. Karel also remembered that his sister Jana worked at Edinburgh Airport in the booking office.

"Duncan, I will call Jana this evening and have a word with her about cheap flights and how to get them. I'm sure she has flown to Nottingham before now."

The train was slowing down on the station approach when Karel wrote down his address and telephone number to hand to Duncan. He then suggested.

"Stall for time and see what options are available for you. If ever you need advice about your income tax, give me a ring and I will help you, but if I were you, I'd keep comments about backhanders and cash-in-hand wages to yourself."

Duncan drew his forefinger over his lips in a mock zipping motion which caused yet another bout of mirth and they alighted the train together and shook hands.

As he sat on the bus for the last leg of his journey, Duncan was digesting the advice from his childhood friend. He concluded that it would do no harm to stall for time so he could make further inquiries into the practicality of commuting to Nottingham.

He arrived at work and was in high spirits as he clocked on. The morning was passing without incident until Bernard Savage strode up raging, "Are you aware that Robertson has not turned up yet? It's 10am and he's still not here. We haven't had a phone call from him or his wife, so we don't know what's happening. I wouldn't be surprised if we never see him again, the bone-idle bastard. Let me know if you hear anything or if any of the other lads know what's going off."

"Certainly. Let's hope it's nothing serious. He might be ill or maybe he's had an accident." Duncan replied.

Bernard marched off back to his office. Duncan had a feeling that it was the last he would see of Robbo at work. He was right. Two hours later, Bernard came charging up to the loading bay where Duncan was supervising the men with a delivery to Addison and Co.

"What did I tell you? That idle bastard has jacked in. He even got his wife to ring the office and say he's got another job, and could we forward his P45 and his outstanding wages? Not a thought of giving us some notice. I wish I'd have sacked him now on Friday. You shouldn't have talked me out of it, Baker."

Duncan looked across at Bernard and noticed the sheer hate in his eyes. He decided it was pertinent not to say anything that might make matters worse. "Sorry to hear that, shall I call the agency for a replacement?" he meekly asked.

"No, I've already done it. Just make sure that none of the others choose to piss off."

At lunch break, Duncan decided it was time to make the call regarding the job offer in Nottingham. The conversation went better than he could expect. Mr Wignall was delighted to hear that Duncan accepted the offer; he was impressed that Duncan actively sought to work a full month's notice as it showed he had a sense of loyalty. When Duncan then falsely mentioned he had a holiday booked in July, he was told that would work out even better. Apparently, they were installing a new computer modem system into the MT & AS building, and the contractors were at least a month behind schedule, so it would work out fine if his start was delayed for about six weeks or so. They agreed on a start date of Monday July 22nd.

Mr Wignall concluded, "We will send you a copy of the contract of employment. If you could sign it and return it in the stamped addressed envelope provided, then it's all systems go, I'm looking forward to meeting you, Mr Baker. I will personally meet you and show you round your new department on the Monday morning. Thank you for calling. See you in six weeks."

Duncan was ecstatic. Although he had lied regarding his supposed holiday in July, it didn't really matter. They were happy for him to start in six weeks and that was all that counted. He would decide by the following weekend anyway, so he had plenty of time to make up his mind.

When Duncan went to the loading bay canteen to eat his lunch, he detected the same sour mood among the men as the previous Friday lunchtime. Nobody spoke to him unless he spoke to them first. Their answers were short, curt and to the point, all delivered with a blank expression. It was obvious the men all blamed Duncan for being a co-conspirator in the downfall of Robbo. Although he was disappointed with the men's demeanour, he thought, "They can sulk all they like; my conscience is clear. I tried my best to keep Robbo in his job, but he's obviously done a bunk. They'll get over it. Mind you, I will miss him. He was as much use as a pox doctor's clerk, but he was good for a laugh, and I loved listening to his stories."

As Duncan was nearing the end of his lunchbreak, the silence in the canteen was shattered by Bernard Savage having yet another monumental angry rant.

"Which one of you loaded up the pallet for the delivery to Parkers on Friday afternoon? I need to know! We've just had a phone call from Frank Parker. There was a dead rat inside one of the boxes. It could only have been put there deliberately. I'll get to the bottom of this, even if I have to sack the lot of you. Well, who loaded it?"

"It was Sammy Robertson, Mister Savage," said Bill Crossley, the longest serving warehouse labourer, who was approaching his retirement. "It was only one pallet, and he said he would sort it out while the rest of us were unloading the big delivery from Woodcocks." Bill continued.

Bernard was seething. He could hardly contain himself, "I knew it, if I ever clap eyes on him again, I'll swing for him. We've lost a regular customer because of this. The directors will have my guts for garters when they have the next board meeting. It comes to something when we cannot trust the staff."

Duncan noticed how the top of Bernard's shirt front was covered in spittle after his explosive tirade. The men all stood there motionless and silent, not wanting to say anything, and then become the victim of his retribution. Eventually, Bernard stormed off back to his office. In a strange way Duncan felt slightly sorry for Bernard. If indeed he was to be made the scapegoat in the eyes of the directors, it just didn't seem fair. There was no doubt in Duncan's mind what had happened. The pallet would have been shrink-wrapped in polythene once the boxes were stacked, and it was an absolute certainty that the rat was placed inside the box beforehand. Robbo had left his mark.

When Duncan arrived home that evening, Elizabeth informed him that the earliest appointment she could get for them to have a meeting with the bank manager was on the Thursday morning. She had also been to the job centre, but there was hardly anything at all apart from part-time bar work.

On the Tuesday morning Duncan and Karel met on the platform as normal. Karel asked how Duncan had fared when he made the phone call regarding the job offer.

"I didn't even have to stall for time. I can start in six weeks if I want to take the job. Other than that, I will tell them next Monday if I decide not to accept it. The phone call could not have gone any better." said Duncan as they boarded the train and found a carriage that was almost empty where they could continue their conversation.

Karel spoke first. "I rang Jana last night and asked her about the costs of flying to East Midlands Airport and back and which are the cheapest tickets. I also asked her how many flights there are and at what time they take off and arrive. She said something about standby tickets, but then she said she is coming up this way on Thursday. She has a dental appointment at two o'clock, so she is taking the afternoon off work. After the dentist, she is driving up to Dysart to see our mum. She will call in and see me about eight o'clock or thereabouts on her way home. She will bring a timetable of the flights and she will have all the information regarding flight fares, so it might be worth your while speaking to her in person if you are really serious about commuting to Nottingham. She will explain everything to you."

"Thanks for that, Karel. I might be off work on Thursday as we have an appointment with the bank manager in the morning to see about a loan, so it won't be a problem to come and see you both. By the way, do you ever see any of the other kids that were in our class at school? I lost contact with everyone when I went to St Andrews."

"I see some of them. Most of them are married with children just like us, but there's one or two of them that things didn't work out too well. Can you remember that idiot who thought he was the best fighter in the whole school? He used to bully all the juniors. 'McMinn the Dim' we called him. Well, anyway, he has been arrested at least three times for indecently exposing himself in front of teenage girls. The last time he received a twelve-month sentence in HMP Perth." Continued Karel.

Duncan was howling with laughter, tears coming down his cheeks at the thought of McMinn the Dim standing there in a flasher's mac in the dock while the magistrates sent him down for a twelve-month stretch. Duncan's laughter was infectious, and Karel also burst out in raucous laughter, much to the annoyance of the few passengers that were hoping for a quiet journey, particularly a large, bearded man who asked them brusquely to "be quiet please." They both buried their heads in the morning newspapers until they reached Waverley Station.

When Duncan arrived at work, he had to see Bernard regarding booking a day's holiday for the Thursday. *"What!"* screeched Bernard. "Now you want the whole day off, do you? You said that you were coming in at lunchtime when you asked me yesterday."

"I'm extremely sorry Mr Savage, but we now have another appointment in the afternoon, so it will not be worth coming in. I've decided to have the full day off." Duncan pleaded.

That evening, Duncan was as relieved as at any time in his employment to clock off and head for home. At the bus stop, Hughie Dwight, one of the labourers was waiting for the bus.

"Duncan, have you heard about Robbo?" Hughie asked.

"No, why?"

"He's now cleaning windows again. One of the drivers, John Anderson, saw Robbo on Monday night in the pub. He told John that you saved him from getting the sack. None of the lads were aware of it until about an hour ago when Anderson came into the loading bay and told us all about it. Some of us owe you an apology, Duncan."

"Water under the bridge, Hughie. No bother."

Duncan arrived home to an empty house. He was glad of the quiet and was looking forward to a restful evening after yet another long and testing day. Elizabeth had left him a note propped up against the kettle to say she would be home about 8.00pm and she would bring him haddock and chips. It was exactly one week since Duncan had opened the letter and received the offer of the job in Nottingham. It seemed as if it had been the longest seven days of his life. He was very tired and could quite easily have fallen asleep, until he was stirred by the sound of Cuthbert pulling up outside.

Duncan ate his dinner and was half asleep as Elizabeth was telling him all about her day at the golf club. By the time she had finished, she noticed his eyes were almost closed. Getting up early for work at 5.30am was taking a distinct toll.

"Why don't you have an early night, Duncan? You look shattered," she said.

The following morning, Duncan met Karel on the platform again at the exact place as the two previous days. They were both carrying a lunchbox and a daily newspaper. As the train arrived, they boarded together and then found two seats for the journey ahead. They even sat in the same format; Karel was seated with his back to the engine and Duncan was facing the engine. Duncan was horrified to think that this could possibly be his daily routine for the rest of his working life. He confirmed that he would be able to go to Karel's home on Thursday evening as he was now taking a day off work. Karel asked him to bring along his tax code or his latest wage slip so that he could work out how beneficial the job in Nottingham was likely to be.

Karel explained. "It's no use earning an extra five and a half grand and then paying it all out in extra income tax and travelling and lodging expenses. If you give me an hour tomorrow night, I'll sort it out and let you know if it's going to be worth your while."

"Thanks for that. I'll be there at eight." Replied Duncan.

The rest of the journey gave them time to reminisce about their childhood days at school. They remembered Mr Thomson, a science teacher who had developed the habit of saying everything at least twice. All the children cheekily called him "Two Times Thomson" behind his back. There was a lady mathematics teacher who was very timid, and she had a particularly quiet voice and spoke in barely a whisper. Her name was Mrs Winfield. Karel recalled how the children all called her "Whispering Winnie." Duncan was amazed at how Karel could recall the teachers' names from over twenty years ago, as he had forgotten them, until he was reminded of them. It was a pleasant journey, and Duncan arrived at the factory in capital spirits. On that Wednesday, Duncan was continually plagued by Bernard, who was constantly wittering about making sure the men knew what was expected of them the following day on the Thursday.

"It's all in hand, Mr Savage. Don't worry." Said Duncan.

"Don't worry!" Bellowed Bernard. "If we don't keep our eyes on the bastards, they'll be sending out shipments of dead rats again, and that'll be more customers we lose. You can't trust them an inch."

Later that afternoon, Duncan was talking to Bill Crossley about his forthcoming retirement.

"Yes, another four months and I'll be gone from here." Said Bill with a smile as wide as the Firth of Forth. "I won't be sorry when I've gone either. There's too much aggravation and backstabbing here now compared to the old days. It used to be a good firm to work for, but it started going downhill when that miserable swivel-eyed shithouse got promoted to manager. The way he's carrying on, he's likely to blow a gasket before too long. He's a prime candidate for a heart attack. You can see it in his eyes. Mark my words."

On the train home that evening, Duncan could not get the final comment of Bill Crossley out of his mind, and he also remembered something else that had been nagging at him for several days. He had not had the chance to rebuke his son, after he had the misfortune to witness the fleeting vision of Alexander with his latest trollop hurriedly trying to get their clothes on. As Duncan was due to have the following day off work, he planned to confront Alexander in the morning before his son set off for school, as he had hardly seen him since the previous Saturday afternoon.

When he eventually arrived at home, Duncan was very tired. He was looking forward to an extra two hours in bed in the morning. Perhaps Bill had been right, the aggravation and stress levels at work had increased significantly, particularly since the incident of the dead rat. It was a stressful and tiring environment guaranteed to sap the energy of even the fittest.

Elizabeth apologised to Duncan as she served his dinner. "Sorry love. We need to do some shopping tomorrow. This is all that we have left. The bairns had chips for their tea."

"Never mind, Lizzie. I'm quite partial to beans on toast." Said Duncan with a deep twist of sarcasm in his voice.

"I can't help it, love; money seems to go nowhere these days. It's high time that I got a job and started earning so I can contribute to our finances. I heard there's a chance of a job at the petrol station. They are looking for a cashier to start next week according to Sue Walker. I was at the garage yesterday for petrol and asked if the job is still on offer. They said it was and the boss will be in tomorrow. What do you think about us going to see him after we've been to the bank?"

"*What do I think!* " Roared Duncan. "I'm not surprised they want a cashier; the bloody place has been robbed twice already this year, *both* times in broad daylight. The last time they threatened the cashier with a knife. If you think that I'd be happy for you to get a job there then you're sadly mistaken. No chance, not a prayer. I'd sooner go and earn more money selling my bloody arse in Edinburgh at the weekends. There must be something else."

"It's either cleaning or part-time bar work, and you've never wanted me to do any of those either; I've got to do something as it's getting me down, as we seem to be getting nowhere. Another thing I am worried about is this business of getting a bank loan. We struggle to get by as it is even without having to pay a bank loan back. How are we going to cope?"

It's late in the day, Lizzie I'm absolutely knackered and I'm finding it hard to think straight. Can we discuss this in the morning? And yes, I'm worried about it too."

They settled down to a quiet night in front of the television. Duncan was fast asleep within twenty minutes and Elizabeth couldn't help but notice how he was twitching about in the chair. She was sure that something was bothering him. She was right, as usual.

The Thursday dawned on what was to be a momentous day for the Bakers. It was June 13th, eight days away from midsummer's day. The weather was glorious, and Duncan awoke galvanized with a fresh bout of optimism. The extra two hours in bed had certainly been beneficial to him. When he heard Alexander coming down the stairs, he took the opportunity to have a serious chat with him.

"Sandy, can you give me a lift with something at the bottom of the garden?"

When they were alone at the bottom of the garden, Duncan began. "I don't need a lift with anything, but me and you need a serious word in private, my lad. I asked you down here because your mother doesn't know what I witnessed last Saturday. I'm not happy about you turning our house into a knocking shop. You're only just fifteen. I hope you know what you're doing, and if you are indulging in that sort of behaviour, I hope you are being careful. Are you aware of sexually transmitted diseases? And another thing: is your girlfriend the same age as you? If she is, you could get into serious trouble. You've got to be more careful."

Alexander replied. "She's not my girlfriend, and I'm sorry but I haven't got a clue how old she is. I'll ask her the next time I see her. And yes, dad, we were careful, or would have been if you hadn't burst in on us."

"What do you mean she's not your girlfriend? What sort of a strumpet is she?"

Alexander burst out laughing and almost doubled up with mirth. "Strumpet? For Christ's sake, where did you get that from?"

"It's no laughing matter. If she's that free and easy you could be catching anything from her."

"Dad, I know all about contraception. It wasn't the first time. Emma is okay. She's one of the lads. Most of my mates have been there before me and they didn't have any problems afterwards."

"*Afterwards!* " bellowed Duncan. "For God's sake, just be careful. We don't want the police knocking on the door if she's underage. Nor do we want you having treatment at the pox clinic. And stop smirking. Your mother would be mortified if she knew what you were getting up to."

"Have you finished, dad? I've got an important exam this afternoon and we've got a free revision period this morning. I could do with not being late today."

"Well, just be bloody careful, and don't be so bloody cheeky."

Duncan stood and watched his firstborn walk back up the garden path and realized how tall he had become. He was only an inch or so smaller than Duncan. He watched him disappear through the conservatory doors into the house. He had a smile on his face as he grudgingly appreciated that his son was not a young boy anymore; he was certainly confident and growing up perhaps a little too fast. He would be alright.

"What did you want Sandy for?" asked Elizabeth.

"Oh, just man's stuff, Lizzie. Nothing worth bothering about." Said Duncan. Elizabeth knew better; the sideways glance and fixed stare was proof indeed of that. When the children had left for school, Duncan and Elizabeth resumed their conversation from the previous evening.

"It's right what you said last night, Lizzie. I don't think we would be able to afford to pay off a bank loan on just my wages."

61

"I must get a job, whatever and wherever it is. Let's go to the job centre after we have been to the bank," she replied.

Duncan did not say anything to Elizabeth regarding the possibility of commuting to England. After all, if he found out later this evening that it would not be worth his while taking the post, there was no point in broaching the subject now.

It was another glorious sunny day when they set off to the bank. They decided to walk, as they had plenty of spare time. The meeting at the bank went very much as they had expected. As they had never been overdrawn on their joint account and had a savings account, the manager was more than happy for them to have a loan. Mr Hennessey explained all their options and they asked him for a few days to decide. As they left the bank, Duncan asked Elizabeth if she wouldn't mind his having a second look at that new Ford Escort.

"Of course I don't mind. We can't afford it, but you can look as much as you like. I think we might have to settle for a cheaper second-hand car in the long run, and only then if I can get a job that will pay enough wages to make a decent contribution to our finances. And remember this: we need to start putting money aside for when the bairns go to university."

Ten minutes later, they arrived at the car showrooms. The brand-new blue Ford Escort was still on offer, gleaming as the mid-morning sunshine was magnified through the large windows. Duncan recognized Stuart, the salesman whom he was speaking to on the previous Sunday.

"Hello, Stuart. We have come for another look at what's on offer. I think that new blue Escort is out of our price range though. You might have to show us round the second-hand cars."

"Hello Mr Baker. I'm glad you have come back. I told Mr Gemmill you were here on Sunday. He was really pleased to hear you may be interested in one of our cars, although he was sorry to have missed you. He's in his office now, and he told me that if you come back, he wants to speak to you personally. If you wait a minute, I'll go and tell him you are here," said Stuart.

Moments later, a beaming Mr Gemmill came over and introduced himself to the couple. "Mr Baker, or can I call you Duncan?

I haven't seen you for at least ten years. Are you going to introduce me to your beautiful wife?"

"Yes, this is Elizabeth. How did you know she is my wife?"

"Mr Bowyer told me you have a wife. You told him on Sunday. You said that you make all your decisions together. Are you interested in anything that you have seen?" asked Mr Gemmill.

"Yes, we are interested, but money is the deciding factor. It looks like we will have to get a loan to get anything decent. I was casting my eyes over the new Ford Escort, but it's out of our price range. We may have to look at a second-hand car if the price is right." Said Duncan.

"Come through to my office. We can talk in private. Would you like tea or coffee?"

Stuart Bowyer was ordered to make three cups of coffee and bring the biscuits through to the manager's office. Stuart winked at Duncan as they set off following Mr Gemmill.

"Take a seat. Did Stuart tell you that I am a director at the Rovers?" said Mr Gemmill.

"Yes, he did mention it when I told him I used to play for the Rovers," replied Duncan.

"I wish you still played for us now; In my opinion you were the best centre forward we've ever had. It was sickening when you had that injury, both for you and the club. When I think back to all the players we've had at Starks Park, you and Jim Baxter stand out well above the rest. This lot we've got now are just obsessed with money. Talking about money, we let you down badly when you had to retire. I stood down as chairman because of it. I was totally ashamed."

"In what way did the club let me down?" asked Duncan.

"It was not long after you had the specialist advice to retire. We had our usual weekly board meeting at the club and one item on the night's agenda was if we should award you a testimonial match. I had already approached Dundee United and Celtic, and both clubs said they would send a representative team made up of former players and youngsters. We were going through a sticky patch financially at the time. I blame myself for not lobbying the other directors before the meeting. The board were all arguing about the costs of a testimonial match being played in midweek. They were moaning about the floodlight costs and who would pay for the stewards and gatemen? They were even arguing about who would pay for printing the programmes. As you know, the chairman only has the casting vote if all the other members have voted and it's a stalemate. They voted unanimously to reject the proposal, just because you were only a part-time player, plus the additional costs to the club of staging the match. I was very angry. I stood down as chairman, but I retained my position on the board. Right, let's see what we can do for you. Did you say you have to take out a loan?"

"Yes, we are looking for a decent car that's going to last a lot longer than our last car. I would love to be able to afford a new one, but it's out of our price range I'm afraid. Would you be able to recommend any of the used cars?" Inquired Duncan.

"Have you thought about buying a demonstrator? I have just the thing if you are interested." Said Mr Gemmill.

"What's a demonstrator?" Asked Duncan.

"We always have two brand new cars of each model here in the showroom that we use for customers to take test drives. We usually sell them after six months to pave the way for brand new registrations. My wife has one of them now. She only uses it to do her shopping and to go to the golf club, it was first registered in April this year, so it's only a few months old. I can do you a good deal on it if you are interested. It's exactly the same as the blue Ford Escort in the showroom, same model, same colour, same specification. I can sell it to you at cost to the garage so long as we break even. As I see it, I will feel a lot better if I can do you a favour, particularly as you should have had a testimonial when you had to retire. How does three thousand pounds sound?"

Duncan looked across at Elizabeth and noticed the glazed look in her eyes, and that her mouth was slightly ajar in amazement. "That sounds fantastic, Mr Gemmill, but we are not here to accept charity. That's almost two thousand pounds less than the new one in the showroom."

"It's not charity. So long as the garage breaks even on this one sale, it doesn't matter, but that's strictly between the three of us. I have lots of the current players coming in buying their motors. I give them all a very good discount because it's good for business. Free advertising, turnover. That's all I care about."

"If that's the case, then yes, we are interested. When could we see the car and have a test drive?" Inquired Duncan.

"I will get the car in tomorrow for a full valeting. Can you come in on Saturday morning, and if you are happy with it, you can leave a deposit and drive it away. The car will be yours."

"Thank you very much, Mr Gemmill. We will see you on Saturday morning." said Duncan.

"I'm so glad I was here when you arrived. Another five minutes and you would have missed me. I've got to go to the Job Centre now, unfortunately Verity is leaving at the end of next week. I don't know how we'll manage without her so I need to go and place an advert immediately. I should have done it earlier, but I've been far too busy."

"By coincidence, we are on our way to the Job Centre." There was stunned silence for a few seconds, but it seemed an eternity. "Elizabeth is looking for a job. That's why we are going there now." Continued Duncan.

"What sort of a job are you looking for, Elizabeth?"

"Anything really, I can't afford to be choosy. Both our bairns are at the age where they are costing us a fortune, to say nothing of the fact that they'll both be off to university soon."

"Have you ever done any secretarial work, Elizabeth?" Inquired Mr Gemmill.

"No, I've never had full-time employment, apart from raising the bairns," she said.

"Oh, I was hoping that you could use a computer and type. I don't hold out much hope of getting someone to replace Verity at the Job Centre: half the people these days can't read or write properly. I might have to advertise to a much wider audience."

Duncan and Elizabeth smiled simultaneously, something that was picked up by Mr Gemmill.

"What's the matter? Have I said something wrong?" he asked.

"No, it's nothing really, it's just that when you mentioned people can't read or write properly, you obviously wouldn't have been aware that I have a Master's degree in English, achieved with honours in 1969 at the University of Saint Andrews. I have also written five books. Three of the books did quite well, so literacy is probably my strongest asset. Also I have my own computer at home, on which I wrote my novels." She continued.

"Elizabeth, you may be the very person I'm looking for. It's a pity Verity isn't in today or she could have explained what's involved much better than I can. Verity is not really my secretary; she is more of an office manageress. She does all the VAT returns; she sends all the requisition orders to head office to replenish parts. She does all my e-mails and personal letters to head office. She keeps a strict account of all the sales and purchases of used cars; in fact, she is indispensable when I come to think of it." Said Mr Gemmill.

"Why is she leaving?" Inquired Elizabeth.

"She is retiring early. She sadly lost her husband three years ago and she's decided that she's going to move to Jedburgh to be with her daughter and her two grandchildren. She has sold her house, and she is moving down to Jedburgh next weekend. She is at her house now, meeting the young couple who are buying it. She is going to offer them all the furniture. Yesterday she said that all she wants to take with her are her clothes, her jewellery and her memories. That's Verity all over."

"She sounds lovely, I'd like to meet her," said Elizabeth, as Duncan sat bolt upright and tight-lipped hoping that their fortunes were about to change for the better.

Mr Gemmill spoke next: "Elizabeth, could you possibly come in tomorrow and meet Verity? She starts work at 8.30 am and finishes at 5.00 pm. I'm sure that after one day Verity could explain everything and show you her role in keeping this place ticking. If it's acceptable, I can offer you a week's trial period next week where you could work alongside Verity until you know the role inside out. Of course, you will be paid for your time even if things don't work out. The salary is six thousand pounds per annum, which is paid on a monthly basis. That works out at five hundred pounds per month. You would also need to have your National Insurance Number and your latest tax code, and we can take it from there."

"Do I need to bring anything else?" asked Elizabeth.

"No, if the trial goes well and you are successful, I will draw up a contract of employment. I would expect you to work along the same lines as Verity. She works four and a half days a week, and she usually takes her half-day off on Wednesdays but that's her choice. We do also pay all our employees an annual bonus according to how the sales figures have done. We have an excellent team here, and teamwork is our byword, eh Duncan?"

"Yes, Mr Gemmill, teamwork is very important," said a red-faced Duncan, obviously grovelling to his wife's prospective employer.

"Another thing you will need to bear in mind is holidays. You will be entitled to twenty-three days per year plus bank holidays. However, we cannot both be off at the same time, and unfortunately you will not be able to have the same weeks off work as me. I have a time-share apartment in Portugal, and Mrs Gemmill and I always have four weeks holiday on the same dates each year."

"That shouldn't be a problem at all. Thank you, Mr Gemmill, everything sounds perfect, I will not let you down," said Elizabeth.

"Brilliant, just one more thing, Elizabeth. Please call me Mr Gemmill in front of the other employees and customers, but you can call me Martin in private. It's so informal being called Mr Gemmill all the time. See you in the morning, and thank you. You've saved me some time and trouble. I was not overly optimistic about the Job Centre."

"Yes, we don't need to go there now either. See you in the morning Mr Gemmill, er sorry, Martin," she replied.

FOREWARNING

As they sauntered across the showroom forecourt, they could not have been in a happier mood. In the last hour their fortunes had changed enormously, Elizabeth had found a job, although she had to work a week's trial period. The bank had agreed they could have a loan, and they had been offered a car that was almost brand new at an excellent knock-down price.

"We could get away with only borrowing three thousand now," said an excited Duncan. However, Elizabeth had always been less spontaneous than him. Where he would make decisions in an instant, she preferred to give matters considerably more thought.

She said. "Whatever we decide, one thing is for sure. We need to start building up our bank balance over the next two years, ready for when Sandy and Lottie go to university. I was talking to Ruth McGugan on Tuesday in the clubhouse. She was saying that her son is at the University of Stirling and he's now in his third year. She said it's costing her about one thousand pounds a year to pay for his accommodation and welfare."

"I heard the same thing from Ronnie Clark. He's got a daughter who's studying at Glasgow University." Duncan replied.

They decided to borrow three thousand pounds for the car and leave their savings account alone as back-up. If the trial period for the job went to plan and Elizabeth secured the full-time post, the repayments for the loan would be well within their capabilities. They went straight back to the bank and arranged the loan immediately while they were both available to sign the forms. Afterwards, Duncan felt very relaxed, and he was looking forward to the weekend for the test drive and possibly to collect their new car. It was an enormous relief to the couple to have arranged everything so easily. But later, as the afternoon elapsed, Duncan noticed that Elizabeth was getting seriously stressed and twitchy for no apparent reason.

"What's the matter Lizzie? he asked.

"I don't know what to wear tomorrow. Do I wear a dress? Do I wear a skirt and blouse? Do I wear trousers and a shirt? I don't know. I've haven't got anything decent to wear anyway; all my clothes are dropping to bits. I don't want to turn up looking like the Wreck of the Hesperus. I need a new outfit for tomorrow. I'll head off to the shops to see what's on offer."

Duncan smiled as Elizabeth charged out of the front door. He was aware of the nervousness that she would be feeling, but he was so happy for her. She deserved to get a decent job. Two hours later, Elizabeth returned from her shopping expedition complaining about the lack of quality and selection of ladies' clothes shops in Kirkcaldy. She would have to go to Edinburgh at the weekend. However, she had bought a new black skirt and a white blouse to wear the following day. Duncan raised a smile as she was unable to sit still. Her nervousness was blatantly obvious.

"Do you think I need to buy a briefcase? Do you think I should buy some new shoes? What shall I do about lunch, should I take a packed lunch? If it's raining, should I go in Cuthbert or should I walk and take an umbrella? What do you think, Duncan?"

"I think we'll have a takeaway tonight, so you don't have to cook. Stop worrying, you'll be fine. After tomorrow, you'll have a better idea of what you need for next Monday, so we can sort it out at the weekend, and you always look lovely anyway."

As the afternoon wore on, there was more of the same. By the time they had dinner, Alexander and Charlotte had been lectured about making more of an effort to get themselves up and make their own breakfast. From tomorrow, Elizabeth would have to prioritize getting herself ready for work. She would be going out of that door at 8.15 am come what may, whether Alexander and Charlotte were ready for school or not. She need not have worried. They were delighted for her and promised to toe the line. As Elizabeth went to the bathroom for a shower, Duncan informed her that he was going to be out for about an hour. He was going to see Karel and Jana (whom he had not seen for over twenty years).

At eight o'clock Duncan was knocking on Karel's door. "Hi, come in. Jana has just arrived two minutes ago. That's good timing." Said Karel with a big smile.

Duncan entered his friend's house for the first time. He was amazed at how neat and tidy everything was. The living room walls were adorned with countless framed photographs of the three children, all taken at different ages and stages of their lives. They were beautiful children and Duncan knew straight away that the parents were very proud of them.

"Hello, Duncan," said Jana, getting up from the sofa to give him a hug, "I've not seen you since you left school to go to university. I was only fourteen then. It broke my heart when you left. You were the very first boy I ever had a crush on; in fact, half the girls in my class fancied you but you were more interested in playing football. Some of the girls even said you wore your shoes on the wrong feet. You haven't changed much since I last saw you: you're still as handsome as ever."

A blushing Duncan proffered an awkward smile and gave her a big hug. It was time to change the subject. "You are looking well, Jana; Karel tells me you live in Edinburgh and work at the airport."

"Yes, I understand you want to know about flying to the East Midlands Airport from Edinburgh. I have the timetable here. Generally, there are two flights a day each way. One is very early in the morning and the other one is in the evening. The flights take about one hour and five minutes," Jana explained.

"I see that there's a flight out of Edinburgh at 6.10 am that is scheduled to arrive at the East Midlands at 7.15 am. That would be perfect on a Monday morning. There is a flight back at 6.10 pm that gets to Edinburgh at 7.15 pm. Beeston is on the easiest side of Nottingham to get to the airport; it should only be about half an hour. Have you a list of the cost of the fares?" inquired Duncan.

"This is where it becomes complicated," said Jana. "You can get a normal one-way single ticket or a normal return ticket. However, we never pay for a normal flight ticket. We always get a standby ticket. They are slightly less than half the price of the normal tickets. There is one drawback though: if the flight is fully booked up, you will not get a seat at all which means you would forfeit your fare. Also, you will not be allocated a seat until fifteen minutes before take-off, then they will give you a seat, but you will not have a choice where you sit. I work in the booking office, so I get to know which flights are likely to be fully booked up. Most of the flights are only operating at between fifty and seventy percent occupancy. If I were you, I would always plump for the standby tickets."

"Have you got a list of the ticket prices with you Jana?"

"I have them here. If you look at the standby ticket cost, you'll see what I mean," she replied.

Duncan and Karel were pouring over the figures. With standby tickets, it would cost about £1,400 per annum to fly each way based on forty-eight weeks working year.

"How much does it cost you in petrol to drive to Leith and back every week Duncan?" inquired Karel.

"Well, it's a sixty-mile round trip and that makes it three hundred miles a week. I reckon it was probably costing about twenty pounds a week on average."

"Based on a forty-eight week travelling year, that is £960.00 pounds. Plus, you would be driving 17,000 miles a year, so you would need at least one service, possibly two. That's another £100.00 at least. There's not a lot of difference. If you factor in wear and tear on the car, it doesn't make a lot of economic sense." Karel explained.

"While you two are talking facts and figures, I'm going now." said Jana. It's been great to see you Duncan, hope to see you again soon, don't leave it too long, just think of all the beautiful babies we could have made together."

With that lecherous comment scrambling Duncan's brain, Jana bade her farewells. She gave both men a big kiss on the cheeks, although she lingered slightly longer when her lips were attached to a red-faced Duncan. She gave him a saucy wink as she headed for the door. He was totally perplexed and slightly relieved when he heard her car start outside, and he didn't know what to say for the best.

It was Karel who spoke first. "Your face, Duncan, it's a picture. She really got you going then, didn't she? She's always been a wind-up merchant."

"I thought she was serious. Is your other sister like that?"

"No, Eliska lives up to her name. It's a divine name meaning 'Pledge to God' in Czech. She's not like Jana at all."

"Do all Czech names have a meaning?" inquired Duncan.

"I think so. Jana means God's gift. My name means a free man," explained Karel.

"Have your children got Czech names?"

"No, the boys are named Andrew and Gordon, but my daughter is named Katrina which is Scottish and Czech. I didn't want my sons to go through the infantile name-calling that I suffered. It amazed me the sheer number of idiots who kept saying, 'why have you got a girl's name?' Then each time I had to say it's K-A-R-E-L, not Carol. It gets on your nerves when you've heard it thousands of times."

"Yes, I remember McMinn the Dim going on and on in the playground one day until you punched him and made his nose bleed. He never bothered you much after that," laughed Duncan.

"Yes, but I didn't want my lads to have to go through the same thing as I went through."

"Where are the children now?" Duncan asked.

"Sally has taken them all to the pictures. There's a new James Bond film on. They won't be back until much later, so shall we press on?" Karel asked.

"Yes, sorry, Jana threw me out and I forgot what I came here for," spluttered Duncan.

Thirty minutes later when all the figures were analysed, it was Karel who did the summing up. "Duncan, currently your salary of £7,000.00 minus Income Tax, National Insurance and travelling costs leaves you an approximate disposable income of £4,800.00 If you took the new job at £12,500.00 and commuted each Monday and Friday, your Income Tax and National Insurance contributions would increase. However, your petrol costs would decrease significantly. If you add the flights and accommodation, it will leave you with a disposable income of approximately £8,600.00. That is a total increase of £3,800.00 a year, not to be sniffed at in my view."

"Yes, interesting, definitely worth thinking about. We are coming up to a very expensive period in our lives where that sort of extra money would go a long way to seeing us through. I'll speak to Elizabeth and see what she thinks. Thanks, Karel. I'll go now, Elizabeth will be running round like a headless chicken; she's got her first day at work tomorrow on a week's trial."

"Before you go, there's another thing to consider. If you decide to take the job in England and commute to work, you don't need to permanently commit yourself. You could stay for about four to five years while you are paying for the bairns at university, and then when they have left university and are earning their own keep, you could pack up and look for something local again. They won't know that you only have the intentions of staying there for a short duration. Think about it; oh, and when you get home and you speak to Elizabeth, tell her good luck from me. Take this sheet with you. It's got all the information on. I'll see you in the morning Duncan."

"Thanks Karel. See you in the morning."

On his way home, Duncan was digesting all the facts and figures on the sheet. One thing stood out: an extra £3,800.00 pounds to put in the kitty. But was it worth it when he would have to be away from home four nights a week? As things stood, he hardly saw much of his wife and children in his current employment. They were all in bed when he got up at 5.30 am and left at 6.25 am, and when he arrived home the children were always out. He saw his wife for a couple of hours each evening, but would things change if her week's trial went well, and she started full-time employment? He knew instinctively that there would be very little chance of discussing things with her tonight. He was right. She was still worrying to excess about her first day at work in the morning. Duncan was tolerant and tried to calm her fears but without much success. They both had a fitful night's sleep. Elizabeth could hardly sleep at all and spent the whole night tossing and turning while repeatedly accidently waking her husband. It was a relief for Duncan when he crawled out of bed at 5.30 am after giving sleep up as a bad job. Twenty minutes later, Elizabeth arose still bleary-eyed and half-asleep. As she dragged herself into the kitchen, Duncan said to her. "I heard you stumbling round in the bedroom. Try not to worry. You'll be fine. After today you'll wonder what all the fuss was about."

"Thanks, Duncan. I hope so," she replied.

As he was up early, Duncan decided to walk to the train station so as to spare Elizabeth another thing to worry about. It was a pleasant, warm but cloudy morning when he ambled across the town, arriving in plenty of time to buy his ticket and purchase a newspaper. He was so glad it was almost the weekend; just one more day to grind through was uppermost in his thoughts.

Karel was waiting on the platform at his usual spot. They continued the previous evening's agenda as Karel suggested that if Duncan could find someone with a spare bedroom to rent for four nights a week, he may even be able to save more money by not having

73

to pay for a B&B. Also, there was the possibility that some landladies would charge a lesser rate for a long-term boarder, all things to consider when making his decision. They then settled down to reminisce about the past.

Karel told Duncan an interesting fact about a lad from their school who was a year younger than the two of them. They called him Arthur, but that was not his real name. He was very small, he had dark hair and he wore big thick-rimmed glasses with dark frames. They all called him Arthur because he looked like Arthur Askey. "Can you remember him now, Duncan?"

"Yes, I can't remember his real name though. I wonder what he looks like now, I'd love to meet some of these characters from our past." said Duncan.

"Well, you don't want to be in such a hurry to meet him," replied Karel.

"Why?" inquired Duncan.

"He's the mortician at the infirmary."

They both roared with laughter, again to the annoyance of the other passengers. Duncan thought of how much pleasure he was having travelling to work on the train. He would sorely miss his daily conversations with his friend. He decided they would keep in touch whatever the outcome of his employment decision. When he arrived at work, he thought about Elizabeth and realized that she would already be on her way to work. He knew for sure she would not be late. He was right: She arrived at work early, looking elegant in her new black skirt and white blouse. Her jet-black hair was neatly curled at the shoulders, and with just a hint of make-up and mascara, she exuded more than a touch of class. Verity had not arrived yet, but Martin Gemmill was there to welcome her.

"Good morning, Elizabeth. It's good to see you nice and early. Verity should be here soon. She's never late. In fact, that's her now walking across the forecourt. She will show you the ropes, much better than I ever could."

When all the formal introductions had been made, Elizabeth accompanied Verity to her office. She noticed the nameplate on the door," Verity Barratt" which gave her a slight feeling of apprehension. Would she ever have her name on the door like that? Time would tell.

Duncan sought out Bernard Savage for a chat to find out if things had run smoothly in his absence the previous day. Bernard was in his office, sitting in his leather chair. Duncan had never seen Bernard looking so scruffy and downtrodden. He had enormous bags under his eyes, his shoulders were drooping forward and his back was hunched. He was unshaven, possibly unwashed, and he looked half asleep.

"Good morning, Bernard. Did everything go okay yesterday?" Bernard did not reply verbally but gave a small nod to indicate that all had been well. "Okay, I'll carry on then, see you later, Bernard."

Duncan left the office and made his way to the loading bay. For the first time in his employment, he felt truly sorry for Bernard. He could not understand how and why he was looking so abjectly pathetic. Had something happened the day before in his absence? The lads on the loading bay would know for sure. It was a grinning Geoff Sutton who told him what had occurred.

"The directors had an emergency meeting yesterday. It looks like we've lost another order. Wilson's have cancelled their monthly order. It sounds like they got wind of what happened on the Parker's order, and they have cancelled now. Apparently, the directors had Savage in their office yesterday and blamed him for the lost orders, and not being able to control the staff. It's not his fault; we all know who's to blame. One of the secretaries who was there taking the minutes told us in the strictest confidence that Savage was blubbering like a baby. At one stage he threw himself on the floor wailing and beating his fists on the carpet. Nobody knew what to say or do, she said. The directors were all staring at each other until one of them told him to get up and pull himself together, or, if he wasn't up to the job then he'd better go home. She said it was awful. She was nearly crying herself when she told us. The sad thing is the girls on the production line were laughing about it when he went to do the fire extinguisher checks later yesterday morning, and that set him off again. He went home at dinner time and didn't come back until this morning. There is a strong rumour that they were talking about redundancies. Last in first out we've heard."

"Thanks, Geoff. I certainly haven't heard anything about redundancies. It's Chinese whispers probably. If I hear anything, I'll let you know. In the meantime, come to me for the delivery schedules, and any decisions that need making no matter how big or small. Let's leave Mr Savage alone for a while," said Duncan.

There was no need for the staff to stay away from Bernard. He had no intention of coming out of his office. Duncan wondered if he ought to pop in and see how he was, and if there was anything he could do for him, but after giving it much thought, he decided that it would be better to leave him alone. Hopefully, with a stress-free day and the weekend to follow, he might feel much better by the following week. Duncan gathered all the men in the loading bay and told them not to disturb Mr Savage. "You can come and see me if there's a problem." He emphasized the point that if one of them was feeling under the weather, then he would expect the other labourers to cover for him. "Let's not make matters worse for Mr Savage please." The men stood silently until Duncan had left to go back to the production area. As soon as he had disappeared from sight, the raucous laughing and mickey-taking started. Bill Crossley (who hated Bernard with a passion) was making cuckoo noises and twirling his finger round in circles near his temple, much to the entertainment of the other men. There would be no sympathy from them.

At lunchtime, Duncan sat in the canteen and his thoughts turned to Elizabeth. He wondered how she would get on at her very first day at work. He need not have worried. Elizabeth had impressed Verity immediately with her knowledge of computers, her vast literal capacity, her organizational skills and her excellent speech and manners. As Verity openly admitted, she expected to find that her replacement would be an eighteen-year-old bimbo with an enormous bosom who could hardly read or write. She was delighted to nurture a competent mature lady who was readily accomplished in the art of grammar. She told Elizabeth that her role in the company had grown dramatically over the years. She had originally started as a secretary in 1959 and she had worked for Martin Gemmill for twenty-six years.

"When I first started here, I was just a typist and a filing clerk. I spent many hours typing letters on the old typewriter. We still have it. It's in the stationery cupboard, but it's never used now. All the accounts back in those days were done by hand in the annual ledgers. I used to help Mr Gemmill with the accounts and do all the filing of the ledgers. But things have changed. Now, everything is computerized and nearly all communication is done by emails. The VAT started in 1973 and I had to take charge of doing the VAT returns. Most people pay by cheque these days, but we still bank what little cash we have every Monday. I don't want to scare you by going over everything in one go, so we'll leave some until next week," suggested Verity.

"Why are you retiring, Verity? Mr Gemmill said you are indispensable yesterday." asked Elizabeth, although she already knew the answer.

"I want to see more of my daughter and grandchildren. She lives in Jedburgh and I'm moving down there to live with them. I'm sixty-two now and I have been on my own for three years since my husband passed away. I miss him so much; I become very lonely, and most evenings I spend hours on the phone talking to my daughter and grandchildren. They have built an extension on the side of their house, all self-contained, so I'm going. There's nothing to keep me here, I don't need to work anymore. I'll have all the money from the sale of my house." said Verity.

"Well, I hope things work out for you. Hopefully, we can keep in touch, but I won't ask you anything about work," said Elizabeth.

"You can ask all you like. I'm not saying you'll get an answer, but you can certainly ask anyway," giggled Verity.

Elizabeth was impressed at how accomplished Verity appeared to be and how naturally she coped with everything. It seemed that nothing could phase her. Without doubt, she was going to be a hard act to follow.

As lunchtime arrived, Verity asked, "Do you want to come for a stroll, Elizabeth? I usually go down to the park and go for a walk round the boating lake and find a bench to eat my lunch. It's nice to get out of the office for a while. I find that if I stay in the office to eat my lunch, I end up carrying on working at the same time. It's good to get away for a break. Well?"

"Okay, so long as I don't get into trouble," she replied humbly.

"You'll be fine. Don't bother shutting down the computer. I'll lock the office door on the way out," said Verity.

A short while later, they were sitting on a bench in the park watching two toddlers throwing bread into the water to feed the ducks, while their proud mothers were standing watch over them.

Verity began the conversation. "Elizabeth, I wanted to get out of the office to have a private word with you. There's an old saying that 'walls have ears,' and you never know who's listening. It might be something or nothing, but I need to tell you anyway. When I first started working for Mr Gemmill twenty-six years ago, I wasn't the grey-haired, wrinkled old battle-axe that you see before you now. I was only thirty-six back then and I could still make a few heads turn. When I had settled in, I initially noticed that Mr Gemmill was giving me regular compliments about my appearance. He would say things like 'your hair looks lovely today' and 'you look lovely in that dress.' One day he said, ' I love the smell of your perfume, it's really nice.' All innocent stuff, until one day it dawned on me: he was getting very "touchy-feely," and it was all getting a bit creepy. I knew what he was really after. Aren't all men? Then one day I was in the stationery cupboard opening the filing cabinet, and he crept up behind me and put his hand on my hand. He tried to make out it was an accident, but I knew it wasn't. I pulled my hand away and didn't say anything, but just gave him a Medusa-like stare that told him I wasn't interested. It seemed to do the trick as he never bothered me that way again, thankfully. It was twenty-six years ago, but I know he's still a lecherous old goat, even though he's about sixty himself. You must swear not to repeat this, but the lads who work in the showroom all call him 'The Bluebottle.'

Elizabeth was shocked. She asked, "Why do they call him 'The Bluebottle'?"

"Every time an attractive female comes into the showroom, he's there straight away, buzzing round like a fly round shit. He can't keep away. Even if one of the other salesmen is already dealing with the lady, he can't resist introducing himself and fawning all over them. It's a standing joke among the staff. I'm telling you this, so you can get yourself prepared mentally if it happens to you. I noticed this morning as I arrived, he was already talking to you, and he had that same glint in his eyes and that awful cheesy smile. He's like all men: if he can get something on the side, he'll take it, and bugger the consequences. I hope I'm wrong, and he's past that sort of behaviour now, but Elizabeth, you are very beautiful, and you have legs to die for. I know women who would kill to have legs like yours, so please be careful. It might be beneficial to dress down a bit in future. You look absolutely stunning in that outfit." said Verity.

Elizabeth was speechless. She was very flattered by Verity's compliments, but shocked into silence to hear of the lecherous slant of her new prospective employer. When she finally gathered her thoughts, she thanked Verity for the advice.

It was Verity that changed the subject. "It's lovely here in this park when the weather is nice. I love seeing all the children enjoying themselves. I like to look at the mothers and see the pride in their faces. It makes me so happy. You see quite a few girls from the offices just down the road. They often come here for their lunch, and I love to hear them all so happy when they are laughing and giggling. I heard from one lady who I know, as she often walks her dog round here, that a man got arrested about two months ago. Apparently, he was hiding in the bushes over there, and he was jumping out in front of all the girls waving his wotsit about. He had nothing on under his raincoat. They ought to have sliced it off for him. She said the police caught him later in the day as they knew who it was likely to be as it wasn't the first time he'd done it. They were waiting for him when he got home. He still had his raincoat on and nothing else bar his shoes and socks."

"I hope they throw the bloody book at him." said Elizabeth, wondering what would come up next. She didn't have too long to wait as Verity continued.

"I hope I haven't put you off working for Mr Gemmill. He's loyal to his staff if you are loyal to the company. He can be very generous when the mood takes him, and so long as everything runs smoothly, he is usually amiable and friendly. However, my advice is don't get drawn into calling him Martin. Get used to calling him Mr Gemmill, always. That will let him know that your relationship with him is on purely professional terms. Sorry, there's just one more thing: try to avoid his wife at all costs. I don't like her. She's condescending, arrogant, obnoxious and she comes into the showroom every now and again, often to swap her car for a new one. She usually changes her car every six months, and then the company then sells them on as demonstrators. She came in about a year ago to get her car valeted because she was going to St Andrews to play golf, and she didn't want to arrive there unless her car was gleaming like a new pin. While she was waiting for her car, she ordered me to make her a cup of coffee, but I totally ignored her. She was livid. She was ranting like a banshee to her husband. Mr Gemmill came and asked me why I didn't make the drink for her, and so I told him straight. 'The only person who can order me to make a drink is you Mr Gemmill. Anyone else would need to politely *ask* me to make a drink. I don't respond to orders or bad manners from non-company personnel.' He didn't know what to say and he ended up making the drink himself, but he's never mentioned it to me again. Anyway, if I *had* made her a drink, I would have spat in the cup, so she was better off without. Shall we head back?"

Duncan's organizational skills had been put to the test, and he had passed with flying colours. It was unusual for every delivery to be packed and loaded by four o'clock. With an hour and a half still to go before finishing time, Duncan went across to Bernard's office to see how he was. He was stunned to find the office empty. Bernard had taken all his belongings and left without clocking off. Suddenly he was interrupted by one of the directors. It was Walter McInally who spoke first, short and sharp: "Mr Baker, follow me!"

When Duncan arrived with Walter at the boardroom, he was shocked to see the other three directors. They were all waiting for him. Walter sat down in his leather chair and shuffled a pile of papers. Yet again, Duncan had that feeling of impending doom. He looked along the line of the four men and instantly thought of the Four Horsemen of the Apocalypse.

It was Walter who spoke first: "Mr Baker, I understand you had a day's holiday yesterday. Are you aware of the events of yesterday regarding Mr Savage?"

"Not really. I heard a few rumours, but nothing official." Duncan meekly uttered.

"Yesterday was a disaster. We lost yet another regular order. This might be just the tip of the iceberg. When word gets around, other companies may lose confidence in trading with us. This has been caused by the wilful act of one or more of our employees deliberately sabotaging a small delivery to Parkers. Yesterday, we had to speak to Mr Savage in harsh terms, as the responsibility for all outgoing deliveries comes under his remit. I'm afraid to tell you that Mr Savage did not take it very well. He went home at lunchtime, and today no-one has seen him, but we know he clocked on this morning. Half an hour ago we received a phone call from his wife. He has been to see his doctor and the outcome is that he has had a nervous breakdown. She said that he must have complete rest and take regular medication. The doctor wants to see him again in six weeks' time. So, as it stands, he is out of the picture for the foreseeable future, perhaps even permanently. So, we are asking you to step in and take full control. If things work out, this position will be permanent, and we may even have to let Mr Savage go."

After a few moments of reflection, Walter continued, "Yesterday, we were discussing ways of saving overheads with Mr Savage. After the loss of two regular orders, we need to make drastic cuts. We were discussing the possibility of removing the manager's assistant role completely to save finances. That would mean that your present role in the company would not exist. We then explored the possibility of upgrading one of the warehouse staff to chargehand status with a rise in salary. This would save the company six thousand pounds a year. It would have meant you being offered the position of chargehand. It was at this point that Mr Savage threw himself on the carpet shouting that he couldn't manage to do his job without you. It's patently obvious he is not up to the mark, and he has relied on you to carry his workload for far too long. So, in effect, one of you has to go anyway. Yesterday's woeful performance revealed a lot about the temperament of Mr Savage, I'm afraid if he does come back to work, he will have to undertake a more menial role in the workforce. We must think about reducing the workforce as we adjust to the capacity of our current order book. We need at least a ten percent reduction in the workforce right across the board. What are your thoughts on the matter, Baker?"

Duncan was stunned. He spluttered. "It's all come as a bit of a shock, I'm sorry, but I don't really know what to say. I wondered what had happened to Buffa er... Mr Savage. He was very sullen this morning and could hardly speak. I know one of the loading bay labourers retires in a few months, but I don't know so much about the production area staff. You haven't mentioned if there's an increase in salary if I take on the extra responsibility. Is there an increase in salary? Do you need me to decide now, or could I have the weekend to think about it?"

"Yes, it can wait until Monday morning. But then we must make a list of personnel to release so notices can be drawn up immediately. And yes, the annual salary for the new position will be one thousand pounds above your current salary. Any questions?"

"No, I'm sorry to hear about the loss of another regular order. Let's hope that's the end of the matter," said Duncan.

"Just one more thing, Baker. No-one, absolutely no-one, must know anything about our loss of orders and impending redundancies. Loose talk can be a death sentence if the word gets around. So we expect total silence on your behalf. We want a decision first thing on Monday morning. Goodbye, Baker." Walter concluded.

Duncan left the boardroom feeling hollow inside. He'd always longed for promotion, but not in circumstances like this. The heartless way Walter McInally had spoken about Bernard sickened him to the core. "Nobody deserved to be kicked when they are down," he thought, "not even Bernard."

Duncan ambled over to the loading bay and politely had a quiet word with Alfie Cooper, the agency man who had replaced Robbo, "I'm sorry, Alfie, but we are overstaffed at the moment."

Duncan informed the agency and let Alfie leave early. He decided to tell the men about Bernard's enforced absence and that he would be in charge until further notice. But that was all. There was nothing spoken about redundancies. However, he was still unsure whether he was interested in the promotion. It was obvious that the directors wanted the manager to do the work of two men with a little help from a chargehand on the coalface.

On his way home, as the train passed over the Forth Bridge, his thoughts turned to Elizabeth. How had she got on? He would have been proud if he had seen for himself how impressed Verity had been with her understudy. During the afternoon, Verity understood that she had total confidence in Elizabeth's capabilities and complemented her by saying to Martin Gemmill, "She'll be alright. She's taken to it much easier than I ever did."

As they were finishing work for the day Elizabeth said to Verity, "My husband and I are coming in for a test drive in the morning. We are looking at the Ford Escort that is currently being driven by Mr

Gemmill's wife. It's been offered at a great price. It's a long story. I'll tell you about it next week."

"Hope you don't mind me asking, but how much have you been quoted for the car?" Inquired Verity.

"Three thousand pounds." said Elizabeth.

Verity was stunned. "Please be careful. He's never reduced the price of a car as much as that before. I don't know what his motives are or what Head Office would think. Anyway, you've done very well today, Elizabeth. I'm sure that next week will be a piece of cake."

Elizabeth left for home feeling on top of the world. She was looking forward to telling her husband all about the day's events, and how well things had turned out. Her only concern was whether to tell her husband what Verity had said about Martin Gemmill being a lecherous old goat, but she thought that perhaps Verity was slightly overenthusiastic in casting all men as being in the same mould. Anyway, she felt sure that if anything of that nature occurred, she would be able to deal with it easy enough. It was probably nothing to worry about, so why mention it?

When Duncan arrived home, Elizabeth was standing, waiting at the door to let him in, and she had a smile that signified that her day had been a success. She told him twice everything about how well her day had gone and how wonderful she and Verity had hit it off and how Verity had said that next week would be a piece of cake. She eventually ran out of breath and inquired as to how Duncan's day had gone.

"Terrible, we've lost yet another regular customer, my boss has had a nervous breakdown, we are having to make redundancies next Monday and I am supposed to be the axeman. The board were going to scrap my job which would have meant demotion for me onto the labour force, but now they want me to do the work of two men and they have only offered me a pittance for my troubles. I understand they must make cuts, but not at the expense of my health. I don't want to end up like Bernard, blowing bubbles down my nose."

"Oh, I'm sorry to hear that. What are you going to do?"

"I don't know yet. They want a decision by Monday morning, so we need to do some serious thinking. There are a few options: I could accept the job as it stands and probably end up going doolally like Bernard, I could tell them I don't want their promotion and end up working alongside the labourers for a cut in pay, or I could pack it in altogether and leave. The way I feel that's the most appealing. I don't want to make a rash decision, so I'll give it some thought over the weekend. Anyway, we have the test drive in the morning, so one thing at a time. I suppose Sandy and Lottie have had their dinner already and gone out?" Duncan said.

"Yes, just me and you now. We can eat, or we can work up an appetite upstairs?" offered Elizabeth.

The following morning, they were up early as there was a lot on the agenda. First to the showrooms for the test drive of the new car, then a shopping trip into Edinburgh for Elizabeth to purchase some new outfits for work. She didn't want to be back too late as Charlotte was at the under-sixteen disco again and Elizabeth would pick her up when it finished at six o'clock. They arrived at the showrooms before any other customers had arrived. Martin Gemmill and four salesmen were hovering inside, awaiting the expected Saturday morning rush.

"Good morning. Good to see you both nice and early. I'll get one of the lads to bring the Escort round to the front. It's been valeted and it's ready to go. In fact, it's got nine months road tax left on it and it's almost full of petrol. If you take it for a spin and you like it, all we need is a cheque for the deposit, and you can drive it away." said a beaming Martin Gemmill.

Elizabeth noticed that most of the time that her boss had been talking to them, he hardly looked at Duncan, but was instead, staring at her intently. It made her feel uncomfortable. However, she said nothing about it as she and Duncan excitedly climbed into the-newly polished, gleaming blue Ford Escort. A twenty-minute drive around the town was not even necessary. Duncan knew instinctively that the car was too good an offer to refuse. He put the car through its paces for ten minutes and then swapped seats with Elizabeth so she could drive back to the showroom. The formality of accepting the deal was confirmed and a cheque for the deposit was duly handed over. Finally, Elizabeth was very keen to introduce her husband to Verity. With the consent of Martin Gemmill, they made their way to her office to say a brief hello, much to Verity's delight. She said. "It's nice to meet you Mr Baker. Has Elizabeth finally calmed down yet after yesterday? She was working at a hundred miles an hour all day and there's hardly anything left for me to do."

"I can't thank you enough, Verity. I really enjoyed it yesterday. See you on Monday," said Elizabeth.

"Yes, and you can bring that gorgeous husband of yours in on Monday and leave him here for me to take to Jedburgh."

The smiling couple set off for Edinburgh feeling elated. While on the journey, Elizabeth was making plans for the number of outfits she would need for next week's trial period at work. Would one skirt be enough if she wore it with different blouses? Would she be able to mix and match trousers and shirts? Would she need a new jacket and some shoes to match? New shoes, how many pairs should she get? Should she get a bigger handbag or a briefcase? Make-up? Do I need to replenish my mascara and make-up while I'm here? Her mind was racing overtime.

At the same time Duncan was thinking. "Bloody marvellous. She'll be spending her first month's salary before she even gets her hands on it. No wonder we can never afford a decent holiday. Mind you, this car is lovely to drive. At least it will make going to work a bit easier from now on. Work, work, what am I going to do about work? If they think they are going to send me to the loony bin to hold hands with Buffalo Breath and blow bubbles down my nose, they've got another thing coming. I just wish that Lizzie had already got that job confirmed one way or another, so that would give me a better idea of what to do. At least the traffic is light today; we'll be there soon."

"What do you reckon then Lizzie?" he asked.

"I was thinking of Marks and Spencer first if that's okay?" she replied.

"The car, the bloody car. What do you think of the car? That's what I'm asking."

"Oh sorry, I was miles away. Yes, it's nice, lovely and smooth. Are you happy with it?"

"Yes, darling, I am. Marks and Spencer it is then."

DECLINE

Duncan understood exactly what Verity had meant when she mentioned Elizabeth "going at a hundred miles an hour" once they arrived in Edinburgh. She flitted from shop to shop and rack to rack, and then back again with the vigour and enthusiasm of a hyperactive locust. Duncan was amazed by her energy, and by mid-afternoon he was extremely relieved to hear she was "calling it a day." His arms were fully loaded with shopping bags, and it was a relief to get back to the car park and unburden his load into the boot.

As he was driving home, Duncan was silently indulging in mental arithmetic trying to work out how much his wife had spent on clothes, shoes, and make-up. His conclusion was that there would be very little change from her first pay packet, if indeed, there was any change. There was no point in griping about it. He knew she would feel more confident if she was dressed appropriately, and hopefully these outfits would last for a long while. Verity had said that her week's trial would be well within her capabilities so she would be fine.

They arrived home to an empty house. Charlotte was at the disco and Alexander was out as usual. Duncan was pleased to see the smile on Elizabeth's face as she was hanging her new outfits in the wardrobe, and for the first time in forty-eight hours she began to relax.

As it was only 4.15 pm Duncan went over to Dysart to visit Jack and Alice McKinlay. He was surprised to see they were now no longer fostering children, although he fully understood as they were both in their seventies. They had fostered children for almost forty years and deserved a happy retirement. They were overjoyed to hear of Alexander's swimming prowess and Duncan promised them that if Alexander was chosen to represent Scotland in the Commonwealth Games, he would get them tickets and take them to Edinburgh to watch his son. The smiles on their faces almost brought him to tears.

When it was time to go, Jack came outside with Duncan on the pretext of having a look at his new car. When they were alone outside, Jack suddenly became very sombre, he said.

"Duncan, we've had to finish fostering because of Alice. I'm afraid she's been getting very forgetful over the last couple of years and it's getting worse, much worse. Odd things really at the start, leaving lights on and forgetting to turn the gas off on the cooker. Then it got worse. We were shopping once, about six months ago, and she walked off without her handbag and purse. Luckily, I was there. She forgets to lock the doors, and she even can't remember birthdays and anniversaries. She had no idea a fortnight ago that it was our fiftieth wedding anniversary. She is having tests now; but the specialist has forewarned me that it might be the start of Alzheimer's Disease. He has advised me to be very vigilant and careful with her. Nothing has been confirmed yet, but we see the specialist again next week on Wednesday and I think I know the outcome already," said Jack.

"I'm so sorry to hear that, Jack. I'll call in next weekend to see what the results are. I hope it's not that serious. You both deserve a wonderful retirement. Say goodbye to Alice for me," said Duncan.

Duncan felt ashamed as he drove home as he had not visited Jack and Alice since before Easter. Meanwhile, Elizabeth had gone to pick Charlotte up at the community centre.

When they arrived home, Charlotte dashed straight upstairs to the bathroom. Elizabeth said to Duncan, "Lottie's in a hurry, Fraser wants to take her to the pictures. There's a new James Bond film on at the cinema but it doesn't finish until half past ten."

Normally, Duncan would have put his foot down that she couldn't go as it finished so late, but he felt very sad already and didn't want any further fuss or bother. Later, as they were watching a video, Elizabeth looked at Duncan and he appeared to be in deep thought. She asked. " What are you thinking about, Duncan?"

"Far too much going on. My heads ready to burst. I keep trying to decide what to do for the best when I get to work on Monday. Also, I wish we knew for certain what will happen with your week's trial at work. If I knew which way that is likely to go, it would help me decide my own position. I'm gutted to hear about Alice: she is my mother; nobody could have had a better mother. Also, I'll feel a lot easier when Lottie gets home. I didn't realize it would be this nerve-wracking when she's out so late on her own. How are you feeling?"

"Pretty much the same about Lottie. However, I'm confident next week will be okay. Verity thinks so anyway, and she has enormous influence with Mr Gemmill. We will just have to wait and see."

"I bloody hope it does go all right. You'd better keep all the receipts for those clothes and shoes just in case we have to take them back," he said, sarcastically.

Eventually, their anguish ended when at 10.45 pm Charlotte arrived home. For the first time in four hours, they both felt relieved. Charlotte told them all about the film before she went to bed. Fifteen minutes later, they followed her. Alexander was not home yet, but he had his own door key.

The next morning after an early breakfast, Elizabeth knocked on Alexander's bedroom door to see if he wanted to go to St Andrews with them. She hurried downstairs in a panic. "Sandy's not at home. His bed has not been slept in. Where the hell is he?"

Duncan angrily exploded. "Here we go again. I go to work all week, we go shopping all day yesterday and now, when we have one day to ourselves and we have a day out planned, he's gone missing, and we don't have a clue where he is. It's not good enough. He should call us. That's what the telephone is for."

"Is that all you're bothered about. Your day out being ruined? Alexander could be out there seriously hurt or even worse. He could be in hospital for all we know, and you sit there moaning because you can't go to the beach," said Elizabeth.

"For God's sake give it a rest. He'll be home when he's hungry or he's got no money, you'll see," he replied.

Duncan was right: two hours later Alexander came casually strolling up the path without an apparent care in the world. He was about to go upstairs when he was intercepted by his fuming father who was on the verge of boiling over.

" Where the bloody hell have you been? Your mother has been worried sick and she's very upset. Why didn't you call us and let us know where you are? And don't give me any of that bullshit about not having any money for the phone. Well, where have you been?"

"Sorry, dad. We ended up at a party and it went on until about three this morning. I crashed out on the sofa because I didn't want to come home that late and wake anyone up. I lost track of what time it was. I'm sorry. I am just going up for a shower, is there anything else?"

"*Anything else?* You stink of booze, there's lipstick all over your neck, and in your hair. We've been ready to go out for the last two hours, but we waited to see if you're okay. One phone call, that's all it would have taken. You could have rung up early this morning. You'd better go in there and apologize to your mother and sister for ruining their day. It's too late to go to St Andrews now."

Ten minutes later, after a grovelling apology to his mother and sister, Alexander was washing off the aftermath of his Saturday night conquest in the shower. He couldn't tell his father the truth. How could he? How do you tell your parents that you have spent the night in bed with a married woman? What would they say? They wouldn't be happy, especially as her husband is abroad serving in the military.

After abandoning the idea of a trip to St Andrews, Duncan, Elizabeth and Charlotte decided on a shorter trip to Leven. It was a relief to get out of the house eventually after such a long wait. While the rest of the family were out walking, Alexander spent the whole afternoon catching up on his lost sleep. He woke up one hour before they returned, and he was deep in thought about the previous night's events. He realized that he had told lies on three separate occasions during the last twenty-four hours, and it hurt him to admit that one of those lies was to his family. He had no qualms about telling the barman that he was eighteen when he and three mates went to a pub that was having a karaoke evening. After all, he was nearly six feet tall, well-built and could easily pass for someone much older.

He had also lied to Mandy, telling her he was eighteen. He had been flattered by her approach, and then startled when she followed him into the gent's toilet. She had one thing on her mind and asked him straight away if he wanted to go home with her. It was too good an offer to refuse, so he kept up the pretence that he was eighteen in case she changed her mind. It was not the first time he had indulged in the carnal act, but he was a sheer novice compared to Mandy. He had very little experience of the many different positions which it was possible to perform, and he had never had oral sex performed on him before. He remembered the wonderful sensation of laying on her bed while it happened. There was an enlarged framed portrait photograph of her husband in his military uniform with a big smile on his face that was hanging on the bedroom wall facing the bed. "You wouldn't be smiling now if you could see what your wife is up to." He thought at the time. But although he had no regrets about last night's events, he was not happy with himself for telling lies to his parents, although the truth would have been considerably worse.

He had only just started doing some revision for his geography exam on the following day when the rest of the family arrived home. Elizabeth was delighted to see him hard at work revising for his exams. Duncan cast him a dubious glance, as he strongly detected a smear of untruth in his excuses earlier. Alexander knew he was treading on thin ice where his father was concerned. "It may be wise to keep out his way," he thought. "Yes, I'll go to my room to do my revision."

The next morning, Duncan bitterly regretted having to get up so early for work, but at least he would have access to the bathroom in the morning. Elizabeth had told him what a scramble it had been on the Friday morning when she and Charlotte were both wanting a shower at the same time and Alexander needed the toilet.

The following day was June 17th. Duncan was supposed to be starting his new job in Nottingham five weeks from today. He arrived at work on time and it wasn't long before Walter McInally approached him on the loading bay and said "Baker, the boardroom, now!" All four directors were present, faces set in stone, looking as welcoming as the Spanish Inquisition. Yet again Duncan was very nervous; his bowels were working overtime trying to stifle an outburst of wind.

It was Eugene Withe who spoke first. "Mr Baker, we need to know your decision regarding the position of manager. We are in dire need of taking immediate action to restructure the workforce and cut down on overheads. Considering the escalating costs of the raw materials, we are now running at a sizeable loss. This calendar year alone the cost of analgesics, antihistamines and decongestants has increased by an average of eight per cent. Our bottle manufacturer has increased the price by five per cent and even the printed labels have gone up by seven per cent. Fuel costs seem to be rising weekly, and the costs are getting out of hand. We cannot put our prices up too much as there is a large competitor in Nottingham that is undercutting us already. Our workforce has remained constant throughout the year, but, if we are to survive, then drastic action needs to be taken, immediately. Unfortunately, we have two options, neither of which are likely to be popular among the staff. We could close the production area for one day a week and put the staff on a four-day week.

Alternatively, we could make staff redundancies. Your decision is crucial in this restructure. What is your decision Mr Baker?"

"Can any of the customers who have cancelled their orders be persuaded to reconsider?" Duncan inquired.

"No, we have tried, even grovelled. It seems they are getting a better deal from Nottingham. Where's the loyalty when they are placing orders with the bloody English?" Eugene griped. "What is your decision regarding the manager's position: yes or no?"

Duncan swallowed deeply before speaking. "Let me say that I am flattered by your offer to become the new permanent manager. Yet, I am worried that I might not be able to fulfil your expectations. Mr Savage took a leading role in the production area and I was left in charge of the loading bay and stores. I am worried it will be too much for me. However, I do not want to let you down, especially in the current climate. I am prepared to give it a trial for a week or two to see if I can cope. If things go well, then I will carry on. If it's too much for me, then it will be your decision as to what happens in the future."

There was complete silence, the four members of the board began looking at each other for inspiration before Eugene spoke first.

"Wait outside, Baker. We'll call you back in a moment."

As he waited outside the office door, Duncan could hear the four of them discussing his proposal. It seemed all four were trying to talk at the same time which caused him to smile, and break wind to his vast relief. After what seemed an eternity, he was hailed back inside.

"Mr Baker, we are prepared to let you have a trial period to see if you can cope. Now that the order book is down, we think it ought to be within your capabilities. Have you thought any further about one of the labourers being promoted to a chargehand?" said Eugene.

"I have, but the only person worthy of that position whom I could trust retires in three to four months, so it's far too late for him to be retrained and adapt now. The rest of them are good workers, but none of them are chargehand material. I'll go it alone if I may, on one condition. You have offered me an initial extra one thousand pounds per annum, but I want an extra two thousand or it's no deal."

"*What! Two thousand. What are you trying to do. Bankrupt us?* You had better leave the office now, Baker. We have to discuss this at length." Said Eugene Withe, as Duncan made a hasty retreat to his office feeling a trifle smug and surprised at his own level of brazen cheek. When he had organised the rotas for the production area, he went to the loading bay where the labourers were standing about gossiping. He had to ask them to appear busy even if there was nothing to do. He took the opportunity to have a word with Bill Crossley. "Bill, can you come to my office? I want to speak to you in private."

A few minutes later Duncan invited Bill Crossley to sit down before he asked him a question he was certainly not expecting. "Bill, last Friday you said that you wished the company would make you redundant. Were you serious or were you joking?"

"No, I wasn't joking. They would be doing me a favour if they laid me off. It would be like retiring early. I don't know the exact figures, but I reckon I would get a massive wedge after forty years' service. If it hadn't been for the war, it would have been nearer fifty. Why, what's going on?"

"It's obvious that we are overstaffed and when I think of the future, you would certainly be the last person I would want to see leave, but after what you said, I thought that if you were happy to be made redundant it would save one of the younger men from being laid off, one who probably needs the job considerably more than you do, do you understand?" asked Duncan.

"Yes, I understand a great deal more than you think I do. We're up the creek without a paddle, aren't we, losing orders hand over fist? Well, go ahead, sort it out, I will gladly go."

"There's another thing. If I arrange for your redundancy, I will have to ask you to not say a word to any of the other staff regarding the company losing orders, or any other particular difficulties we are experiencing, is that clear?" Duncan asked.

"Certainly, Duncan, and thanks," Bill replied. As he was leaving Duncan's office, Bill nearly collided with Eugene Withe in the doorway. Eugene composed himself before he reluctantly stated." Baker, we have come to a decision regarding your request for an increase in your salary of two thousand pounds. We feel it is too much at this stage, but we are prepared to give you an increase of one and a half thousand straight away, rising to the two thousand in six months according to your adaptability in the new role. Basically, it will be a trial period of six months. What are your thoughts?"

"Yes, I'm happy with that, but I will need a new contract of employment stating my adjusted title of manager, along with the details of my improved salary." Duncan replied.

"Of course. By the way, who was that old chap who was just leaving your office as I arrived? Does he work here?"

"Yes, it was Bill Crossley. He has just agreed to take voluntary redundancy, so that's a start. I am about to start looking at the files of the production and assembly line personnel. The only way I can reduce numbers will be last in, first out. I'm not sure what to do about the delivery drivers. We have three good permanent drivers, and I don't think we can afford to lose one of them, unless we make up an occasional shortfall with an agency driver. I'll give it more thought."

"Excellent. Carry on, Baker," said Eugene.

At lunchtime, Duncan was not in the mood for eating. An hour earlier, he had the unenviable task of giving redundancy notice to two ladies in the production area. It was traumatic. One of the ladies took it reasonably well, although he could see she was upset. However, Rose Curran was another matter. She was absolutely distraught and sobbed her heart out and became hysterical, so Duncan had to get one of the other ladies to take her home. Although he hated handing out the dismissals, he was relieved to get it over and done with in one morning. As he sat at the canteen table drinking his coffee, he realized with disgust that one of the directors didn't even know who Bill Crossley was, the same Bill Crossley who had worked for the company for over forty years. He thought that was appalling. It was while he was deep in thought that Jeff Sutton walked by him and put a gentle hand on his shoulder. Jeff knew what was going on and his reassuring pat on the shoulder gave Duncan a slight measure of comfort.

If Duncan was having a day from Hell, then things were the exact opposite for Elizabeth. It was her first official day at work, and Verity spent the morning teaching Elizabeth the Spares Department ordering system and the Service Department booking procedure. Elizabeth took everything in her stride and amazed Verity with her levels of efficiency and organization. As Verity had said to Martin on the Saturday morning. "You have struck gold there, Mr Gemmill. She's extremely intelligent, diligent, and competent, and you were lucky to find her so easily."

Elizabeth asked Martin if it would be okay for her to take her half-day off on a Tuesday afternoon, as she normally played golf on Tuesdays as it was Ladies' Fourball Day. She was relieved to receive confirmation from Martin that it wasn't a problem. The day went much better than Elizabeth could have ever imagined: she didn't have any difficulties getting to grips and understanding the various systems that were in place, and for two hours in the afternoon Verity sat back and allowed Elizabeth to take a leading role. As she was shutting down the computer at five o'clock, she thought about Alexander for the first time in the day. "How had he got on with his Geography exam?"

Alexander had left home with Charlotte to make their way to school discussing her upcoming birthday on the Friday. He asked her what he could buy her for her birthday that didn't cost a lot of money. She asked for a Madonna CD.

"Okay, I'll see what I can afford when I get my pocket money. What are Mum and Dad buying you?" Alexander asked.

"I don't know. I've not asked them yet. I know what I want, but I'm afraid to ask them." Charlotte said nervously.

"Why, what do you want?"

"I'd like a tattoo, just a heart with an arrow through it and Fraser's name underneath, on my shoulder," she explained.

Alexander laughed sarcastically. "Well good luck with that. I can't see them letting you have a tattoo. Anyway, that's crap, you've only been going out with him for five minutes.

"It's not five minutes, it's three weeks and two days now since we met, and anyway I love him." said an irate Charlotte.

"Well, it's up to you, but don't expect them to be happy about it, especially Dad."

Alexander's class were allowed a one-hour revision period before their exam. Unfortunately, no matter how many times he scrolled through the capitals of all the countries of the world and all the states in the USA, his mind kept going back to the events of Saturday night and Sunday morning. It was a unique experience, the most exciting in his whole life. He kept thinking of how insatiable Mandy was once they came to grips in her bed, and he understood that all the novice conquests and juvenile fumbling that he had already indulged in, paled into insignificance compared to Mandy. He knew it

94

was dangerous, but he wanted more. He felt a stirring in his loins at the thought of her, which made him quite uncomfortable while sitting at the desk, but that made him even more determined to see her again, although he was not so sure if Mandy felt the same way.

On the Sunday morning after a brief two-hour sleep, she had roused him for a "farewell performance" before she told him to go afterwards. She wanted a shower and some breakfast before her husband was due to phone her at noon. It all felt a bit abrupt, but he didn't linger. He was totally spent and worn out. He didn't enjoy the fact that he had lied to her about his age, but he had the faint impression that she may well have had an idea that he wasn't really eighteen, but didn't give a damn anyway.

If he was concerned about lying to Mandy, then he need not have worried. Mandy had been lying to him. Mandy was not even her real name; it was a name that she used to be discreet, one that she adopted for "just this sort of occasion," and furthermore she was determined that he would never get to know her real name. Mandy was twenty-nine years old, almost twice the age of Alexander and she was very used to getting her own way. She lived by the philosophy of what Mandy wants Mandy gets. She had taken a tour of the pubs and bars on the Saturday night to find a man, any man, someone to fulfil her needs, and when she spotted Alexander at the bar, she fancied him immediately. She knew that she was taking a risk by taking him home, something she had never done before. On the half dozen previous occasions when she had been unfaithful to her husband, it was usually in the back seat of a car, but this was different. It was still light outside at 10.15 pm when they arrived at her home, and they could have easily been observed by the neighbours. She had been reckless, and it added to the thrill. She had been very disappointed in his first effort at performing the carnal act: the ammunition in his cannon exploded before the gun was primed. But after the initial disappointment of his premiere, he had performed admirably, impressing Mandy with his powers of recovery, his stamina, and his ability repeatedly to "rise to the occasion." She could not recall making love so many times in one night. The truth was, she was captivated by his youthful zest, and she wanted more. She also knew it was dangerous, but she wanted him more than she had ever wanted a man before, including her husband.

Alexander finished the last question of the exam just as the time-limit expired and shrugged his shoulders in a manner that said, "I could have done better." It was too late to worry now. The class would have an English exam tomorrow at the same time, and he resolved to concentrate harder and revise when he arrived home. Yet, as he walked home, he still could not get the thought of Mandy out of his mind. He wanted her, but what could he offer her apart from his body? He lived with his parents; he had no money save his weekly pocket allowance. On the other hand, she had an enormous house, fabulous clothes, a sports car parked on the drive and almost certainly plenty of money. She was also fantastic in bed, and he yearned for more.

It was a tortured teenager that arrived home and went to his room. Later Elizabeth arrived home feeling slightly tired but mentally on top of the world. Work was going exceptionally well. As the sun was still blazing, she called Alexander to ask if he had any dirty clothes that wanted washing. He brought down a pile of clothes and went back upstairs to continue his revision. Elizabeth detected a strong smell of ladies' perfume on one of his T-shirts and the alarm bells rang immediately. She decided to wash the clothes and get them on the line as the sun would have them dry before nightfall, but she would certainly speak to Duncan about her suspicions.

Duncan was just clocking off from work around the same time after a day that had been a war of attrition. He hoped that he would never have such a traumatic day again: gruelling and distressing. As he was driving home, Duncan had an awful feeling of emptiness inside. He felt as though he had the weight of the world on his shoulders, and he vowed that if this was to be the outcome of a day's work now that he'd achieved promotion, he would leave his employment.

As he arrived home, Elizabeth noticed the torment etched all over his weary face.

"Are you having a shower before dinner?" she asked.

"Yes, I'll be down in ten minutes." he said.

In the shower Duncan scrubbed his body with a vigour that he had never employed before. It was as if he was trying to wash away the misery of the day's events. A sullen forlorn husband sat down at the table for his meal. It was his favourite. He loved shepherd's pie, but he could hardly face eating it.

"You're popular today, Duncan. You've got three letters to open when you've had your dinner." said Elizabeth.

Duncan couldn't manage to eat all his dinner. He apologized for not being hungry and being wasteful.

"Never mind. Open your letters and let's see who they are from." Elizabeth said.

The first letter contained a cheque from the DVLA for the rebate of the unused road tax of his scrapped Morris Marina; it didn't even raise a smile. The second letter was from Mr Burkett of the Scotland Swimming Association formally inviting Alexander to training and coaching regarding the Commonwealth Games in Edinburgh. The training would commence on Saturday June 29th at the Edinburgh University Commonwealth Pool. Duncan asked Elizabeth if it was wise to tell Sandy about the invitation straight away, as he was taking exams all this week, and they didn't want him to take his mind off his revision.

"I agree. We'll tell him on Friday evening when you get home from work. I'll make a special celebration meal as it's Charlotte's birthday as well. She's still not asked for anything for her birthday yet. I'll go upstairs and ask her while you see who the other letter is from."

The third letter had a Nottingham postmark, so Duncan knew exactly who it was from and what was enclosed. It was a contract of employment, to be signed and returned immediately in the stamped addressed envelope provided. A brief letter was inside, formally welcoming Mr Baker to the staff. He was not in the mood to deal with it tonight; it would have to wait until tomorrow.

His mood did not improve a few minutes later when Elizabeth came back downstairs.

"I've just spoken to Charlotte. She would like a tattoo for her birthday. What do you think?"

"*A tattoo! What do I think!* " he bawled. "No, no chance, and that's final. She can do what she likes when she leaves home, but while she's still under sixteen and living under our roof, she'll do as we say."

Elizabeth went back upstairs to tell Charlotte that her father said no. Charlotte flew into a rage. She screamed hysterically at the top of her voice. "It's my birthday, my decision, my body. I can do as I want, tell dad *I hate him!* " She was sobbing uncontrollably. Elizabeth tried to comfort her, without success. Charlotte pushed her away screaming, "Get out, *out!* "

Duncan had heard most of the conversation leaving him very upset. He'd never envisaged the possibility of hearing his daughter screaming that she hated him. When Elizabeth came back down to tell him of Charlotte's reaction, he already knew.

"That just about sums my day up today. I've had the day from Hell at work, and now my daughter hates me. Is there anything else that can go wrong today?"

"She doesn't hate you, Duncan. It's just her way of showing her disappointment because she cannot have her own way. She'll calm down. It might take a day or two, but she'll get over it. She doesn't hate you; she worships the ground you walk on; I know that for a fact. Let's go out for a walk. There's something I need to tell you in private."

It was a beautiful summer's evening, and they decided to walk down to the quay. Elizabeth was slightly on edge and Duncan knew that something was wrong. He asked, " What's the matter Lizzie?"

"Oh dear. Where do I start? It's Sandy. He's not telling us the truth about Saturday night. I did his washing earlier this evening, and the T-shirt that he wore on Saturday night reeked of perfume, not any old perfume, but Louis Vuitton perfume. It has a very distinctive aroma of saffron and jasmine, and it's very expensive, and it's not the sort of perfume girls of his age could afford to buy. The sort of woman who uses that perfume would be much older than Sandy, and certainly not short of money. I'm worried that he's been lying to us. He certainly didn't spend the night with his mates. There was lipstick on his T-shirt as well. What shall we say to him?"

"Leave it to me, I'll have a word with him later in the week. Let him get these exams out of the way first. We don't want anything to put him off. Was there anything else?" Duncan asked.

"Yes, can I have the new car tomorrow and you catch the train one more time? When I finish work, I will have to go straight to meet the girls for lunch before we go to the golf club. I don't really want to turn up at the car showrooms in Cuthbert, especially as it leaves an oil stain where it's been parked.

"Yes, okay. I can put up with it one day a week."

Duncan was still thinking about work as they arrived down at the quay. Elizabeth treated him to a pint of lager at the quayside bar, and Duncan sat motionless staring out to sea as Elizabeth set his drink in front of him. For fully two minutes, he was gripped with inertia and didn't move a muscle, leaving Elizabeth to joke that he looked like the statue of "The Thinker."

"Sorry, Lizzie. I'll be glad when this week's over. There's far too much going on. I hope tomorrow goes better than today. If I have another day at work like the one today, I'm jacking up and that's final."

"You say that every week. In fact, you've been saying it for about ten years. I've lost count of the number of times that you've said that you're jacking up on Friday. They ought to re-name you Jack Friday." sniggered Elizabeth.

For the first time in the whole day, Duncan managed a smile. Elizabeth always had the ability to bring him down to earth, and he knew at that precise moment, why he loved her so much.

The following morning Duncan met Karel on the platform again and they talked for the entire duration of the trip to Waverley Station. Karel was very concerned for Duncan, but he kept his thoughts to himself on this occasion. He thought that the writing was on the wall for Duncan's company, particularly as they were experiencing cash-flow problems and having to make staff redundant.

Duncan arrived at work and then went to the canteen to see the labourers. Disappointingly, there were not many deliveries for the following day that were on the schedule, and that meant that at least one driver would be spare tomorrow. He was concerned about a late delivery of twenty-thousand bottles from Keane's that were for the production area, as they were due yesterday. He had checked in the stores, and they were running very low. He decided to ring the supplier and to find out what was the delay, and he was shocked by the answer. He was told by Mr McDonald that all deliveries were put on hold until further notice. "You haven't paid us since February, and now March and April's invoices are well overdue, and May's invoice is imminent. We will only release deliveries after we receive payment."

Duncan knew that without the bottles, there would need to be a halt on the production lines. He immediately went to the accounts office to see if payment could be made, but he was told they could not authorize payment without instruction from a director, so he was advised to see Mr Withe who was dealing with financial matters. Two minutes later he was in Eugene Withe's office explaining the problem. "Sit down, Baker. I'm afraid it's not possible to settle the Keane account at this particular time as we have a slight cash-flow problem. It's the same old story: suppliers want paying straight away and customers withhold their accounts as long as possible. Mr McInally is in Glasgow this morning looking at a new bottle supplier. We are aware of the importance of the bottles, and if we can get some supplied from an alternative source then we won't have to rely on Keane's as much in the future. I'm on my own today holding the fort, as Mr Storey and Mr Moore are also both out canvassing new customers. It's as simple as this: if we cannot get some new customers, then there will have to be further cutbacks. If it means shutting down the production lines a couple of days a week temporarily, then so be it. You are probably not aware, but we have had confirmation this morning that the delivery to Morgans on Thursday will be their last delivery . They have cancelled all future orders after this week, yet we have been supplying them for over twenty years and they have cancelled without an explanation."

"How serious is the cash flow problem, sir?"

"It's not good, not good at all. During the last five years, our meagre profits have rapidly dwindled and completely disappeared and now we are now running at a sizeable loss. Inflation is the main problem. We've been hoping to turn the corner, but we need to acquire more loyal customers and we need to cut our cloth accordingly just to survive. In February we (the board) all had to put two thousand pounds of our own money in the account just to pay wages. In April we all put another three thousand in the accounts, but we have now agreed that we cannot continue to keep doing this as we will end up bankrupt ourselves. Company expenditure must be cut down by about sixty to seventy thousand pounds a year I'm afraid. Mr Savage was aware of this in March, yet he didn't make any progress in reducing our expenditure. He let us down badly. It seems that you are already making more significant progress on the matter than Savage ever achieved. It goes without saying, Mr Baker, everything you have heard in this office is strictly confidential and must not be repeated outside of these walls. Do you understand? Is there anything else you need?"

"I'm sorry to hear all that. I have checked in the stores, and I think there is just about enough bottles to last until tomorrow night. But what are we going to do about Thursday and Friday if we can't get any more bottles?" Duncan asked.

"We will have to stop production and send the staff home." said a dejected Eugene.

A crestfallen Duncan slowly made his way back to his office. The promotion he had craved for all these years was turning into a nightmare. He now knew that Bernard Savage had been aware of the predicament of the company, and he understood how it must have affected him, eventually leading to his nervous breakdown. He knew that there was very little or no chance of getting a new bottle supplier immediately and it was a cast-iron certainty that production would have to cease by Wednesday night. His mind was in torment as to what to say to the men on the loading bay. He had got to know them all personally, and he counted them as his friends.

At the morning break, he was in the canteen when Vic Woan, one of the labourers, came over to speak to him.

"Duncan, can I have a word? I had a phone call from my mate last night. He's on leave this week, off the oil rigs. He's been asking his gaffer for months if I could have a job, and now they need more men so I can start next Monday. Is it okay if I finish on Friday?"

"Certainly, Victor. It would be harsh to insist that you work out a two-week notice period and miss an opportunity like that. I'll sort it out with the wages office to get your notice official. I hope it all goes well for you on the rigs. Good luck."

Although Vic was leaving of his own accord, Duncan wondered what effect it would have on the morale of the rest of the labourers. Bill Crossley was already serving a four-week notice period and Vic was leaving on Friday. Soon there would only be four labourers left. However, if they didn't get any bottles delivered by tomorrow afternoon, then they would all be in deep trouble. Duncan felt his stomach churning. He desperately wanted continuing production. "There must be something we can do," he thought. In a last anxious effort, he went back to see Eugene Withe.

"Mr Withe, would it be possible to speak to Keane's and ask them that if we paid the March invoice today, could they at least send us five thousand bottles which would keep us going for another week or so? Tomorrow is quiet for outgoing deliveries, and we could send one of our own drivers to Keane's to collect them. Is there any hope?"

"That's a good idea. Our priority has been to withhold funds to ensure we can pay salaries, but we may have enough in reserve to settle one month of Keane's account. I'll check the figures. Come back after lunch and I will see what we can do."

So, there was hope. It would depend on Keane's benevolence, but anything to maintain production and deliveries going out was preferable to a temporary closedown, which in all probability would have signalled a permanent closure. During lunchtime, Duncan was relaxing in the canteen when he cast his thoughts to his family. "How is Elizabeth getting on at work? I hope she's okay. How is Alexander going on with his English exam? He'll be alright. I wonder if Charlotte has calmed down yet and if she still hates me?" he wondered.

Elizabeth was enjoying an easy morning at work. With Verity at the helm and Elizabeth as a willing understudy, they were cruising through the day's tasks. At 1.00 pm as Elizabeth was leaving the showroom, she was aware that Martin was following her to the car.

"Elizabeth, just a quick word, I won't keep you long. Tomorrow Verity is having her half-day off in the afternoon. I want you to do a favour for me. As she is leaving on Friday, I want to get her a nice farewell present. I would like you to engage her in chit-chat tomorrow morning and find out what type of jewellery she likes. Don't make it obvious that you are probing her for information. Just do it casually. Anyway, once she has left, I will give you a hundred pounds to go into the high street and get something nice. Also, if you can get the shop to gift-wrap it that would be brilliant." Martin continued. "Additionally, can you get one of those big retirement cards for us all to sign. There's just one last thing. On Friday, you *must* keep her in your office between 3.30 and 4.30. Can you do that for me Elizabeth?"

"Of course, I can be discreet. It's good of you to trust me. For a hundred pounds I should be able to get something very special. Thanks, Mr Gemmill. See you in the morning."

Elizabeth felt on top of the world: Martin had given her the impression that she was now completely trusted. She was one of the staff, and surely the job would be hers. He had shown a high level of generosity in his appreciation of Verity's service to the company, and Elizabeth thought that he was not the total ogre that Verity had made him out to be.

She met up with the girls for lunch ten minutes later and was introduced to Bobby, a new member to the club who was a friend of Colette. Her real name was Roberta, but "Everyone calls me Bobby," she said shaking hands with Elizabeth.

As they arrived at the golf club, Elizabeth and Sylvia were just getting out of the car when they heard the shrill vitriolic voice of Maud Gemmill. She was in the carpark admonishing a humbled greenkeeper who was standing to attention in front of her. It appeared he had left the sprinkler on too long on the seventeenth green and part of it was slightly waterlogged. She berated him for fully two minutes as all the ladies stood there in amazement.

"She's a nasty piece of work," said Sylvia in a whisper that only Elizabeth could hear. Maud noticed the registration of the car that Elizabeth and Sylvia had arrived in.

Caustically she sneered, "I see you came in my old cast-off."

It was Sylvia who replied, curtly, and with a trace of spiteful irony: "Yes, it now belongs to Elizabeth and her husband, but at least they *paid* for it."

Maud was totally speechless. She was not used to anyone answering her back.

Elizabeth spoke next. "Well, many thanks for looking after it so well. We are really pleased with it."

The ladies all walked off into the clubhouse before Maud could come back with a riposte. Three of them were smirking, but Elizabeth was concerned that word of Maud's humiliation would get back to her boss. Her concern was unfounded. In Maud's egotistical mind, she was vastly superior to all of the other ladies, and she could never admit that she was on the losing end of a verbal exchange. Whether or not the little *tete au tete* with Maud had inspired Elizabeth, she had the best round of golf in her life, and for the first time ever she completed a round in under eighty shots.

ANXIETY

Wednesday didn't start well for Charlotte. As she walked to school with Alexander, he said that she was "out of order" shouting like that at her parents. He explained that they would have her best interests at heart, and she was selfish to ignore her father's wishes.

He was not expecting her reply: "I don't care, I hate him. I want a tattoo; It's my birthday and I can have what I want. I'll save up my pocket money if I have to and pay for it myself. Fraser wants me to get a tattoo to show how much I love him, so I'm going to get one."

"Well, I think you are being stupid. You hardly know him. He shouldn't be asking you to have his name tattooed on your shoulder.

It was probably the first time in Alexander's life that he had shown any real concern for his sister. He didn't know anything about Fraser, but what he had heard made him feel very uncomfortable.

His English exam went quite well, as he concentrated hard not to keep thinking of Mandy as he had done on the previous day. Later, as he walked home after the exam, he was determined to find out a lot more about his sister's boyfriend; something wasn't quite right.

Back in Leith, Duncan's stress levels were reaching a new peak. During the afternoon, one of the delivery drivers Barney Middleton knocked on his office door to complain that he had just been to the garage to fill up with diesel, but the account was now on hold.

"They wanted me to pay for the diesel with cash, so I couldn't fill up. Can you sort me out some money from the petty cash, or that wagon's going nowhere?" griped Barney.

"Give me ten minutes, Barney. Get your wagon loaded up and I'll go to the accounts office and see what's happening."

Once again Duncan was advised to see Mr Withe. Eugene was in a state of high anxiety after Duncan inquired, "Sorry to inform you, sir, but one of the drivers has just told me our account at the garage is on hold. He needs to fill up for tomorrow. Is there any chance that we can pay them and get this sorted out?"

Eugene replied. "Sit down. Baker. I have just found out that we are not able to increase our overdraft at the bank, and we are now running at a loss of about one thousand pounds a week. There is a slim possibility that we can get through this, but it means we all have to pull together and tighten our belts. If we can see more business on the order books and make reductions in the weekly staff expenditure, then we have a fighting chance. Unfortunately, I have been going over our existing funds and we just have enough to pay the final two week's wages in June. We are then expecting monies from our clients for the May accounts and that should see us through July. However, there is very little money left to pay our suppliers. We will have to do a balancing act and pay whoever and whatever is the most critical to maintain production and deliveries. I have spoken to Keane's and promised them payment for the March account tomorrow, and they will release four pallets of bottles. That should keep us going until this time next week. Unfortunately, there is nothing left after Keane's have been paid. The garage account will have to wait. If I give you twenty pounds, give it to the driver and tell him it's out of petty cash. He *must* fill up at another garage and bring the receipt back for me to claim on my expenses. At least that keeps us going. I want you to consider laying off one of the delivery drivers and that will give us the opportunity to sell one of the lorries to raise funds. That should help us through this crisis. Have you any further questions?" Eugene concluded.

"No, sir. There is one problem however: quite a few of the men have got wind of something and consistently ask me, 'What's going on?' They are not as gullible as we think. I hate telling them lies. All that I've said so far is that the company is readjusting the labour force to accommodate the reduced order book, which is basically the truth anyway. However, I didn't know that the situation was as bad as this. Is there anything else I can tell them?" Duncan asked.

"No, definitely not! You must keep it to yourself. It's a temporary glitch, that's all. Let me know when we can sell one of our wagons. We should be able to raise at least eight or nine thousand for one of those. That's all Baker."

Feeling deflated, Duncan went back to his office. He was poring over the delivery schedules and routes to see if it was possible to manage the deliveries with just two vehicles, so in the morning he could decide which driver would have to go.

Duncan got a lift to the train station with Jeff Sutton and managed to catch the earlier train and meet up again with Karel. After they were seated together, he told Karel all about the day's events. While he was talking, he noticed that Karel was shaking his head from side to side and continuously tutting.

Karel said. "I can't believe you're putting up with all that crap. What an outfit! I'd be off like a shot; you've got another job to go to in a few weeks anyway. Why make yourself bad sorting all that shit out? You need to take a good look at yourself or you'll end up being carried away by the men in white coats."

"It's not that easy, Karel. There is nobody else there who could do the job. They can hardly advertise for somebody to come in and supervise through these current difficulties. I feel that I would be letting them down if I left now. I'll give it to the end of the week to see how it goes. If it doesn't improve, I will hand in my notice next week."

When Duncan arrived home, Elizabeth said that Alexander was in his room revising and that Charlotte had gone to Rebecca's house for the evening. She would pick her up at ten o'clock. Duncan had his dinner before slumping in his chair to read the paper. Elizabeth had never seen him look so downhearted in the nineteen plus years they had been married. Discretion told her not to disturb him for the rest of the evening. Later, Elizabeth left the house to collect Charlotte and Duncan didn't even notice she had gone.

Fifteen minutes later, a frantic Elizabeth returned, alone. She cried, "She's not there. Rebecca's mum said she popped in for five minutes and left about 7.30 . I then went to Kerry's house, and she wasn't there either. She's taking us for idiots. I bet she's out there somewhere with Fraser. What are we going to do?"

Duncan groaned. "Why can't they be honest and tell us the truth? I know what I'd like to do: ring her bloody neck. That's it, she's grounded now until further notice."

" I'd like to see her home safely before I make any judgement, as you should too," said Elizabeth.

"Er, that's what I meant; I was talking about when she *does* get home. She wants her arse tanning for a start, and then she wants grounding. It's out of order lying to us." He moaned.

It was a torturous wait as they sat in stony silence, staring blankly at the television screen. At 11.15 pm the deathly hush was broken by the sound of the front door opening and the sudden rush of

Charlotte running upstairs to her room. Duncan rose from his armchair seething with anger, but Elizabeth bade him to wait while she went upstairs to have harsh words with her daughter.

Ten minutes later Elizabeth came down to find Duncan pacing up and down the living room.

She said, "She's done it to spite us. She's upset because she can't have a tattoo for her birthday. She's stayed out late to get back at us as revenge."

"*Revenge?* She'll know what revenge is when I get my hands on her;" Duncan snarled.

"Duncan, it's late. You have to be up at six in the morning. I will deal with her tomorrow. Let's leave it for now and go to bed, I've got work as well in the morning, remember?"

They were not in the mood for sleep, and they both endured a restless night. The next morning Duncan crawled out of bed to get ready for work, and his thoughts were piecing together the hideous events of the previous day. Surely today could not be any worse.

During the drive to Leith, he was mulling over recent events when he recalled how his daughter had lied to them and deliberately set out to spite them both. It saddened him enormously. She wasn't speaking to him and all he could think of was her screaming, "I hate him," when he denied her the gift of a tattoo for her birthday.

Duncan was now faced with the unenviable task of finishing one of the company's delivery drivers. He eventually decided to finish Wes Gaynor. Fortunately Wes was able to find alternate employment immediately with a company in Dalkeith.

I'll be sorry to see you go Wes, but there's not enough work for three drivers. By the way, how much fuel is in your wagon?"

"It's over three-quarters full, luckily I filled up last Thursday."

"Good, we can use your wagon for the Aberdeen run.

Feeling pleased by the morning's events, Duncan called in to see Eugene Withe to explain that one of the drivers was finishing today and one of the delivery wagons would be spare as from tomorrow.

"Well done, Baker. I wish you had been at the helm long ago. We wouldn't be in this bloody mess that we are now. Mind you it's as much our own fault for having our heads buried in the sand. That's all, Baker, and stop looking so smug."

Back in Kirkcaldy, Elizabeth's day had started with a massive argument with Charlotte. She told her that she was disgusted that she had deliberately lied to her parents concerning her whereabouts the previous evening, and as a result, she was now grounded until further notice. Charlotte flew into a rage screaming and shouting that "you can't stop me going out if I want" whilst crying hysterically.

"We can stop you going out, and we will stop you going out until you show us that you are sorry and show us a bit more respect. If you go out against our will, don't expect any pocket money, or clothes, or make-up, or anything else for that matter," Elizabeth said.

Alexander had also been disgusted with his sister's behaviour, and on the way to school he admonished her for throwing tantrums at their parents. He said. "You don't realize that they love you to pieces and worry about you all the time, especially when you are out at night with boys. You're not fourteen yet until Friday, and it's only natural for them to worry. You need to cut them a bit of slack and stop being so selfish. It's embarrassing. How do you think they would feel if they found out that you had got yourself pregnant?"

"Don't be such an idiot. I'm not *that* stupid. They can't stop me going out. If I want to see Fraser, then I'm going out to see him and they can't stop me." Charlotte replied.

"If Fraser had any respect for you, he would make sure you were back home at the time that your parents requested. He shouldn't keep you out until after eleven o'clock," Alexander explained.

Alexander was wasting his breath; Charlotte was not remotely interested in anything he said, and as a result they departed in opposite directions in stony silence at the school gate. Alexander was to have a gruelling day with a history exam in the morning and a biology exam in the afternoon.

Charlotte was in a very spiteful and insolent mood, and eventually after several hostile comments talked her way into trouble with her teacher. She had always been a diligent student and it came as a surprise to Miss Walsh to hear Charlotte being so abusive and aggressive. The threat of a detention made no difference to Charlotte's behaviour and a frustrated Miss Walsh asked Charlotte to come with her to the head's office.

As they were walking down the corridor to the head's office, Charlotte suddenly bolted for the exit door and tried to escape. Unfortunately, as she reached the door she stumbled and fell. She was not badly hurt, but the fall winded her and shocked her to her senses.

"You silly girl, Charlotte, are you okay? It's no use trying to run away and getting yourself in deeper trouble. Come with me to Mister Hart's office and let's get it over and done with." Miss Walsh said.

A red-faced Charlotte begrudgingly followed her teacher to the head's office. Miss Walsh explained that Charlotte had been a bad influence on the rest of the class. She was contradicting everything her teacher said, she was making rude and offensive noises and gestures and disrupting the whole class. When she was asked to behave herself, it made no difference as she became even more abusive.

"Thank you, Miss Walsh. You may return to your class now. I will deal with this."

Mister Hart was an experienced head teacher with over thirty-five years' service in education. He was aware of how temperamental teenage girls could suddenly become owing to the changes in their body and infatuation with boys.

"Sit down, Charlotte. I'm surprised to hear of your behaviour today. There's obviously something the matter with you at the current moment. Do you think that you could talk about it with me, or would you prefer that I invite your parents into school and explain the matter to them? We can't have you disrupting classes, so it's your choice: Is it me, or your parents? Well..., it's up to you." said Mr Hart

"I've fell out with my parents. My dad won't let me have the birthday present that I want. My mum has told me I cannot go out to see my boyfriend. I hate them; they can't stop me going out, it's not fair. All my friends have got boyfriends, and they don't get stopped from seeing them."

"Yes, there's usually a boyfriend involved somewhere. Tell me, what did you want for your birthday that your father doesn't want you to have?" Mr Hart inquired.

"A tattoo, sir," she explained.

"Oh, I see, and why are you being stopped from seeing your boyfriend? Have you been up to no good giving them a good reason to stop you seeing him?"

"I was late in last night sir, that's all."

Mr Hart continued. "That's all? Well, that's more than enough. If I had a daughter that was your age, I would be worried sick if she was late in at night. I bet your parents were worried sick too. You must stop being so selfish and start thinking of others. I've met your parents quite a few times on open evenings and they are very attentive and responsible parents. They are always keen to know about your progress and very proud when you attain good exam results and end-of-year reports. You have always been a model student; it would be futile for you to throw it away now and discard your chances of a higher education. I want you to sit there quietly, for ten minutes. Don't say a word, just think. Think of everything that your parents have done for you in your lifetime, think of the better life you could achieve with a higher education. Then, when you are ready to return to your class, you *must* apologize to Miss Walsh, and you *must mean it*. If you do that, then that's the end of the matter and we will forget all about it. Is that a deal, Charlotte?"

"Yes, sir, sorry sir."

Meanwhile Elizabeth was having a good day at work. In the morning she instigated talk about jewellery and perfume without Verity having a clue what her motives were. After Verity left to take her afternoon off at lunchtime, Martin Gemmill came to see Elizabeth with the money to get Verity's leaving present. Elizabeth had established that Verity was very fond of rubies and red was her preferred colour, particularly Garibaldi Red, which was her favourite.

She wandered into the town centre exploring the jewellery shops until she found exactly what she was looking for. It was a beautiful ruby necklace and matching set of earrings in Garibaldi Red costing eighty-three pounds. The shop assistant was only too pleased to gift-wrap the presentation box for her. Elizabeth then went to another store to buy perfume which was to be her own gift. She had established that Verity liked Christion Dior perfume, so she bought some with her own money. She bought a large farewell card, and she also had time to call in at the bank where she discovered that the loan had been cleared into their joint current account earlier that day so it would be possible to pay off the balance for the car.

Martin was delighted with Elizabeth's choices of the jewellery and farewell card and especially the gift-wrapped presentation box. He asked Elizabeth what the other small present was.

"Oh, it's just some perfume that I have bought to thank Verity for being so kind and teaching me everything I needed to know about the job. I could not have picked it up so easily without her considerable help. I can understand why you hoped she would stay."

"How much was the perfume?" Martin asked.

" It cost nineteen pounds." Elizabeth explained.

" Keep the change out of the hundred pounds I gave you, then we have bought it between us," he said.

"Well, okay if you insist, but while we are talking about money, I can pay the outstanding balance on the car now that our loan has been cleared. I will write the cheque now."

Martin had all the staff sign the retirement card and leave a little personal message to say a farewell to Verity, and Elizabeth was very impressed by the generosity shown by her boss to the retiring employee. She was beginning to see him in a different light.

Back at Leith, Duncan was slowly beginning to enjoy his day. Where yesterday there had been a gruelling torturous grind that only a masochist would relish, today was turning out to be quite pleasant. The production lines were in full swing, one wagon was loaded and fuelled up early for the following day, another reduction in the labour force was achieved without detriment to operations and nobody was giving him any grief. Work was going along nicely for a change.

In the afternoon he was checking the fire-extinguishers in the production area when Ada Barron caught his attention and gave him a thumbs up. He returned a polite smile and a courteous wave and felt enormously relieved to witness her pleasant temperament. "Things are looking up, at last," he thought.

The afternoon passed without incident and Duncan left work in good spirits ready for the drive home.

When he arrived home, Elizabeth stopped him in the doorway. "Charlotte has apologized for last night. She's been told that she is now grounded until further notice. She wanted to go out tonight, but I told her no. Could you please leave it at that?"

"Okay. Did the loan come through today?" Duncan asked.

111

"Yes, I've handed in the cheque for the outstanding amount. It's paid for now. Sausage and chips okay for you?" Elizabeth asked.

"Smashing. Where's Sandy?"

"He's out at football training, on the park. I asked him if he has another exam tomorrow and he said he has a French exam in the afternoon. He hates French, he said it's a total waste of time."

Alexander had been looking forward to start training for the following season. He was glad to get away from the grind of daily revision and he was the first to turn up at the park. As the other players started arriving, he was met by a barrage of questions.

"Oi, Alex, where did you get to on Saturday night? One minute you go to the toilet, and next minute you've disappeared. What happened?" asked Sean Lyall.

"Er, I went to the toilet, and I felt as sick as a dog. I think we had some dodgy prawns for dinner in that seafood curry my mother made. Anyway, I felt lousy, so I went home."

"You're a lying hound; Nathan saw you leaving out the back way with a good-looking woman, years older than you. C'mon, out with it, where did you go?" Sean continued.

"I've told you; I went home. That lady must have been leaving at the same time as me. She wasn't with me. It's just a coincidence."

"You're still lying; if you were going home, why did you go down the street in the opposite direction?" Sean persisted.

" I was just getting some fresh air after being sick, I felt lousy."

"Then why was that woman talking to you as you were walking down the street?"

"She asked me if I had any matches or a cigarette lighter as she wanted a cigarette. I told her I didn't smoke, that was all."

Although he had managed to come up with feasible answers for all the questions, he got the impression that no-one believed him. It was ironic, he thought, that if he had told them the truth, they would have been less likely to believe him.

However, Alexander had questions of his own to ask. He would wait until they had a break in training. Three of the lads in the team lived in the north of the town and they went to a different school from Alexander. While they were having a welcome drink, Alexander asked them if they knew anything about Fraser. "I think his surname is Burley, but I'm not sure," he said.

"Yes, he goes to our school. He's a right arsehole. He leaves school in a few weeks and we'll be glad to see the back of him. He's a nasty piece of work. Why do you want to know?" Said Andy Starbuck the goalkeeper, as all the other boys gathered round laughing.

"He's going out with my younger sister. She's fourteen on Friday and the silly cow thinks she's in love with him. I knew there was something dodgy about him. He wants her to have a tattoo on her shoulder with his bloody name on it." Alexander explained.

"Not that again, he's obsessed with that. There's a girl called Denise in our year at school, and she's already got a tattoo on *her shoulder* with his name on it. He's got a reputation for going out with younger girls and as soon as he gets what he wants he finishes with them. Your sister needs to be careful," Andy said.

"Thanks, Andy. How old is he?" Alexander inquired.

"He's a year older than us, so he must be sixteen."

Alexander had heard everything he wanted to know. His suspicions were correct: Fraser was trouble. He would tell his sister the verdict when he next saw her. He wondered whether he ought to tell his parents, but he would try Charlotte first. If she didn't take any notice, then he would tell his parents.

The football training went on until it was dark, and Alexander didn't get home until the rest of the family were in bed. He had thoroughly enjoyed the work out, but he was ready for a drink and a shower which refreshed him enormously. He was wide awake as he went to his bedroom, so he decided to do "just a little" revision for his French exam as he hoped it would help him get to sleep.

The next morning, it took three attempts from Elizabeth to rouse him, and as she left for work Alexander was still getting dressed. Charlotte was also leaving as she preferred a slow steady walk to school, but today Alexander was not ready in time to walk with her. He was angry with himself as he wanted to tell Charlotte exactly what he had heard on the previous evening concerning her vile boyfriend. He eventually had to run to school to get there on time. He was not happy; of all things it was French revision that caused him to be late.

Elizabeth was mulling over the events of the last two days as she walked to work. She concluded that Charlotte now regretted the deceit and disrespect she had shown to her parents. "It's her birthday tomorrow, we don't want anything to spoil her day," she thought.

After the morning coffee break, a bemused Verity was scanning the computer screen studying the monthly accounts when she suddenly exclaimed. "Look at this. How much did you say you and your husband paid for the car Elizabeth?"

"Three thousand pounds." Elizabeth confirmed.

"Well, I'm looking at the car sales figures for this month and your purchase has just been entered in the sales file this morning. It says here that the cost was four thousand five hundred pounds, which is probably nearer the true value of the car, and that the account is paid in full. How is that?" asked Verity.

"I can assure you we only paid three thousand. It's a mystery to me as well. The only other thing I can think of is that he mentioned something about the football club should have given my husband a testimonial match when he had to retire. I wonder if the football club has paid the balance."

"I wonder if *he* has paid the balance. I don't like it. Either the balance has been paid from an alternate source or he is 'cooking the books.' I hope he's not got any ulterior motives in mind."

"Oh dear, I wish you hadn't told me. We don't want to cause any trouble," said Elizabeth.

"Don't worry, you've done nothing wrong. I'll have a word with him at lunchtime and find out what's going on." Verity said.

Later, when Verity asked Martin where the additional money came from, she was told, "It's all legal and above board so there's nothing for you to worry about. Anyway, you retire tomorrow, there's no need for you to get involved."

Both ladies were bewildered when Verity explained the conversation with Martin. "I suggest we carry on and forget it," was the final comment by Verity, but Elizabeth was going to find it hard to forget. She had been hoping for a proper explanation.

The day had started well for Duncan. Production was in full swing, and the warehouse staff were well on top of the day's tasks. They even had time to jet-wash the lorry that was surplus to requirements, and so he decided to tell the directors it was ready to be sold. He went across to the office area and found Walter McInally's secretary Hayley Carr waiting outside the director's boardroom.

"You can't go in, they're having a meeting, I've been told to wait outside and not let anyone enter." She explained, then continued. "Shush!! They're arguing. I'm trying to listen."

Duncan could hear raised voices, then short periods of silence, then the voices would be raised again. It wasn't easy to hear anything through the stout oak door, but he thought he could make out one of the directors say, "I don't care how long we have been in business; I'm not re-mortgaging my house and that's final."

As soon as he heard that, if indeed that was exactly what he'd heard, he said to Hayley that it was not sensible to eavesdrop, and they should wait a little further down the corridor.

Hayley replied, "Why, what are they going to do, sack me? I've already had my notice and I finish tomorrow anyway. If they want to sack me today, I'll go and do my shopping instead."

"I'm sorry to hear that, Hayley, but if I were you, I would serve my notice professionally so that I could secure a good reference. You don't want to be dismissed and leave without one," he explained.

"Yes, you're right. I'll move away until they call me in. I'll be glad when I've finally gone."

"Why's that, Hayley?" he asked.

"When I first started, I was Mr Storey's secretary and there were three other girls doing secretarial work for the other three directors. Now me and Maureen O'Kane are finishing tomorrow, and the other two girls will be rushed off their feet. It's not just the secretary's either that are leaving tomorrow. Nicola McGovern in the wages office has also been laid off."

"Oh, I see. I'll come back later. Remember what I said Hayley: stay here." he demanded.

Duncan walked back to his office with the wind well and truly taken out of his sails. "It seems we take one step forward and two steps backwards," he thought. If the comment that he assumed he had heard was correct, then things were looking bleak. He was determined to find out later when the directors' meeting finished. He was kept busy for several hours and eventually acquired an audience with

Gerald Moore. Gerald was the elder statesman of the four board members whose great grandfather was one of the three original partners who started the business. He was looking forward to retiring in eighteen months. Gerald said.

"Come in, Baker. What can I do for you?"

"Well, sir, it was just to let you know that one of the delivery wagons is now surplus and it's ready for sale. I've been told there's a commercial vehicle auction centre in Livingston."

"Okay, Baker. Anything else?" said Gerald.

"Yes, there is sir. I'd like to know if everything's okay regarding the company's future. There's a lot of worried people out there. It seems that we have been doing nothing but fire-fighting this last couple of weeks. Is everything okay?" Duncan asked feebly.

"The company's welfare is our concern, *not yours*. You are paid to do a job. I suggest you return to the shop floor and get on with it. Close the door on your way out," snarled Gerald.

Feeling grossly insulted, Duncan trudged back to his office and locked the door for ten minutes to calm down. He was livid. Perhaps it was not his place to speak with the directors regarding the future of the company, but Gerald Moore had been extremely rude. Again, his thoughts turned to handing his notice in next Monday. He had another job to start in four weeks anyway. Clocking out could not come soon enough and Duncan dashed to his car to get home as quick as possible.

Alexander was surprised at how easy the French exam had been. He was not expecting to do so well, but amazed himself as he was the first student to finish the exam fifteen minutes before the cut off time, and he was allowed to go home early. As he was walking towards home a white sports car pulled up at his side. The window opened slowly, and a lady's voice ordered him to, "Get in,"

He hesitated at first as he didn't recognize her voice. She was wearing a headscarf and very large sunglasses, but as he opened the passenger door all became clear, it was Mandy. She drove the car without speaking towards Kinghorn, until she found a quiet lay-by to pull in. He was embarrassed to be wearing his school uniform but excited at the thought of what was to come. He spoke first: "How did you know where to find me?"

"I didn't find you; I have just been to the hairdressers to get my hair done. I was driving home and noticed you as I went past. I turned round and came back because I wanted to see you to let you know I won't be around for a while. My husband was due to have four days leave and come home tomorrow for a long weekend, but he rang me on Tuesday to say he has wangled two weeks leave and he has booked us a holiday in the Greek Islands. We are going on Saturday morning. I was wondering if I would see you again and there you were, walking down the street on your own. If you had not been on your own, I wouldn't have stopped."

"Did you want to see me again, Mandy?" he asked.

"Yes, last Saturday night was fun, I will come and find you when I get back from holiday when I know it's safe. I can't risk taking you back to my place again though."

"Do you want to give me your phone number?" he asked.

"Don't be such an idiot. You must *never* ring me, *never* come to my house, and *never* even speak about me to anyone. Is that clear?" Mandy ordered harshly.

"Yes, I haven't said one word about you to anyone,"

"What are you doing tonight?" she asked.

"I was going to do some revision for a maths exam tomorrow."

"Would you like me to give you a proper lesson tonight, instead?" Mandy said seductively.

"Of course. Where, when?"

"Meet me on the Esplanade. Wait near the telephone box, I'll pick you up at about seven."

"Where will we go?" he asked.

"My friend has a flat overlooking Seafield Beach. She's on holiday this week and I've got the keys to her flat as I go every two days to feed her pet cockatiel. It's a good job she comes back on Saturday as I would not have been able to look after her bird when we go away. She asked me to let it out the cage every other day for some exercise, but the stupid bird never wants to go back in its cage. It flies round for a couple of minutes and then starts shitting all over the place and I end up cleaning the mess up. I'd like to wring it's neck." .

Mandy set off back towards Kirkcaldy and on the way dropped a bombshell of a question for which he was totally unprepared. "You look so much younger in that school uniform. How old actually *are* you? and don't tell me any more lies."

"I'm seventeen, I said I was eighteen because I was in the pub,"

"I still don't believe you. You haven't started shaving yet, but never mind. I don't care so long as nobody knows what we get up to, and it had better stay that way, is that clear, do you understand?"

"Yes, I'm not an idiot, Mandy."

Mandy dropped him off near his home and Alexander was ecstatic at the thought of what was to come later in the evening. He knew there would be no trivial conversation or petty foreplay as it was likely to be straight "under starter's orders." He quickly showered and bolted his dinner down before cleaning his teeth and taking a slow walk down to the Esplanade.

While waiting at the phone box, he realized that he forgot to speak to his sister about her vile boyfriend, but with the anticipation and excitement of meeting Mandy later, he had forgotten all about it. She arrived on time and ten minutes later they were getting undressed in her friend's flat. If Alexander's body had been punished the night before during the football training, it was as nothing compared to the arduous grind he endured at Mandy's pleasure. The first hour was exciting, but three hours later he was totally spent. He was about to admit defeat and say he couldn't manage it again when his blushes were spared as Mandy got out of bed and ordered him to do the same. She pulled the sheets off the bed and took off the pillowcases declaring that "These will need to be washed; we've made a right mess of them. It's your fault, you horny sod. Make yourself useful and go and feed that bloody bird, and don't let it out."

Alexander went into the living room stark naked and switched the light on to find his way. As he approached the cage, looking for the birdseed, the cockatiel suddenly chirped loudly, "Who's a pretty boy?

Mandy was just entering the room as the bird chirped, and they both burst out laughing. Alexander couldn't remember feeling as happy than at any other time in his whole life. He was becoming deeply enamoured of Mandy, and he was desperately hoping to continue their relationship.

After they locked up the flat, Mandy took the laundry to get it washed and dried. She drove back to town and dropped Alexander off at the phone box. After they had a brief goodnight kiss, Alexander said to Mandy. "I wish we could be together all the time. I've really enjoyed tonight. It's great being with you. I've never felt like this before." Mandy replied. "Don't be ridiculous. You can forget that; you're just a kid. What can you offer me? You're still at school for goodness's sake. Look, I like you, but it's only sex; I'll find you when I'm back off holiday. On Saturday nights go in that same pub and I will come and find you. That's if you want me to find you, but if you don't, I will understand. You'd better go."

Alexander watched the sports car all the way down the road until it was completely out of sight. He was feeling hurt at the things that Mandy had said, totally deflating his ego, and he realized he had learnt a harsh lesson when it came to the art of adult relationships. She was right of course; what could he offer her other than his body?

If Alexander was feeling hurt and upset at their parting, it was nothing in comparison to how rotten Mandy was feeling. She was devastated at the things she had said and at how she had spoken to Alexander. It was purely her defence mechanism that had taken over, nothing more, and the fact was, she was rapidly becoming infatuated with her teenage lover. She was attracted to him physically: he was good-looking, his body was smooth and supple, and, despite his tender years and lack of experience, he was an excellent lover. He had more stamina than any man she had ever known, and she wanted more of him. Much more.

Duncan and Elizabeth had spent a boring evening in front of the television, Charlotte had spent the night in her room listening to music, but they were all in bed when Alexander arrived home just before midnight. Earlier that evening, he had totally forgotten that he had wanted to warn Charlotte about her boyfriend, but he resolved to tell her in the morning. He made a cup of tea and decided to do just a little revision again, but within ten minutes he had climbed into bed and was fast asleep. Exhausted, spent, drained.

RETRIBUTION

It was midsummer's day, and It was to be a monumental day in the family's lives. As Duncan left to go to work Elizabeth went in the shower feeling slightly nervous as today she would receive the result of her week's trial at work. It was Charlotte's fourteenth birthday, and she was excited to see how many birthday cards and presents she had received. Alexander was still asleep, and was virtually in hibernation. His worn-out exhausted body was badly in need of rest.

Charlotte opened her cards and presents and asked Elizabeth if it was "possible" that she could go out tonight to the cinema with Fraser, as he wanted to treat her for her birthday: "I promise I'll come straight home afterwards when the film ends," she begged.

"Charlotte, you have put me on the spot. This is very awkward; you are grounded until we are satisfied that you are sorry for telling us lies. Your father would not be happy with me if I let you go out before speaking to him. If he says you can go out, then you can, but I'm not giving you permission until he gets home and we discuss it."

"But he doesn't get home until half-past six. I'm supposed to meet Fraser outside the cinema at seven o'clock."

"I'll ring your father at work later and speak to him. You will be home from school early, so I will call you then. Other than that, I should be home for ten past five, that's all I can say for now."

"Please ask him. It is my birthday and I want to see Fraser. I'm sorry for telling lies. I won't do it again, I promise."

Alexander was still in bed and Elizabeth went upstairs to wake him for the final time just before she left to go to work. It was like waking a corpse. "C'mon, wake up. I'm going in five minutes. You'll be late for school. Haven't you got another exam today?"

Alexander crawled out of bed while trying to decide what day it was. "Shit, I've got a maths exam today," he remembered. He came hurtling downstairs as his mother and sister were leaving together.

Charlotte cleverly decided to leave at the same time as her mother so she could walk with her for five minutes before they parted to go their different ways. She used this additional opportunity to badger her mother relentlessly about letting her go to the cinema.

Unfortunately, Elizabeth was not persuaded. She stuck to her guns and said the situation could only be resolved after speaking to her father.

Meanwhile, Alexander was in a panic, skipping breakfast and getting ready for school. He was aware that the mathematics exam was very important to him, and he needed to get a good grade. For the second consecutive day, he ran to school just to be there on time.

Duncan arrived at work and was amazed to see a large crowd of employees milling about in the car park, all talking in groups while looking very concerned. He asked Bill Crossley, "What's going on, Bill?"

"We've all been stopped from clocking In. Nobody's allowed in. There's a gang of men in posh suits saying we've all got to wait out here until our names are called. They might be bailiffs or receivers or something like that. It looks like the company's in shit street."

"I'll see what I can find out," Duncan replied. He approached the two men in the doorway, stating that he was the production and distribution manager, and could they say what was happening?

"You'll not be producing anything today I'm afraid. If you wait until your name has been called out, everything will be explained to you." Said one of the suited men standing in the doorway.

Duncan ambled back to where the labourers were standing all looking like condemned men. "Sorry, lads. They won't say anything."

Duncan was looking round the loading bay for a sign of the directors, without success. He did notice Ada Barron glaring at him, menacingly, and his heart skipped a beat. It was a sad drawn-out wait as one by one names were called and employees were escorted into the building. Ten minutes later, they would reappear with a large white envelope containing a letter of termination of their employment. The receivers had been called in by the bank. It appeared that the company had an overdraft that exceeded the limit, so the bank had instructed a foreclosure. It was heart-breaking to see some of the production line ladies weeping as they came out. Most of the men came out with sombre faces, resigned to their fate. Some came out swearing and shouting, and several were clearly very angry that they would not be receiving this week's wages which were due to be paid today. Geoff Sutton summed it up perfectly. "The bastards. We're not even getting paid this week. Why didn't they leave it until Monday? At least we would have been paid today."

Duncan was the last to have his name called out. He was escorted to the boardroom where he noticed the company directors were seated in the corner of the room on plain chairs while two of the receivers were sitting at the big oak desk. Duncan looked across at the four directors and he was reminded of naughty schoolboys being made to sit in the corner. Everything was explained to him regarding the termination of his employment. He asked one of the receivers about his salary as he was a salaried employee paid on a monthly basis and his wages were due to be paid today.

The bespectacled receiver spoke: "I'm sorry, Mr Baker, but there will be no salaries paid out today. We will send you a form to fill in as you will now become one of the company's creditors. When the company's assets are wound up you will receive a percentage of any monies recovered. I'm sorry."

"Not as sorry as me you're not. Who's going to put food on the table when I've just lost a month's wages? You sit there with a smarmy face sacking people left right and centre without a care in the world. I sincerely hope that one day you get to feel exactly like I feel now."

"Mr Baker, it's not our fault. We are just doing our job. There's no need for you to be so offensive," he continued.

"Oh, says he, no need to be offensive, well you can bollocks, the bloody lot of you. And another thing: there's two of our drivers out there making deliveries after making an early start, and the poor sods won't have a clue what's going off. They will be working all day for bugger all. I don't suppose you've had the common decency to try to intercept them and bring them back." There was silence as the receivers were dumbfounded and looked at each other for inspiration. "Yes, I thought so. You haven't got a bloody clue." raged Duncan.

As he was led back out of the building, Duncan remembered that he had some personal belongings in his office. He was allowed to retrieve his brief case and a big framed family photograph that was on his desk. He stood silently, taking one last look around his office before shrugging his shoulders and slowly trudging out of the building. "Why of all days are they shutting us down today on the 21st when my salary is due?" he asked himself. He knew that losing his month's salary was going to hit the family hard. He was hoping that his wife was faring better today. This was the day she would find out if her week's trial had been successful. "How would she feel if she was turned down? "What are we going to do for money?" he thought. It was a torturous drive home to Kirkcaldy.

Fortunately, Elizabeth was faring significantly better. She went to see Mr Gemmill in his office during her morning coffee break. She inquired, "Sorry to bother you Mr Gemmill, but I was wondering how my week's trial had gone?"

"Oh that? Forget about that. When Verity told me how well you were doing last Saturday morning, I knew then that you were the person we were looking for. I'm sorry, I should have said something earlier instead of keeping you on tenterhooks. Be assured, Elizabeth, you are now part of the team, I knew from the moment I first saw you that you were the right one for me."

Elizabeth smiled, and thanked him gratefully, before returning to the office. Disappointingly, she had an uncomfortable feeling about Martin's final comment and voiced her concern to Verity.

"He's at it again. I told you; he can't help himself with his double entendres. Make sure you're on your guard at all times and let him know you're not interested at the earliest opportunity, or he'll keep going on and on until he's stopped," said Verity.

The day went exactly to plan as Martin had requested. Verity was unaware that a presentation was taking place later in the day and Elizabeth kept her in the office all afternoon. Verity sat back watching her *protégé* doing all the work, and subsequently when Elizabeth asked her if she would "go through everything one last time," shook her head and said she didn't need to. "You're better at it than I am."

At 4.20 pm there was a knock on the office door. It was Stuart Bowyer. "Ladies, Mr Gemmill has asked that you turn the computer off, lock the door and come to the showroom." A few minutes later Verity was in floods of tears. In the showroom there was bunting and balloons, and a large table spread out with assorted party food. Martin had supplied a few bottles of sparkling white wine, and there was soft drinks for the non-drinkers and drivers. All the staff were present, even the mechanics, including one optimist who quite clearly had his eye fixed on Elizabeth until he was gently let down. Verity was overcome with her gifts of perfume and jewellery, and for once she was speechless. However the one thing that really opened the floodgates was the final presentation. Martin Gemmill had instructed one of the mechanics to take down the name plate on the office door. It was hurriedly wrapped in gift paper and Martin composed himself before making a small speech: "Verity, on behalf of the company I would like to present you with this final token of our appreciation. I know that you are not taking any of your furniture to Jedburgh, but you may wish to consider taking this small reminder of your time with this company, a company that has been enriched by your presence and is eternally grateful for the hard work and endeavour you have shown over the years. We all wish you a *very* long and happy retirement."

After a prolonged round of applause, Martin's few words nearly had Elizabeth piping her eyes as she was overcome at how much Verity was appreciated. She realized how generous Martin could be to his loyal staff and she didn't want to think too unkindly of him for his persistent semi-suggestive comments. Martin booked a taxi to take Verity home with her personal belongings and her farewell gifts, and Elizabeth went with her to the taxi to say goodbye. Verity's final words to Elizabeth were, "It's been lovely to know you, briefly as it's been. Look after yourself Elizabeth, and *never ever* drop your guard. Remember, they don't call him the Bluebottle for nothing."

The taxi pulled away as Verity waved goodbye. A misty-eyed Elizabeth waved goodbye until the taxi left the forecourt.

Alexander left school after his maths exam totally unaware that this evening he would find out about the invitation to train with the Scottish swimming squad. Duncan also had the intention of grilling his son regarding the previous weekend when he came home on Sunday morning reeking of perfume after staying out all night.

As Alexander arrived home, he was surprised to see his father sitting in his favourite armchair. "You're home early, Dad. What's the occasion?" he asked.

"Trouble at work. We were all laid off, the company's gone bust. Don't worry lad, something will turn up. We have something to tell you when your mum's home. I think you will be very surprised."

Alexander went up to his room and laid down on his bed. He was asleep as his head hit the pillow, and snoring within minutes.

Charlotte arrived home a few minutes later and her first thought was to ask if her father had spoken to her mother.

"No, Charlotte. We haven't spoken to each other today as she would not have known I have been at home since mid-morning. I'm afraid I'm now out of work. Anyway, what did you want to know?"

"As it's my birthday, please can I go to the cinema with Fraser tonight? He wants to treat me for my birthday. I promise I will come straight home afterwards when the film finishes, please, *please.*"

"On one condition: don't *ever* lie to us again. I mean it. If you ever lie to us again, I will never forgive you."

"Thanks, dad." Charlotte rushed to the phone to make her arrangements with Fraser before going to the bathroom.

Later, Elizabeth arrived home and complained that she had tried to ring him at work, but she couldn't get an answer. Duncan had to go through the whole explanation of events at work yet again.

"I'm not hungry at all. I've just had some sausage rolls, some *vol au vents* and a slice of chocolate cake. I feel stuffed. I'll do you and Sandy sausage and chips, but I don't want anything, she said.

"Oh, by the way; I've told Lottie she can go out tonight as it's her birthday. She's promised never to lie to us again," he explained.

A strikingly dressed Charlotte went out early to meet Fraser as her father now recognized what a mature and beautiful young lady she was rapidly becoming. Elizabeth eventually woke Alexander up at seven o'clock to tell him his dinner would be ready in five minutes. When Alexander came downstairs, he cursed himself because he had missed his sister yet again, although he was reassured when he heard she had gone to the cinema with Fraser. He thought to himself, "What harm can he do in the cinema?" He was not to know that Fraser had no intention of watching a movie tonight. He told Charlotte that he and a few friends had organised a surprise birthday party for her.

"I'll give you your birthday present later," explained Fraser.

They made their way to East Burn onto a patch of wasteland where Fraser and his cronies would often congregate. On the way, Charlotte told him all about getting into trouble at school and how she fell over when trying to run away.

When they met up with Fraser's pals some of the boys were already in high spirits. They had been drinking cheap cider and cans of strong lager. Fraser persuaded Charlotte to try some of the cider, but she had never sampled cider before in her whole life. She didn't want to be shown up as a party-pooper, so she joined in with the others in drinking the cider and the lager. It wasn't too long before her head started spinning and she felt dizzy. The boys were all laughing at her, and she had to sit down on the grass before she fell over. One of Fraser's friends then opened a tobacco tin and produced a joint of marijuana that he had rolled earlier at home. When it was lit, the boys all took a deep inhalation before Fraser passed it to Charlotte.

"Try this. It will make you feel better." Fraser said.

"What is it? I don't feel very well," Charlotte complained.

Fraser held the joint to her lips and cajoled her into taking a deep inhalation. Afterwards, she instantly regretted it as she felt as if she was about to pass out. Her head was spinning round in circles, and she unsuccessfully tried to stand up, but it was no good: her legs felt like jelly. She started retching as though she would be sick, but it wouldn't come out. She was rapidly losing control of her senses and momentarily passed out. A minute later, she came to her senses to find Fraser on top of her. He had pulled her skirt up and taken her pants down, leaving them hanging on one ankle, and he was fumbling, trying to insert his erect penis inside her. She screamed. "Stop it. What are you doing? No, no, please stop it."

"Stop moaning, I told you I was going to give you a birthday present. Well, this is it." Fraser said sneeringly. He had been holding her down using brute force with both hands, but he released one hand to try to assist his attempt at entering her body. She was crying and screaming hysterically. "No, no, no, stop. I don't want to."

With her free hand she successfully managed to claw at his face, leaving four deep horizontal scratch marks across his cheek which drew blood and startled him with the pain.

"You bitch!" he wailed, and instantly punched her in the face as hard as he could. He stood up and pulled up his jeans while his mates were all laughing uproariously.

"She's made a right mess of your face; we could play noughts and crosses on it now Fraser." Said the boy who had produced the joint. At that point Fraser lost all control of his temper and violently kicked Charlotte twice on the body, causing her to be sick. All his friends were disgusted with him and said they were going, so the impromptu party broke up and the boys skulked off, leaving Charlotte alone in an extremely bad way. She was in terrible pain, and she was struggling to breathe. She couldn't manage to stand up, and it was an effort to pull her pants back up as she cried for an eternity, wailing for her mother. With the effect of the alcohol, the marijuana, and the beating, it was dark before she could even stand up and she had great difficulty in walking home. It was almost eleven o'clock when she arrived home, sobbing hysterically. She went straight into the living room and threw herself into her father's arms, holding him tight round the neck so he couldn't move.

"I'm sorry dad. I'm sorry." She kept repeating the words while crying her heart out. Despite repeated requests made by her parents of "What's the matter? Have you fell out?" she said nothing, but kept insisting how sorry she was. Duncan and Elizabeth could not see the swelling that was beginning to come through on her cheek as she had kept that side of her face buried on her father's chest.

After half an hour, Elizabeth persuaded her daughter that she would be "better off in bed," and Elizabeth took her upstairs to her room. Charlotte was able to keep her head turned away from her mother so Elizabeth was unaware of the swelling that would surely be much worse in the morning.

When the worried mother came back downstairs, she said to Duncan, "Well, it looks like the end of her relationship with Fraser. That didn't last very long, did it?"

"Lizzie, could you smell her breath? It stank of alcohol, and I think she had been sick as well." Duncan exclaimed.

It was a sombre end to their evening, an evening that had started off with the proud parents showing their son the letter from the Scottish Swimming Association inviting him for the special training. Alexander shocked his parents by not showing much enthusiasm. He said that he didn't want to be in Edinburgh so late in the afternoon as he wouldn't be able to get back in time to play football. When it was pointed out to him that they may be able to manipulate the hours of his attendance, he brightened up considerably. Duncan was surprised at his son's nonchalant reaction as he was a far more accomplished swimmer than he was ever likely to be as a footballer, but Alexander loved his football considerably more, and nothing would get in his way of the enjoyment of playing football. He was also worried that the swimming might be all-consuming of his leisure time, and he didn't want anything to spoil the occasional opportunity of seeing Mandy. Not that he could say that to his parents.

Later in the evening, Alexander was asked to explain how, on the previous Saturday night, his T-shirt was tainted with the aroma of expensive perfume. He said that he had met a girl in the pub, but not that she was nearly twice his age and that she was already married. He admitted that he stayed the night in her flat. His parents were utterly mortified at the frankness of his explanation and his father was extremely angry with him. "For goodness' sake, you're only fifteen. You shouldn't be up to behaviour like that. I hope you were careful. How old was she?"

"Eighteen, but don't worry, we had a big argument in the morning, and I won't be seeing her again. Anyway, dad, I'm tired and I think I'll go to bed."

Alexander went to bed leaving his parents speechless. Their night did not improve when Charlotte arrived home later. It had not been a good day all round for Duncan, after losing his job and a month's salary. "Let's go to bed, Lizzie, I'll be glad when today's over."

On the Saturday morning, Duncan and Elizabeth went to the supermarket to do the weekly shopping. Alexander and Charlotte were still in bed. Later in the afternoon, Duncan hoped to have time to visit Jack and Alice McKinlay to hear the result of the medical tests for Alice.

Alexander was up and dressed before his sister, and he noticed that she was not downstairs. She appeared to be in her room, so he went back upstairs and knocked gently on her door.

"Charlotte, are you up and are you decent? I am sorry I missed you yesterday. I've got your present here, can I come in?" After he got a positive reply, he went in to give her a Madonna CD. "I'm sorry it's not wrapped up. Hey, what's up with your face?"

Charlotte was still in bed, feeling awful with a blinding headache and severe pain in her ribcage where she had been kicked. Her left cheek was badly swollen, and the bruising was just beginning to turn a light shade of blue. She had forgotten to pull the sheets right up over her face so he could not see her.

"What happened? C'mon, you can tell me. How did you get a bruise on your face like that?" he asked.

Charlotte sobbed gently. She was feeling as though she was at death's door. Her morale was at rock bottom. She told her brother the full story, begging him not to tell her parents. "I'm going to tell them I fell over. Please don't say anything else, but what happened was we didn't go to the cinema. Fraser said we were going to a birthday party for me. It was just him and his mates. They were all boozing, and they gave me some. It made me feel dizzy. After that, they asked me to smoke something called a joint and it made me feel all wobbly. Then, after I had one puff of it, I couldn't get up and I must have passed out because a minute later I realized he was on top of me holding me down with both hands trying to put his thingy inside of me. He let go of my arm for a moment and I clawed his face and pushed him off. He hit me very hard, then he kicked me twice in my stomach. It really hurt, I hate him, I wish he was dead. They left me on the ground, and it took ages before I could manage to get on my feet again and walk home. I was very scared, and I'll never forgive him. As far as I'm concerned, I'm finished with boyfriends now. Don't tell mum and dad what happened, please, please, promise!"

"Charlotte, it's not up to me to tell them what happened, it's up to you. You need to tell them. They will find out eventually. Get it over and done with. You can't hide that face forever."

Alexander went downstairs, leaving his distraught sister still weeping gently and trying to go back to sleep, possibly trying to erase the memory of the previous night as though it never happened and may eventually go away. Of course, it would not.

While Alexander was downstairs, there was an incoming phone call. He took the call, writing down the name and number of the man who was asking for his father. When his parents returned from the supermarket, Alexander told his father, "There was a phone call for you, dad. A man called Jim Storey; he's left a phone number for you. It's on the pad at the side of the phone." Duncan knew that Jim Storey was one of the directors and out of sheer interest he called the number back. He was amazed at the conversation.

Jim began, "The receivers are asset stripping the company and have already got a buyer for the three lorries. There is a company coming in next week with a view to purchase the machinery in the production area. However, we have evaluated the stock that is already in the stores. There is approximately thirty to thirty-five thousand pounds worth of merchandise ready to be dispatched. The receivers want to sell these goods as it would recover about twenty percent of the overall debt. We have spoken to many of our customers, and they are prepared to accept deliveries until the supplies have been exhausted. Obviously, that will give them time to look for a new supplier. We want you to come in and sort out these deliveries. You have all the details of each delivery on your computer, which is still here. It will take several weeks to exhaust the supplies and we will pay you a daily rate of forty pounds. You would be, in effect, working for the receiver, as I am. I can promise you that you will be paid either on a daily or weekly basis if you take up this offer but you will not be paid the outstanding salary that is owed to you. Well, what do you say?"

"How are the deliveries to be made if the receivers have sold the delivery wagons?"

"We will hire a big Transit van, that should be enough. That way we won't need anyone with an HGV licence. The fuel will be paid for by the receiver, so it's a matter of loading them up and delivering as soon as possible. Well, what do you say?"

"Okay, I'll be there on Monday morning."

Duncan replaced the receiver and for the first time since Friday morning he managed a slight smile. He told Elizabeth. "The receiver has just offered me a few weeks work clearing all the stock. The wages will be better than the wage I received before. I'll take it just to tick over as they have guaranteed payments. It's better than nothing."

"Good, will you need the car?" Elizabeth asked.

"No, you can have it. I'll go on the train on Monday morning and come home in the hire van."

The rest of the day didn't seem so bad with the knowledge that Duncan had acquired some work for a few weeks. They would obviously miss his month's salary, but it wouldn't be too long before Elizabeth received her first wage. Duncan visited Jack and Alice later in the afternoon and received the verdict that the specialist's suspicions were confirmed. Alice had Alzheimer's Disease. Duncan thought that she looked no different and didn't really look unwell: she made him a cup of tea exactly how he liked it and the piece of cherry pie she served him was delicious. As he was leaving, Jack came out to see him off and explained, "This is one of her better days, but I don't like to leave her on her own too long, so I'll say goodbye and hopefully see you soon."

Duncan left and he was looking forward to a quiet night in front of the television with a couple of cans of lager. When he arrived home, he was shocked to see Elizabeth had a worried look on her face.

"What's up Lizzie? You look bothered," he asked.

"It's Lottie, her face is swollen up and badly bruised all down one side. She said that she fell over last night, but I don't believe her. There's no grazing, just an enormous bruise and loads of swelling. Something's up, I don't know what, I asked her if she was seeing Fraser today, but she said she never wants to see him again. I am worried that something very serious went off between them."

"Is she still in her room?" Duncan inquired.

"Yes, she doesn't want to come downstairs looking like that. She says she's not going to school next week, and she won't go until her face is back to normal. I didn't know what to say."

"We'll say nothing. She has to learn by her mistakes and she'll be a bit wiser now. I reckon that she had some booze last night and fell over and banged her face. Anyway, what's for dinner?"

"Is that all you think about, your stomach?"

The following morning, Duncan and Elizabeth were having a late breakfast after a long lie-in when there was a knock at the door. Elizabeth said alarmingly, "Duncan, there's a police car outside. I'm worried, will you come to the door with me?"

They answered the door together, and were shocked to see a policeman and a policewoman standing on their doorstep. It was the policeman who spoke first as they showed their identity badges.

"Good morning, I am PC Farnsworth, and this is WPC Sharp of the Fife Constabulary. We are here to investigate the complaint by Mr and Mrs Burley of an alleged assault on their son Fraser. He was attacked yesterday evening, and he suffered many injuries, one which will require dental surgery. Can we come in?"

"Yes, come in. What's his attack got to do with us?" A bemused Duncan asked.

PC Farnsworth waited until they were all inside the lounge before he spoke again. "It is alleged that the attack was made by Alec or Alex, someone who is the older brother of Charlotte Baker. We have been given this address by the victim who does not know the alleged attacker, but he knows the sister lives here. Is there an Alec or an Alex who lives at this address?"

"Yes, our son. His name is Alexander. He's still in bed, I'll go and wake him up," said Duncan.

"Alexander came downstairs wearing a pair of shorts and an old T shirt with nothing on his feet. He gave the impression he didn't have a care in the world. "Yes. What can I do for you?" he asked.

"We are here to investigate an alleged assault that took place yesterday evening at about 6.15 pm. Could you tell us of your whereabouts at that time?"

"Certainly, of course I can. At about that time I was beating the crap out of a slimeball called Fraser Burley. He got off lightly. I felt like killing him, so he's lucky to just get a good hiding."

A bemused WPC Sharpe spoke for the first time, "So, you don't deny carrying out the assault Alexander."

"No, I hammered him, good and proper, and I'll hammer him a damn sight worse if he ever tries to rape my sister again."

"What?, Tried to rape her!" Bellowed Duncan with a voice that could be heard in Glasgow. *"Tried to rape her? I'll kill the bastard!"*

An open-mouthed WPC Sharpe looked across at her partner. They were both momentarily speechless. It was the PC who regained his composure first. "Sir, you need to calm down. Threats to kill someone are not helping. Alexander is facing a charge of assault, which he has admitted. They are also suing for costs for his dental treatment. Apparently he had a crown knocked off one of his teeth."

"A crown!" roared Duncan, *"A crown, he'll never need a dentist ever again when I get my hands on him, he'll have no teeth left. He'll need an embalmer."*

WPC Sharpe quietly whispered in her partner's ear and said, "I think we need to go back to the station immediately and speak to the superintendent. There's far too much going off here than we can deal with, they'll have to call the special unit out."

The pair left to go back to the station as a raging father was looking for an explanation from his son. "Sandy, what do you mean 'he tried to rape her.' What the hell has been going on, and why doesn't anyone tell us?"

Alexander explained the whole events of Friday night. Then Elizabeth ran upstairs, hoping to comfort her daughter.

"You silly girl, why didn't you tell us? Is that how you got that bruise on your face?"

Duncan was pacing up and down the living room, seething and finding it very hard to control himself. "Sandy, when did you find out about this? Why didn't you tell me?"

"I found out yesterday morning. I didn't tell you because you would have ended up in serious trouble. I'm only fifteen, they won't lock me up. Besides, I quite enjoyed pasting him."

In mid-afternoon, two police cars arrived at their house causing consternation with some of their neighbours. PC Farnsworth and WPC Sharpe were joined by three other officers of the Specialist Sex Crime Unit comprising two experienced female officers and one male officer. The female officers wanted to interview Charlotte but insisted that Elizabeth be present. "Hello, Charlotte. Don't be afraid! I'm Superintendent Elspeth Charles and this is Inspector Shona Hill. You're not in any trouble. We just need to ask you a few questions regarding an accusation by your brother that Fraser Burley made an assault on your body and tried to rape you. Is this correct?"

It was harrowing for Charlotte. It was bad enough to admit she had been drinking alcohol in front of her mother and that she took one draw of a marijuana joint, but to relive the attempted rape ordeal was a heinous experience. She spoke slowly and deliberately, "He was holding me down with both his hands, but he couldn't manage to get his thingy inside of me. Then, he let go of my right arm and he put his hand down to his thingy to try to guide it inside of me. Then I managed to claw his face with my right hand and my nails scratched his face quite badly and when he lost his balance, I pushed him off. He then punched me in the face and then he stood up, and then he kicked me, really hard, twice. I was sick, then they all went away and left me, on my own, I couldn't breathe, I was in lots of pain, I was really scared."

"Charlotte, when you say he tried to put his thingy inside of you, do you mean his penis? Was he trying to insert his penis inside of you?" enquired Elspeth.

"Yes, it was horrible. I was screaming, 'no, please no!' but he took no notice. He said it was my birthday present."

"Can you please say, he was trying to put his penis inside of you." Elspeth continued.

"Yes, he was trying to put his penis inside of me, I hate him, I'm sorry, mum, I'm sorry."

Mother and daughter were both sobbing and hugging each other. Even Elspeth Charles was becoming misty eyed, and she had dealt with sexual assault cases like this for eight years.

She asked. "Charlotte can you be brave. We have bought a photographer with us. He's downstairs. Before I call him up, can you show us where he kicked you?" Charlotte was still wearing her pyjamas and pulled up the top to reveal enormous bruising on the left side of her ribcage. The bruising was already turning a nasty vivid bluey-black colour. Shona Hill went downstairs to fetch the photographer; he was advised to be as quick as possible but get as many photographs as he could in that time. The photographer was efficient and courteous, and he was finished in four minutes.

Downstairs Alexander was making a statement to WPC Sharpe and PC Farnsworth. It came to light that Fraser had told his parents he was savagely attacked without any warning or provocation by his ex-girlfriend's elder brother, because he had fallen out with his sister.

"Is it true that you viciously attacked him in the street without warning?" WPC Sharpe enquired.

"No, I beat him up after we had an argument. I asked him why he punched and kicked my sister. He denied it saying he didn't attack her. He reckoned she was drunk and attacked him, and he just pushed her away. 'She must have fallen over and now she's trying to blame it on me,' the lying toerag said. I then asked him how he got the scratches on his face, and he lied again, saying she went mental and attacked him. I then asked him why he tried to rape her. He said she was lying. I told him that I believed her more than I believed him, and he was a stinking liar. He threw a punch at me that just clipped the side of my chin as I ducked sideways. Then I came back up and smashed him in the mouth with my right fist. After that it was easy. I gave him a good hiding. I admit that it was me and me alone, but he threw the first punch. It was bad luck for him that I threw the rest."

"Right, Alexander, we need your date of birth and signature on this statement. Could you sign here please?" PC Farnsworth asked.

A few seconds later PC Farnsworth exclaimed, "Is that your date of birth? That makes you... you're only fifteen, and not that long as a fifteen-year-old either. Is this right? You look about eighteen or nineteen I'd say."

"Yes, officer. Shall I fetch my birth certificate?"

"Don't be cheeky. I didn't realize that you were so young. Have you ever been in trouble before?" A bemused PC asked.

"No, officer, but I'll tell you something: if that slimy toerag ever comes near my sister again, I *will* end up in serious trouble, and that's not an idle threat."

"Take my advice, young man, keep comments and thoughts like that to yourself. It's our job to deal with anyone breaking the law. And, if he is guilty as you have stated, then he will be dealt with by the courts, is that clear?"

"Yes, officer, sorry"

As PC Farnsworth was passing Duncan he whispered, "He's a big lad, what do you feed him on, ... raw meat?"

Prior to leaving, Shona Hill asked Elizabeth if she would bring Charlotte to the laboratory at the headquarters. Hopefully they could find and take samples of any human skin that may have accumulated underneath her fingernails. They also wanted to take blood samples. They explained how important this might be in obtaining a conviction. Charlotte didn't want to go initially, but was persuaded by her parents.

Elizabeth was impressed at how kindly her daughter was treated at the station, gently, and with enormous compassion, and they were back at home by the early part of the evening feeling relieved that the police seemed to believe Charlotte's version of events, and they appeared to be on her side. It was a day the whole family were glad to see the back of.

DEPARTURE

The next morning Duncan arrived at work and went straight to the production area where he was met by an eerie intimidating silence. He stood quietly for about a minute, staring, thinking, "how has it come to this?" He was totally dejected; he could visualize all the ladies working on the lines with the conveyor belts and the machinery making a deafening noise. He could visualize Ada Barron with her enormous, tattooed forearms working like a trojan while barking orders at the other ladies to "get a move on." He could see a scatter-brained Dorothy Ingram whistling merrily to the tune of "The Archers" and Shirley Lyons, who thought she had a voice like Shirley Bassey, instead of a voice like a ship's foghorn, singing her heart out. His thoughts then turned to Bernard Savage, walking alongside the conveyor belt, checking up on progress while most of the ladies were sticking two fingers up behind his back and giggling. That made him smile and improved his mood. He was joined by Jim Storey who was wondering where he had got to.

Duncan sadly reminisced. "Four days ago, this area was bustling with activity. Now look at it. What a waste! When I think about it, after Bernard first went off sick, and I was chucked into the deep end, I absolutely hated it. But every time I managed to sort a problem out, it gave me enormous satisfaction. I reckon that's the real reason Bernard went doolally; he knew the writing was on the wall and he couldn't cope. Let's see if the van is here yet?"

He concentrated on local deliveries only as he had made a late start, and while on the deliveries, he was wondering what sort of day his wife would have at work now that she was working under her own steam. His worries were unfounded.

She breezed through the day working on nervous energy and hardly left her office apart from visiting the ladies' room. As she was in the new car, she was home just after five o'clock, and went upstairs to see Charlotte who could not be persuaded to go back to school.

When Elizabeth saw her face, she understood the reason why. The swelling and bruising looked hideous, as the bruising had now turned black. She told her mother not to worry as she had kept herself busy by reading and listening to music. She had made herself several cups of tea and a salad for her lunch. "I'm okay, mum, don't fuss."

Elizabeth then asked Alexander how well he had fared in his Chemistry exam.

"Not bad, mum. Glad it's out of the way. It's not my favourite,. One more to go tomorrow, Physics. I hate that nearly as much as I hate French. Don't worry though, I'll revise all night and do my best."

As the family all sat down for a meal together, Duncan was thinking that if he eventually took the job on offer in Nottingham, moments like this would be few and far between. He loved his family dearly. He was exceptionally proud of his wife for attaining the post at the car showrooms, and although he was a trifle miffed at the police knocking on their door, he was very proud of the fact that his son had dished out retribution to his daughter's attacker. He was immensely proud of his daughter; she had been put through a terrible experience and her fortitude in dealing with the matter was admirable.

The week was passing by quietly for the family. Charlotte took the whole week off school and spent the days reading and playing music. Alexander finished his last exam on the Tuesday and settled back into normal lessons. Elizabeth was coping well in her new role and keeping herself busy. She occasionally had to contact her boss, but generally tried to stay as remote as possible. Duncan was enjoying doing something completely different for a change, and he thought it was wonderful driving to remote towns like Aviemore and Inverness.

They had a visit from Elspeth Charles on the Friday evening, who called in on her way home from work. Duncan was pleased she was not in a police car; he had been annoyed at the "curtain twitchers" staring at their house on the previous Sunday. Elspeth informed them that the police had taken a statement from Fraser, who had denied attacking Charlotte. She continued, "He said that it was Charlotte's idea to get the alcohol as it was her birthday. He then said she got drunk and went berserk, attacking him for no reason. Then he pushed her away, but that was all. He denies attempting to rape Charlotte, and said the bruises must be from when she fell over at school, running away from one of the teachers. Did you fall over at school, Charlotte?"

"Yes, but I didn't hurt myself. It just knocked the wind out of me. It was nothing really."

"Well, unfortunately that doesn't help our case in trying to get a conviction. However, we know he is telling lies because he said that the scratches on his face were from when he was attacked by Alexander. What he doesn't know is that we will analyse the samples of skin from underneath Charlotte's fingernails, and we are sure they will match the samples we have taken from Fraser. We can tell he's lying. It would help if we knew the names of the other boys who were there, and we could question them and possibly get a witness. Do you know any of the other boys?" Elspeth asked.

"No, I'm sorry, but I think I heard one of them say the name Bing. I heard that twice. He was the one who passed that horrible thing round to smoke."

"Mm, the less said about that, the better Charlotte." Elspeth frowned while writing a few notes.

On the Saturday morning it was time for a family trip to Edinburgh. Elizabeth and Charlotte were going to the castle while Duncan took Alexander to the Royal Commonwealth Pool.

The first week's training was more of an introductory meeting to meet the coaches and interview all the swimmers. Alexander was introduced to Graham Quigley who was taking a very keen interest in the progress of the teenager. He surmised that it was paramount to further Alexander's significant potential by him having regular one-on-one intense coaching as Alexander desperately needed to master the tumble turn. It would benefit no-one by his trying to learn among a host of competitors during race conditions. Graham was sympathetic to Alexander's request to be allowed to finish early during the football season, but he strongly advised that he ought to consider packing up playing football as he was risking injury and potentially jeopardizing his chances of international selection. One of the coaches, who lived in Cowdenbeath, volunteered to help. He would coach Alexander on a personal basis if Alexander could get over to the pool in Cowdenbeath, which is about ten miles from Kirkcaldy. Duncan took his details saying that it would be possible in a few weeks as Alexander would be breaking up from school for the summer vacations.

The family met up at the pre-arranged venue at the bottom of the Royal Mile. On the way home Duncan could hear Alexander and

Charlotte talking in the back of the car, and he heard Alexander say, "today had been a waste of time," which was probably about right.

It was a quiet night in for the whole family with a takeaway meal. Alexander was brooding over Mandy's absence, and he was also trying to save a bit of money for the school holidays. Charlotte's face still had a little bit of swelling and bruising on her cheek, although it had nearly disappeared, but she would not go out in Kirkcaldy until it was completely back to normal. It seemed a shame to Duncan to stay in on a nice Saturday evening such as this.

The next morning, they loaded the car and left after breakfast for a family day out to St Andrews. The weather was beautiful and the whole family enjoyed a dip in the sea together, although Charlotte wore a white T-shirt over her bikini to cover the remaining bruising.

Later in the afternoon, the parents left Alexander and Charlotte at the beach for an hour as they had a quick look round the castle adjacent to the university to re-kindle old memories of twenty years earlier when they lived in St Andrews. They stayed until the evening and had a meal in a restaurant in the town centre before leaving for home. It had been a fabulous day out, made all the better because the whole family were together.

The following morning was the start of a new week where events were quietening down considerably for the family. Alexander went to school on the Monday, apprehensive about the results of his exams. He wasn't remotely worried regarding the assault on Fraser. Indeed, he was more concerned counting the days until he would see Mandy again. Charlotte returned to school on the Tuesday as her facial bruising had completely disappeared. She vowed that she would never ever have a boyfriend again, which made her parents smile, but she absolutely meant it at the time. Elizabeth was coping admirably in her new vocation, staying mainly isolated in her office.

Duncan arrived at work on the Monday morning to see "For Sale" signs posted at the gate and contractors' lorries in the loading bay. There was a team of engineers stripping out the machinery and conveyor belts from the production area, piece by piece and section by section. "That's it," he thought, "there's no going back now."

By the Wednesday afternoon, the contractors had finished stripping out all the machinery and had left the area virtually bare.

When Duncan went in for a look round, he stood silent, staring into the emptiness. He was surprised that the inside of the building looked smaller now than it looked before when all the machinery was there.

Elspeth Charles came to see them on the Thursday evening. She said that there had been progress in the evidence against Fraser Burley. She explained, "He has now changed his statement, again. We have tracked down at least one of the other boys who was present on the night, and he has given us a statement. His name is William Crosby. If you remember, Charlotte heard the name "Bing." Well that's what led us to him. He has confirmed pretty much what Charlotte said but he denies knowing anything about supplying marijuana. He's obviously worried about his own skin. Unfortunately, the blood samples taken from Charlotte are inconclusive and do not contain sufficient positive traces of alcohol or marijuana. It's a pity we didn't get them much earlier on the Saturday morning instead of the Sunday afternoon. However, we have a very positive result from skin samples taken from under Charlotte's fingernails. They contain conclusive particles of skin that match the skin of Fraser Burley. Along with the witness statement from Crosby, we are going ahead with a prosecution. Hopefully, the statements from Charlotte and Crosby will be enough for a conviction. Fraser Burley is sixteen now, he's not a minor, he's in serious trouble. I will keep you informed of any progress. Any questions?"

"No. What will happen to Alexander?" Duncan inquired.

"My department is only dealing with the alleged sexual assault; but I don't think that you will have a lot to worry about. As Alexander is under sixteen, he's likely to get a warning letter as to his future conduct. This would not be a caution and would not mean he has a record, but he needs to take notice and behave himself in future. It's our job to punish offenders and it makes our job harder if people are going round like vigilantes administering their own punishment. However, strictly off record, if he was my son, I would be proud of him, but that's another matter."

On the Friday afternoon, Duncan was assessing the remaining stock. He worked out there would be four more days of deliveries before the stocks were exhausted. That would leave him only six more days during which he would not have any employment, because now he had made up his mind, *he would be* taking the job in Nottingham.

The following Monday, Alexander received his exam results and was pleasantly surprised at how well he had done in most of them. He had even excelled at French, something he could not understand. He would have been happy enough if he had failed French abysmally, but he received the third highest mark in the whole class.

Charlotte's return to school passed without incident. Her classmates were unaware of the traumatic events on her birthday and Charlotte was determined it would stay that way. The school would be breaking up for the summer holidays in less than two weeks, and she was looking forward to it immensely.

On the Wednesday evening, Duncan was driving home in the Transit van. He had a few deliveries to make on the Thursday and would return the hire van and come home on the train. When he was nearly home, he was about to pass under an old disused railway bridge when it hit him like a thunderbolt. There painted on the bridge in letters eighteen inches high was written in bright white paint.

CHARLOT IS A HARLOT

It was like a knife through his heart. He knew who it was meant for, and what's more, who was responsible. Obviously, he knew that his daughter would not be the only Charlotte living in Kirkcaldy, but it was more than a coincidence that this graffiti had appeared just now. It was certainly aimed at his daughter. He felt sick to the pit of his stomach. When he arrived home, he was determined not to mention it to the rest of the family; he would go to the police station on Friday after he had finished work and report his suspicions.

There was little the police could do. They could make an enquiry, but without proof or a witness their hands were tied. He was advised to report it to the rail company as the bridge is their property, and they might be able to get it cleaned off, but that was all. When he left the police station he felt as though he was ready to commit murder without any regrets. He would be having a week's holiday before setting off for Nottingham, and he had been looking forward to a nice relaxing week. Now his stomach was twisted in knots. He was seething. His main hope was that it would get cleaned off before his wife and daughter got to know anything about it.

Elizabeth had a surprise of her own when she arrived at work on the Friday morning. As she approached her office door, she was delighted to see her name on a new wooden sign in gold lettering. She felt enormously proud: now anyone who entered her office would realise that she had acquired a position of respectability. She thanked Martin very sincerely, causing him to brandish his trademark cheesy smile. She was now beginning to see him in a totally different light.

Alexander and Charlotte broke up from school the following afternoon, both with very favourable school reports, and looking forward to their six week vacation.

Elizabeth received her first salary, and Duncan had also been paid, so the family were in a buoyant mood for the school holidays.

On the Saturday morning, Duncan and Alexander went to the second session of swimming training, which was an improvement on the first. The men's and lady's training was now separate, and hourly slots had been allocated for each stroke. Alexander was delighted that the men's freestyle was allotted the hour from 10am until 11am. There were several races packed into the hour in which Alexander came no better than third, but he was less than a half a second behind the two men in front of him.

During the afternoon, Duncan and Elizabeth were washing the conservatory windows when Duncan suddenly came straight out with his decision, stunning Elizabeth.

"Lizzie, I've decided that I'm taking that job in Nottingham. They have offered me a start date on the 22nd, which is only a week away. It's not going to be permanent; I only intend staying there for a maximum of three or four years while we build our money up to pay for the bairns to go to university. In fact, if a local job comes along before the four years are up, I will pack up even earlier. They won't know that I'm only using it as a stopgap. I have done all the sums, and I will be nearly four thousand pounds a year better off. I will fly from Edinburgh airport; the flights work out just right. It will be an early start on a Monday morning, and on a Friday evening I'll be home at a similar time to now. I hardly ever see Sandy and Lottie in the week, so that won't make much difference anyway. The only worry I have is that I will miss you, and hopefully you will miss me, but that will make the weekends all the sweeter. Well, Lizzie, what do you think?"

"What do I think? Duncan, you started off by saying 'I've decided,' which sort of makes anything I say pointless. Of course, I'm not happy about you going all that way for work, but I understand we need the money, desperately. I realize that we will struggle on one wage, especially now we have the car loan to pay back. But please, please, promise me that as soon as you can get a suitable local job you come straight back."

"Of course, I don't really want to go, but hopefully it'll all turn out for the best," he said.

"How are you getting there and back?" Elizabeth asked.

"I will drive to Nottingham the very first week, and then on the Friday leave the car at the airport car park. When I get to Edinburgh airport on the way back, I will get a taxi to Dalmeny Station which isn't far from the airport, and from there get the train home. They run every half hour. It's only thirty minutes on the train from Dalmeny. On the Monday I will do the reverse."

"I do understand. It's just that it couldn't have come about at a worse time. This business with Lottie and Fraser, to say nothing of Sandy getting into trouble. I just hope I can cope while you're away."

"I will phone every night. It's only four nights a week, and I'll have lots of holidays to look forward to. I'll have eight bank holidays and twenty-five days off at my own leisure. The time will fly by." Duncan said with an optimistic smile.

"Yeah, well, we'll see about that," Elizabeth grimaced.

Duncan was not looking forward to telling his children about commuting to Nottingham, but Elizabeth put him on the spot as they were eating their evening meal together and he was forced into it. Alexander nonchalantly shrugged his shoulders, but Charlotte reached across the table and gripped her mother's hand, something she had not done for a long time.

Duncan was determined to make the most of the time he had left at home before setting off for his new job. He was delighted to be able to persuade the children to join them for a day out on the Sunday to Pittenweem to see St Fillan's cave and the wonderful harbour, and then on to Crail, another beautiful fishing village. Charlotte was impressed by the quaint charm of the small fishing villages, and she took many photographs, which pleased her parents immensely to see her so happy. Alexander was daydreaming and wondering how Mandy would be getting along with her husband in the Greek islands. He was pining like a love-sick puppy, although he did well to hide it from the rest of the family. While driving home, Duncan realized that today was likely to be the last time the whole family were available for a family day out for a very long time. Both he and Elizabeth would be working full time towards paying for their children's studies at university, and by the time they graduated they would be adults. The thought of it sent a chill down his spine.

On the Sunday evening, Duncan telephoned George Vowden, the coach in Cowdenbeath. Duncan explained that he was off work the following week and that he could bring Alexander across to the pool in Cowdenbeath at George's leisure. It would be difficult now that the schools had broken up and the swimming pool would be far busier. However, from 7am until 9am on Wednesday and Thursday it was possible for private tuition as these times were set apart for club members. George could arrange membership for Alexander if he could attend during the early session to which Duncan agreed.

During the first week of the holidays, Duncan and Elizabeth noticed that Charlotte seemed very reluctant to want to go anywhere without her parents. The events on her birthday had made a severe dent in her confidence, and when her friends Kerry and Rebecca invited her for a day out at the ice-skating centre on the Tuesday, she seemed very reluctant to want to go. Duncan knew she was normally very keen to go ice-skating and he could only persuade her to go by promising to meet her outside and walk home with her after the skating had finished.

Alexander wasn't happy to have to get up so early on the Wednesday, and grumbled the whole way to Cowdenbeath. But once in the pool he worked hard at trying to master the tumble turn. It was a matter of timing the distance to the wall before beginning the turn. Several times he made a mess of it, but after ninety minutes he had managed to achieve the turn on three consecutive occasions. It was going to be a matter of continual practice until he could achieve the turn without thinking about it. As George said, "Alexander now needs to be able to do it under race conditions when the pressure is on."

The following morning, Duncan and Alexander set off early again but today Alexander was not moaning; he seemed excited at the prospect of seeing if he could improve on the previous day. George was very pleased with his progress, as he seemed to be getting the timing of the turns exactly right, but the acid test would be in the Commonwealth Pool under race conditions.

On the Thursday evening, Charlotte asked her parents if they were happy to let her go with her friend Kerry for a week's holiday in Leven. Kerry's mum had booked a big caravan for seven days, and she was more than happy for Kerry's friends Rebecca and Charlotte to accompany them. Beatrice came to see Elizabeth and Duncan during the evening to explain how it would be preferable for the girls if they had company of their own age. Beatrice asked if it was possible to help them with the transport, so Duncan agreed to take them all on the Saturday morning. It would be a "bit of a squeeze" but they'd manage.

After he'd dropped them off at the caravan park and came back from Leven, Duncan visited Jack and Alice McKinlay, before returning home to find Elizabeth in a sombre mood.

"I'm dreading you being away. Please make sure you call me every night," she said.

"Of course, I will call you at about seven every night. If that's not enough, I'll call you in the morning at seven as well to make sure you are up for work. Don't worry, you'll be fine."

On the Saturday night, Alexander went out leaving Duncan and Elizabeth alone to enjoy a blissful evening in bed together.

The following morning, as Duncan was packing a bag for his first week in Nottingham, he felt a nervous sickness in the pit of his stomach. He knew, or thought he knew, that he would be okay once he was there and started the job, but leaving his family, even on a temporary basis, was something he had never done before, and he wasn't sure how it would affect him, or them.

Elizabeth made a roast dinner at lunchtime, and by two o'clock Duncan was putting his bag into the boot of the car while Elizabeth was standing on the pavement looking forlornly at him through misty eyes. After a big hug and a long slow kiss, it was time for him to set off. He wanted to make the most of the daylight hours and not arrive too late in Nottingham. As the car pulled away from his home Duncan was thinking, " I hope I'm not making a big mistake."

After a seven-hour journey, an exhausted Duncan arrived in Beeston at the B&B. He had been very fortunate to arrive just as the landlady was locking up and leaving to go to her local for a drink. "I didn't think you would turn up at this godforsaken hour. Never mind, come in. You're in room number five. Breakfast from seven until nine. If you go out, make sure you lock up," she said.

Duncan dropped his bag off and went out to find a public payphone. He knew Elizabeth would be pleased he had arrived safely. Unfortunately, the conversation was static, as neither knew what to say, not having been in this situation before.

"Do you want me to call you at seven in the morning to make sure you're up?" he asked.

"Please, I probably won't sleep much tonight with you not being here," Elizabeth replied.

Although he was tired from the long journey, Duncan didn't sleep well at all, and as a result he was up and dressed by six o'clock. He went for a walk around the local streets to familiarize himself with the area, before calling Elizabeth at seven o'clock. Disappointingly, she had suffered a similar night's lack of sleep.

"Perhaps by tonight we'll both get back to normal," he said.

"Good luck. Hope it goes well," she replied.

Duncan had his breakfast and left for work in plenty of time. He was at the new MT & AS department twenty minutes early, and he was the first person there. It wasn't long before a crowd of men and women had joined him, all standing outside the locked doors. At eight o'clock, Joseph Wignall arrived and asked if there was a Mr Baker present. When the introductions were over, Jospeh unlocked the doors and led all the operatives on a guided tour of the department. Everything was brand new, installed to a very high specification. Duncan felt nervous; he was wondering if he had bitten off more than he could chew. All the operatives were then taken to a lecture room for an induction, and then they were instructed to the company's expectations with several lectures and demonstrations regarding the new computer system. This took all morning, and by lunchtime there were many worried blank faces among the operatives. The lectures resumed in the afternoon, while Duncan was escorted to Joseph's office for a private consultation.

He was advised by Joseph, "Mr Baker, or can I call you Duncan? As this is your first day, I need to make you aware of a few things that you ought to know. First and foremost, when we initially advertised the post for the manager's position, we were determined to engage an operative who doesn't already work for the company. There are several employees who are as qualified as yourself already working here in other departments in the company, but we wanted a brand new start. As you can imagine, jealousy can be detrimental to morale when one person is jealous of a promotion that another person has achieved, that they think they should have had. We have two men and a lady who will be working under your leadership who are very highly qualified, and my advice is to try to allocate as much responsibility as you can across the board. Don't try to take on too much yourself. You will be in overall control, so try to spread the workload equally among all the operatives. Do not be afraid to discipline operatives for bad timekeeping and any form of malpractice. You will need to keep a tight watch on holidays. For example, you will find that the majority want a week off at Christmas and a week at Easter and then a fortnight in August. It will be your responsibility to ensure we are not understaffed at these popular holiday periods, so you will have to organise these periods on a rota basis. There is one more thing: you will need to use your judgement in acquiring an understudy, someone you trust implicitly to take over the reins when you have your vacations. This is critical; you must make the right choice. Any questions Mr Baker?"

"No, sir. That all sounds exactly as I expected. Who are the three operatives that are very highly qualified?"

"Des Pearce, Ted Hector, and Olive Mackay. All three are long-serving and have a good record with the company. We have made you a folder with the files of each of the operatives in your department. You would be advised to get to know their capabilities immediately. Good luck, Mr Baker."

Duncan knew straight away he would be well advised to heed the advice afforded to him. As an "outsider" he had no doubt that he would have to earn respect from his staff. After two more lectures in the afternoon, the first day had passed in a whirl and he was back at the B&B before he even had time to speak to any of the new staff.

He spent a couple of hours going through the employee files before going out to call a crestfallen Elizabeth. She was already missing her husband immensely; Charlotte was also away for the week at the seaside with friends and she only saw a fleeting vision of Alexander going out to meet his mates while eating a sandwich as he left. The house was eerily quiet. It was not normal, and she couldn't help but show her disappointment when speaking to Duncan, which didn't improve his morale. It was the first of many such phone calls that would become routine. Elizabeth had told Duncan that her work was going well, and she felt comfortable now that her first few weeks were behind her, which pleased him enormously. Duncan explained that it was going to be a delicate matter to designate tasks to each individual as he was starting from scratch, and he didn't really know anyone, but time would tell if he would be successful.

Over the next two days, Duncan had the chance to meet all the operatives, and he decided it was preferable to split the workforce into small teams, each with their own specific targets and agendas. He appointed the senior employees as section leaders and hoped that he could eventually make the right choice as to who would be his understudy. He was conscious of the fact that he didn't want to be classed in the same mould as Bernard Savage, and he spent as much time as possible getting involved with each team's progress.

Duncan was certainly looking forward to going home on Friday: he was finding the evening telephone calls to Elizabeth frustrating as generally they had little to say except how their work was progressing. Elizabeth reminded him on the Thursday evening that Sandy had swimming training on the Saturday morning, and they would have to go to Edinburgh in Cuthbert unless they caught the train. Also Charlotte was due home from her holiday in Leven. She told Duncan that she had seen very little of Alexander: "He spends most of the time down at the beach with his friends. He's getting a good tan. In the evenings he goes out to meet his mates without saying a word of where he's going, but he's always home by about eleven o'clock."

Duncan replied. "It would be nice if *we* could get away for a beach holiday, Lizzie, but, as we have both only just started in our new jobs, it's hard to ask for holidays already. I have to sort out a rota for the holidays with the staff that is fair for everyone, but it's not going to be easy. Many of them want their holidays in August, and most of them have applied for a holiday at Christmas. I know that I've got to upset some of them, but what can I do?"

Although he was finding some of his responsibilities very stressful, Duncan recognised that he was enjoying the work more than at any time during the eleven years of his previous employment in Leith. He had occasionally found some of the operatives begrudging in their respect of his authority, but generally most of them were usually very co-operative and respectful, and he was overjoyed to be in a position of senior management.

As he finished work at five o 'clock on Friday, Duncan was amazed at the frantic rush to get out of the gate that was akin to the stampede at his previous employment in Leith. What's more, he was right in the middle of it as he was in a rush to get to the airport. He arrived at the airport and parked his car, and then dashed into the booking-hall to buy a standby ticket. He was at the departure gate ten minutes before programmed take-off and, as all the other passengers had already boarded, he was allowed through, much to his vast relief.

The flight landed on time at Edinburgh, and as he was walking into the arrivals area, he was delighted to see Elizabeth standing there waiting for him. It was a pleasant surprise. They stood hugging and kissing for two minutes as dozens of passengers swarmed past them. The very fact that Elizabeth had made the effort to drive twenty-five miles to meet him showed him how much she'd missed him, and with the prolonged stirring in his loins, how much he had missed her.

"I came in Cuthbert, it's in the short-term car park. Will you drive us home?" she asked, and ten minutes later they were on their way home, occasionally holding hands when the car was held up in traffic or waiting for traffic lights to change.

"Sandy's already gone out tonight with his mates, so we have the house to ourselves when we get home. I haven't got anything ready for dinner yet, so if you're hungry we can pick up a takeaway on the way home. You can have whatever you want, it's your choice."

"Sod that, who's bothered about food? There's only one place I want to go, up that wooden hill to bed, and when you have rogered me senseless, we can eat later."

The couple spent a blissful evening together wallowing in their love for each other. The light was beginning to fade before they eventually came back downstairs and had a slice of toast and a cup of coffee. Duncan vowed to himself he would never get into trouble and end up in prison, as being away from his wife for less than just one week was absolutely torturous.

The following morning, Duncan and Alexander left in plenty of time to get to Edinburgh for swimming training. The old Morris Minor made reasonable time, and they were twenty minutes early for the freestyle coaching. Alexander was changing into his swimming trunks when Duncan was approached by the senior coach Frank Burkett.

"Mr Baker, I've been speaking with George Vowden who has informed me that Alexander has made significant progress in mastering the tumble turn. It will be good to see if he can adapt it into race conditions when his adrenaline will be pumping. It's much harder when there are seven other swimmers alongside you all going flat out. Let's hope he remembers everything that he's learned."

Duncan watched from the spectator's balcony as the first race began. Alexander stormed down the first fifty metres and was in the lead at halfway, but he made a complete hash of the tumble turn by attempting it when too far away from the wall, and, consequently, he eventually turned in last place but recovered to finish fourth. Graham Quigley was delighted to see that he had tried it under race conditions and gave a "thumbs up" in Duncan's direction. The coaches were keen to see Alexander have another attempt, and forty minutes later he was afforded another try. The second race started exactly like the first with Alexander leading coming to the halfway turn. This time he was slightly too close to the wall before turning but made a much better job of it and turned in third place. He eventually dead-heated for first place much to his own disgust and to the delight of the coaches.

Frank Burkett said to Duncan, "He's almost there. He must have lost at least half a second on that turn, but he still got up to finish in a dead heat for first place. He needs to keep practising; I reckon he can take a full second off that time by next year. Look at him. He's a colossus, and he's getting faster. He's only half a second off the British record already."

"This morning on the way here, he told me he's been swimming in the sea every day this week with his friends. They're on their school holidays now. Unfortunately, his mother and I both work full-time and we can't get him over to Cowdenbeath to see George, but I'll have a word with Alexander to see if he will go by bus. I don't know how he will react to that though. Anyway, see you in a fortnight."

On their way home, Duncan told Alexander all about his conversations with the coaches, and was surprised at Alexander's reply: "Not a chance dad. I'm not getting up at daft o'clock to go on the bus. There's plenty of time until next July. I'll master it easy by then, don't worry."

When they arrived home, Elizabeth came out to meet them in a panic. "Duncan, can you go straight up to Leven to the caravan park to pick the girls up? Lottie and Beatrice rang me this morning to ask if you could pick them up. I didn't know what to say, so I agreed. They have been spending the whole morning cleaning the caravan, but they hand the keys in at one o'clock so by the time you get there they will be waiting for you."

"Bloody hell, Liz. It was tight in the Escort; we'll be like bloody sardines in Cuthbert. We will not get all the bags in the boot either, so some of them will have to sit with their bags on their laps. Good job it's not that far."

As Duncan pulled away in Cuthbert Alexander smiled at his mother and said, "One thing for sure, Mum: he'd make one hell of a miserable taxi driver."

ADVERSITY

Duncan arrived back at home later with Charlotte. She told the family all about the holiday, and how she had spent most of the time on the beach swimming and sun-bathing. Elizabeth was overjoyed to see how happy and relaxed she was. While having a cup of tea, Duncan couldn't help but notice how both his children were looking very tanned and healthy, yet he and Elizabeth were pallid by comparison. It made him pine for a seaside holiday, yet he knew that he wouldn't be able to have time off work after just one week in employment. He had also falsely told Joseph Wignall that he had a holiday booked before he started in his new job. He now wished that he hadn't.

Later that Saturday afternoon, they had a visit from Elspeth Charles who informed Duncan and Elizabeth that they would soon have confirmation of a court date for Fraser Burley. She said, "He Is to be charged with attempted rape, assault by beating, supplying alcohol to a minor and also giving false information to a police officer. He has now changed his story three times, but each time his lies are getting him into more trouble. His parents have now secured the services of a barrister which personally I think is a waste of their money. Fraser already has two previous convictions for minor offences, one was for theft and the other vandalism. I contacted the barrister, and I told him that our case is watertight, so with that in mind I hope that Fraser will be persuaded to plead guilty. If that is the case, then Charlotte will not be cross examined. I hope so. I will keep in touch with you."

On the Sunday morning, Duncan, Elizabeth and Charlotte all went to Earlsferry and Elie to spend the day on the sandy beach while Alexander and his friends were on the beach at Kirkcaldy.

While swimming in the sea, Alexander was thinking that Mandy would be back home yesterday, but her husband would probably still be with her over the weekend. He was hoping that he and Mandy would meet up the following weekend, while at the same time he appreciated he was getting obsessed with her.

Later that day, one of his friends Paul Woods was telling all the lads about how he had "gone all the way" with a girl he met while he was on holiday. Alexander smiled in acknowledgement, yet he was yearning to upstage him with tales of Mandy and himself.

Duncan was in bed early as he had to be up at 4.30 am, but he had another one of those nights when it was hard to sleep. His back had caught too much sun, and he spent most of the night trying to get comfortable, without success. He was delighted that Elizabeth got up at the same time so she could go with him to the airport.

During the flight, Duncan was going through the notes he had made the previous week regarding progress so far. He was aware that the majority of the staff were respectful when he was allocating their tasks, but he was not so sure about Ted Hector and Olive Mackay. Ted seemed positively resentful and surly, and would not speak to Duncan unless he was spoken to first, even then begrudgingly with a degree of uncivility. Although Olive was more talkative, she also appeared to be harbouring a grudge, possibly because he was a newcomer to the company and because in her opinion, she was considerably more qualified for the post. It was a challenge that Duncan would relish over the following weeks, and he was determined that he would gain their respect in the fullness of time.

As the summer passed into autumn, he eventually made the decision to promote Des Pearce to be his understudy. Des was very reliable; he would get on with his work with the minimum of fuss and he would always keep Duncan up to date with his team's progress. The decision further infuriated Ted Hector who did not try to hide his disappointment. It came to a crunch one lunchtime when Duncan overheard Ted saying to some of his team, "I don't know how that sweaty sock got the job in the first place. Fancy him making Des Pearce his second in command, I've worked here much longer than Des, and I have got more qualifications than him. It's not right."

Duncan waited until the afternoon before he called Ted into his office. After asking him to sit down, he casually confronted him with the comments he had heard earlier. "Ted, I overheard you complaining to members of your team concerning my decision to promote Des Pearce to assistant manager. The fact that I overlooked you should be obvious. You have displayed a negative attitude ever since I came here. I would point out to you that if you are not happy working in this department, you have several choices. First, you can apply for a transfer to another sector. Second, I could demand that you are transferred elsewhere. Third, you can leave the company and go somewhere else. Fourth, you can grow up and take that chip off your shoulder and get on with your work. Finally, if I ever hear you calling me a sweaty sock again, I'll knock you into the middle of next week. It's your decision. Let me know by close of play this afternoon."

"You can have my decision now. I will put in for a transfer." Ted replied through a nervous smile..

"Yes, I think that's wise. As far as I am concerned, I don't even want you in this building anymore, I would appreciate you collecting your belongings and saying your goodbyes as soon as possible."

The transfer of Ted Hector seemed to have a positive effect on Olive Mackay. She no longer gave the impression that she harboured a grudge against Duncan, and she now became positively co-operative and very respectful towards him. Possibly, she was beginning to see him in a new light, or maybe it was a case of self-preservation, or even a combination of both, but she became an enthusiastic team leader and a very important employee in the running of the department.

As the weeks passed by, Duncan was delighted how his initial worries about working in a new environment were totally unfounded. However, he did have one worry; he had put on almost a stone in weight in the first six weeks, mainly owing to eating a fried breakfast in the B&B and takeaway meals on weekday nights. He was horrified when Elizabeth pointed out that he was acquiring a paunch, and, after he weighed himself, he resolved to address the matter immediately.

He was determined to leave the B&B, and he put a card on the notice board in the company canteen asking if anyone had a spare room. Luckily his request was answered positively and he had an offer of rental accommodation by Wilf, a maintenance section employee.

Wilf had recently sadly become a widower. He was in his early sixties and looking forward to his retirement. Wilf would be glad of the company, and, as he said, the extra money would "come in handy" He told Duncan that he would be selling the house in four years' time when he retired. This was exactly what Duncan needed as he was able to change his diet completely. As he was used to waking up very early from his time working in Leith, he began doing more exercise by going out most weekday mornings, jogging down to the river and along the footpath towards Attenborough. Slowly his improved diet and daily dawn run had a marked effect on his weight, but he noticed that it took much longer to shed the extra pounds than it took to put them on.

Back in Kirkcaldy as the summer elapsed and the autumn continued, Elizabeth was becoming yet more concerned regarding the number of occasions Martin was visiting her office for nothing more than mindless chit-chat. He had started to make comments on a daily basis regarding her appearance and attire. On one occasion he had said, "I wish my wife had your dress sense and your good looks."

Many more complements were forthcoming over the weeks regarding her hairstyle and even her perfume. Elizabeth was becoming very concerned at his over-familiarity, especially remembering the counselling afforded her by Verity. Her work was going splendidly, and now that she was earning a good salary, she didn't want to do or say anything that might upset the status quo. It was all-consuming in her thoughts, and she was becoming very frustrated at her own lack of ability to nip it in the bud. So she carried on regardless, just offering the occasional smile whenever he gave her a compliment, but inwardly hating his excruciating back-door advances.

It wasn't the only thing that was giving Elizabeth concern. Charlotte was becoming quite reclusive, spending most evenings in her bedroom listening to music and not wanting to go anywhere. She had stopped going to the under-sixteen disco, and furthermore she had very little contact with Kerry and Rebecca. Elizabeth understood that the awful experience she endured on her birthday with Fraser had a marked effect on her, and had severely dented her confidence.

Elspeth Charles came to see Duncan and Elizabeth one Sunday to tell them that, "The court date is set for Thursday September 26th." Fraser's barrister had advised that his client would plead guilty to the charges of assault by beating, supplying alcohol to a minor and giving false information to a police officer. However, he emphatically denies the charge of attempted rape. His fourth statement now said that,

'He was only trying to frighten Charlotte as she was drunk, and he was hoping to shock her and show her how vulnerable she could be by getting herself in such a state.'

"I'm afraid, as penetration did not take place, it will be difficult to gain a guilty conviction on this. Basically, it would mean Charlotte having to go in the witness box to be cross-examined by the barrister. I can assure you that it would not be very nice for her. It would be extremely traumatic. Being questioned by a very experienced barrister who will try to make her look foolish and apportion all the blame on her would be a torrid experience for anyone, let alone a fourteen-year-old girl. If we decide to drop the attempted rape charge and he pleads guilty to the other charges, then Charlotte will not be called as a witness. I think this would be preferable for Charlotte. But be assured, Fraser Burley will be on our radar from now on."

Charlotte was relieved to know that a date had now been set for Fraser's court appearance. She had been back at school for just one week and she was suffering torment and ridicule from her classmates. The graffiti on the bridge was now common knowledge, and several girls were now calling her "The Harlot." When she tried to explain to the girls that it couldn't be her as she had never even let a boy touch her or even get to first base, the ridiculing increased. All the other girls had achieved first base, at least half of them had reached second base and three of the more adventurous girls had "gone all the way." Charlotte took the ridicule and name-calling very hard, particularly when her friends Kerry and Rebecca became involved, but she had her dignity and her principles, and she would stick by them.

Elizabeth certainly did not have any worries concerning Alexander. She had never seen him happier than he was during that summer. He worked very hard on mastering the tumble turn until he could do it without even thinking, and during the fortnightly coaching sessions in Edinburgh, he was able to win his races with considerable ease. The coaches were delighted with him but once again they made a point to Duncan regarding their concerns about his playing football.

Alexander had made contact with Mandy again early one evening in late August. He was walking home from spending an afternoon on the beach when her car pulled up at his side. She was wearing a blond wig neatly trussed in a headscarf and she was sporting the same enormous dark sunglasses. He didn't recognize her at first until he heard the familiar "get in." Mandy drove out of the town and pulled up in a quiet layby on the road to Auchtertool so they could talk.

She had not seen him in a month, and she had missed him enormously. Her holiday on the Greek islands with her husband had

156

been a disaster as they had spent most of the time arguing. They argued about every trivial thing, and Mandy had reached the stage where she was only staying with her husband for financial reasons. Although she had money of her own by way of a monthly allowance from her father, it was her husband who owned their house. She knew that she could not afford to be divorced, but she longed for a fresh start, and one thing she had realized was how much she wanted Alexander to be part of a new chapter in her life.

They happily concurred that they wanted to see more of each other and arranged a regular meeting place and time at a phone box near the railway station on Saturday nights. Mandy booked them into a cheap hotel for the night and it was a rarity if they ever got any sleep.

Alexander missed one of the training sessions in September because Mandy had left a plethora of scratch marks on his back. He was afraid to go into the pool wearing just his swimming trunks as everyone would be able to see the scratches. He made an excuse to his parents that he wasn't feeling too good, so they were unaware of the real reason. When he attended the next training session, two weeks later, Frank Burkett was very relieved. He told Duncan that Alexander was a certain starter for Scotland in the Commonwealth Games. He was now achieving an unofficial time that was better than the Scottish record and on a par with the British record.

As Frank said, "In another nine months he'll be nailed on for a medal if he continues like this. He's getting faster as he gets bigger and stronger, I can foresee a gold medal around that neck."

Alexander was taking everything in his stride. He was ecstatic with his social life, his work at school was progressing steadily towards his exams, his improvement at the hundred metres freestyle was way beyond his own expectations, and also his team manager had made him the team captain for the new football season. Alexander went on to be a formidable captain, leading by example with a never-say-die attitude that inspired his teammates.

He received an official letter from the Fife Constabulary that warned him as to his future conduct. The letter confirmed that it was not a caution and that he did not have a criminal record.

Fraser's day in court finally arrived, and the Baker family were in attendance. Duncan booked two days holiday and came home on the Wednesday evening for a four day break. Elizabeth also had a day's holiday to chaperone Charlotte who fortunately was not called as a witness. Despite his reluctant admission of guilt and desperate pleas for leniency by his barrister (as his client had now started work and acquired an apprenticeship), he was duly sentenced to six months detention in a young offenders' institution. Charlotte's parents were happy to see him convicted, but disappointed in the lenient sentence. As Duncan said to Elizabeth, "That guttersnipe should have got five years. What good is six months? With good behaviour, he'll be out by Christmas. Still, hopefully, Lottie will be able to relax a bit now."

As the court case had finished by lunchtime, Charlotte decided she wanted to go to school in the afternoon, which gave the couple the opportunity to spend time together alone. Elizabeth desperately wanted to talk to her husband regarding the underhand advances being made towards her at work, but somehow, she could not bring herself to begin the conversation, so they spent the afternoon in bed and only arose just before the children arrived home from school.

During the four-day break, Duncan noticed that his daughter did not go out of the house except to go to school. It was something that Elizabeth had already observed, and he too became worried that she was becoming too reclusive.

On the Saturday night, after Alexander had gone out, Duncan knocked on Charlotte's bedroom door for a quiet word with her. He was worried that she was being bullied or picked on and that she might be afraid to go out, but she explained to her father, "No, it's nothing like that. I'm fed up with all the other girls in my class, even my friends Kerry and Rebecca. All they ever talk about is boys and all they are interested in is boys. They all brag about how far they've been and rubbish like that. I hate it. I'll never ever have a boyfriend again. I'm going to get my degrees and go to university and either become a vet or get a job somewhere where I can work with animals. I trust them more than I trust boys. I'm all right, Dad. Don't worry about me."

"Of course I worry about you, Charlotte. You and Sandy are my whole life, that's why I go all the way to Nottingham for work as the extra salary will help us pay for you and Sandy to go to university. I wouldn't bother otherwise. Your mother and I love you dearly, and we just want to see you happy." Duncan replied.

"I *am* happy, Dad; I'm looking forward to Christmas when we all have a holiday together."

Christmas was also painfully on Duncan's mind. More than half of the staff in his department had put in a request for a holiday that included all of the Christmas and New Year period. Duncan desperately wanted to have some days off during this time and it was a situation that would seriously test his resolve and powers of leadership.

On the Monday morning, Duncan called a meeting with his senior team leaders, Des Pearce, Olive Mackay, and Jack Francis who had replaced Ted Hector. Olive wanted a holiday over the Christmas period as she had worked the same period the previous year, but Des Pearce and Jack Francis were available as cover if Duncan wanted any time off. Duncan was pleased that his senior staff were co-operative as he had been worried that it may lead to conflict. He spent a whole afternoon sorting out the Christmas holiday rota before letting all the staff know the outcome. It did not please everyone, which was to be expected, but the majority of the staff were understanding and aware that they couldn't all be off at the same time.

Elizabeth was able to book a slightly shorter holiday than her husband, as she would have to work on two of the days between Christmas and the New Year. This was disappointing for them as they wanted to take the family away for the whole festive period.

Alexander and Charlotte both worked very hard at school towards their important exams. However, on most Saturday nights, Alexander would be out with Mandy. They were becoming more like a newlywed couple and always held hands when walking together. Mandy had found a small hotel a few miles away down the coast in Kinghorn where they would not be recognized and she regularly booked them in for the night, paying strictly by cash after giving a false name and address. It was a heavenly period in Alexander's life, and he hoped that he and Mandy would be lovers forever. She was becoming to feel that way too. When she had initially met him, she had only been selfishly interested in her own sexual fulfilment, but she had rapidly become besotted with her young lover. She forever thought about him when they were apart, and she often found herself pining for him during her lonely days at home during the week. She had stopped calling him an idiot whenever he asked a simple question, and she was enjoying having adult conversations with him. Even on one occasion when he innocently asked her, "Does it ever bother you, being unfaithful to your husband?"

She replied, "No, he's probably doing the same thing right now. About five years ago, he came home on a fortnight's leave with a dose of gonorrhoea. He had to take antibiotics and use cream on himself. I wouldn't go near him. His saving grace was that at least he had the decency to tell me, so we didn't sleep together. Would you believe it, he tried to make out that he must have caught the pox off a toilet seat while abroad. He must think I'm stupid. I know what he gets up to when he has some leave. He's more than likely at it now."

As the autumn days were getting shorter and the nights considerably longer, Duncan started going to the pub on Wednesday nights with his landlord as Wilf was a member of a local darts team and Duncan was getting fed up watching television every night. He found it boring at first, as he didn't know any of the players, but he enjoyed listening to all the conversation and watching the darts. Wilf's partner was a man that everyone called Lonely, whose real name was Lester, and during a match one night Duncan asked Wilf why they called him Lonely, as he was quite a well-presented man about his own age, clean, well-dressed, and certainly not unattractive.

"Ask him, he won't mind," replied Wilf.

Duncan waited until a quiet period later in the evening during a break in play when the sandwiches were served and asked the question. "Excuse me. Why do all the lads call you Lonely?"

"Because I live on my own. All this lot have got wives or girlfriends, but I don't bother with that now. I tried it once. It was about twenty-five years ago in 1960. I was going out with a girl called Lucinda. One night I took her to the pictures to see the film *Psycho*. I paid for the tickets and bought her some candy floss and I thought she would enjoy the film as I had seen it two nights earlier with all my mates and we really enjoyed it. Anyway, when it came to the shower scene where the girl gets stabbed to death, I turned to Lucinda and said "this is the best bit" ... then, she just stared at me, gone out! A few seconds later, she got up and walked out. I thought she might have gone to the toilet, but she never came back. I never saw her again. If that's women for you, then you can keep them."

Duncan struggled to stop himself from howling with laughter. He had to go to the toilet to regain his composure. Later that night, Wilf asked him if he spoke to Lonely regarding his nickname, and he was mischievously chuckling even before Duncan could answer.

It was odd little moments like this that made the weekdays more bearable as the winter approached. He was coping easily with the responsibility of senior management, but finding the travelling on Mondays and Fridays to be very stressful. On several occasions he was only just in time to catch his flight to Edinburgh on Friday evenings, as traffic was becoming a problem owing to roadworks on his route.

Elizabeth was looking forward to the festive period as Duncan manipulated twelve days holiday and would not be back at work until January 2nd. She made inquiries about a short holiday for the family, but was disappointed when Alexander said he didn't want to go, and then Duncan said he did enough travelling already. He was happier to spend time at home with his family and furthermore push the boat out with the celebrations. Charlotte also said she wasn't bothered either way, so a family holiday at home it was.

The swimming training was cancelled for the holiday period, and Alexander found himself at a loose end as Mandy had told him that her husband would be home for a month at Christmas and they had booked a three-week holiday at Cape Verde. She promised that she would see him again as soon as Joe went back abroad on duty.

On Christmas eve, as Elizabeth was just about to eat her lunch, Martin Gemmill came into her office and said, "We are finishing early; we haven't had one customer in the showroom today, so log off your computer and call it a day. Oh, by the way, I have bought you this little gift. It's not much, but it's my way of saying thank you and I hope you have a very happy Christmas... Are you going to open it?"

Elizabeth was mortified. She never expected that she would receive a present from her boss. She had not even considered buying presents for the staff, as she barely knew most of them, and she felt ashamed when unwrapping her present. It was beautiful. A matching green emerald necklace-and-bracelet set in a presentation box. Green was her favourite colour and she had never envisaged owning anything as exquisite as this. Her eyes suddenly began to mist up and she was momentarily speechless.

"Try them on. Let's see if they suit you." He said as Elizabeth was trying to regain her composure. She tried to put the necklace on, but her hands were shaking with the unexpected shock of the present. Martin stepped forward. "Here, let me help." Martin took hold of both ends of the necklace and slowly and deliberately slipped it around her neck. He gently clipped the hook and eye as Elizabeth was conscious of his warm breath passing over her neck. She was mightily relieved when he took a couple of steps backwards to pass judgement.

"That looks wonderful. Try the bracelet, Elizabeth." When the bracelet was in place Martin smiled at the result. "You look beautiful, Elizabeth. I hope you like them."

"They're wonderful, Mr Gemmill. Thank you so much. I'm very sorry, but I haven't bought any presents," sighed Elizabeth.

"It doesn't matter. You look gorgeous in green jewellery; it matches your eyes and your dark hair. It's nice to see an elegant lady with class. That jewellery would be wasted on my wife."

As Martin left the office, Elizabeth removed the jewellery and placed it straight back in the presentation box. She felt extremely uncomfortable, and she was positive that he was furthering his lurid advances towards her. But one thing was for certain: she could not refuse his gift; it would definitely insult him.

She locked the office door and quickly walked through the showroom in a slight panic and a concerted rush to get in Cuthbert and go home. She did not want to be alone in the showroom with Martin when he locked up. Yet again she was contemplating telling Duncan about her fears, but she decided against it as she did not want to spoil the mood of the festive holiday. However, how was she going to explain the beautiful set of jewellery without telling him the truth? She would avoid it for as long as possible, as she decided to hide it away until a special occasion arose.

It was a wonderful holiday for the couple. Both children were at home on school vacations and the whole family had a fabulous time. They all went together to Edinburgh for the New Year's Eve street celebrations, returning to Kirkcaldy at three o'clock in the morning.

As with most holidays, the time seemed to fly by for both Duncan and Elizabeth, and far too soon they were back at work and the teenagers were back at school.

Training at the Commonwealth pool resumed in January, and Alexander was in splendid form. He finished his first race well in front of the rest of the swimmers, and although there was not an official timer, and it was only timed with a handheld stopwatch, Frank Burkett assured Duncan that his time was very close to the Commonwealth record and there was potential for further improvement. Duncan was very proud and he couldn't get home soon enough to tell Elizabeth all about the morning's training: "Mr Burkett has told me in private that Sandy will definitely be picked for the Scottish team. We must keep it quiet for the time being. The official squad announcement isn't until May, but Sandy is much faster than all the other swimmers in his event. I haven't said a word to him about it. He has to carry on as though he is still aiming to get in the team."

The weeks passed by slowly as the harsh winter eventually elapsed, and late in March, Alexander received some staggering news from Mandy. She had picked him up near the train station and they were sitting in her car when she explained, "You've often said that you wish we could be together all the time. Do you still feel that way now?"

"Yes, of course I do. I never think of anything else. There's lots of girls my age in Kirkcaldy who want to go out with me, but I'm not interested in any of them. I know you think I'm only a kid, but I think I make you happy. Anyway, why do you ask?"

"Sadly, my father has passed away. He was killed in a skiing accident in the Swiss Alps. At least he died doing something that he loved. That was how he lived his life, skiing, fast cars, horses, pheasant shooting. He divorced my mother twenty years ago when he caught her having an affair. She's somewhere in America now and I never hear from her. Anyway, his solicitor has been in touch and informed me that I am the sole beneficiary of his estate. It's ironic, he couldn't wait to get rid of me and pack me off to boarding school when I was eleven, which was not long after he divorced my mother. But as I was their only child it was inevitable that I would inherit his estate. I just didn't think it would be so soon. He was only fifty three," said Mandy.

"I'm sorry to hear of your father, but how will that affect us?" Alexander inquired.

"My father owns a large country estate in Perthshire. There's a big manor house, a visitor's hotel, a pheasant farm, a water sports centre, horse riding stables and an alpaca farm. The problem is my father spent some of his time on the estate, but most of his time away enjoying himself. He employed an estate manager who ran the place when he was away. On Monday, I have to go up to Perthshire to see Mr Mulligan and ask him to carry on doing his work on a permanent basis. Anyway, I'm not interested in being the Lady of the Manor and I'm going to look at selling the whole estate as a going concern. I will try to get the new owners to keep all the staff, as there are about forty permanent staff employed on the estate. Most of them live in cottages on the estate; even they are part of the package that I inherit. I haven't got a clue how much the whole estate is worth, but it could be quite a lot of money. The solicitor said it could be several million. When the estate is sold and I receive the money, I can do as I want. I am going to divorce my husband by any means possible. I will even admit adultery with you if it means getting rid of him. Afterwards, I will buy a nice big house somewhere so we can be together, if that's what you want?"

Alexander was shocked, "Yes, of course," he spluttered.

Mandy continued. "I haven't got a clue how long it will take to sort out all his affairs. I haven't even arranged the funeral yet. First, I've got to organize getting his body back home. Then I've got to get the estate valued and put it up for sale. We might not see each other for ages until after the funeral and the sale of the estate."

"That's okay, I understand you have a lot of things to do. I can wait. The important thing is that we will eventually be together."

"I'm sorry to say there's no point in us booking in the hotel tonight. It's that time of the month I'm afraid. I only came to the meeting place so I could see you and let you know where I will be for the foreseeable future. I'll drop you off back in town now if you want."

"No, that's not what I want. I'm happy enough just to be with you. It's not just about sex, I am happy just sitting here talking with you. If you want to go for a slow walk somewhere or maybe go to a pub and have a drink, I'm perfectly happy. Mandy, if you're not going away until Monday can I see you tomorrow? Perhaps we could even go out for the day as we won't be seeing each other for quite a while."

"Okay, my husband is calling me tomorrow evening so I need to be home by six. We can go to Edinburgh for the day. Be at the usual place by ten in the morning and I will pick you up."

On the Sunday morning, they arrived in Edinburgh and went to a car park located on Blackfriars Street. As Mandy opened the glove compartment to get out her handbag, a postcard dropped on the mat near Alexander's feet. Mandy didn't notice the postcard falling out. She got out of the car to pay for the parking, leaving Alexander alone in the car. The inquisitiveness of youth made him pick up the postcard and look at the picture. It was a view of the Matterhorn Mountain taken from the balcony of a Swiss mountainside chalet, sent by her father. He innocently turned the postcard over and was shocked to see the correspondence begin "Dearest Henrietta." He put the postcard straight back in the glove compartment before Mandy returned.

Later that morning, he could resist the temptation no longer: then he asked Mandy, "who's Henrietta?"

She was caught completely off guard, "What do you mean?"

"You accidently dropped a postcard on the floor when you took out your handbag, and as I picked it up, I couldn't help but notice it said, 'Dearest Henrietta.'

Mandy began to blush. She waited a few seconds before her composure returned, "All right, so now you know. That's the name I was christened by my parents, but I don't like it. I prefer to be called Mandy. I've never got round to changing my name officially, but you will always call me Mandy, okay?"

"Whatever you say. I think Henrietta is a nice name. Now I can love you twice as much: I can love Mandy and Henrietta."

"Call me Mandy, or you'll be walking home," she joked.

They enjoyed a blissful day out together, laughing and fooling around and spending much of the time holding hands and passionately kissing. Alexander was very sad when Mandy dropped him off a few streets away from his home in the evening as he knew that it would be a long time before he could see her again. He had thought about admitting to her that he was still only fifteen, but his birthday was only four weeks away and it was possible he would be sixteen the next time they met, so he decided to keep it to himself.

Alexander would be having a very busy April, as owing to the extremely harsh winter, his football team had a lot of matches to complete because of cancellations caused by frozen football pitches. The manager informed them that they would likely be playing every

Saturday afternoon and Wednesday evening from now on until the end of the season now that the days were getting longer and lighter. His team were also still in a Fife County Cup competition. Duncan and Elizabeth were very concerned by their son playing so many football matches in a short period as he would be risking being injured and ruining his big chance of representing Scotland in the Commonwealth Games in the summer.

That wasn't Duncan's only concern as Easter elapsed. After nine months, his department was running like clockwork, but now it was expanding to accommodate the creation of a new range of ladies anti-wrinkle creams, and it would mean additional responsibilities. He had four good candidates for the team leader, and he eventually appointed Susan Jemson, who had achieved a BS in Pharmaceutical Sciences and a Master's degree in Biochemistry. She was hardworking, diligent, and respectful, and although she was considerably higher qualified than Duncan, she was respectful of his seniority.

While Duncan was totally engrossed with all the additional responsibilities, Elizabeth was extremely worried that her daughter was becoming ever more reclusive and spending all of her free time alone in her bedroom. Charlotte and her two friends had not fallen out, but Kerry and Rebecca now had boyfriends and would spend their leisure time courting. Charlotte repeatedly told her mother that she was okay and that being on her own did not bother her, but Elizabeth was not so sure. She wished that her husband was not working away from home so he could give the family more moral support, but she understood that he was extremely happy in his new vocation and his additional income was helping to build their savings enormously.

Alexander's football team finished their league games, eventually finishing second in the league, sadly losing by only one point, but having the satisfaction of defeating the champions in the semi-final of the Cup. The Cup Final would be the last game of the season, and it was programmed for Wednesday April 30th, two days after Alexander's sixteenth birthday. Duncan and Elizabeth had both been pleading with their son to stop playing football until after the Commonwealth Games, but they were extremely pleased to know that he was to captain the side in the Cup Final which would be his final game until September, by which time the Games would be over.

Duncan booked three days' holiday off work, and came home on the Tuesday evening excited at the prospect of seeing his son play in a cup final. Elizabeth also booked a day's holiday, and the proud parents and Charlotte went to watch the match that was to be played at Starks Park with the second half to be played under floodlights. The evening was misty and wet, but it did not dampen the enthusiasm of the players and supporters. There was a small crowd of approximately two hundred at the game, with the majority of them being family and friends of the players. Duncan could not disguise his pride as his son led the team out, but his beaming smile was momentarily stifled by a sudden startled gasp from his daughter. He inquired, "What's the matter Charlotte?"

"Dad, look, over there, it's Fraser. He is playing for the other team," she cried.

Charlotte pointed to one of the opposition's players who was speaking to his parents near the touchline. His parents were wearing matching turquoise shell suits and white trainers, and the father was sporting a white headband although his head was shaved. Duncan was horrified. The last he had seen of Fraser was almost eight months ago when he was sent to a young offenders' institution for six months.

"Take me home mum, I don't want to be anywhere near him." sobbed Charlotte, and Elizabeth could see the panic and the tears welling in her eyes. She said. "Duncan, I'll pop back home with Lottie and be back soon. Please don't start any trouble."

The game started well for Alexander's team, and they raced into a four-goal lead by half time, and it seemed a foregone conclusion that they would win the trophy. At half time, Elizabeth came back and she was pleased to hear how well the game was progressing.

The second half was slowly drifting towards the inevitable conclusion, and with just a few minutes to go, Alexander's team were winning the match by six goals to one. Alexander had purposely kept out of the way of Fraser which was quite easy for him as both players were defenders for their respective teams. When Alexander's team won a corner with two minutes left to play, he threw caution to the wind and charged up into his opponents' penalty area to see if he could score a goal. He had been teased beforehand by his teammates that he was their only outfield player who hadn't scored a goal all season.

The corner was taken and the ball came over to the middle, and there was a hectic scramble as the ball broke loose.

Alexander was just about to kick the ball into the goal when a flying two-footed drop-kick that was worthy of winning a Martial Arts contest caught him on his standing left leg that was planted on the ground. The horrendous blood-curdling scream was enough to make time stand still, and suddenly everyone in the ground was stunned into silence and inertia. Everyone, that is, except for Duncan. He raced across the pitch consumed with the memory of his own career-ending injury and the realization that his son might have suffered the same fate. He was hoping it might just be bruising or something trivial, but on reaching his son he knew that was not the case. Alexander was barely conscious and in chronic debilitating agony. He spoke to his son, but he was mortified when he didn't get a reply. Most of the players couldn't bear to hear the awful guttural whining noise coming from the stricken player, and many of them gathered round in small groups near the halfway line. Duncan was leaning over the prostrate body of his son when suddenly he was engulfed by the red mist of anger. He looked round to see the referee talking to Fraser Burley and writing something in his notebook. "It was that bastard" he realized and suddenly rushed towards Fraser with murder on his mind. Fraser saw him coming and raced off towards his parents while the referee and two linesmen were struggling to hold Duncan back from getting at his son's nemesis. Fraser and his parents jumped in their car and left the ground immediately as the referee was in tears. He had been so proud to have been awarded a match of this stature and had been pleased with how the game had gone up to that point. With only two minutes left, and a small amount of extra-time to be played, the match was almost over. Now everyone was just standing about waiting for an ambulance. He vowed he was finished with football and would never referee a match again.

"I've sent him off, and I shall send in a report to the SFA. That was not a tackle, it was deliberate. I'm so sorry for your boy, but if you get into trouble, it won't help him." said the referee to Duncan as he tried to placate him.

When the ambulance arrived, Alexander could not be moved for what seemed an eternity, as initially morphine was administered and an oxygen mask applied. There were several members of the Fife Football Association committee present who told the referee to inform all the players that the game was over. The Paramedic team advised everyone to leave the pitch before they could begin to get their patient on a stretcher as it was likely to be very harrowing for anyone to be near when the patient was moved. Duncan told Elizabeth to go home and be with Charlotte and he would go with the ambulance and call her later from the hospital.

It was a night of sheer hell for the distraught father. Nearly five hours after arriving at the hospital, Duncan had been waiting patiently in the corridor when the specialist orthopaedic surgeon came out of the theatre to see him.

He said, "Mr Baker, I'm very sorry but it's not good news. There are two areas of heavy impact trauma on the left leg. I have only experienced this much leg damage previously after road vehicle accidents. Your son has a double compound fracture of the tibia and fibula in the lower leg. They will heal in time, but the big problem is the damage to the knee. His left knee is severely impaired. The anterior cruciate ligament, the medial collateral ligament and the meniscus are all badly ruptured. We have had to heavily sedate Alexander, and during our examinations we found, and then had to remove, a blood clot that could have caused a serious risk to his life. There is no point in you staying here any longer tonight. Why don't you go home and get some sleep? At this time, we cannot set the leg in plaster or fit a knee brace as we have to keep an eye on the operated area where we removed the blood clot. It's early days yet, but with time and physiotherapy we will get him back on his feet eventually."

Duncan slowly walked back to the reception area where the kind lady on the counter phoned a taxi for him. It was 3.05am and it was the saddest point in Duncan's life. He now knew that there was no chance of his son representing Scotland at the Commonwealth Games. He strongly suspected that his son would never be able to play football again as he himself couldn't after his own injury many years earlier. He was heartbroken for his son and disappointed for the rest of the family who would have felt so much pride in his achievement of representing Scotland. He certainly was not looking forward to breaking the news to Elizabeth and Charlotte.

When he arrived home, he quietly unlocked the front door and crept in, hoping not to wake anyone up. He need not have bothered being so careful. Elizabeth was down the stairs in a flash as she had found it impossible to sleep. Charlotte was not far behind her. Duncan did his level best to explain Alexander's injuries while at the same time putting a positive spin on them talking about physiotherapy and recovery. He omitted to tell them about the blood clot, as he knew they would both be mortified to hear about that. Charlotte put the kettle on, and they all had a hot drink before going up to bed, but as it was nearly four o'clock in the morning, they had little or no sleep.

On the Thursday afternoon, Duncan went back to the hospital in Cuthbert. He was disappointed to hear that his son was still heavily sedated and virtually comatose, but he was allowed in at the bedside to see him. Alexander looked very vulnerable, and Duncan felt as though he wanted to sweep him up in his arms just like he had done when he was just a baby.

Duncan sat for an hour holding his hand, he was just about to leave when the orthopaedic doctor came to see him. He introduced himself: "Hello, I'm Doctor Laws and I have been looking at the results of the X-rays of Alexander's knee. We hope that the swelling on the knee will have reduced sufficiently in the next two days to enable us to start treatment. The big problem we have is the severe damage to the ACL that may require further surgery, it's impossible to tell right away. We will keep Alexander heavily sedated for the time being before we put a cast on his leg and a brace on his knee. It's very important to keep the pain levels down to a minimum, so the longer he is sedated the better it will be for him as rest is the most effective remedy in the short term. It's important to start physiotherapy and build the strength up in knee before we can assess whether the ligaments will fully recover or whether he will need a further operation on the ACL. You can be assured that we will be doing all we can to get your son mobile again, but it is likely to take quite a long time."

" How long will he be in hospital?" Duncan asked.

"It's hard to say at the moment, but as he has had emergency surgery to remove a blood clot, we would like to keep him under observation for a while. I can only say that we will keep you informed of progress as to when he is likely to be sent home."

Duncan cast one more forlorn glance at his son and trudged out of the hospital back to the car to find a parking ticket placed on his windscreen under the wiper. He had forgotten to go to the pay-and-display machine in his haste to get in the hospital. "The lousy stinking rotten bastards," he muttered to himself, but he knew it was his own fault. He drove home, and lay down on the sofa and was fast asleep within two minutes. He awoke as Charlotte arrived home from school stating that it was raining. He decided to go and pick up Elizabeth from work at five o'clock so she at least would not get soaked.

Elizabeth was delighted that her husband had come to pick her up from work, but that was the only crumb of pleasure they had over the rest of the week. Duncan spent as much time as he was allowed at the hospital at Alexander's bedside, only leaving the ward temporarily while his son was examined, and, on another occasion, when he was given a bed bath by two ladies of the auxiliary staff..

After his son had been thoroughly washed from head to toe, Duncan returned to the bedside just as the two ladies were about to leave. One of the ladies said to Duncan, "Is he your son?"

"Yes, it was his sixteenth birthday last week. Why do you ask?"

"He's a big lad, isn't he?" She said lecherously with a heavy sigh and a twinkle in her eye.

"Yes, he certainly is a *very big* lad," said her partner, licking her lips with a saucy grin, and they both scuttled off smartly, sniggering like a pair of naughty schoolgirls.

ISOLATION

Duncan was back at work on the Monday morning, cursing the fact his son was still in hospital. Elizabeth visited the hospital after finishing work in the evening, and was informed that Alexander would be discharged within a couple of days. He was now conscious, with his lower left leg encased in plaster and a knee brace fitted. Elizabeth tried her hardest not to look upset as she didn't want to distress her son any further. He told his mother that he couldn't even remember how he ended up in hospital. Elizabeth stayed until visiting hours were over, gently holding his hand and smiling at him while engaging in small talk and inwardly feeling her heart strings being wrenched apart. She used up some of her holiday entitlements so that she could visit Alexander every day, and she even missed playing golf on Tuesday afternoon, which was usually the highlight of her week.

Alexander was brought home by ambulance on the Thursday morning. He understood the magnitude of his injury, and he was very upset that all the training for the Commonwealth Games had been in vain as he was unlikely to be swimming again for quite a while. His leg would be in plaster for at least six weeks, and then he faced months of physiotherapy on the shattered knee.

The following day, a letter arrived that confirmed Alexander's selection for the Scotland team in the upcoming Commonwealth Games and Elizabeth realized that they had not informed the coaches regarding Alexander's injury. She phoned Frank Burkett on the Friday afternoon with the heart-breaking news: her son was unlikely to be able to swim again for at least two months, possibly longer, and it was unlikely he would be fit enough to compete in July. Frank Burkett was horrified. He was extremely sorry for Alexander, especially that his injury came as a result of playing football. He offered words of comfort that maybe it would be possible for Alexander to be fit and then compete in the Seoul Olympic Games, but Elizabeth had the distinct impression that he was downright angry that Scotland was being deprived of a potential gold medal at the Commonwealth Games.

After Elizabeth ended the call, she was struggling to contain her sorrow. It had been heart-breaking to see her son's face when he first saw the commode in his bedroom. The realization that he could not even get to the bathroom unaccompanied hit him very hard.

The next few weeks went by in a whirl for the family. Duncan was tortured at work thinking only of his family and how they would be coping without him, while Elizabeth was taking the brunt of the stress of caring for their stricken son. Their front doorbell continually rang with a succession of friends and teammates turning up to offer their support and best wishes. After two weeks, there wasn't any room left on the plaster for anyone else to sign their autograph and leave a message. Every player from the club had already visited before the manager, Eric Chettle, came on the third week. It was on a Saturday morning and Duncan was at home as Eric arrived..

When Eric spoke to Alexander, he told him he had a surprise for him: "I know it's not much comfort now, but the SFA have said that the Cup Final does not need to be replayed as the result was conclusive with so little time left to play. So, I am pleased to be able to give you the Cup Winners medal which you so thoroughly deserved. I only wish you would have been able to lift the trophy on the pitch that night."

"What happened? How did my leg get broken?"

"It was an horrendous tackle. The lad that did it has been thrown out of his club. Their manager rang me last week to offer congratulations to us for winning the Cup and said that the SFA will hopefully make that lad sine die, meaning he'll probably never play again. Here's your winner's medal. Congratulations, Alexander."

Before leaving, Eric was having a quick chat with Duncan at the front door when they both heard a very loud metallic clang come from upstairs. Duncan rushed upstairs to see what had made the noise, and when he entered his son's bedroom, he saw Alexander laying on his bed reading as though nothing had happened.

"What was that noise?" Duncan asked.

Alexander pointed to the floor where the medal was laying on the carpet underneath the radiator. There was a chink of paint missing from the radiator where the medal had struck it forcibly. Duncan picked up the medal and put it on the dressing table while shaking his head. He decided not to say anything that might upset his son further.

Later, Duncan told Elizabeth about Alexander's blatant apathy concerning his medal. "He threw it away, as though it was just a sweet wrapper. Is he always like this?"

"Yes, mostly, it's hard work communicating with him. He is really depressed and living in a world of his own. I can't get through to him. I wish you were here more often as he takes no notice of me."

Alexander's depression increased as each day passed and to make matters worse, he was sorely missing Mandy. He knew it would be ages before he would be back on his feet and be strong enough to walk to their meeting place. He cursed the fact that she did not trust him enough to give him her telephone number as she was scared that he would call her and her husband might answer. Additionally, she didn't even know where he lived as she had never been anywhere near his home. It was constantly on his mind wondering if she had organized her father's funeral and completed the sale of the Perthshire Estate? It was torture for him lying on his bed unable to contact her.

While her parents' attention had been firmly set on the rehabilitation of their son, Charlotte was becoming ever more isolated. She spent all her spare time after school alone in her bedroom and depression was gradually taking a firm hold on her being. She only came out of her bedroom at mealtimes, and Elizabeth repeatedly asked her why she was not mixing with her friends or going out to the disco or ice-skating, but Charlotte stubbornly re-iterated that she preferred to be alone, and she was far happier in her own company. Elizabeth knew it wasn't right to spend so much time on her own, but what could she do? She couldn't force her daughter to go out and enjoy herself, so it was a constant worry to the exasperated mother.

Each week that passed became a torturous grind for Elizabeth while holding down full-time employment and trying her very best to look after her extremely moody son and her reclusive daughter. She was always physically and mentally worn out by the time Duncan arrived home on Friday evenings.

In June, Alexander had his plaster and knee brace removed. Initial examinations confirmed that the lower leg breaks on the tibia and fibula had both healed relatively successfully, but it was heart-breaking news regarding the damage to the left knee. His ACL had been torn very badly, the MCL was only moderately damaged but approximately twelve months physiotherapy and rehabilitation were necessary. It was possible that the physiotherapy alone would not be enough, and it was more than probable another operation would be required on his knee. Alexander sat staring at the floor, head bowed, distraught. He knew that he would not be able to play football the following season, but he asked the orthopaedic doctor if his leg would be okay to play football sometime in the future.

"It's far too early to give a decision on that, Alexander. A lot depends on how your knee responds to the physiotherapy. It's important to get you back on your feet first and walking again. Time will tell how much your knee has healed. But be assured, we will do our utmost to get you mobile again." Dr Butlin stressed.

Alexander was almost in tears; he knew deep inside that it was unlikely he would be able to play football again. He was given a programme of physiotherapy exercises and advised to start slowly and try to build up the strength in his knee gradually. He was given a new smaller knee brace that he could remove himself to use the bathroom. It was also a minor comfort to him now that the plaster was off his leg, and he was able to use the family bathroom again. He was anxious to have a shower, which would be his first in almost seven weeks.

When Elizabeth and Alexander arrived home, Alexander went straight upstairs for a shower. Almost immediately their phone started ringing, "Hello, is that Mrs Baker? Hi, I'm Thora Hinton. I am the secretary at Charlotte's school. Mister Hart has asked me to contact you and ask you if it's possible for you to come to the school to see him regarding your daughter Charlotte. He say's don't worry, she's not in trouble, but could you come at your earliest convenience?"

After speaking to Alexander, and establishing he would be okay on his own for an hour, a frantic Elizabeth set off for the school in a state of high anxiety. Obviously, she knew there would be some sort of problem, but she had no idea what it would be. She was escorted through to Mr Hart's office by the secretary, and, after a brief wait, she was sitting facing him across his desk.

"Mrs Baker, firstly your daughter Charlotte is not in any sort of trouble. However, her class teacher Miss Walsh and I are increasingly worried about her welfare. Academically, she is doing exceptionally well, and she is one of the brightest students in the whole school. But we are worried that she usually appears to be on her own. She has always been a popular student in the past with many friends, but not these days we have observed. She always finds an excuse to skip the sports lessons and prefers to study alone when the other girls are out of the classroom doing exercise. She uses the excuse of her menstrual cycle far in excess of what is normal, and we know that she is just avoiding physical exercise. I'm afraid there's more. One of the teachers caught her in the girls' toilet with her fingers down her throat forcing herself to be sick. She denied it, but it probably explains why she often looks pale and pallid the longer the day goes on. Also, Miss Hindley reported to me that she caught sight of her in the girls' toilets with her jacket off and she thought that there were blood stains on the sleeves of her shirt. Have you witnessed any of this behaviour at home?"

"No, certainly not. But I must admit that recently she seems to be spending more and more time alone in her bedroom. I'm not aware of her being sick on purpose and I don't know anything about blood on her sleeves. However, she does her own washing and ironing as I now have a full-time job. Unfortunately, her father is working away and he is only home at the weekend, and with our son being badly injured and needing plenty of attention, it's possible that we might have ignored Charlotte's welfare over the last few months. Oh God, I feel so guilty. What do you think I should do?" Elizabeth asked.

"Well, we need to establish if our suspicions are correct, and if they are then we can either tackle the problem together or seek professional advice. I wanted to find out if you knew that Charlotte was self-harming. Speak to her father first and let's take it from there."

Elizabeth left the school feeling absolutely deflated. She had a noxious feeling deep inside and she felt that she was a failure as a parent. It should have been a happy day with her son coming out of hospital, but she couldn't remember ever being so sad at any time in her life. She worshipped her children and would feel their hurt tenfold.

Later, when Duncan phoned she spoke in hushed whispers so that Alexander and Charlotte could not hear her conversation. She stopped short of telling Duncan the whole story, but made it clear she was desperate for him to get home as soon as possible.

Duncan was mortified. Knowing that there was a problem but not knowing what it was seemed torture. He arranged a day's holiday for the Friday so he could come home on the Thursday evening. After he had a quick shower he spoke to Elizabeth regarding her concerns. She explained that she was struggling to cope with all the stress of holding down full-time employment and the additional problems she had with Alexander who had become very insolent and increasingly aggressive towards her. He picked fault with everything including his meals, which was something he had never done before. Then there was the worry of Charlotte. She told Duncan about the meeting with Mr Hart earlier in the week and the school's concerns regarding Charlotte's welfare, but she admitted that she did not want to speak about it on the phone and she had not approached Charlotte regarding the matter as she was waiting for him to be home. He was shocked.

"What do you think we should do, Duncan?" she asked.

"We need to find out what's going on with Lottie, I suggest we go up and speak to her now. I will speak to Sandy in the morning."

"I agree, I'm so glad you are home. It's been tearing me apart with all the worry. Before we go upstairs to her room, you must be aware that she doesn't like anyone to go in her bedroom. She usually makes her own bed and does all her own cleaning and washing. We will have to go about it gently and not charge in like a bull at a gate."

Two minutes later, Elizabeth knocked gently on her daughter's bedroom door while asking, "Charlotte, your father is home. Can we come in and speak with you?"

"Wait a moment, … Okay, you can come in now."

As they entered Charlotte's bedroom, they were surprised to see her lying in her bed wearing her pyjamas with the sheets pulled up right up to her neck and just one wrist visible holding the blankets up.

"What do you want?" Charlotte asked aggressively.

Duncan replied, gently and amiably, "Well, that's not a very nice welcome home for your father when he's just travelled three hundred miles to come and see you. You know how much I miss you all when I'm away. You could at least give me a smile."

"Sorry, dad, but why are you here?" Charlotte asked.

Duncan continued. "We're very worried about you, Charlotte. We've had a report from your school that one of the teachers saw you with your fingers down your throat making yourself sick. Plus, another teacher noticed some blood on the sleeves of your shirt. We have also noticed ourselves that you never go out to meet your friends anymore and we never see Kerry or Rebecca nowadays. You don't even go to the disco anymore. You need to speak to us if you are having problems with anything. We can't help you if we don't know what's going off."

"There's nothing to tell you or nothing for you to worry about. I'm perfectly okay. I did make myself sick once, as one dinner time I had mistakenly eaten a sausage made of meat that I thought was a vegetarian sausage. The blood on my sleeve was from a nosebleed caused by the strain of me retching to be sick. I don't see Kerry and Rebecca in the evenings now because they both have boyfriends, and I don't want to hang out with them like a gooseberry. Okay?"

The stunned couple looked at each other in amazement. Either Charlotte was telling the truth or she had concocted a succession of lies on the spur of the moment. Duncan spoke gently with a big smile on his face. "Okay, sweetheart. Give your dad a hug and we'll leave you in peace if you want to be alone."

As Duncan stooped over her bed and gave her an affectionate hug and a kiss on her forehead, he purposely pulled down the blanket and slid the sleeve on the arm of her pyjamas to reveal her forearm. The sight of her scarred forearm shocked him to the very core. Duncan recoiled in horror, momentarily speechless. He looked at Elizabeth. She had also noticed the number of wounds on her daughter's forearm, obviously caused by a blade of some sort.

Charlotte screamed hysterically. *"Get out, leave me alone!"*

Elizabeth rushed over to her tearful daughter to give her a consoling hug. Duncan stood with his mouth agape not knowing what to say or do, until Elizabeth made up his mind.

"Duncan, leave us. Go and pour yourself a beer."

As Duncan was having a drink, Alexander came into the lounge and Duncan inquired, " Hi Sandy, how are you going on?"

"Not as good as I hoped. The breaks in my leg have healed okay, but it looks like my knee is knackered. I can hardly walk ten paces without loads of pain. I don't know when I'll be able to walk to school and back. I've missed two months already and they'll be starting to do exams soon. The worst thing is I've got a nasty feeling I won't be able to play football again. The specialist said I have to build the strength up in my knee gradually, without overstretching it. Another thing is that I won't be swimming for Scotland in the Commonwealth Games. I'll just have to hope I can get ready for the next Olympic Games."

"That's the spirit, Sandy; we have to look to the future and not worry about the past," replied Duncan.

As Alexander went upstairs to his bedroom, he was thinking about Mandy yet again. It had been almost eight weeks since he last saw her, and he had no idea if or when he would see her again. He was very worried that he would not be able to walk to the railway station without considerable discomfort. He toyed with the idea of telling his father in confidence about Mandy and asking for a lift to the station on the Saturday night, but after considerable thought he decided not to bother.

Since Mandy and Alexander had last met, she had arranged for her father's body to be repatriated back to Perth from Switzerland and then organised his funeral. She had the estate valued by three different agents, and subsequently it was put up for sale at offers in excess of two million pounds. She had driven back to Kirkcaldy from Perthshire on three separate Saturdays hoping to see Alexander, but each time she went to the station at the allotted meeting time, she had been disappointed by his absence. She was beginning to wonder if he had found a girlfriend of his own age or indeed if he had tired of her. However she was prepared to keep trying for a while longer until the estate was sold, as for the first time in her adult life she actually cared for someone else and not just selfishly for herself. It wasn't just the lovemaking she was missing: although he fulfilled that part of their relationship with flying colours, it was his tenderness and compassion, his youthful zest and energy, his respect, and manners; and above all he loved her for who she was as a woman. She would then return to the estate on Mondays feeling quite depressed, but thankful that Mr Mulligan was a very competent manager, and the estate was in good hands.

Duncan had been alone in the lounge for almost an hour when Elizabeth came downstairs wiping tears from her eyes. She exclaimed, "Duncan, I feel so guilty. Lottie has been very depressed since her birthday last year when that horrible boy assaulted her. We've been side-tracked with everything that's been going on with Sandy that I reckon she feels totally ignored. I don't know what to do. She hates herself and thinks that nobody loves her or wants her as a friend. She hates boys and will never trust a boy ever again. It's so sad. She has been inflicting cuts on her arm, and she told me she didn't care if she lived or died. I feel like I'm a failure as a mother."

Duncan put his arms round his wife, and they stood hugging each other until Elizabeth regained her composure. "What shall we do? Mr Hart said we might have to seek professional counselling.

"I'll go and have a chat with her and we'll talk about it later."

Duncan quietly tapped on Charlotte's bedroom door and then talked gently with her for about an hour. He didn't raise his voice, but encouraged Charlotte to do most of the talking. It was obvious that the problems all stemmed from her bad experience with Fraser. She had trusted him implicitly and she had been besotted by him and thought he was in love with her. She would never forget the attempted rape and the physical assault, and she felt that it was her own stupidity and naivety that contributed to the assault, and that she was partly to blame. Duncan assured her that not all boys are the same, and there are lots of boys who would be grateful for a girl as beautiful as you.

He went on. "You have so much going for you: you are pretty, you are intelligent, you are kind and caring, you have good manners; in fact, if I was a boy of your age, then you would be just the sort of girl I would want as a girlfriend. Your mother and I worship the ground you walk on, and we want to help you and see you happy. I wouldn't swap you for any other girl in the whole world. Please let us help you. We could make a start by you coming downstairs and having a cup of hot chocolate with us. Then we can start making plans for our summer holidays. Your mother and I would love it if we all went somewhere nice together for a change."

"Okay, I'll come down in five minutes, but one thing first: don't tell Sandy. It's bad enough as it is, I don't want him to know."

"Of course, but please, *please* talk to us in the future. It's probably our fault for giving Sandy so much attention over the last six months, particularly since he ended up in hospital. We have been concentrating so much on him that we have been ignoring your problems. Can I have a hug?"

Charlotte thrust out her arms and Duncan and his daughter held each other tightly before he went back downstairs.

It was a tense wait until Charlotte came down. When the hot drinks were made, they sat talking in the lounge with Elizabeth and Charlotte snuggled up alongside each other on the sofa. The parents made a concerted effort to let Charlotte do most of the talking regarding places they might go for their summer vacation. It looked like a holiday to the Italian lakes was favourite as the parents were in a mood to agree with anything that Charlotte suggested.

At ten o'clock Charlotte and Elizabeth were ready for bed as they had school and work in the morning, so they both bade their goodnight. Duncan sat quietly alone for what seemed an eternity wondering if he should leave his employment in Nottingham and get a local job somewhere, whence he could get home each evening. It was obvious to him that his daughter needed more support, and Elizabeth was struggling to cope. He would discuss it with her over the weekend.

The following morning, Duncan took Elizabeth to work and came home in Cuthbert after promising to pick her up later. He arrived home and found that Alexander was still in bed. He was determined to spend as much time with his son as he could now that he was at home. Alexander came downstairs, with great difficulty, an hour later, and Duncan made him some breakfast before settling down for a long talk with his son. He was interested in knowing how Alexander was coping with the physiotherapy, but disappointed to hear it was not going well.

"It's torture dad. It really hurts, I've never had so much pain in my life. The worst thing is I only started on the easy programme, and I've got to build it up over the weeks, but if the pain gets any worse than it is already, I won't be able to cope."

"Sorry to hear that, Sandy. Is there anything I can do to help?"

On the spur of the moment, Alexander thought about Mandy and wondered if she would be home this weekend. He just wanted to see her and let her know about his injury, and then tell her that if she could wait, he would hopefully be back to normal in a few weeks. He decided to take a liberty with his father.

"There is something you can do to help, dad. Would you be able to give me a lift to the train station on Saturday night and get me there before seven o'clock?"

"Of course, it's only a few minutes in your mother's car, why do you need to go to the station?"

181

"I need to meet someone, I don't know if she'll be there and I might be coming home again if she's not, but I want to try."

"Who's she, is it someone special?" Duncan asked.

"Yes, she's someone special, that's all I can tell you for the moment. I don't like keeping things from you, but on this occasion, you'll just have to trust me. Anyway, if you drop me off and then come back in half an hour and I'm still there, I'll have a lift home. If she turns up, I won't be there."

"That all sounds a bit weird, Sandy. Hasn't she got our phone number or isn't she on the phone so you could call her?"

"Sorry, dad. I've said enough. We have to keep things secret for the time being. As soon as I am able to say anything, you'll be the first to know."

Duncan was no fool. He knew, or thought he knew, that his son was guarding the fact that *she* was either a married woman or someone in a similar relationship and Alexander was keeping it a secret. He decided not to broach the subject further after agreeing to his son's request.

On the Saturday afternoon, Duncan went to Dysart to see Jack and Alice, and was delighted to see them both in good health. Jack assured Duncan that he kept Alice quite busy, and her condition was only marginally getting worse which was to be expected.

Jack had been thrilled to see Duncan, and as they were shaking hands outside, he asked Duncan if he would call in more often as he noticed that Alice was ecstatic when he visited, and he was sure it was "doing her good." Duncan promised he would call in more often, but pointed out it was harder now that he was working away.

Later that evening, Duncan took his son to the station as requested and then left him for half an hour, before returning to find a despondent Alexander standing in exactly the same spot he had left him earlier. Mandy had not come home this weekend as she had prospective purchasers for the estate coming on the Sunday for a second viewing. They had already put in an offer of one and a half million pounds that had been rejected, but were keen for another viewing. Alexander was very worried that he might never see Mandy again, but he would keep turning up at the meeting place as often as he could and live in hope. It was a cruel twist of fate that Mandy had tried to contact Alexander and she had been at the meeting place on the two previous Saturday evenings. Duncan and Alexander arrived home to a bemused Elizabeth who asked where they had been.

"Sandy just wanted a lift across town to see one of his friends, that's all," explained Duncan, which in effect was half truthful.

After a visit to see his friend Karel on the Sunday morning and a relaxing afternoon and evening at home with the family, it was time for Duncan to pack his bag and have an early night in preparation for work the following day.

On the Monday morning, Elizabeth assured Duncan that all would now be well now that the problem with Charlotte had been uncovered and she could monitor the situation and spend more time with her daughter. Duncan was not convinced, and it wasn't until later that night that he managed to put it out of his mind.

Elizabeth met her three friends on the Tuesday afternoon for their weekly round of golf, and when they had finished playing, Sylvia had some dreadful news for her. Their former golf partner and friend Maggie had passed away, succumbing to her long-term illness during the previous weekend. Elizabeth was heartbroken. It hit her very hard, it all seemed so unfair. When they were getting changed in the ladies' locker room, Elizabeth told the ladies captain Maud, who shrugged her shoulders in a gesture of indifference and didn't say a word. Elizabeth felt a sudden urge to grab her by her throat and throttle the living daylights out of her, but luckily she somehow managed to retain her composure, especially as Maud was married to her employer.

When the ladies were in the car park saying their farewells, Elizabeth vowed that one day she would take the starch out of Maud and bring her down a peg or two. "She's an evil witch, I swear to God that she will get her comeuppance one day" she said, and everyone agreed, unanimously.

Maggie's funeral was on the following Friday and dozens of ladies from the golf club were in attendance. Maud didn't attend, and Elizabeth was disgusted with her as she was the captain of the club. Sylvia said that she was glad the vinegary old trout didn't show up, which caused a slight moment of mirth in an otherwise very sad day.

As the seasons passed, Duncan was becoming bored staying with Wilf, as the evenings became a routine of watching inane television programmes, soap operas mainly. Wilf would record all the ones in the daytime , and then watch them in the evening in between watching the evening soap operas. It was becoming extremely tedious, and so Duncan renewed his keep-fit regime in earnest as a way of passing time and quenching boredom.

Often during the summer months he drove down to the river, and then he would run along the river footpath from Beeston Weir past Attenborough Nature Reserve towards Trent Lock at Long Eaton. Gradually, as the weeks went by and he became fitter, he would time himself in an effort to beat his previous best time.

It was one particularly cool dawn when he set off from the weir feeling fitter than he had for a long time that he noticed another jogger going in the same direction as himself. She was quite a long way in front of him, but he gradually caught up and passed her about halfway towards Trent Lock. He had a shock on his way back as she was laying on the footpath in obvious pain and distress. It was 6.15am and there was no-one else around. He stopped to see if he could help as she was struggling to stand up with a very badly sprained ankle, and he then half-carried her as she hopped along the footpath on one leg back to Beeston. She was in considerable pain, and Duncan drove her home to her flat in Beeston and advised her to take things easy.

"If I were you, I'd ring your employers and tell them you're not coming in today." he said.

"I will. Thanks, you're so kind," she replied.

Duncan went back to his lodgings and thought nothing of it for several weeks until one Thursday he was sitting in the works canteen having his lunch when he was gently tapped on the shoulder.

"Sorry to disturb you, but I just wanted to thank you again for helping me out the other week. I could hardly walk for about eight days, but my ankles okay now," she explained.

"Oh, no problems. Glad to see you're okay now. I didn't know you worked here," he said.

"Been here since I left school eight years ago, incidentally, when I hurt my ankle, if you hadn't come along, I might have been there for ages. Anything could have happened. It's really bothered me and I don't think I have the confidence to go out so early in the morning on my own again," she said.

"Well, I go for a run most weekday mornings except Mondays usually as soon as the sun's up, and you're welcome to join me. What's your name by the way?"

"Venetia."

"I'm Duncan, I won't be at the weir until next Tuesday. I'll be there at six o'clock if you want to try and have a gentle trot up to Attenborough and back and see how your ankle holds up."

"Okay, I might take you up on that," she said.

Duncan put the matter straight out of his mind, as he was looking forward to going home for the weekend.

On the Saturday afternoon, Duncan took Charlotte to the ice-skating arena and he tried skating for the first time. He was pleased to see how accomplished Charlotte was at skating, but by comparison he was completely hopeless. After falling over for the umpteenth time, he was ecstatic to see his daughter craning over him and howling with laughter, and it was the most enjoyable outing he had experienced with her in a long time.

When they left the ice-skating arena, Duncan decided to call in briefly at Dysart to see Jack and Alice, who were delighted to meet Charlotte and made an enormous fuss of her. Alice produced two large slices of home-made toffee and walnut cake for her guests, and took great pleasure in seeing them wolf down the cake with hardly a break for air. Jack was thrilled to see Alice so happy, and when it was time for their guests to leave, Jack came outside briefly to have a word in private with Duncan as Charlotte was waiting in the car.

"Duncan, it's been great to see you again. I can't tell you how happy it makes Alice feel, but there's something I need to tell you. We're getting on a bit now and so we decided to sort our wills out with a solicitor. As you know, we have no immediate family of our own. I was an only child and my parents passed away years ago. It's the same with Alice. We were going to leave all our estate to charity when we've passed, but now we have decided to include you and your family in the will. It won't be for a long time hopefully and it won't be a lot, but I can't think of anyone else I'd rather see having something to remember us by. That's all, I hope you are not offended."

"No, Jack, I'm not offended. You're very kind, but as you say, let's hope it's not for a *very long* time."

As they were driving back home Charlotte said to her father, "I'm not surprised you like to visit them, dad. They are lovely. That cake was awesome. If they were your foster parents, then you couldn't have wished for better parents."

"Yes, and whatever you do, don't tell your mum about the cake, agreed?" said Duncan.

"Yes, dad, agreed."

On the Saturday evening, Duncan took Alexander to the train station again with the same disappointing result. Mandy was not there. Unbeknownst to Alexander she had accepted a basic offer of £2,000,000 for the estate, but she had to be in attendance for the valuation of all the fixtures and fittings in the hotel and the country manor as she had been hoping to sell everything all in one lot. Negotiations for the said items went on over two weeks, but were eventually agreed, and the total sale was marginally over £2,150.000. Mandy now had what she had always wanted: her own means of finance to live her life exactly as she wanted, and what she wanted most was to share her life with Alexander. She would be back in Kirkcaldy on the following weekend and her priority was to meet up again with her lover. Alexander was unaware of her whereabouts and whether she had resolved the sale of the estate, and he was becoming increasingly depressed and angry. He cursed the injury to his knee, and furthermore cursed the person who inflicted the injury.

On the way home from the station, he told his father that he had an appointment with the physio on the following Wednesday, and he was disappointed to have to tell the physio that despite all his efforts in exercising his knee and keeping to the strict training regime, it didn't appear to be getting any better, and if anything, the pain was getting worse. Duncan felt desperately sorry for him; he could see the pain and anguish etched all over his face.

On the Sunday, Duncan and Elizabeth's relationship was slightly strained as both parents were feeling very worried about the welfare of their children. Elizabeth was also coping with the constant strain of the innuendo and advances of her employer, who had recently tried to persuade her to accompany him to a business conference in London with an overnight stay. He was disappointed when she refused to go, and he went about the showroom sulking for hours. She had still not told her husband anything about her concerns, and often the strain would gnaw away at her, leaving her deflated.

On the journey to work on the Monday morning, Duncan sadly reflected that although he and Elizabeth had slept together the whole weekend, Elizabeth had just turned her back towards him and said goodnight. It was a rarity he couldn't understand. They had always enjoyed a full comprehensive sex-life in the past, and Duncan was desperately hoping that this weekend's lack of activity was not a portend of the future.

Duncan was not in the best of spirits as he awoke early on the Tuesday morning. His phone call to Elizabeth the previous night had upset him as his wife appeared to be subdued and lacking in conversation. He felt sure that he detected that she may have been weeping, and it made the frustration of being so far away notably worse. When he parked his car near Beeston Weir for his early morning run, he noticed Venetia was waiting for him. She was wearing a tracksuit and jogging on the spot.

"Hi, I thought I'd take you up on the offer and see how my ankle is." Venetia said.

"Sure, no problem. Have you been waiting very long?"

"No, just arrived about two minutes ago. It's a bit nippy, shall we begin?"

They set off together at a very casual pace as Duncan was aware he didn't want to push it too much in case her ankle took a turn for the worse. As a result, they spent most of the time talking and getting to know each other. Venetia worked in the accounts department at the same company, and she lived in a flat in Beeston. She was unattached, which amazed Duncan as she was very attractive and well-spoken. By comparison, she was not surprised to hear that he was married with two teenage children, but she *was* surprised to hear that he still lived in Scotland and travelled home each weekend. They casually jogged most of the way towards Long Eaton before turning round at Cranfleet Lock, and then they agreed to increase the pace on the way back, which put an end to the conversation. Venetia was very pleased when they arrived back in Beeston as she had no pain in her ankle and so she asked Duncan if it would be okay to meet him again the following morning. Duncan agreed as it made the workout more enjoyable, and he was glad of the company.

They met again the following morning and jogged all the way to Trent Lock, and Duncan was impressed at how Venetia could keep up the pace. It was the start of a casual friendship that was to grow over the coming months.

On the Wednesday, Alexander had an appointment with the hospital physio, and after the initial examinations and a scan, he was given the bad news that he would need further surgery on his knee. He was distraught. He had already missed the chance to represent Scotland in the Commonwealth Games, and he had no idea when, or even if, he would ever play football again. He was extremely worried about whether he would ever see Mandy again, and additionally, he had been off school for three months and missed taking his exams. He was advised that the sooner he had the operation the better it would be for him. They would book him in as soon as possible.

The following morning, he hobbled across the town to Mandy's house on the off chance that she would be at home, although he had no idea what he would say if he knocked on the door and her husband answered. Her car wasn't parked on the driveway, and it appeared that no-one was at home. He was in considerable pain trudging back home and had to rest for several hours with a bag of frozen peas on his knee.

When Elizabeth arrived home from work, Alexander gave her the bad news regarding the need for another operation. She was very upset for her son, but tried hard not to show it by trying to put a positive slant on it, about "getting back to normal."

They didn't have long to wait, as within a week Alexander was back in hospital to have his additional surgery. After the operation, Alexander was kept in hospital for observation which turned out to be a blessing. He was taken seriously ill during the following night and rushed back into emergency surgery where another blood clot was removed from one of his main arteries.

Even while Alexander was laying on the bed recovering, Elizabeth was given the news that his knee was very unlikely to fully recover, and he would be strongly advised never to participate in contact sports again as another injury to the knee would almost certainly cripple him for life. she said, "I think he knows that already."

The timing of Alexander's second operation and hospital convalescence was very unfortunate. Mandy had returned home after contracts had been signed and all her business in Perthshire had been concluded. She had the intention of finding her young lover with whom she wanted to start a new life. She had not told her husband that it was her intention to leave him and seek a divorce, as she wanted to get away from the marital home first. She tried many times to contact Alexander by going to their allotted meeting-place and then trawling the bars and pubs of Kirkcaldy in the evenings. In desperation, she went to the road near the school where she saw him previously walking home from school, but after three consecutive days with no sightings, she assumed he had left the school and he was now at work or college somewhere. She was heartbroken. Had Alexander found another girlfriend? Had he gone away to university or college? Was their relationship over? She had no idea. She decided to wait until the weekend and continue searching for him while cursing herself for not giving him her phone number. She was not to know that Alexander was in hospital until the Tuesday morning of the following week, by which time she had given up on any hope of their ever getting back together again. She packed her suitcases with all her best clothes and jewellery, her passport and driving licence, and left Kirkcaldy for good after locking up the house and pushing the keys through the letter box. She would never return.

As she drove south towards Edinburgh, she was mulling over the idea of eventually going to California or maybe Monte Carlo via a brief stay in London. She would sell her car in London and leave to start a new life on the coast somewhere either in the USA or the French Riviera, where she could live among the rich and famous and not have any cares in her life. Her one regret was that Alexander was not at her side, and, furthermore, would not be sharing her bed.

DECEPTION

During the autumn, Charlotte was now back at school and there seemed to be a distinct improvement in her well-being. Her friend Rebecca had finished with her boyfriend and she recommenced her close friendship with Charlotte, and they often would spend many evenings together after school. Charlotte even attended the Saturday afternoon junior disco again as she had been assured that Fraser was no longer welcome there. He was overage anyway. Charlotte appeared much happier now that she was socializing with her peers again and she was spending less time alone in her bedroom.

It was vastly different for her brother: Alexander would usually stay at home watching television and he didn't show any inclination whatsoever to return to school. He repeatedly told his mother that the pain in his knee was too severe for walking to school and back. He said, "What's the point? I've missed my exams and I'm months behind the rest of the class, I might as well give it up as a bad job."

"That's ridiculous, you can catch up if you try hard enough. You've got to start motivating yourself again. We can't do it for you," said a frustrated Elizabeth.

The problem was that Alexander now had no motivation whatsoever. He had an empty feeling inside, compounded by the fact he was struggling to walk without suffering pain, and he was showing a slight limp. He went to watch his team play football one Saturday afternoon, but left early after becoming envious of the action.

He tried repeatedly to find Mandy's whereabouts, but it was to no avail. One Saturday, he even went to the flat overlooking Seafield Beach that was owned by Mandy's friend bringing back fond memories of the night he and Mandy spent in bed together, but when Sophie answered the door, she couldn't help.

Sophie explained, "Mandy told me she was leaving, but that's all. She said that she would go to London first and stay in a hotel while she made up her mind where she is eventually going. Anyway, how did you know this address and come here to ask about her?"

"When we were out together once, we came here to feed your bird. I'm Alexander, and I'm desperate to get in touch with her. Did she say that she would forward you an address or phone number when she eventually settled into a new home?"

"Oh, so you're Alexander. She told me all about you. She told me that you are the only person she has ever really loved, and she was heartbroken because she couldn't contact you again. She said that she tried dozens of times to find you, but then she decided that you must have gone away to university or something like that and she gave it up as a bad job. We weren't that close really. We only got to know each other because our husbands are away in the forces. When she rang me to tell me she was leaving, she just said goodbye. She doesn't want her whereabouts known as she doesn't want her husband to track her down and find her. I think we've seen the last of her."

A crestfallen Alexander made his way home feeling that his world had fallen apart. The following morning, he walked over to Mandy's house that appeared to be eerily empty. A neighbour came out to ask what he was doing staring at the house.

"I was looking for the lady who lives here. Do you know where she is?" asked Alexander.

"No, sorry. I know she cleared off and left her husband. He was at home last weekend, and he told me he's going to put the house up for sale. Anyway, why do you want to know?"

"Er, I did some work for her. I washed her car a few times. She still owes me ten pounds." Alexander lied.

"I think you've lost that. From what her husband says we won't see her around here again. Apparently, she inherited a fortune and she's cleared off."

"Okay, thanks," said a dejected teenager.

With his misery sinking to new depths, Alexander slowly trudged home. Over the following months, his depression slowly and steadily increased as he spiralled deeper and deeper into a nadir of misery. He felt that his life was ruined. Mandy had left and he probably wouldn't see her again, his knee was wrecked and he had no specific hopes or ambitions for the future.

As the weeks passed by, it was torture for Elizabeth to see her son so abjectly unhappy. He would often sit morosely staring at the television for hours during the day, and then in the evenings he would beg money off his mother so he could go out. Later, he would come home reeking of alcohol and go straight to his bedroom. Elizabeth could not persuade him to go back to school, and no matter how many times she begged Duncan to intervene and influence Alexander to return, Alexander would promise to go back, but then renege on the Monday when his father was back at work. It was having a detrimental effect on Elizabeth's nerves, and she often spoke to Duncan about him finding a new job and being at home more to support her.

Duncan sympathized and usually said he would start looking for a local job, but the truth was he was extremely happy in his current employment. He had been working in Nottingham for a little over a year and their bank account was beginning to look much healthier than it had been for many years. The loan for the car had now been paid off in twelve months, and with the addition of Elizabeth's salary, they had a little over four thousand pounds in the savings account. Duncan thought that one more year would easily double their savings now that the car loan was paid off, and he would be in a better position to acquire a local job, even with a reduced salary, then.

Elizabeth received a letter from the school asking if Alexander was ever likely to return, and when he was confronted by both parents about the letter, he promised to go back after the October half-term holiday. The promises meant nothing; he had learnt how to become an accomplished liar and he had no intentions of going back. Elizabeth thought it ironic that not that long ago she was worried sick about her daughter's welfare, but now Charlotte seemed to be back to her old self, while her son was causing her nothing but heartache. Duncan suggested to her that she ought to stop giving him money every time he asked and try to show him that he had to start standing on his own two feet, but she knew it would be hard, if not impossible. The selfish attitude and behaviour of her son was having a very marked effect on Elizabeth morale, as he never took any notice of her encouragement and advice, and she felt her parental authority was being totally undermined. He was just over six feet tall, and very intimidating as he towered over her during an argument. Her nerves were getting worse, and more often than not she would end up sobbing herself to sleep. What concerned Elizabeth the most was that Duncan was not showing any interest in finding local work, and she was carrying all the burden on her own shoulders during weekdays. Each weekend seemed to pass by quickly and Duncan always made time to visit Jack and Alice, leaving less time with his own family. Alexander continually made sure he was never at home at the weekends, thereby avoiding any confrontation with his father which added to Elizabeth's irritation.

Her frustration increased as on a Friday in October, Duncan was held up in a massive traffic jam owing to roadworks and a bad accident on the motorway near the airport. Despite his best efforts, he failed to get to the airport in enough time to catch his plane home. He pulled up at a phone box in Long Eaton and called Elizabeth as she was expecting him to be home in a few hours.

"Elizabeth, disaster; horrendous traffic and I've missed the plane. I didn't get anywhere near the airport by take-off time. I don't know what to do. I can drive home which will be nasty and take me about seven hours, or I could get the plane in the morning. However, I've got a lot of paperwork to do this weekend that's urgent. What do you think I should do?"

"I don't want you driving home; that would be very tiring for you. There's not much point in you getting home in the early hours exhausted and fit for nothing, and then you would be off again at dinnertime on Sunday. Either catch the plane in the morning or give it a miss this weekend. Call me in the morning and let me know if you're on your way," Elizabeth said forlornly.

Duncan went back to Beeston where a bemused Wilf was wondering what he was doing back at the house. He explained, "I missed the plane, Wilf, If I get up early enough in the morning, I will try again tomorrow."

"I see. Sorry but there's no dinner. I called in at the chip shop on the way home. You'll have to sort yourself out,"

Duncan decided to go out for a meal and have a couple of pints. He knew Wilf would be engrossed in his soap operas, so a bit of personal leisure time seemed quite appealing. He walked into Beeston town centre where he had a pizza, and afterwards he called at a pub for a drink. While he was leaning on the bar, he noticed a lady at the pool table taking her shot. It was Venetia. He had not seen her during the last three weeks as she had now joined a gymnasium and was training there on weekday evenings now that the days were growing shorter and colder, also the footpaths were becoming quite muddy.

She looked completely different in her skin-tight black leather trousers and a mustard yellow top as he was only used to seeing her in a baggy grey tracksuit. When her game of pool had finished, she came to the bar to get a drink and noticed Duncan casually leaning on the bar, alone, with a near empty glass in front of him.

"Hi, what are you doing in here? I thought you went home at weekends. Can I get you a drink? I owe you a favour for helping me that day when I sprained my ankle," Venetia said.

"Hi, I missed my plane because of the traffic. It looks like I'll probably stay for the whole weekend now as I have some paperwork to get on with. If you're buying, I'll have a pint of lager please."

This would be his third pint and already he was feeling relaxed and comfortable although he was a stranger in the pub. They talked for a while until the pool table became vacant again and Venetia challenged him to a game. He had never played pool in his whole life, and he was soundly thrashed by Venetia who, unbeknownst to him, played for the pub team. Duncan got the next round of drinks while Venetia set up the rack for the next game, but he was heavily beaten again although he did manage finally to pot one ball.

"You need more practice," she said jokingly.

"Aye, football was my game, I was half decent at that."

As they sat down together, Duncan told Venetia all about his football career and how it had finished tragically early while he was still in his prime. She was fascinated to know about his career, and he then further enlightened her with some of his old pal Robbo's exploits coming to Wembley to watch Scotland play, but he strategically left out the bits where women were involved, especially the part where Kenny McKenzie caught the crabs. He had Venetia in hysterics, and it was a very enjoyable night, spoilt only by the landlord calling time.

As they left the pub together, Duncan suggested he would escort her to her flat before heading off to Wilf's house. It was only a two-minute walk to her flat, and she unexpectedly invited him in for a night cap. He had already consumed five pints of lager, but he was looking forward to another drink as he was in an excellent mood and enjoying the night immensely. She poured him a large gin and tonic with at least a triple measure of gin. He had never been a big drinker, and it wasn't long before the mixture of lager and gin had him feeling light-headed. It wasn't just the alcohol that made him intoxicated. He was also overcome by Venetia's beauty and the alluring aroma of her perfume. He knew it was a big mistake being alone in her flat with her, but he felt a carefree streak overpower him. When Venetia went into her bedroom to get changed out of her leather trousers, he pondered the idea of getting up from his chair and leaving smartly. It was out of the question. He could hardly muster the strength to get up out of the chair. She was now wearing a pair of flowered pyjama bottoms, but she still looked extremely alluring.

"I'm sorry, Venetia. I feel a bit tipsy. Can you make me a coffee or a cup of tea?" he asked.

When Venetia went into the kitchen, Duncan could feel his eyes getting heavier, and he was struggling to stay awake. When she returned with his hot drink, he was almost asleep.

"Wake up," she said, while prodding him in the ribs.

Duncan humbly apologized. While drinking his coffee he was very embarrassed as he struggled to stay awake. When he had finished his drink, he asked Venetia to help him out of the chair as his legs felt like jelly. Her first attempt failed, so she slipped her arms under his shoulders and round his back before pulling him up with a great effort. For a split second as they were standing opposite each other, time stood still, their faces were almost touching, and simultaneously they both leant forward, and their lips embraced in a passionate kiss.

Duncan did not fly home the following morning. He didn't return to Wilf's house until Saturday afternoon and he was totally exhausted. He and Venetia had spent the night together engaged in activities akin to a newly married couple on honeymoon. Duncan felt ashamed of being unfaithful to his wife, but he had enjoyed the night immensely. When asked by Wilf where he had been, he made up the excuse of meeting two lads from Scotland and taking a carry-out back to their place where he slept on the sofa. Wilf gave him a dubious stare and pursued it no further.

Duncan called Elizabeth and told her he had been up very late working hard on his reports and he had overslept in the morning so he wouldn't be home until next weekend.

"Ah well, we'll have a long weekend to look forward to," she said, but the disappointment was apparent in her voice.

On the Saturday, Wilf spoke to Duncan about the possibility of early retirement. He still had three years to go before his sixty-fifth birthday, but he was thinking of retiring the following year and moving to the east coast. "Obviously, I will let you know well in advance that I will be selling the house before moving, but I found out that there are a load of new bungalows planned for a site in Skegness and one of those would be just right for me if I can afford it," Wilf explained.

"I hope it works out for you, Wilf. Don't worry about me, I can always go back to the B&B."

Duncan did not want to tell Wilf that he was more than likely leaving before Wilf retired anyway, as he didn't want anyone to know about it in case the information was picked up by his employers.

Later, as he sat down at the table to start his reports, his mind was comprehensively scrambled with the events of the previous night. He was in a state of confusion as whether to go and see Venetia and apologize and tell her it was a mistake because he had taken too much alcohol on board. But then again, would she then be insulted thinking that it was only alcohol that made him fancy her? Alternatively, should he play it cool and keep out of her way and hope that the whole episode was just a one-off and would be forgotten in time? What about Elizabeth? Should he own up and beg her forgiveness, or should he keep it to himself and hope his infidelity was never found out? He knew that the truth would probably be uncovered eventually. His head was throbbing, he couldn't think straight, so he decided to leave the reports until the following day. He would go to bed early and try to catch up on the sleep he missed the previous night.

Back in Kirkcaldy, Elizabeth's patience with Alexander was stretched to the limit as he brought a girl home on the Saturday night, and without even saying a word to his mother, took the girl straight to his bedroom where she stayed the night. Elizabeth caught a glimpse of her on the Sunday morning as she was leaving and was not impressed. She had a leery wanton look in her eyes and her mouth was working overtime while she was chewing on some gum. Elizabeth noticed that her fingernails were dirty, and she felt disgust that her son could bring home a girl such as that. When he eventually came downstairs asking what was for breakfast Elizabeth snapped. "Breakfast! It's nearly half past twelve and you want breakfast. I'm very disappointed in you,

Sandy. I don't mind you having a girlfriend, but please don't bring a tramp like that into my house ever again. God knows where you found her. You're better than that. What would your father say?"

"I don't give a shit what he would say, it's my life. I can do what I want and see who I want, and you can't stop me," he replied.

"We'll see about that. Wait until your dad comes home next weekend and let's see what he has to say. I'm disgusted in you. And another thing. Until you show me some respect you can forget about me making you any breakfast or any other meal for that matter. If you are going to carry on behaving like this, you can look for somewhere else to live," an angry Elizabeth cried.

Alexander came face to face with his mother and for a brief second she was terrified that he would hit her. He glowered at her menacingly before saying, "You're bloody pathetic." Then he went back upstairs to get ready and went out without saying a word. Elizabeth was shocked and trembling, and all the strength had left her body as she sat on the sofa weeping profusely. Charlotte had been in the kitchen and heard the whole conversation, and after her brother had left, she came into the lounge to console her mother. They held each other tightly sobbing in unison.

Later the same evening, Elizabeth was relating the day's events to Duncan and once again tears were streaming down her face. Duncan was fuming. He was over three hundred miles away from home and he would not be home for another four days. He said angrily, "I'll be home as soon as I can on Thursday and I'll sort him out. Even if I have to swing for the ungrateful bastard, I swear he won't ever talk to you like that again."

Duncan went to work on the Monday after a fitful night's lack of sleep thinking about events at home and his deceitful behaviour on the previous Friday night. His mind was in total disarray, and he badly wanted Thursday to arrive so he could go home to support Elizabeth.

In the company canteen at lunch on the Monday, Duncan saw Venetia for the first time since their night spent together. She joined him at his table as he was sitting alone. Venetia spoke first. "Hi, how are you? did you manage to get all your reports done?"

"Fine thanks, yes, got them all finished on Sunday. How are you?" he asked.

197

"I'm okay, I really enjoyed Friday night. It was fun. I have to say though, you need a lot of practice at pool. You were hopeless. Mind you, you made up for it in other ways. In fact, you more than made up for it," she said provocatively.

"That's nice of you to say. However, you do know that I am married, and Friday night should not have happened, but I don't regret it. You are gorgeous, and it was wonderful."

"Well, there's no harm done then is there? I enjoyed it, and your wife will never find out unless you tell her. If you fancy a night out in the week, we have a pool match on Wednesday. Don't be afraid to come and watch, I won't ravage you in the pub. Mind you, I can't vouch for what happens afterwards," she teased.

Duncan felt a thrill of excitement shiver through his body and a stirring down below. He was blushing and eventually managed to splutter out, "Okay, I'll probably come in later as I don't want to have too much to drink during the week. I hope you won't be offended if I decline the offer of afterwards."

Venetia giggled and reached her hand forward and rested it on Duncan's wrist. "That's okay, come out for a drink anyway. We can still be friends."

That evening, Elizabeth called at the shops on her way home from work to buy something for dinner. She was very confused at the checkout counter when she opened her purse, and although the loose change was there, she was sure that there should have been a ten pound note also. She could not remember spending it and she was beginning to doubt her own sanity. She wrote a cheque for the groceries and left completely at a nonplus. When she arrived home, she emptied her handbag and looked everywhere where there was a possibility the note could have been, but she couldn't find it. She eventually gave up and decided that her memory was playing tricks on her, and she had probably spent it over the weekend.

Elizabeth and Charlotte ate dinner together and spent the night watching a video, which was comforting for Elizabeth after she had endured another blazing argument with her rebellious son after telling him she would not make him a dinner until he apologized to her for his aggressive behaviour. She told him, "You can have some money for the chip shop, or I'll make you some sandwiches, but that's all; I'm not cooking for you until you show me some respect."

"Stuff your sandwiches, I'll have money for the chippie," he snorted. He did not return home until the following morning.

When Duncan called Elizabeth after work on the Tuesday, she complained that she was becoming increasingly disturbed by her son's attitude and aggressive behaviour. "It's as though he just doesn't care anymore. He lies in bed until mid-day, then sits watching television or videos or he plays games on his computer and then he goes out without saying a word. I'm ashamed of him. Even Charlotte tries to avoid him now as he's so aggressive."

Duncan was feeling the strain himself being so far away from home. All he could do was repeat that he would "sort it out at the weekend" when he came home. It was reaching the point where he was not looking forward to his phone calls with Elizabeth as each call was a repetition of the one before. The call on the Wednesday evening followed the same pattern, and it was at that point he decided to go to the pub to watch the pool match. Perhaps a couple of pints would help him relax and forget his problems at home, he thought.

Despite his best intentions, Duncan ended the night taking Venetia back to her flat. He did not leave until two o'clock in the morning after another prolonged bout of primeval lust. While walking back to his lodgings, he was half-stricken with guilt and half-elated at his rejuvenated infidelity. He couldn't fathom out how a gorgeous sexy woman like Venetia who was many years his junior, could fall for a man of his age. Still, as she said, they could still be mates. He told her he was going home on the Thursday night, but was really looking forward to seeing her again the following week. She teased him suggestively, "You know where I live. Come round anytime."

Duncan arrived home on the Thursday night, and as soon as he walked through the door, Elizabeth ran straight up to him and threw her arms around his neck hugging him very tightly. He noticed she was trembling slightly.

"Oh, I'm so glad you're home. Lottie's upstairs in her room with her friend, but *he's* out, thank goodness. I'm at my wits end with him. It's no use waiting up for him as he comes in anytime in the middle of the night."

"Calm down, Lizzie. There's not much I can do about it now."

On the Friday lunchtime, Alexander came downstairs to find Duncan quietly sitting alone reading a newspaper.

"Me and you need a talk, Sandy. First of all, why are you giving your mother all this grief? That's all I'm bothered about. I don't give a damn if you want to ruin your own life, that's your choice. But you are not going to ruin other people's lives in this house. Even your sister stays out of your way now. What's up with you?" Duncan asked.

"I don't know, I don't mean to upset her, but I'm sick to death of being nagged at. Nag, nag, nag, that's all I get," Alexander moaned.

"Oh, so when you can't even be bothered to go to school or - God forbid- get a job, and your mother shows you some concern and worries herself sick and cries herself to sleep ... *you think that's nagging.* When you were doing really well at school and looking forward to going to university and now you are throwing it all away and your mother begs you to go back to school ... *you think that's nagging.* When you've lost all your self-respect and bring sluts home to share your bed and your mother shows concern for your welfare ... *you think that's nagging.* "When you've lost all your manners and become rude and aggressive to your parents, and we show some concern ... *you think that's nagging.* You need a big reality check, my lad. It stops right now. Go and get showered and changed. We're going out, and afterwards you will apologize to your mother."

Duncan took Alexander along the Esplanade to the bar near the quay where they sat together talking over a few pints of lager. He encouraged Alexander to get things off his chest and get everything out in the open, and it was obvious that he had many personal grievances, all stemming from his football injury. Alexander told his father all about Mandy, although he left out some of the more lurid details. He told him how much they were in love and how they would start a new life together. She had now left, and he was hurt. He was also devastated by the long-term effect of the injury to his knee, which meant in effect his football and swimming careers were over. He had no inclination to go back to school and resume learning, as he candidly pointed out, "I can't see the point, I'm too far behind now."

"What if we go to see Mr Hart, and he arranges for you to recommence your studies? I'm sure you'll be able to catch up. Nobody ever achieved anything without hard work. You can do it, Sandy. We have faith in you. Though you need to have faith in yourself."

When Elizabeth came home from work, Alexander apologized to her for his recent boorish behaviour much to his mother's delight. She was praying that he would now get back to be like the boy she was so proud of one year ago.

Later that same evening, Elizabeth was very quiet and very thoughtful, and Duncan asked her what she was thinking about.

"I was just thinking about earlier today when Sandy apologized to me. On reflection, it just didn't seem like him. There was no feeling in his voice, and when he spoke, he could have been reciting from a script. He just stared at me. I hope I'm wrong, but I have the feeling he was apologizing under duress, just to keep the peace."

Later they decided to treat themselves to a special night out on the Saturday. Duncan booked a table at their favourite restaurant in town, and they would leave Cuthbert at home and walk to the restaurant so they could share a bottle of wine.

Duncan spent the Saturday morning at the ice-skating arena with Charlotte, and after lunch they visited Jack and Alice. On the way home Charlotte said that she thought Alice was not looking very well; it had not escaped Duncan's attention also.

All through the day, Elizabeth was looking forward to their night out, and she decided she would wear the brand-new dress that she had bought for special occasions. She was also looking forward to sporting the new emerald necklace and bangle that she had received the previous Christmas as a gift from her employer. She had an appointment in the afternoon at the hairdressers, and later, when she donned her new dress, she felt on top of the world. Fifteen minutes before they were due to leave home, she went to her wardrobe to put on her new emerald jewellery, but she couldn't find it anywhere. Nor even the presentation box. In a hectic panic, she went through the whole wardrobe including the underwear drawers anxiously throwing everything on the bed and doubting her own sanity. Duncan didn't even know she had the two-piece emerald set as she had been saving it for a special occasion. She had a numb feeling inside. Where had she put it? Why couldn't she remember where it was? What was happening to her? Was she losing her memory? She put on an old pair of earrings and a necklace and went downstairs feeling traumatized.

"Are you ready Lizzie? You look lovely. Is that a new dress?" asked Duncan.

"Yes, it's new, and I had a new two-piece jewellery set that I was going to wear, but I can't find it," she replied.

"Don't worry. It'll turn up. You've probably hidden it away somewhere. Let's go, I'm starving."

After a wonderful night spent together, the next morning was disappointing for Elizabeth when after two hours frantic searching, she concluded that the jewellery set was missing. There was nowhere else it could have been. Where could it be? Had she thrown it out by mistake when having a cleaning session? Did it get mixed up with some of the other items she took to the charity shop? She was very worried that she may be starting to lose her mind.

Elizabeth came downstairs and told her husband, "I can't find that jewellery set. It's gone."

"Never mind. I'm sure it'll turn up one day," he said.

On the Monday morning, Duncan was up very early for his trip back to work. Previously, he hated Monday mornings' and was always miserable to be leaving his family, but not anymore. He felt a thrill of excitement about seeing Venetia again. He understood how wrong it was to be feeling this way, but he just couldn't help it. He still loved his wife and children, but the expectation of further infidelity with Venetia was all-consuming in his thoughts.

On the same Monday morning, Alexander went back to school and to the surprise of Mr Dwight his teacher, appeared keen to resume his studies. Mr Dwight was stunned, because he knew that Alexander had missed almost six months of studies including his exams. It was going to take an enormous effort from Alexander to catch up on his curriculum, and Mr Dwight promised he would give as much help as he possibly could. He was offered the opportunity to take the exams in November, and for two weeks he worked tirelessly trying to garner as much information as he could. However, it was to no avail, Alexander's initial burst of enthusiasm did not last all that long, and on the week before he took the exams, he was almost ready to give it up as a bad job. He carried on reluctantly with very little hope and even less enthusiasm until he finally came to terms that it was beyond his capabilities and he failed all the exams. He was advised by Mr Hart to carry on in his current class but then re-sit the exams again the following year, which meant dropping down one year. He said he would think it over, but he had no enthusiasm to go through the whole process again, and so he planned to wait until the Christmas holiday when he would speak to his parents about leaving school for good.

His father certainly didn't have leaving on his mind. Duncan was feeling happier at work than he had ever felt before. The MT & AS department was performing admirably, and it was very noticeable that he had made some excellent choices of the individual team leaders, with each team striving to outperform the others. His relationship with Venetia was permanently at the forefront of his thoughts, and he was determined the affair would last as long as possible, while at the same time he was wary of trying not to get too emotionally involved.

One morning in November, he suddenly realized that he was going to have to work through the period between Christmas and the New Year as he had taken that same period on holiday the previous year. He was worried about telling Elizabeth that he could only have the three Bank Holiday days off, yet he felt a thrill of anticipation about spending more time with Venetia. He knew how perilous it was, but he couldn't resist the temptation, so the affair continued.

On a wet and cold Monday evening in early December, he arrived at Wilf's house after work to find Wilf was waiting to speak to him with a solemn face. "Hello, Duncan. Sorry, but I've got some bad news for you. I had the house valued over the weekend, and if I get the price the estate agent said, then I can easily afford one of those bungalows in Skegness. They will all be available from next March. Anyway, I need to do some decorating first to smarten the place up before I put it up for sale, and I have a mate starting the decorating next week. I'm afraid that this week will be your last one here, as next week he will be doing the bedrooms, I hope you don't mind."

"No, certainly. I hope everything goes to plan. I was very fortunate that you put me up for so long. I will clear all my belongings out by Friday," Duncan said.

When he went up to the bedroom, he recognised that clearing out all his belongings was not such a trivial task. He had accumulated a lot of clothes and shoes over the many months during his stay at Wilf's house, and he knew it would be very difficult to carry all his luggage home on the plane.

Later that night, he told Venetia about the situation and she asked him what he would do the following week.

"I'll book myself in at the B&B for next week, at least it's clean and the beds are comfy."

"What's the point of paying for bed and breakfast? You can move in here if you want. You spend more time here than you did at Wilf's anyway," she said.

Duncan had not expected Venetia to invite him to move in, and he was caught unawares. He said, "Nothing would give me greater pleasure, but are you sure that's what you want? I'm much older than you, and you know I'm already married. It's very risky for me as the less people that know about us the better, and I don't want gossip about us living together getting all round Beeston."

"It's up to you. I don't mind that you're married, and I have never considered you as being old. You're in your prime, at least you are in the bedroom department. Think about it, and tell me later."

"What would I do about paying rent?" Duncan asked.

"The rent, rates and electric bills are paid on standing order. You can help by buying all the food if that's okay and you don't mind."

"Perfect, when is it possible to move in?" he asked excitedly.

"Anytime. Bring your stuff round at your own leisure. If things don't work out, you can always look for somewhere else then."

Duncan felt that all his birthdays had arrived together. He moved in with Venetia, and over the following weeks leading up to Christmas he eased himself quite comfortably into two separate domestic arrangements. His affair with Venetia had initially been based on lust, but he was now becoming besotted with her, and it came to a crunch just before the Christmas holiday. Venetia wanted him to spend it with her, but Duncan was adamant he would have to go home to his family. It was only going to be for four days. Venetia was not happy, but accepted his decision.

Christmas Eve arrived, and Duncan made his way back to Kirkcaldy. On the flight to Edinburgh, he remembered that he had not bought his wife a Christmas present or even a card, and he was aghast as there would not be an opportunity for him to buy anything appropriate. He arrived home at 8.30 pm feeling very embarrassed. Elizabeth threw her arms around him, and she was delighted he was home, as she was looking forward to their short holiday together. She was excited to tell him that her Christmas bonus of £290.00 had been paid into their bank account, and she had done all the Christmas shopping and bought presents for Alexander and Charlotte. Duncan stood motionless looking round the lounge that had been decorated quite exquisitely. The spruce Christmas tree was festooned with new fairy lights, and everywhere looked like a winter wonderland palace. Duncan felt ashamed. He had not expected everything to look so welcoming, and his insides were churning over with guilt. Charlotte came downstairs to give her father a big hug and a Christmas card, and he felt a tear beginning to well up in his eyes.

"So glad you're home, Duncan. There's a beef casserole in the oven. I'll get you a drink, lager okay?" Elizabeth inquired, as her errant husband was racked with guilt with his insides turning somersaults.

Later in the evening, Alexander came in unexpectedly early and joined the family in the lounge, where they all spent a pleasant night in each other's company. Elizabeth and Duncan poured their teenagers the occasional alcoholic drink and spoke to them as the adults they were rapidly becoming. Elizabeth was so happy she wanted the night to last forever, but tomorrow would be Christmas day and she was also looking forward to the morning. Charlotte and Alexander both went to bed just before midnight, and Duncan said that they also ought to go up as he was tired from all the travelling.

"You go up, Duncan. I'll be about ten minutes. I've still got some wrapping up to do. I won't be long. By the time you've been to the bathroom I'll be right behind you," Elizabeth said.

Duncan went upstairs, slithered into bed, and he was almost asleep straight away. Ten minutes later, he was startled awake as Elizabeth entered the bedroom and turned the light on. "Sorry. Were you asleep? What are you doing on my side of the bed?" she asked.

"Er I always," Duncan realized in the nick of time that at home he always slept on the far side of the bed so Elizabeth could be nearer the door. It had been ever thus since the children were small. But during the week in Venetia's flat it was exactly the opposite, and he slept nearer the door. His heart was pounding as he rolled over to the opposite side and in a flash of inspiration he said, "I was warming up your side of the bed for you, it was bloody freezing when I first got in."

"Oh, that's so sweet of you. I'll warm *you* up in a minute."

It was a blissful holiday for the couple. With Christmas Day being on the Thursday and the weekend to follow, all thoughts of work went completely out of their minds and Elizabeth was determined they would have the best Christmas ever. During the four days of the holiday, each meal became a feast and each evening and night became a party. Elizabeth really surprised her husband as she had acquired an insatiable appetite for his body over the four days, and on the Monday morning he felt as though a good gust of wind would blow him all the way back to Nottingham.

They travelled together in Cuthbert to the airport as Elizabeth wanted to speak to Duncan in private about something serious and she hadn't wanted to spoil the family holiday.

"Duncan, I don't know how to tell you this, but something is wrong. Can you remember a few months ago I told you about that missing jewellery? Well, last week I was on the High Street walking past a pawn shop, and I noticed it was for sale in the window. It was still in the presentation box. I went inside and asked the shop owner how it got there. He said it had been pawned four months ago and it was up for sale as the owner had not returned for it. I asked him what was the name of the person that brought it in, but he wouldn't, or couldn't tell me. I can only assume it's one of our bairns, and it gets worse. There has been at least three times that money has disappeared from my purse. First, there was a ten-pound note went missing, secondly a fiver, then yet another tenner. All on separate occasions, and they are the ones that I am definite about. Recently, I have started taking my handbag and purse up to the bedroom at night and never leave it unguarded. I didn't want to say anything while we were all having such a good time. What do you think I should do?"

"I'll try to sort it out next weekend. There's not a lot I can do now. You're doing the right thing by removing the temptation. Just be on your guard until I get back," he said.

After Elizabeth dropped him off at the airport, she left for the journey back to Kirkcaldy. While on her way home, she was confused as it seemed that Duncan wasn't as authoritative as usual, and she had noticed that he had occasionally appeared distant as though he was daydreaming. She couldn't understand why he didn't fly into a rage when she told him about the missing money, which is what she would have expected. Perhaps it was her woman's intuition, but something didn't seem quite right, and she couldn't put her finger on it.

While on his journey back to work, Duncan was thinking how hard it was becoming to live this double life. Over the festive period he found it very difficult when he was talking to his wife not to call her Venetia. He had bitten on the word on at least two occasions, and he became very scared that he might eventually make a big mistake. He wondered if Elizabeth had suspected any skulduggery when he fell asleep on the wrong side of the bed, but he hoped that he had got away with it. He was concerned that money was being taken from his wife's purse and it would be a priority to get to the bottom of it when he was next at home. Duncan didn't come home for the New Year's Eve celebrations as the New Year Day holiday was on the Thursday and he had to work on the Friday, so he told Elizabeth he would be back on the Friday night. Unfortunately for him, he was put into an impossible situation when Venetia and he were talking on the Monday night.

She said with authority, "Duncan, I want you to stay over this weekend. One of my dearest friends is getting married on Saturday and I have been invited plus, a guest. Can you stay this weekend and come to the wedding with me?"

The request left him dumbstruck. He was not expecting to be asked to go to formal functions with Venetia as a couple. He froze temporarily, while trying to regain his composure.

"I wasn't expecting that. I'm supposed to be at home this weekend. We have big problems with money being stolen from my wife's purse. You've put me on the spot there," he said.

" I need to know straight away so I can tell my friend. She wants a decision immediately as she needs to sort out the seating arrangements for the reception. Obviously if you don't come with me, I would have to sit on my own with strangers. I'll be very disappointed if you don't come," she said.

"I'll go and phone home and see what I can sort out." Duncan strolled down to the nearest payphone from where he usually called his wife. It didn't go down very well when he falsely claimed that he had an enormous amount of work to do and he was likely to be busy all weekend in order to catch up.

Elizabeth was very angry and burst out, "I'm sick to the teeth of you being away, it's driving me mad. This will be the fourth time you won't be coming home. I want you to pack that job in. Sod the money, it doesn't matter. The important thing is I want you to come home and the family needs you at home."

"My intention was to leave when we have enough money in the bank to pay for them both to go to university. What is the savings account worth now?" Duncan asked.

"There's about five to six thousand pounds, but it doesn't matter how much we have in the savings account; I want you to pack up and come home. I need you here. We all need you here. Stuff the money. We will get by so long as you are back at home, and we can live a normal life again. I don't care if you're stacking shelves at the supermarket or emptying dustbins so long as you come home every night. You don't realise how hard it is for me to cope with everything, especially with Alexander being such a problem."

"Lizzie, be patient for just a while longer until we have another three or four thousand put by then I'll look at packing up. I'll call you tomorrow and let you know about this weekend."

Duncan trudged back to the flat feeling the weight of the world on his shoulders. His wife and family needed him at home, yet, he had never been happier at work in his whole life, and he was also ecstatic with his new domestic arrangements as he was besotted with Venetia. He desperately wanted to continue the affair for as long as possible although he knew deep down inside it couldn't last forever. When he arrived back at the flat, Venetia was waiting expectantly for a positive answer from him. She needed a decision immediately and was pleased when he agreed to accompany her to the wedding. He said that it would be a one-off weekend and he would have to make more of an effort in the future to go home at the weekends.

Duncan did not enjoy telling Elizabeth the news on the following evening, and he was on the receiving end of a fearful tongue-lashing. He worried that his wife was almost at breaking point, a fact not helped by Alexander's blunt refusal to return to school after the Christmas holiday.

Elizabeth explained, "Alexander said that he's not going back to school because there's no point. When I asked him what he intended to do in the future, he just shrugged his shoulders and went out without saying a word. What can I do? I need you to sort him out, desperately, for my sake and my sanity."

Duncan was growing to dread the evening phone calls, as during each call he was feeling under more pressure to return home, and he was becoming resentful at the pressure being put on him. Each evening he would try, usually in vain, to calm the troubled waters and encourage Elizabeth to stay relaxed until he came home. Nevertheless, Elizabeth repeatedly pointed out to him, "If you were here in the first place, I wouldn't need to be asking you all the time. Sandy is clever enough to know how to keep out of your way at the weekends when you are at home, I haven't got a clue where he stays, probably with one of his new floozies, but as soon as you have gone, he makes my life a complete misery again."

Duncan then promised he would start looking for alternate employment the next weekend he was at home, but secretly he knew he wouldn't be looking too seriously as the chance of a similar post was extremely remote. He certainly didn't want to accept employment of a menial nature as he had become used to the lofty heights of senior management, and the thought of being at the bottom of the ladder again appalled him. His labouring days were over as far as he was concerned.

REVELATION

The weekend arrived and Duncan accompanied Venetia to her friend's wedding. She looked stunning in a sky-blue two-piece suit with a royal blue hat. He had a shock as they arrived when he noticed that his senior assistant Des Pearce was the father of the groom. He was also aware that many of the other guests were from his workplace, several of whom worked in his department. Alarmingly, his former adversary Ted Hector was at the evening reception with his wife.

Later in the evening, Duncan slipped out of the reception to find a phone box and called Elizabeth. She recycled everything they had already spoken about on their previous calls, and he cut the phone call off short with a simple, "I'll call you tomorrow."

Elizabeth was heartbroken, it was the first time that he had called her while working away without finishing the call by saying, "I love you, goodnight, Elizabeth."

Whether it was the tone of his voice, the abrupt ending or just plain woman's intuition, she knew something was not quite right.

Duncan walked back briskly to the reception, half feeling guilty at his lack of patience with his wife, but equally looking forward to getting back, just to be with Venetia. As he arrived back at the reception, he was met by Des Pearce in the lobby.

"Hi, Duncan, I didn't expect to see you here," said Des.

"Hello, Des, I saw you were on the top table. I presume that is your son who is the groom."

"Yes, one down, two to go. I've also got two daughters, Nina and Rachel who are both teenagers and I suppose they'll be getting married one day. It's all bloody expense when you have kids. Can we have a word outside? There's something I need to say to you and I don't want anyone to hear." Moments later they were in the car park. "Duncan, I noticed you earlier on the dancefloor with that lady, I know that you have a wife and family in Scotland, so I thought I ought to warn you. You're playing with fire if you're seeing her."

" I'm not seeing her. We're just good friends. We go running together when the weather is okay, but now in winter we go to the gym. Anyway, what's the problem with *her*, as you so harshly put it?"

"There's no problem with her. She's lovely and any man would be delighted to be with her. But please be careful. I'm not as gullible as you think. I saw you both earlier on the dancefloor smooching and you were squeezing her arse and she loved it. I saw the way you were looking at each other, that's not how casual friends look at each other. Anyway, that's not the point. The fact is she used to go out with a right horrible bastard who's a real nasty piece of work. He's in prison now. I think he got about six or seven years. He's the type of evil swine who might consider her to be his property, which probably explains why all the younger local lads who know about him won't even go near her. The reality is, he has friends and cronies living in this neighbourhood who keep in touch with him. The rumour is, he's still responsible for most of the crime round here. I know he's been in prison for about three years now, but he's dangerous, so be careful, very careful. Don't say you haven't been warned. I'm sorry if I have ruined your night."

Duncan went back inside not knowing what to make of Des's advice. He didn't want to spoil the rest of the night, so he decided to wait until the following day and casually bring it up in conversation. Despite the warning from Des, and being continually stared at by Ted Hector who couldn't take his eyes off the couple, Duncan and Venetia had a wonderful night, and they were among the last guests to leave when the reception was over. A slightly tipsy couple finally made their way back to the flat where they made love like a demented pair of newlyweds, eventually falling asleep about 3.00 am in the morning.

It was almost noon when they surfaced the following day, and Duncan's first thoughts were of the conversation with Des Pearce. He decided to leave it until later in the afternoon and ask Venetia what her intentions would be when her boyfriend was released from prison.

Later on the Sunday evening, he asked the question, "I've heard that you used to have a boyfriend who's now in prison. Is it your intention to get back together with him when he comes out?"

"No, I'm well shut of him. When he was sent down, I wrote a letter and sent it to his prison, but he's never even replied. Surely, he can't expect me to wait for him. To be honest, I'm hoping my future is with you. I didn't want to put pressure on you, but it would be nice if we were permanently together. I've never felt like this about anyone before. I know you're married, but we have something special, and I'm sure you feel the same way about me, don't you?" Venetia asked.

"Of course, I love you, so much it hurts, but the problem is, I still love my wife and children as well and sometimes I feel the whole situation is tearing me apart. I want to be with you, but I also want to be with my family as well."

"Well, let's leave things as they are for the time being, but you will have to make a decision eventually. I don't want you to string me along and keep me waiting forever," she said.

"Does the fact that I'm seventeen years older than you come into the equation?" he asked.

"No. My friend Bryony who got married on Saturday thinks you're a real catch, and she asked me if she could be a bridesmaid at *our* wedding. I told her it's early days yet, but fingers crossed. I didn't tell her you're already married."

Duncan appreciated that he would have to make a decision that would change his life for ever, or, he would have to break up his relationship with Venetia. He knew he was burning the candle at both ends, and it couldn't last. Later, it was a weary husband who went out to call his wife. As he trudged towards the phone box, it started raining heavily and he was drenched as he dialled the number. When Elizabeth replied, neither of them were in a talkative mood, until Elizabeth eventually bitterly complained about Alexander who had brought another girl home again on Saturday night. "They sat downstairs drinking and making lots of noise until they went to bed about two o'clock. She was a filthy slut; she wore black fishnet stockings that were full of holes, and she wore a leather jacket with skull and crossbones on the back. Her hair looked like it had never seen a brush and she had horrible black mascara all round her eyes. She didn't leave until late on Sunday afternoon. When I spoke to him, he was very rude and said that 'It's none of my business and he can see who he wants.' It's getting to the stage where I am frightened to say anything to him as he always gives me an aggressive stare when I speak to him. I'm scared of him. I thought he was going to hit me. Please try and sort him out when you next come home."

Duncan stopped his morning calls to Elizabeth but continued his evening phone calls which all followed a similar pattern through January and February. Whereas he had initially looked forward to

212

speaking to his wife and just hearing her reassuring and loving voice, he was now beginning to dread the daily torturous ritual. He did not confront Alexander in the next two months as his son would go out on the Friday evening and not come home until Monday after his father had returned to work. It was a desperate time for Elizabeth who was becoming increasingly fraught with her shredded nerves.

Towards the end of February, Duncan and Elizabeth received a letter from Jack McKinlay with the news that Alice had succumbed to her illness and passed away. The funeral would be on Wednesday March 11th. Duncan booked a week's holiday and told Elizabeth not to let Alexander know he would be home for the whole week.

When Duncan informed Venetia that he was going home on Friday and would be back in Scotland for nine days she was none too pleased. She complained, "Oh, I see. You want to go back to Scotland and leave me on my own for a whole week. I'm not happy about that. It's time you made your mind up. You need to decide, is it her or me?"

Duncan agreed that he needed to make a decision and he promised that when he returned to Nottingham, he would have made up his mind. It was to be a pivotal week in all their lives.

It started badly for Duncan as it was an awful flight back to Edinburgh with heavy clouds and stormy weather causing lots of turbulence, and it was a mightily relieved set of passengers that scrambled across the tarmac to the arrivals lounge in pouring rain. Later, as Duncan arrived at Kirkcaldy station, he was relieved to see several taxis outside available for hire. Within five minutes he was at home hugging his wife. He could sense that Elizabeth was trembling, and she appeared to be a nervous wreck. He tried to calm her with a reassuring kiss on her lips, but it was to no avail. It was obvious she was very seriously distressed.

"Hey, Elizabeth, please calm down, I'm home now. What's the matter?" he asked.

"It's him again. I can't take it anymore. When I arrived home from work, he tried begging off me for some extra pocket money and I refused; then when I had shower, he must have crept in our bedroom and rifled through my handbag. He has emptied my purse. I know there was at least forty pounds in notes and change. Now it's all gone. What are we going to do?"

"I'll ring his bleeding neck when I get my hands on him. Does Charlotte know anything about it?"

"Probably. He's stolen money from her recently and she tries to avoid him because he's always on the scrounge. He's not the same boy who we loved and were so proud of a year ago. He's changed: he's scruffy, rude, aggressive and I'm ashamed to be his mother. I feel as though I'm a failure as a parent,"

"No, you're not a failure. It's more my fault for not being here. I don't think I've even seen him for two months, probably since the New Year. I'm home now for the next nine days, and one way or another I will sort him out," Duncan explained.

"Please don't give him a good hiding. The last thing I want is to see you both fighting. I'm not bothered about the money; I just want my son back to the boy we loved and the boy he used to be."

As Duncan sat down at the table and Elizabeth served his dinner, he noticed the few strands of grey that were showing through in her hair. He had never noticed them before, but they were certainly visible now. His thoughts changed to Venetia, and he wondered what she would be doing now. He was already missing her and wishing he was back at the flat while at the same time relieved to be at home with his dysfunctional family. He told Elizabeth that he would go to Dysart tomorrow and visit Jack McKinlay although he expected it to be distressing and a harrowing experience.

He was right. When he arrived at the bungalow, he was stunned at how thin and gaunt Jack was. He had expressionless eyes peering out of a sullen face. His skin was pale, and Duncan noticed his skeletal-like bony fingers as he poured a cup of tea. They spoke for an hour, and it was a relief to Duncan when he eventually left.

On the way home, Duncan felt ashamed that he had not been to visit the McKinlays for over four months and Alice was quite poorly the last time that he saw her. She had been in a palliative care home for the final six weeks of her life, and it seemed to Duncan that Jack had ceased to look after himself properly. He was obviously not eating sufficiently, and he had lost a lot of weight. Duncan was very worried that Jack appeared to have "given up the will to live," and when he expressed his fears to Elizabeth later, he thought that he heard her mumble quietly under her breath, "I know how he feels."

Discretion dictated that Duncan pretended not to hear the comment and he changed the topic of conversation.

On the Monday morning Duncan gave Elizabeth a lift to work in Cuthbert and then went over to Dysart to see if Jack needed any help before the funeral on Wednesday. Jack was very pleased by Duncan's offer but he'd already organized everything including the catering for the wake, which would be back at his bungalow.

He said to Duncan, "There's only a few people coming. There'll be just a few neighbours and friends, but I'm so glad that you'll be coming as well. Alice was so proud of you. She worshipped you as if you had been our own son."

Duncan replied, "She was a very special lady, you were both fantastic parents and I couldn't have wished for a better childhood. I feel so ashamed that I hadn't seen her since before last Christmas."

"Don't worry yourself. She wouldn't have recognized you at the end. I think she didn't recognize me in those last few weeks."

When Duncan was on his way home, he called at the bank to pick up some money for Elizabeth. When he arrived home, he crept in quietly, and he was aware that there were voices upstairs. He went upstairs to Alexander's bedroom and opened the door to witness his son with his latest female companion sharing a cannabis joint.

He was livid, and demanded loudly, "*What's going off here? Right, you, get your things and bugger off, now!*"

Sheepishly, Alexander's girlfriend grabbed her handbag and coat and hurriedly fled down the stairs. She slammed the door on her way out as Alexander was trying in vain to stop her.

"Oi, dad. That's not right, she's done no harm. You can't just chuck her out like that."

"Oh, can't I? Well, I've got news for you, my lad: you'll be next if you don't stop thieving money off your mother and making her life a misery. Look at the state of you. You look a mess, and why don't you come home at the weekends, eh? It's because you know I'll be here and you're keeping out of my way. And another thing, why aren't you back at school? If you think you're just going to leave school and scrounge about the house poncing money off your mother, you're sadly mistaken. It stops now! You either look for work and get a job or go back to school, if they'll have you, which I doubt looking at the state

215

of you. And how long have you been smoking those horrible things? It stinks in here. Get yourself showered and come downstairs, and you can have a bloody haircut this afternoon."

Duncan went back downstairs, allowing his son time to think what he would say when he came down after his shower. Half an hour later, Alexander appeared as Duncan was reading the local newspaper with a particular interest in the "Situations Vacant" section.

"Well, what have you got to say for yourself? Why have you been stealing money from your mother's purse?"

"Because she always gives Charlotte anything she wants, but she never gives me anything. She gets all new clothes, new shoes, trainers, books, make-up, she's even bought her a new computer. If I need any new clothes or shoes, she takes no notice of me, and I have to go without. Well, it's not fair, I only..."

"*Not fair!*" Roared Duncan, with his temper rising by the second, "*Not fair!*, I'll show you what's not fair, you scruffy bone-idle scrounging bastard. You will apologize to your mother when she gets home from work. You can get your hair cut this afternoon and I will take you back to see your headmaster in the morning. If they don't take you back, then you can look for work and start paying your board. If you're not happy with that, you can pack your bags and leave now. Oh, and don't ever bring a scrubber like that into my house again."

Alexander stormed out of the lounge and went back upstairs. Duncan was still seething, and as he picked up the newspaper, he was aware that his fists were clenched as though he was almost ready to hit his son. He sat down, shocked by his own temper, and he wondered how close he had come to thrashing his son. As he was trying to wind down, his thoughts were, "Do I really need all this aggravation?"

His thoughts turned to Nottingham and the domestic bliss he was sharing with Venetia. It was only midday on Monday, but he was already yearning for the taste and pleasure of her femininity.

On the Tuesday morning, he gave Elizabeth a lift to work in Cuthbert and the children a lift to the school. Charlotte went to the assembly while Duncan and Alexander made their way to the head's office where they were told by the secretary they would have to wait half an hour for an audience with Mr Hart. As they sat in the corridor waiting, neither of them spoke a word and the tension was palpable.

Eventually, they were admitted into Mr Hart's office and Duncan was the first to speak.

"Alexander would like to apologize for all his recent non-attendance and he would like to resume his studies if that's possible."

After half a minute of silence Mr Hart replied. "With the look on his face and the fact that you are doing all the talking, Mr Baker, am I to assume that Alexander is only here under duress? Would you please wait outside, Mr Baker, while Alexander and I talk in private?"

Fifteen minutes later, Alexander came out of Mr Hart's office as the headmaster bade them both farewell. When they were outside the school, Duncan promptly asked his son what had happened.

Alexander explained. "He said it will probably be okay, but he needs to speak to the school governors first. He said something about not wanting to disrupt any of the existing classes, but he will get in touch by Thursday as he needs the governor's approval first. He thinks I might be able to start again next Monday."

"Good. Right, here's the next thing: when your mum gets home from work tonight, you apologize, yet again, for your recent behaviour. You were someone we were very proud of until recently. Now your mother is even frightened to speak to you because of your aggressive attitude. Will you do that for me?"

"Yes, I'm sorry I took the money from her purse. I'll pay it back when I'm at work, I promise."

"The money is not the issue; your mother wants your respect, she just wants you to be honest and someone she can be proud of again, that's all. For a start, you can give her this forty pounds back, but don't tell her I gave it to you. That will be our secret. Just say you are returning it as you didn't spend it."

Later in the afternoon, Duncan went to collect Elizabeth from work. She came out of the showroom delighted to see Cuthbert parked near the door. On the way home, Duncan told her all about the day's events, especially regarding her son. He was hoping that Alexander's apologies would soothe the troubled waters and all would now be calm in the Baker household.

To Duncan's immense satisfaction, a humble Alexander duly apologized profusely to Elizabeth and Charlotte before returning the forty pounds to his mother. It was the start of a quiet night for the couple before tomorrow's funeral, which Duncan was dreading.

Elizabeth had also booked a day's holiday and accompanied Duncan to the funeral. Luckily, the rain held off, and after the service they all returned to Jack's bungalow for the wake. Duncan and Elizabeth kept busy making tea and coffee and serving the buffet for the elderly mourners. Later, when all the friends and neighbours had bade their farewells, Duncan and Elizabeth did the washing-up and helped Jack to tidy up the bungalow. Eventually they sat down for a tortured conversation with Jack that seemed to last forever.

It was as they were speaking that the reality of Alice's death and the big impact it had on him became apparent to Duncan. As his thoughts had been previously preoccupied with the dilemma of his own domestic arrangements, he had not fully appreciated the effect it would have on him, and for the first time he could feel tears welling in his eyes as Jack was saying that "he had nothing left to live for." Duncan and Elizabeth tried to soothe his depression with talk of his going on holidays and cruises and enjoying himself, but his abject apathy was too deeply rooted and he dismissed all suggestions out of hand. As they said goodnight, Duncan promised to visit Jack more often although he knew it would be difficult to uphold the promise.

On the way back to Kirkcaldy Duncan said, "I don't know about you, but I could do with a drink; Have we any cans in the fridge or shall we go to the pub?"

"There are four cans of lager in the fridge, I don't want a drink as I've got work in the morning. I wonder how Sandy and Lottie went on making their own dinner. I bet they are sitting there starving waiting for me to get home."

To their surprise, Alexander had made them both a mushroom omelette with baked beans and had even done the washing-up. Elizabeth was both astounded yet elated. "I'm really proud of him, he even had the sense to take into account that Lottie is a vegetarian when he made the meal."

Duncan poured himself a can of lager and switched the television on although he found that there was nothing on of any interest. He sat staring at the screen through misty eyes feeling a large part of his life was now confined to history. When Elizabeth spoke to him several times during the evening, he was not in the mood for conversation and usually responded with one-word replies, so at ten o'clock Elizabeth went to bed alone as she had work in the morning. She understood how the death of his foster mother had affected him, but she was very disappointed that Duncan did not want to go to bed at the same time. When she thought about it, he had been at home since the previous Friday night, and they had only made love on the one occasion during the five previous nights and tonight was going to be another night of neglect. Her fears that something was wrong were growing by the day. Normally, Duncan couldn't wait to get to grips with her in bed, but it seemed he was losing his carnal appetite for her, and she felt a deep sense of rejection. She was awake until almost midnight before she eventually fell asleep with no sign of her husband.

Duncan had sat quietly thinking of Alice and what would be Jack McKinlay's future now that he was on his own. His thoughts then turned to Venetia, and he longed to be back with her in Beeston. He thought of his wife and children. He loved his family so much that he felt ashamed of his infidelity, but he couldn't help feeling that he loved Venetia even more. He was trying to think of how he could get out of his marriage without causing too much heartache for his family, but it wasn't going to be easy. He thought, "Perhaps, if the mortgage is fully paid up and there's enough money put by to pay for Alexander and Charlotte to go to university, at least I can leave the house and the savings to Elizabeth to soften the blow. But then again, what if things don't work out with Venetia and she finishes with me, and then I end up losing my marriage *and* my relationship with Venetia? What if I lose my job in Beeston and end up on the scrap heap looking for any sort of work just to feed myself? What if…?" his head was spinning like a top, and he knew there wasn't an easy solution.

Alexander interrupted his turmoil when he came in later, and Duncan asked his son to sit and have a drink with him, just the one for a nightcap. He poured them both a large brandy and they talked for over an hour, about sport mainly, football being the main topic. Duncan could see how much his son was missing playing football; he had experienced the same thing through injury albeit at a much older age than his son, but with Alexander it had been a major part of his life to lose at such a young age. Losing Mandy at the same time had an even bigger effect on him and Duncan could see the reasons his son had been going through a rebellious period caused by the tremendous disappointment that his injury had caused. It was the first time that Alexander had opened up his true feelings about how much he was in love with Mandy and Duncan was surprised how much it still hurt his son almost a year since he last saw her. Duncan suggested that he start swimming again as he previously excelled at it and the exercise would surely be beneficial for strengthening his left knee. He could see the disappointment etched all over his son's face as Alexander explained that he had tried swimming at the local pool on several occasions, but he had lost a lot of speed as he had to slow down to compensate because one leg was much stronger than the other, and he couldn't keep a straight line when going flat out.

They both went to bed quietly at half past twelve with the expectation that school would give them a positive answer regarding Alexander resuming his studies.

Duncan received a phone call at 9.30 in the morning from the school secretary asking if he and his son could be at the school to see Mr Hart at 10.30 am prompt. Fortunately, it was good news regarding Alexander resuming his studies, which was rubber stamped for the following Monday. It was made clear that any further protracted periods of unauthorized absence would result in permanent expulsion.

Duncan dropped Alexander back at home and drove over to Dysart to see Jack McKinlay. When Jack opened the door, Duncan was delighted that he could smell the aroma of bacon and toast, so at least he knew that Jack was feeding himself. Jack was delighted that Duncan had made the effort to come and see him again, and they sat together looking through all the old photograph albums that the loving couple had made over the years. There were many photographs taken of Duncan during his childhood, and Jack garnered an enormous amount of pleasure going through them trying to remember where they were taken and what age Duncan was at the time.

He startled Duncan as he said, "Duncan, when I've gone to be reunited with Alice, I want you to have these photograph albums. I don't care what happens with everything else in the bungalow, they can burn the lot as far as I'm concerned. Alice and I want you to have the bungalow though. You can do what you want with it. If you want to sell it, then sell it. It's up to you. We spoke about it before she was ill and it's what we want." Jack had told him previously about the bungalow, so he already knew but Duncan had dismissed it from his thoughts hoping that it wouldn't happen for a very long time. However, Jack was talking about it as though it was imminent and talking about Alice in the present tense which confused him.

"I'd be delighted to have the photograph albums, Jack, but I'm not expecting to own them for years."

Later in the afternoon, Duncan was at home drinking a cup of tea while mulling over the conversation with his son the previous night. He thought it strange that Alexander had been madly in love with a woman almost twice his own age, yet here *he* was, besotted and in love with a woman almost half his age. It raised a smile for the first time in days.

After yet another quiet night in front of the television, Duncan and Elizabeth went to bed at 10.30 pm and marital harmony was restored, much to Elizabeth's delight. They had to be very quiet as Charlotte had only just gone to bed and Alexander was watching television downstairs. Nevertheless, the couple were totally absorbed in one another, and after a prolonged encore, they drifted off to sleep in a blissful stupor.

The next morning, Elizabeth was full of the joys of spring especially as Duncan gave her a lift to work and promised to collect her later. Duncan passed the day doing some gardening with Alexander's help. The postman had been with the usual pile of advertising and bills, but there was also a letter for Elizabeth that was simply addressed to Mrs Baker. The writing on the envelope was done in capital letters with a child-like scrawl which was very unusual. If Duncan had known the content, he would have burned the letter immediately, but he wasn't to know. He would find out later that evening after Elizabeth was home from work and she had opened her mail.

Duncan was upstairs asking Alexander and Charlotte what they wanted from the Chinese takeaway as Elizabeth digested the letter. It was scrawled in capital letters as though a small child had written it: MRS BAKER, YOUR HUSBAND IS HAVING AN AFFAIR WITH A YOUNG WOMAN IN BEESTON. HER NAME IS VENETIA. THEY LIVE TOGETHER NOW. LOOK AT THESE PHOTOS FOR PROOF.

There were three polaroid photographs that were taken at Bryony's wedding accidently catching sight of the couple together. They were not the focal point of the photographs but on one they were in the background walking along holding hands, and on the other two they were in the background dancing closely together, in one of them, he was actually squeezing her backside. Elizabeth read the short letter three times and scoured the photographs with misty eyes, misty eyes that turned to hysterical crying when the reality of the content of the letter and the photographs became blatantly obvious. Duncan came back downstairs moments later to see her howling uncontrollably.

He inquired, "What's up, Lizzie?"

"You swine, you filthy cheating dirty swine, how could you?" she wailed.

"What? what have I done now?" he asked.

Elizabeth showed him the crumpled letter but withheld the photos; she would possibly need them as her trump card.

"Oh, Lizzie, you don't believe that sort of rubbish do you? It's obviously from someone at work whom I've given a damn good roasting, or someone that I've sacked, and they want revenge. When you're in charge of a department with lots of people, there's always someone trying to knife you in the back. Ignore it, it's total garbage."

"Who's Venetia then?" Elizabeth demanded.

"I am friendly with a girl called Venetia. I helped her one morning when I was out running, she had a fall and twisted her ankle and I helped her to get back home. We sometimes go running together down by the river when the weather's good and we go to the gym when the weather's bad, that's all."

"So, nothing else. You don't go out with her at all on social occasions, and you don't live with her, is that right?" she demanded.

"Yes, of course it's right. I wouldn't cheat on you, ever."

"Well, these photographs tell me something different. Look at them, and then tell me you aren't messing about with another woman. She doesn't look much older than Charlotte either."

Duncan was totally dumbstruck. It was quite clear that the photographs had innocently captured Duncan and Venetia in the background, but they were at the wedding together as a couple. He knew it was completely futile to continue denying the allegations. He sat down, staring at the photographs, speechless, wondering who was so evil as to be responsible for this disclosure? He was not to know that Ted Hector had a nephew who worked in the wages department and had access to every employee's personal home address. Neither would he ever find out.

It was Elizabeth that shattered the silence. "As far as I'm concerned, you can clear off back to her and rot in hell. Oh God, when I think of what we did last night, how could you?"

Duncan was ashamed, embarrassed at telling lies, and totally lost for words. All he could think of was, "I'm really sorry, Elizabeth. Where do we go from here?"

"You can go wherever you want, but you'll never share my bed again. We're finished. Go on, pack your bags and leave, *now,* and don't bother saying goodbye to the bairns and telling them a pack of lies. I'll tell them later what a cheating swine you are. Go on, leave, *now.*"

"I don't want to leave. I promise I won't see her again. Can't we sort it out between us and start again if I jack the job in and come home?"

"You can leave now and don't bother coming back. I can't force you to go, but I will tell you this: the first time you fall asleep I will take a knife to you, and you will wake up minus a few parts of your body. You'll never have the chance to cheat on another woman ever again. Go on, get out."

Despite his grovelling apologies, Duncan knew that he was getting nowhere. Elizabeth was enraged and she was not in the mood to forgive and forget. it was pointless humiliating himself any further and increasing her anger, so he decided to leave and give her time to calm down so he could try again in a couple of days. He went upstairs and packed his bag without even saying goodbye to Alexander and Charlotte. As he walked down the path to the gate, he looked over his shoulder to see Charlotte at her bedroom window looking at him.

As he was forlornly walking to the train station, Charlotte rushed downstairs to speak to her mother. "Where's dad going? He's supposed to be taking me ice-skating on Sunday. Why has he left carrying a bag? Mum, why are you crying?"

Elizabeth was filled with an intense loathing of her cheating husband, but, even then, she couldn't bring herself to besmirch his name in the eyes of their daughter. "Work have been in touch with him and he's got to go, he's going to be very busy. We might not see him again for a while."

"Oh, that's horrible mum. No wonder you're upset. He must have been in a rush as he never even said cheerio to me." Charlotte complained.

Duncan made his way to the station and caught a train to Edinburgh where he stayed the night in a hotel before getting an early morning call and a taxi to the airport. The Saturday morning flight back to East Midlands Airport contained an ashen-faced passenger who barely moved a muscle as he sat staring with a blank expression at the seat in front of him. He was exhausted from lack of sleep as he had spent the whole night trying to fathom what to do to try to rescue his marriage, for he was certain, that now that it was all probably too late, it was his family that should be his priority. No matter how much he loved Venetia, he loved his wife and children considerably more. The pain he was suffering from the hurt he had inflicted on Elizabeth was something he had never experienced before; he was deeply ashamed, and he knew that his wife would not forgive him easily. He vowed that he would persist in trying for however long it would take and however much humble pie he would have to eat; that one day she would forgive him, and they would be reunited.

An hour after the flight had landed, he was parking his car outside Venetia's flat resolving to let her down gently over the weekend and move out into the B&B by Monday after work. As he entered her flat, Venetia was amazed to see him. "Hi, Duncan. I wasn't expecting you back until Monday. What a wonderful surprise, and talking about surprises, I've got another surprise for you, well, for both of us really. I think you'd better sit down."

Feeling totally exhausted, Duncan sat down on the sofa wondering what this "surprise" was likely to be that Venetia had mentioned. It wasn't long before he found out.

She explained, "Duncan, when you left last Friday, I was already about a week late and nothing's happened while you've been away, so on Thursday I bought a home pregnancy testing kit, and it appears that I am pregnant. I don't know for certain until I see the doctor on Monday, but it's a safe bet that we're going to have a baby. What do you think of that Duncan?"

Totally stunned, Duncan barely managed to splutter out the words, "Erm… that's wonderful. Erm… I thought you were taking the pill."

"I am, or I was. If I am pregnant, there's not much point in me taking it now, is there? It looks like I probably forgot to take it one day. Either that, or you're blessed with superhuman powers. I've often told you that you are good in the bedroom department, and now you know what I mean."

He rose from the sofa to give her a big hug, but inwardly he was wondering if he was in the middle of a bad dream, one that was rapidly turning into a desperate tragic nightmare. He felt feeble and weak and apologized for his lack of enthusiasm, explaining that he had not slept since Thursday night, and would she mind if he went and had a lay down for a couple of hours?

"Okay, I'll wake you at lunchtime. We can go out tonight and celebrate," she said.

Duncan collapsed on the bed desperately hoping he could have some sleep and then wake up to find it was all a bad dream, but unfortunately, he knew it wasn't. The reality dawned on him: in less than twenty-four hours, he had been thrown out by his wife, losing his marriage of almost twenty-one years, and now he was discovering that his lover appeared to be pregnant. He wondered if the whole world was conspiring against him and perhaps Venetia wasn't pregnant but it was just a plot to ensnare him. Another thought occurred to him, that perhaps Venetia was using her womanly wiles and she didn't take her pills on purpose in an attempt to get herself pregnant and entrap him. His mind was racing overtime, and he only managed to get about half an hour's sleep before Venetia woke him up at twelve o'clock by easing herself into bed at his side with one thing on her mind.

"Before we eat, I thought you'd like to work up an appetite. I've missed you."

VIOLATION

While Venetia was thrilled that Duncan was back two days early from his stay in Scotland, he exuded a zombie-like demeanour that he explained was due to extreme tiredness. The torture he felt about his predicament was all-consuming and he couldn't think of anything else but trying to make things up with his wife.

He was surprised at how ecstatic Venetia was at being pregnant. He even wondered if she now took it for granted that he would end his marriage and move in with her permanently because she was expecting his child. He knew there was no point in calling Elizabeth too soon: he thought that it was sensible to give her a period of reflection and hope that her temper abated. If she wouldn't have him back on any terms, there would be lots to sort out. For a start, his wages were paid into a joint bank account held between him and Elizabeth. The mortgage still had four years left to pay and he would own his half-share of their house. They had a joint-deposit account currently containing about six or seven thousand pounds. It was a mess. Why had he let his own stupidity and lust bring him to this?

Elizabeth was more concerned with keeping things on an even keel in the family household and trying to stay as busy as she could. She knew that when she sat down and relaxed, she couldn't think of anything else other than Duncan's treacherous betrayal and his affair with a younger woman. It was like a knife through her heart.

As they were having their evening meal on the Saturday, Alexander and Charlotte asked their mother why she looked so unhappy, and Alexander explained that he heard them both having a tremendous argument the previous evening. Elizabeth's futile excuse about Duncan returning to work brought raised eyebrows from her son as he knew that his father would not leave on a Friday evening to go back to work. He said nothing but shook his head in Charlotte's direction when Elizabeth was clearing the plates away. He was not as naïve as his mother thought.

That night, Elizabeth and Charlotte were watching television after Alexander had gone out. Charlotte eventually noticed the tears tumbling down her mother's cheeks. She said nothing, but snuggled up alongside her mother on the sofa for comfort.

On the same Saturday night, Duncan and Venetia went out in Beeston for a meal and then on to a pub for celebratory drinks, as Duncan thought, there was no point in keeping a low profile now that the cat was out of the bag and his wife knew of the affair. Venetia received the impression that Duncan didn't share the same level of enthusiasm for the pregnancy, but she put it down to his tiredness, particularly as she had put him "through the gallops" all afternoon. By ten o'clock he was a spent force, and when they returned to the flat, he was in bed snoring within five minutes.

The next day saw both Elizabeth and Duncan thinking of the other, for vastly different reasons. Duncan hated the deceit he had inflicted on Elizabeth and wished he could make amends. Elizabeth was hoping *he* would rot in hell. They were both back at work on the Monday morning, and the weekend's events would have a marked effect on them both. A crestfallen Elizabeth was in her office after a terrible night with a lack of sleep and she hardly had the energy or inspiration to face a day's work. She was sitting at her desk sobbing gently and staring at the computer with tears tumbling down her cheeks when her boss entered her office.

"Good morning, Elizabeth. I hope you had a good weekend. I just need you to enter the ... whatever's the matter? Why are you crying? Is everything okay?" he asked.

The misery and depression that had built up over the whole weekend suddenly exploded and a distraught Elizabeth broke down crying hysterically. The tears were raining down her cheeks and dripping on her skirt and the desktop. Martin briskly stepped forward and put his arms around her to comfort her as he said sympathetically, "There, there, Elizabeth, don't cry, nothing's worth getting yourself into a state like this. Whatever's the matter?"

Elizabeth struggled to get the words out: "My husband, ... he's been ... cheating on me, ... we've ... split up."

"Well, he must be an idiot, that's all I can say. Do you want to go home and come back when you feel a bit better?"

Elizabeth was feebly trembling in his arms and he kissed her compassionately on the forehead and repeated his offer.

"Thanks, Mr Gemmill, I'll be alright in a minute. I didn't sleep last night and it's all getting on top of me."

"Elizabeth, I've told you many times, call me Martin when we're alone, leave that Mr Gemmill formality for when we are in front of the staff and customers."

Elizabeth slowly began to stop crying and Martin took out his handkerchief to assist in wiping away the tears. As he was doing so, he kissed Elizabeth yet again on the forehead.

"I can't have my favourite member of staff feeling unhappy. Sit yourself down and take as long as you like."

Martin held her hand and gently helped her back into her chair before leaning over and kissing her on the cheek. As he left the office, Elizabeth didn't notice the self-appreciative smile etched on his face. She had been happy just for a few words of comfort and a reassuring gesture of tenderness.

Martin came into her office on another five occasions during the day and each time he was pleasant without being overbearing. He told Elizabeth to leave early and try to get a good night's sleep and see how she was in the morning, "If you don't feel any better, take the day off. It's your half-day tomorrow anyway," he said.

"Thanks, Mr Gemmill."

"Martin, call me Martin."

"Thanks, Martin. See you tomorrow."

Duncan had spent most of the day sitting at his office desk trying to decide what to do for the best. He knew a lot would depend on the results of Venetia's appointment with the doctor, especially if she *was* pregnant. He thought it was best to keep his options open and remain with Venetia until he knew for definite whether Elizabeth would have him back. If Elizabeth decided to let him return and then forgive him, how could he finish with Venetia if she was carrying his child? The more he thought about it the more confused he became, and he cursed the fact that he originally left his home and family life to work in England in the first place.

His self-enforced solitude behind his locked office door did not go down well with several members of the staff. Olive Mackay was desperate to see him on two occasions and she sent a junior member of staff to knock on his office door to ask for his attention, but, on both occasions, he ignored the request.

Olive said to one senior researcher Brian Rees, "If he can't be bothered to shift his arse, why should we bother? Sod him!"

As the working day was drawing to a close, Duncan took a brief walk round his department oblivious to the fact that in some specific quarters he was losing respect. He could only think about Venetia and Elizabeth, and he was praying that the consultant had given Venetia a negative result concerning her pregnancy test.

When he arrived back at the flat, he discovered that his prayers were in vain and Venetia's suspicions were correct. She was expecting a child that was due in November.

She said excitedly, "Isn't it wonderful! We must look for a bigger place before the baby is born. It would be nice if we can get somewhere with a garden for the baby to play in as well. Oh I'm so excited. What do you think, Duncan?"

"Erm, yes, that's great news," he said through gritted teeth with his insides doing the Hokey Cokey. "I'm just going to have a quick shower; we'll go out for a drink to celebrate after."

Whilst he was in the shower, his thoughts were, "I wonder if things can get any worse. If Elizabeth does have me back, I'm still going to be saddled with maintenance payments to support Venetia's baby. What a bloody mess!" He decided to let things stay the same for the time being, but make a concerted effort to speak to Elizabeth over the weekend and beg humbly for her forgiveness.

Back in Kirkcaldy, Elizabeth was not in a forgiving mood. She was adjusting her life to the fact she would never see her husband again unless it was in a divorce court. She had been touched by Martin's tenderness and kindness when she was distraught at work earlier in the day, and she just wanted to get on with her life now that she was alone with the children.

Martin was in the same compassionate mood on the Tuesday, visiting her office early to give her another reassuring hug and a quick peck on the cheek, but Elizabeth wasn't aware he was becoming too over familiar with her and she would have been wise to remember the words of wisdom spoken nearly two years earlier by Verity.

On the Thursday there was an unexpected start to Elizabeth's day. She was upstairs in her bedroom putting on her make-up when there was a knock on the front door which Charlotte answered. A man was standing there with the biggest bouquet of beautiful flowers that Charlotte had ever seen.

He inquired, "Elizabeth Baker?"

Charlotte took delivery of the bouquet and set it down gently on the table. Elizabeth came down a few moments later as her excited daughter pointed to the bouquet.

"This is for you mum. I wonder who it's from?"

Elizabeth knew instinctively who it was from. There were very few people who knew it was her birthday, and when she read the card her suspicions were correct: it was from Duncan.

HAPPY BIRTHDAY TO MY DARLING WIFE, I WILL CALL YOU TONIGHT.XXXX

Elizabeth didn't say anything, but inside she was thinking, "The two-faced cheating rat. He needn't bother calling me, I've got nothing to say to him." She picked up her car keys and left to go to work, leaving a surprised Charlotte looking for a vase to put the flowers in.

Later, when Duncan had eaten his dinner, he told Venetia that he had to go out and call home to speak to Elizabeth because he needed to sort a few things out concerning the money in the bank and the mortgage payments. His heart was pounding as he dialled the number, and when he got through it was Charlotte that answered.

"Hello, sweetheart. Is your mother there?" he asked.

"She's in the kitchen, I'll fetch her in a minute. Are you coming home this weekend, dad?"

"I don't know yet, it all depends, I'll know tomorrow."

Elizabeth sharply inquired, "What do *you* want?"

"I just wanted to know if the flowers arrived. Happy birthday Elizabeth. I wanted to speak to you and just to hear your voice. I'm so sorry about everything. It's not been easy for me being away from you all, but what I did was inexcusable, and I will go to the ends of the Earth to try to make things better. I know I don't deserve it, but I would like to make a start by coming home this weekend if that's possible."

After a protracted silence Elizabeth replied, "I can't stop you coming home. This is your house as well as mine, but don't expect any welcome from me. You will never share my bed again. I will not speak to you, I will not cook for you, I will not clean for you. You can sleep in the shed as far as I'm concerned, then you can explain to the children that you supposedly love, why you are there. And remember, if you come near me in the bedroom, I'll take a knife to you."

After another period of silence Duncan asked, "What will the bairns think if they see me sleeping in the shed? Be reasonable.

"*Reasonable? Reasonable!* You think whoring yourself all over Nottingham is *reasonable?* I've a mind to change the locks so you can't get in. Go back to your whore and rot in hell."

"I've moved back in with Wilf and I don't see her anymore. How many more times do I have to apologize? I'm so sorry, I'll do anything to make things better."

"Anything … anything? The only thing that will make things better is if you throw yourself in the River Trent, or under a bus. Either way I don't care, now get lost."

With that insult still ringing in her husband's ears, Elizabeth slammed down the receiver, however it did not go unnoticed that although she had given him a fearful barrage of abuse, it didn't have the effect of making her feel any better.

Duncan trudged back to the flat, shocked at the level of Elizabeth's caustic vitriol before he explained to Venetia that his wife was not in the mood to discuss the formalities of the separation and he would try again the following week.

As he sat watching the television, he realized that he had lied to both his wife and his lover yet again in the space of ten minutes and he felt a profound sense of shame at his deceitfulness. But what could he do? He couldn't admit to his wife that he was keeping his options open by remaining with Venetia, and he couldn't own up to his lover that he had just begged his wife to give him another chance. One thing was for sure: he would not be going home this weekend.

He and Venetia made a start looking at the range of properties that they assumed they would be able to afford, although Duncan was quick to point out that he didn't know what would be left for him after his divorce and after the parasitic lawyers had taken their spoils. Of course, it was all for show on Duncan's behalf, and he was just flowing with the tide because ultimately he desperately wanted to go back to his wife. Venetia impressed on him that she was quite prepared to be cast as the other woman if it meant his getting a divorce, but there was no pressure on them to get married even though she was pregnant. She would be happy if they just lived together.

During the weekend, the realization that he might end up getting divorced was slowly grating away at him, and he thought that perhaps he ought to take the house hunting more seriously. They saw three properties that they assumed would be in their price range, and Venetia was quick to mention that the sooner Duncan made a clean break, and he knew how much he would be left with financially, the sooner they would be able to see properties in their price range.

When they were back at the flat on the Sunday evening, Venetia asked Duncan if he wanted to know if the baby was a boy or a girl. She didn't know herself at that time, but said that if she did want to know she could find out when she had her following scan. It was at this point that Duncan fully understood how deep this relationship was becoming. "Was it a boy or a girl? We are talking about the birth of a child here, and all I can think of is buggering off back to Scotland." He fell silent for a moment before replying, "I'd sooner not know for the time being until we get a bit nearer to the birth. What about you?"

"I'd like to know before I'm too big to help with the decorating. When we get a new place, I'd like to decorate the baby's bedroom before the baby's born. We'll need to get a new cot and bedding and lots of baby clothes, I'm so excited," she said.

" I'm excited too," he agreed, through gritted teeth.

Duncan was back at work on the Monday with a renewed sense of vigour, and soon found himself engrossed with the progress of his department. His temporary blip of the preceding week had to be put behind him, and he apologized to Olive Mackay, explaining that he had a lot of personal problems that needed to be dealt with. She said that she understood, and she was glad he was back to his usual self.

In Kirkcaldy, things were about to take a calamitous turn for the worse. The day had started normally with Elizabeth arriving at work ten minutes early and making a cup of coffee to take through to her office. Monday was normally a very busy day, so Elizabeth was surprised that by lunchtime she virtually had nothing left to do. While she was having her lunch, Martin came into the office to ask how her weekend had gone. She explained that she had a quiet weekend and that she had told her husband that he was not welcome in their home anymore and she just wanted to get on with her life. Martin patted her hand, smiling approvingly and said she was doing the right thing.

"Another thing, Martin, I haven't got a great deal to do this afternoon. I seem to be on top of everything, but I don't want to take this afternoon off as I am taking my half day off tomorrow afternoon and me and the girls are playing golf."

"No problem, I'm sure I can find you something to get on with, I'll see you after lunch."

One hour later, Martin came into Elizabeth's office without his jacket and tie. He said, "There's something I've been meaning to do for ages. The stationery cupboard is full of old junk including a typewriter that's not been used in donkey's years. Shall we give it a good tidy up?"

"If that's what you want. You're the boss," she replied.

Moments later, they were alone in the stationery cupboard and Elizabeth in her innocence had forgotten all about the warnings she had received from Verity.

"Where shall we start, Martin?" she asked.

"Let's get rid of that old typewriter first," he replied.

Elizabeth moved over to the shelf where the old typewriter had been stood gathering dust for many years. As she stretched her arms up to get it down, she realized it was just too high and slightly beyond her reach. "I can't quite reach it."

"Let me help you." He said as he positioned himself behind her, trapping her body against the shelves as he reached up over her shoulders towards the typewriter. Elizabeth could feel his warm moist breath passing over her neck, and she began to feel slightly uneasy. As she was trapped between him and the shelves, he too could not reach up on the angle to get the typewriter, and then he slowly shuffled forward even closer to Elizabeth, pushing against her rear until she could feel a hard protuberance pressing firmly against her backside. She stood motionless, traumatized, praying that he would pull himself away, because it was obvious to her that he was already in a state of arousal. She was shocked and horrified and couldn't move. Panic swept over her, like an invisible cloud, and she felt utterly violated. Martin's breathing became much heavier and deeper, and after

233

initially just pressing against her, he then began to rub his member gently up and down against her backside before lowering his arms and taking a breast in each hand, tenderly caressing them in a slow circular movement. For a few seconds, Elizabeth was paralyzed with fear and horror until her natural defence reflexes kicked in and took over. With all her might she swung her right elbow round catching him fully on his upper lip and nose. He jumped back startled and in considerable pain with blood beginning to pour from his nose while he fumbled for his handkerchief to staunch the flow. He already had specks of blood dotted down his white shirt and his trousers.

Elizabeth immediately dashed out of the stationery cupboard sobbing hysterically and went straight to her office, grabbing her coat and handbag before racing through the showroom where the startled salesmen watched with open mouths. Nobody even had time to ask her what the matter was. She climbed into Cuthbert and left the forecourt, vowing never to return.

When she arrived home, she was shaking so she poured herself a large gin and tonic and sat in reflection at how in the space of a few weeks she had been betrayed by her husband and violated by her boss. She wondered what drove Martin to think it was acceptable to abuse her in such a fashion, and if indeed she had given him encouraging signals by letting him hug her and kiss her on the cheek and forehead when she was at a low ebb. She had told him about the split with her husband, but she had not deliberately led him on; but it was patently obvious that he thought the coast was clear for his lustful advances. She was wondering whether she ought to call the police and report the assault, but then she remembered how Fraser had got away with a sexual assault on her daughter, and how that attempted rape had been considerably worse, but was eventually swept under the carpet, so she decided it would be a waste of time.

Later, Alexander and Charlotte were surprised to see their mother home before them until she explained, falsely, that she walked out at work because she was bored with the job and had fallen out with her boss.

The following morning, Alexander and Charlotte had already left home to go to school when the phone rang. Elizabeth answered apprehensively, wondering who it was likely to be. It was Martin, he inquired, "Hello, Elizabeth, are you coming in today?"

Elizabeth was totally flabbergasted, she could not believe his brazen cheek and the manner of his inquiry, "Are you serious? Do you think I'd really come back after what you did yesterday?"

"I'm sorry about that. It was just a misunderstanding on my behalf. I'm sure we can put things behind us and carry on as though nothing happened," Martin grovelled.

"I can't believe what I'm hearing. I can never forgive you for what happened yesterday. I don't think you understand the severity of what you did."

"Well look, I know it's your usual half-day off today, so take the whole day off and have a good think about it, and then please turn up tomorrow morning. We desperately need you here, and if you do come back, I promise it won't happen again and I will raise your salary another one thousand a year. What do you say to that?"

"You don't get it do you? It's not about money, it's about respect. You can't just abuse someone then sweep it under the carpet with an offer of more money. You are lucky that I have not reported it to the police, and I don't think I will ever be able to trust you again."

"Well, see how you feel in the morning. Hope the golf goes well and I sincerely hope we see you tomorrow, Elizabeth."

Martin hung up leaving a bewildered Elizabeth shaking her head and wondering if her blow to his face had completely scrambled his senses.

Later, as the ladies were walking down the first fairway, Elizabeth was telling them everything about the previous day's events. "He's totally lost his marbles; he thinks it's okay to grope and molest me and then beg me to go back with an offer of more money, another one thousand a year."

"The dirty lecherous swine," said Sylvia.

Then Colette said jokingly, "For a thousand pounds, he can squeeze my boobs anytime."

As they were all howling with laughter Bobby said: "Me too. Mind you, I'd want a thousand for each boob."

It was the start of a very enjoyable afternoon for all the ladies, and the laughs continued all the way to the clubhouse. They each ordered a drink and were sitting in the packed bar reflecting on how badly they had all performed after such a long winter's absence, but how good it was to be playing again and in each other's company. Elizabeth had ordered a pint of shandy to quench her considerable thirst, and after she had taken a few sips she saw the ladies' captain Maud Gemmill marching over to their table with a face like thunder and looking as friendly as the grim reaper.

Maud bellowed loudly at Elizabeth, "You've got a damn nerve showing your face in here. You ought to be ashamed of yourself."

Elizabeth stood up and smiled as the rest of the ladies in the clubhouse stopped talking so they could all listen, and everyone's eyes were directed to the table where the girls were sitting. She replied, "I have nothing to be ashamed of so you're barking up the wrong tree, would you mind leaving us so we can finish our drinks in peace?"

It was Sylvia that spoke next: "What are you on about, Maud. You can't just come over here and start insulting people for nothing."

"*Nothing? Nothing!,* That's all you know. She's been flirting with my husband for months, wearing short skirts and low-cut tops with everything on display. She's been leaning over him and rubbing her body against him and now that her husband has left her, she's desperate for a new man. When she tried it on with my husband yesterday, and he rejected her, she hit him in the face. His shirt was ruined with all the blood. She's nothing more than a backstreet slut that belongs in the gutter," said Maud, frothing at the mouth.

Elizabeth looked at her and shook her head. She spoke calmly and effectively: "Maud, I have always considered that you are a truly despicable odious creature. I knew you had a big ego, and you think the world evolves for your benefit, but I never for one minute thought that you were totally, utterly, stupid."

"Stupid? Stupid? It's you that's stupid, if you think anyone will believe the word of a dirty slut like you instead of a respectable man like my husband, who is a pillar of virtue, you're the one who is stupid."

"You haven't got a clue, have you? If he told you black was white, you'd believe him, you bloody halfwit. Go to the showroom and speak to Stuart or Sean or John or any of the other salesmen and ask them why he's called the 'bluebottle.' Go on, ask them, then you'll find out what a lecherous pervert you're married to."

"I don't have to speak to anyone. We've been married for nearly forty years and I know my husband wouldn't touch a slut like you with a bargepole."

"It's probably *because* he's been married to you for forty years that he seeks his perverted pleasure elsewhere." Elizabeth retorted.

Maud then continued her rant about how her husband had tried his best not to besmirch Elizabeth's name by throwing his shirt in the dustbin and saying he had fallen over before finally admitting that he was assaulted by Elizabeth. It was at this point that Elizabeth lost her temper and threw the glass of shandy all over her head. Maud screamed and stood motionless, stunned, and soaked to the skin. Her previously neatly coiffured hair was drenched, hanging in straggles. There was a collective sound of gasps of amazement from the host of ladies before the clubhouse fell silent, silent that is, except for Sylvia who was in fits of hysterical laughter. Bobby and Colette were finding it hard not to join in with Sylvia's infectious laughter, and both had to grit their teeth firmly as their shoulders were pumping up and down. Elizabeth smiled as she picked up her handbag and calmly walked out, closely followed by Sylvia who was still laughing uncontrollably.

When they were outside in the car park, they were joined by Colette and Bobby who both burst out laughing also. They decided not to let the incident spoil their day and they went into the town centre for a drink, whereupon Elizabeth was feted as the hero of the day.

"I wish that I'd have given that sour-faced witch a damn good soaking," said Sylvia.

Bobby added, "Me too. There's nothing that I would have enjoyed more than drenching that swivel-necked cow."

Colette had them all in fits of laughter when she said, "Well, there's one thing for sure, Elizabeth: you can whistle goodbye to that extra thousand now."

As the ladies were all in fits of giggles, Elizabeth reluctantly accepted that Maud would go home and tell her husband Martin how she got drenched. She knew there would be no point in turning up at work in the morning because Maud would have put the knife in for her and demanded her dismissal. She was unhappy that the decision of her leaving would be taken out of her own hands because she had been harbouring the thought of going back into work and demanding that it would be on her own terms. It was out of the question now. "The damage was done" she thought.

In fact, she was wrong: the damage wasn't completely done. On the Friday, she received a letter from the secretary of the golf club informing her that she was to appear before a disciplinary committee at 7.30 pm the following Monday.

In Nottingham, Duncan and Venetia were discussing finances and their future, and they recognized that she would not be able to work for a considerable time after the birth. Also they would have to consider her loss of earnings along with the additional cost of all the items the baby would need. Duncan thought, "Do I really want to go through all this again at my age?" and the stress was getting him down.

They had an uneventful week before resuming looking at properties again the following weekend. Venetia consistently urged Duncan to get in touch with a solicitor to accelerate his divorce or, alternatively, she would be happy if Duncan and Elizabeth agreed on an amicable permanent split so long as the finances were agreed.

She said, "Then we'll know where we stand financially, so we can cut our cloth accordingly."

Duncan tried calling Elizabeth over the weekend, but she was not in a forgiving mood and wouldn't even engage him in a reasonable conversation.

Duncan asked, "Have you told the bairns anything yet?"

"Yes, they now know what a lying, two-timing cheat you are, don't worry about them. I'm looking after them as always. I won't desert them like the lying two-faced rat that you are."

"I haven't deserted them; I've told you before, I would come home like a shot if you will have me back," he begged.

"And I've told you, there's plenty of room in the shed. That's as close as I want you near me."

Duncan was slowly coming to terms with the fact that Elizabeth would never forgive him under any circumstances, and he seriously thought about filing for a divorce. It wasn't what he wanted, but he had brought it upon himself, and he would just have to live with the consequences.

On the Monday evening Elizabeth arrived at the golf club for her expected slap on the wrist by the committee members. When she was admitted into the club president's suite, she was taken aback to see Maud among the seven committee members who were seated in a semi-circle round a large desk. Her first thought was that she was attending a kangaroo court, and she felt a deep sense of foreboding.

It was the club president, Hamish Proctor, who spoke first. "Mrs Baker, you obviously know why you're here. We cannot accept a lowering of behavioural standards either on the golf course or in the clubhouse. I have read several witness statements and a written report from your captain about your assault on Mrs Gemmill last Tuesday afternoon. What have you got to say for yourself?"

Elizabeth replied, "I'm quite surprised that I seem to be the person on trial here. I was sitting quietly with my friends having a drink when Maud came over and started insulting me by calling me all sorts of horrible names. She called me a backstreet slut that belongs in the gutter, among other things."

"Have you got any written witness statements that would corroborate your accusation?" he continued.

"Well, no, I didn't think I'd need anything like that. Ask her. She knows what she said. Look at her, she's even sneering at me now," Elizabeth replied.

"Mrs Baker, we have three independent statements that concur that you and Mrs Gemmill were "having words," but none of them mention about the insults you have stated. Indeed, the written statement from Mrs Gemmill admits that you were having a heated argument, but she cannot remember the content of the argument. The fact remains that you assaulted Mrs Gemmill by throwing your drink over her head in an unprovoked attack. What have you got to say?"

"Yes, I'm not surprised she can't remember calling me a dirty slut. I think it's called selective memory. If you ask any of the ladies who were at the table with me, they will tell you the same. It's her that should be on trial, and, furthermore, if she insults me again she'll get a damn sight worse next time."

It was Maud that spoke next, "Mr President, I have already told you that I tried to be polite and courteous and help her with her problems, but there's no speaking to her at the moment. I feel very sorry for her. Her husband has left her for a much younger woman, and I think she's temporarily unbalanced and going through a very disturbing period in her life. I think we ought to be quite lenient when administering her punishment."

An enraged Elizabeth couldn't keep her temper under control and railed, *"You two-faced lying cow. You said nothing of the sort, and you know it. How could you sit there lying through your teeth?"*

Maud's false show of compassion and tolerance was enough to tip the scales decidedly in her favour and enough for the president to call proceedings to a halt. He asked Elizabeth to wait outside, and they would call her in a few minutes with the results of their findings. As she left the room, Elizabeth could see that Maud had a satisfied smug grin on her face. She received a severe reprimand, a suspension from the golf club for a minimum period of six months and a warning that any further noted incidents involving herself would result in her permanent dismissal from the club. It was a monumental blow. It wouldn't have bothered her so much if it had been through the winter months, but it now meant she would not be able to play again until October when winter was beginning to set in, and she would miss the whole of the summer and autumn. In the last few weeks, she had lost her husband, her job, and now she was suspended from the golf club.

As she was walking out with her head held high, she stopped and turned to look at Maud for a few seconds. Maud could not return the look and she turned her head to look away. Elizabeth smiled, and under her breath she whispered, "Yes, look away you horrible lying cow. One day you'll get what's coming to you."

Elizabeth went home and rang Sylvia to explain what happened, and Sylvia was appalled at Maud's duplicity. She offered to write a statement for the committee explaining exactly what was said, but Elizabeth explained that it would be a waste of time as the whole thing was a stitch-up from the start.

She said, "The committee had written statements presumably from her friends and partners that said they didn't hear her insult me. They didn't tell me that I would need any witness statements and they probably wouldn't believe it now anyway. There's nothing I can do, but one day I'll get even with that lying toad if it's the last thing I do."

It was the start of a very depressing period for Elizabeth, as her children were at school, and she was at home on her own almost constantly. It grated on her enormously as she came to terms with just how much she was missing her job after nearly two years. The employment had given her independence and a high level of self-esteem. Furthermore, it was an occupation she was exceptionally good at, and she derived a great deal of satisfaction from the fact that she had been virtually left alone to do it in her own fashion. She knew she would probably never get a position like that again.

Tuesdays were especially hard for her as her friends would be playing golf without her, and as the weeks dragged on and she was often sitting at home in solitude, she even started to pine for her cheating husband. She cursed him for taking the job in Nottingham. If he hadn't gone to Nottingham, he would never have met that trollop and they would still be together. It was because they split up that Martin got close and affectionate towards her, which ultimately cost her the job, additionally resulting in her temporary ban from the golf club. It all stemmed from his two timing her with his trollop, but she wished he was here now. "I miss him so much." It was strange that she still loved him, but she hated him with a passion at the same time.

Most evenings, Charlotte stayed at home and would sit with her mother to watch TV for a few hours before doing her homework and revising for her exams. She was hoping her mother would give her permission to go away for a week during the Easter holiday for work experience at an animal rescue centre in Angus. Elizabeth agreed while at the same time regretting that the house would be even quieter without her daughter.

During the early part of April, Duncan had given up on any hope of saving his marriage. He stopped phoning Elizabeth completely because he was fed up with all the abuse he received. As Easter approached, he told Venetia that he was going back to Kirkcaldy over the weekend to finally sort his finances out "one way or another."

He said, "If she won't speak over the phone, she'll have to talk to me face to face, I'll drive up early on Saturday morning and then come back on Sunday afternoon."

On the Saturday, Duncan left very early for the 300 mile drive back to his former marital home. He arrived as Elizabeth was in the kitchen making lunch, and he was delighted to see Alexander look out of the lounge window with a broad smile on his face as he arrived.

Alexander called out to his mother, "Mum, dad's home."

"What does he want?" Elizabeth shouted.

"I don't know, ask him yourself." Alexander replied.

Elizabeth came through to the front door. She could see that Duncan was very tired from the long drive, "I suppose you'd better come in; you look shattered."

Duncan thanked Elizabeth, and even before they sat down, Alexander went to his room so they could talk in private.

Duncan spoke first, "It's nice to see you both again, Elizabeth. Sandy seems to get bigger every time I see him. Where's Lottie?"

"You've just missed her. She's gone away earlier this morning on a work-experience week. It's at an animal rescue centre in Angus. She will not be home until next Friday. Anyway, you haven't come all this way to ask about the bairns. If you actually cared for them, you could ring them after school and talk to them yourself, if you can be bothered. What do you want?"

Duncan was shocked at the aggressiveness in his wife's demeanour. However he replied after a moment to recover his composure, "Elizabeth, we need to talk, and I'm hoping we can sort things out amicably between ourselves. For a start, if you want a divorce, I will not fight it. You can sue for adultery which I will freely admit. I will give you her name and make it as easy as I can for you. Secondly, we need to talk about the financial situation. It's a mess as you are probably aware. I don't want a protracted court case where the lawyers bleed us dry and we're left with virtually nothing after they've taken their spoils, so I'm hoping we can come to an agreement. As you know, we still have four more years left on the mortgage, but I think we could pay that off now with our deposit account and still have a decent bit left. Then there's the house, half of which is mine. Then I've got to consider that my salary is paid into our joint current account, and I need to stop that arrangement because my situation has changed now as we are having to look for somewhere bigger to live. You might as well know: Venetia and I are expecting a baby. It's due in early November, and I cannot continue paying for this house if we get divorced. That's why I want to pay off the mortgage so at least that's settled. What do you think?"

There was a long silence, Elizabeth couldn't think straight. She was shocked by the news that her husband was to be a father again with another woman. She was heartbroken. The reality hit her that now there would be no chance of their re-conciliation. She was also aware that he would not know that she was now unemployed and would be relying on his salary until she found another job, if indeed she could find alternate employment.

Elizabeth spoke sarcastically through gritted teeth, "I suppose I must offer my congratulations to you both."

It was at this point that Elizabeth burst out crying. It was all too much for her; she couldn't contain her sorrow and sobbed her heart out. Duncan got up and went over to offer a consoling hand, but Elizabeth said bluntly, "Get off. Don't ever touch me again."

Duncan sat back down as Elizabeth regained her composure and continued, "All you've spoken about is what *you* want. You care nothing for me and the bairns. Are you even aware that without your salary being paid into our joint account we will have nothing? I'm unemployed now, on the scrap heap. The only thing I have left is the children, and I don't suppose you want to see them starve, do you?"

"I'm sorry, Elizabeth. I didn't know you'd lost your job. How did that happen?"

"He was another man who had no respect for me and thought he could abuse me and do as he pleased. He got a busted nose for his troubles, the dirty, filthy, lecherous swine."

"I'm sorry to hear that. That puts a different slant on things."

"To make matters worse, his wife has got me suspended for six months from the golf club, now I have no husband, no employment, no money, no social life, but don't you worry, just shuffle off back to your little love-nest with your whore. We'll get by even if I have to go out on the streets and sell my body," she said cynically leaving Duncan feeling completely numb.

"Well, we are going to have to work something out, Lizzie. I'll nip into town and look for somewhere to stay tonight and then pop over and see Jack McKinlay. I'll come back later. Have a think about it."

"There's no need for that. Stay here in Charlotte's room if it's only one night," she said.

Duncan left Elizabeth to visit Jack which would enable her to digest all of the options available to them, but every option she could think of had drawbacks.

Duncan arrived at the bungalow in Dysart and was appalled to see Jack looking so frail. They spoke for an hour before Duncan left after making feeble excuses regarding meeting his wife. He was very upset at seeing Jack's skeletal appearance.

After he returned, Elizabeth told him she did not want a divorce until after the mortgage was paid in full, which she would try to sort out on Monday. She would go to the building society and pay off the remaining mortgage out of their savings. As she had no current source of income, Duncan agreed to keep his existing salary going into their joint current account for the family to live on, but only for the time being he stressed, as he and Venetia were looking for a place of their own and would have to take out a mortgage. He generously told her that as far as he was concerned, she could have the house. If they ever divorced, he would not seek his share of it. It was a great relief to Elizabeth to know that at least she would still have a roof over her head, especially for the sake of the children.

Duncan also agreed: "After the mortgage is paid up, you can also keep what's left in the deposit account. It'll help as a start for when the bairns go to university. You are probably going to have to get yourself another job though, Lizzie, and yes, I do know it won't be easy. There's nothing round here."

Elizabeth showed him the local paper and he noticed that her former job was being advertised at the car showrooms.

He said, " I'm so sorry it ended up like that for you."

"Yes, so am I. It's one disappointment after another for me these days, all caused by you cheating on me."

Later, after Duncan had a shower, Elizabeth made him some dinner, which he didn't expect. He was pleased that they were at least on speaking terms. He kept looking at Elizabeth during the evening while they were watching TV and he felt very sorry for her. During the twenty-one months since he had been working and living away from home, she appeared to have aged disproportionately. She looked vulnerable and downtrodden, and he knew that it was his fault and he hoped that he could protect her from any more disasters that would heap misery on her. He thought it was ironically tragic that the main reason he had left to work in Nottingham was their need for a bigger salary to finance the children's further education, and now it was likely that he would soon be receiving a windfall from the estate of Jack McKinlay.

When Duncan returned to Nottingham the following day, he told Venetia that he and Elizabeth had agreed on their financial affairs and would not be having a divorce for the time being. Venetia was just happy that they were making progress. However, she insisted that because he had forfeited the house he must stop paying into their joint account where most of the money was being spent for his ex-family's welfare.

She continued, "We need to start saving for a deposit for our own house. Either that, or look for a bigger rental with at least two bedrooms and a garden. You are too soft, Duncan; we've got to start thinking of ourselves and our own future."

DESPAIR

Charlotte had three good reasons for enjoying the work experience at the animal rescue centre. It was the first time she had travelled on her own and stayed in accommodation by herself and she really enjoyed the independence and adult experience. Secondly, the work dispelled any doubts that she may have had about her ability to work with sick and injured animals: she excelled and thrived where several other students fell by the wayside and dropped out as it was too harrowing for them. But most of all, she met a boy whom she was instantly attracted to. He was seventeen and lived in Carnoustie, and he was also a vegetarian. He was quiet, well mannered, intelligent, well-built and extremely handsome once he had taken off his glasses. Everyone called him Clark because he was a doppelganger for the mild-mannered reporter Clark Kent in the superman films and his initials were C K, but his real name was Campbell.

He'd always wanted to work with animals, but his real love was rugby union where he played as a centre when wearing contact lenses. As he and Charlotte were both of a similar quiet nature, it came as no surprise that they always worked together as a team. Charlotte was overjoyed at the end of the week as they swapped phone numbers and addresses and promised to keep in touch. Campbell drove an old mini car and he gave Charlotte a lift to the train station on the Friday afternoon. There they kissed for the very first time.

Elizabeth was delighted to see Charlotte so happy when she arrived home after the Easter holiday. She had sorely missed her company, and she had spent far too many hours miserably brooding in solitude, with the gin bottle her only companion.

As the weeks passed by slowly towards Whitsun, Elizabeth's loneliness escalated as Alexander and Charlotte were spending many hours revising in their rooms for their exams in June and July.

In May Elizabeth received an official-looking letter addressed to Duncan from solicitors Cottam and Serella which she was afraid to open. Five days later, Duncan called her to ask how they all were and she told him about the letter. He asked Elizabeth to open it and read it to him and he was distraught to hear that Jack McKinlay had passed away in April, and, according to the will, Duncan was the sole beneficiary of the estate, which included the bungalow and all its possessions and a post office savings account. Elizabeth gave Duncan the details so he could get in touch with the solicitors. Later, as he was telling Venetia all the news, he was annoyed that he didn't know about Jack any earlier because he had probably missed the funeral. He hurriedly booked two days holiday for the following week so he would be back in Kirkcaldy on the Wednesday night and have two days to try and sort out what to do with the bungalow and Jack's possessions.

After catching the evening flight, he arrived home on the Wednesday night and collected the letter from Elizabeth before she told him he could sleep on the sofa for one night. Tomorrow he would get the keys to the bungalow from the solicitor's office and then he could stay there.

By the Friday afternoon, Duncan had resolved all his business. The bungalow was to be sold by estate agents Mills and Glover with a proviso that if not sold in eight weeks it would go to auction. The furniture was collected by a local charity and the phone and television licences were cancelled along with Jack's pension. He went back to Kirkcaldy in order to catch the train to Edinburgh, but realized he would be much too late for the evening flight back to East Midlands Airport, so he decided to call back at his former home to say goodbye to Elizabeth and the children. He explained, "I've missed the flight this evening, so I'll look for accommodation for tonight and leave early in the morning to get to the airport."

"You might as well stay here as waste money in a hotel, I'll get up early and give you a lift to the airport," said Elizabeth.

"Will you? That's really good of you. I don't deserve it for how I've treated you."

"No, you bloody don't," Elizabeth said.

Elizabeth made him a meal and they then spent a few hours browsing the photograph albums that Duncan collected from Dysart. Elizabeth was amazed at how skinny Duncan was as a child, as on many of the older photographs on the beach his ribs were prominent.

For the first time in months they enjoyed each other's company, but by ten o'clock Elizabeth said they ought to call it a day as they had to be up very early in the morning. She made him a bed up on the sofa and bade him goodnight before going up to bed. Alexander and Charlotte had stayed in all night and were in their respective rooms, politely leaving their parents to be alone, and Elizabeth tapped on their doors and said goodnight.

As she crawled into bed, Elizabeth knew she wouldn't get to sleep. She lay awake wondering if she had been at fault for causing her husband to stray and look for another woman. She tortured herself for refusing his first proposal of leaving Nottingham and coming home for a second chance; she now regretted it more than anything in her life. She was hoping that he would be brave enough to creep upstairs and chance his luck to see if he was welcome in the marital bed. She applied her most alluring perfume and donned her flimsiest negligee whilst considering going downstairs to invite him to join her. After much deliberation, she finally lost her nerve, as she was frightened of being rejected, especially if he saw her as a poor substitute to his new younger girlfriend. She sobbed for hours, soaking her pillow.

Meanwhile, Duncan was lying on the sofa with his eyes wide open unaware of his wife's frustration. He remembered all the happy times they had together building their home, and he desperately wanted to go upstairs to be with her; just to hold her; just to feel her breath and her warmth and cuddle up to her. The thought of sharing her bed once more caused a thrill of excitement and he was trying to build up the courage to sneak up to her room. Suddenly, he recalled her previous comments of her taking a knife to him, and he waking up minus a few body parts. It made him shudder. Ultimately the sofa didn't seem such a bad option.

The next morning, back in Nottingham, Venetia was delighted when Duncan was telling her all about his affairs over the last few days and the expected windfall of money he would be receiving. To Duncan, it appeared she was more interested and excited about the amount of money he would receive and didn't show any sympathy for the passing of his foster parent.

She said, "With a bit of luck there'll be enough money for a proper house with a garden."

A statement that took him by surprise. For the first time, he saw her in a different light, and he was not impressed, but he decided that in her excitement she wasn't thinking properly.

One Monday late in May, Elizabeth was shopping for new underwear in the big department store in Kirkcaldy town centre. She had selected two new bras and five pairs of pants and was browsing along the handbag shelves when she spotted her hated nemesis from the golf club looking in the jewellery section. Maud was wearing sunglasses and she had a big brown leather holdall bag draped over her left shoulder. She had her back to Elizabeth and didn't see her coming as Elizabeth walked over briskly in her direction. Where the inspiration came from, Elizabeth never understood; it just happened, spontaneously. As she passed behind Maud's back, she gently dropped two pairs of pants out of her basket into Maud's holdall and casually walked away unnoticed. She stood for a moment hiding behind a pillar, watching to see if Maud noticed anything unusual, but she was not aware of her extra baggage. Elizabeth then approached a shop assistant who was carrying a walkie-talkie.

"Excuse me, I've just seen a lady over there and I think she's stealing. She's carrying a basket, but she has put some items straight in her bag. She's in the jewellery section. She's wearing sunglasses and a blue cardigan. She has a big brown holdall on her shoulder."

"Thank you, madam. I'll let security know straight away. They'll wait until she's outside before they challenge her, so please don't go anywhere near her and unsettle her."

Elizabeth had no intention of alarming her. She quickly made her way to the checkout and paid for her remaining items before waiting outside to see the fun. It was fifteen minutes later when Maud came out of the shop, and she hadn't walked more than ten paces when two security men caught up with her.

"Excuse me, madam. We would like to check the contents of your bag as we have reason to believe that you have items that have not been paid for," said the tallest security man.

"I beg your pardon," Maud replied indignantly, "Who do you think you're talking to? Don't you know who I am? Get your hands off."

The security men persevered and threatened to call the police unless she went back inside with them to the manager's office. At this point, Elizabeth approached them and walked by looking at Maud before she said in a very sarcastic tone, "Hello, Maud. Having a spot of bother are you?"

Maud's face was beetroot red as she was escorted back inside the store mouthing oaths and curses that she would sue the shop for every penny they had. Elizabeth was ecstatic. It was the best thing that had happened to her in this awful year. Her day improved considerably when twenty minutes later a police car arrived and Maud was arrested for shoplifting. Later that evening, Elizabeth called Sylvia to tell her about Maud's disgrace and her own satisfactory role in the vendetta.

She said to Sylvia, "I bet she won't show her ugly face at golf tomorrow. I'd love to be a fly on the wall when she's trying to explain it to her husband. It felt good to get my own back on the lying cow."

Sylvia was howling with laughter and said that she wished she could have been there to see it happen, "I'm glad you brought her down a peg or two," she continued, "Elizabeth, on Thursday it's May 28th, and it will be exactly five years since I lost my husband. Do you fancy going out, just the two of us, and we can paint the town red just like we did in the old days when we were daft young students?"

"Of course, it'll be fun," agreed Elizabeth.

They decided to have an Italian meal and Sylvia booked a table as both ladies were very excited and looking forward to the evening.

On the same Monday, Venetia experienced a dreadful bout of morning sickness and her supervisor sent her home at lunchtime. Amongst her mail was a letter from HMP Wakefield simply addressed to Venetia. She had to read it twice to digest it as she could not believe the content. The letter was from her ex-boyfriend informing her that he was up before the parole board in July, and he was desperately hoping for an early release as he was missing her tremendously, and he hoped they would be together soon if he was granted an early release. The letter was full of misleading platitudes, stating that he was now a reformed character, and it contained lots of sentimental flannel vowing his undying love, obviously intended to impress the prison officers who would monitor the mail. She had sent him a letter years ago saying she wanted to get on with her life and their relationship was over; furthermore, he probably wouldn't know she was expecting a child with another man. She couldn't understand how he had the audacity to think that they would be able to continue a courtship after so long an absence. She could almost believe it was a joke or a wind-up if it wasn't for the official prison stamp on the envelope.

She had to sit down, immediately as her sickness escalated. Duncan came in five hours later and she was still sitting in her chair, looking pale and feeling decidedly light-headed. She told Duncan about the letter while reassuring him that he was the man she wanted to spend the rest of her life with, not a jailbird who thinks he could come and go as he pleased. Venetia felt too ill to eat, so Duncan made himself some dinner before they sat together discussing their future. He explained that he should have the money from Jack McKinlay's estate soon, probably no later than August if the bungalow went to auction, and they would be able to look for a new home then.

The following day, Venetia went back to work after a broken night's sleep deeply worried about the letter and her ex-boyfriend. She was hoping that his parole would be rejected, and she wondered if it was wise to send him another letter telling him that she was now in a relationship with another man, and she was pregnant. She was aware that the letter would be monitored, and it might influence the outcome of his meeting with the parole board. Her mind was in total disarray, and she was struggling to think straight, and unfortunately as a result of her light-headedness and fatigue, she carelessly tripped down a small flight of stairs.

She was taken to hospital where fortunately nothing was found badly broken, but she had several cuts and severe bruising along with a dislocated shoulder. Worst of all, she lost the baby. She broke down crying hysterically when she was told of the miscarriage, begging them to fetch Duncan who was unaware of proceedings. Eventually the hospital contacted Duncan via the company switchboard, and he left work immediately to go straight to the hospital. Venetia was in a lot of pain after her shoulder had been re-set, but the pain was nothing compared to the anguish of losing her child.

When she saw Duncan, she wailed, "I'm sorry. I'm sorry, it was a boy. It's my fault, I'm sorry"

Duncan tried hard to reassure her that there would be plenty of time for them in the future to raise a family, but Venetia was utterly heartbroken. She repeatedly said, "it was her own fault, and she shouldn't have gone in to work as she didn't feel too good earlier in the morning and would he forgive her?"

"There's nothing to forgive. It was an accident." Duncan said.

Venetia was kept in hospital under observation for two days and was taken home in an ambulance on the Thursday.

On the very same day that Venetia was discharged, Elizabeth and Sylvia went out in Kirkcaldy to try and relive their youth. They had a meal with a pleasant bottle of Rioja, and then set off to visit as many pubs and bars as they could manage before closing time. Eventually, they were both roaring drunk after mixing wine with gin and tonics. After the pubs closed, they had to hold each other up while singing and giggling, and they slowly managed to walk back to Elizabeth's house where Elizabeth made them a nightcap of coffee with brandy. The ladies were maudlin drunk and talked for over an hour about their past and the men who had been a monumental part of their lives.

Elizabeth told Sylvia, "I still love him, but I hate him at the same time. I should have forgiven him and took him back when I had the chance and he begged me, but I wasn't ready then. I wish I had swallowed my pride and took him back though. It's too late now, his new trollop is pregnant."

After their second nightcap, Sylvia tried to stand up saying she had to call a taxi to make her way home. Elizabeth suggested she stay for the night and save a taxi fare and she would give her a lift home in the morning. Sylvia said she could sleep in the chair or on the sofa, but Elizabeth replied that there was plenty of room for them both in her king-sized bed. As they went upstairs giggling and making lots of noise, Charlotte awoke and came out onto the landing to assist them into the bathroom and then to the bedroom.

She said indignantly, "Mum, get in bed and sleep it off. God knows what you'll both be like in the morning."

What happened next was never meant to happen. It wasn't planned or pre-conceived. It wasn't normal behaviour for either of them, but it happened. It started innocently enough, as Elizabeth leaned over and gave Sylvia a good night kiss on the cheek, as she had done previously with her husband thousands of times. But with the alcohol undermining their inhibitions, they were soon spontaneously engrossed in a passionate kiss. The next ninety minutes were spent engaged in activities that neither lady thought they would ever experience. After their animalistic carnal lust was finally sated, they fell asleep in each other's arms as tiredness and the vice-like grip of alcohol held the upper hand.

As Elizabeth awoke the next morning, Sylvia was already putting on her clothes. Slowly, the realisation of what befell the night before swept over her like a filthy black cloud and she could barely speak with the shock.

"Oh God, Sylvia. *What were* we doing last night? I'm so sorry, it shouldn't have happened."

"I'm sorry too. I feel dirty. I've always loved you, Elizabeth, but not in that way. I'm disgusted with myself, especially as it was on the anniversary of my husband's death. I'll never be able to look at myself in a mirror ever again."

"Don't rush off, Sylvia. The kids will be at school now so I'll make us a coffee and I'll give you a lift home if you want."

"No, I want to go home and have a shower. I feel disgusting. The walk will do me good." Sylvia said forcibly.

Slowly, more events of the previous night came trickling back into Elizabeth's memory. She could still taste the femininity of her best friend, and after she had taken two paracetamols and drunk several cups of coffee, she went upstairs for a shower in the futile hope that if she scrubbed herself clean it may erase the memory of the events of the night before. As she was about to step in the shower, she looked in the mirror and noticed three strategically placed love bites close to her intimate parts. It was then that she remembered the silly game of dare they were playing as to who could place a love bite nearest to the bullseye on the other. The memory of it all gave her a nauseous feeling inside and she tried to be sick in the toilet bowl, without success.

Things deteriorated for Elizabeth as Charlotte arrived home from school and walked straight past her without even speaking while giving her a stare of utter contempt.

Elizabeth asked, "Hi, Lottie. Have you had a good day?"

"How could you? I'm ashamed of you. No wonder dad doesn't come home anymore."

"Charlotte... sweetheart... what are you talking about?"

"You know what I'm talking about, You two, behaving like a pair of bitches in heat. It was bad enough when you woke me up with all that noise, but when I came in to ask you to be quiet your bedroom door was wide open, and I saw you both... *at it*... You're disgusting."

"No, we weren't doing anything like that. We were just playing. We had far too much to drink last night," Elizabeth said.

"Don't lie to me. I know what I saw. I'm ashamed of you. What will dad say when I tell him?"

"Charlotte, please don't say anything. We were drunk, that's all. It was a mistake; I promise it'll never happen again. Please don't tell your dad, or Sandy," begged Elizabeth.

Charlotte walked away shaking her head and went to her bedroom. Fortunately for Elizabeth, Alexander had been soundly asleep the previous night and was unaware of the night's events, so he at least was still talking to his mother.

Elizabeth was so sad that she cried herself to sleep night after night. She wondered what she had done wrong to deserve all of this, and if it was possible for life to get any worse.

It was on the following Thursday, that Elizabeth found out that life *could* get worse... *considerably* worse. It started with a knock on the door after her children had left to go to school. There was a policeman and a policewoman who were waiting patiently.

Once inside, the officers advised Elizabeth to sit down, then the policewoman delivered the devastating news. Her friend Sylvia appeared to have taken her own life, possibly sometime over the weekend. The alarm was raised by a neighbour, who noticed that the lights and the television were on all day and all night, so something must have been wrong. It appeared Sylvia had taken an overdose and passed away alone, sitting in a chair. She had left two letters, one for a brother in Canada and the other for Elizabeth, which the officers had brought to her. Elizabeth broke down, tears cascading down her face. She tried to speak, but words wouldn't come out. She feebly rose from the chair, and then her legs folded as the saturation of trauma caused her to faint, and she hit her head on the corner of the coffee table.

PC Rice immediately rang for an ambulance as Elizabeth had a bad cut on her scalp that would require medical assistance as WPC Fleming staunched the flow of blood with a tea towel.

Elizabeth was taken to hospital where she had seven stitches inserted in the wound. She was left with a very nasty headache, but

Doctor Tiler tried to reassure her, saying that the stitches would heal the cut, and on removal, the small scar would be unnoticeable as it would be under her hairline. Her ghostly white face never even flinched as he spoke. Her eyes were glazed, staring into a vast void of dark emptiness. She didn't hear a word that was spoken. All Elizabeth could think of was Sylvia, her friend, her pillar, her rock, Why?

Alexander and Charlotte arrived home from school and Charlotte found the letter on the floor in the lounge and the blood stains on the carpet. Elizabeth's car was still parked outside the house, and she began to panic. She called Alexander downstairs and they were just discussing whether to call the police when their phone rang. It was Elizabeth calling from the hospital. Alexander picked up the receiver and his mother told him about the fall. "But I'm okay, I've had a few stitches and the doctor said I could be discharged when he does his late round. I'm hoping to be home soon. I'll get a taxi."

Charlotte had the letter in her hands and wondered if she ought to read it. Alexander urged her to read it aloud so they both knew the contents and then put it back on the floor exactly where she found it. The letter said,

"Dearest Elizabeth, by the time you read this letter I hope to be re-united in another world with my Hector. The five years since he departed this terrible world have been a living hell for me, made only bearable by your truly wonderful loyal friendship. The days we have spent on the golf course during this bleak period are the only times I've been truly happy, and nobody could have had a better friend than you have been for me. I cherished our days at university together and the many scrapes and adventures we had together. I sincerely hope that you and Duncan get back together. You were made for each other in the same mould that me and my Hector were made to be together. I can't live without him, I've tried, but he was my life. Please don't be sad at my passing. At least I will be away from all the misery and suffering in this horrible cruel world. I hope in the future that me and my Hector can look down on you from Heaven as you and Duncan are back together again. God bless you, Elizabeth. I dearly loved you, always. You are a truly wonderful person. Sylvia XXX."

Alexander took a deep breath and sighed heavily before telling a tearful Charlotte, "Put it down and let's forget we ever read it. If mum wants us to know what it's all about then it's up to her to tell us. Anyway, what do you reckon we ought to do about dinner?"

In Nottingham, while Duncan was playing the waiting game for Jack McKinlay's estate to be resolved, he was totally unaware of the proceedings back In Kirkcaldy. He had problems of his own as Venetia had been feeling very depressed since the miscarriage, which had slightly taken the edge off his fulfilment with their relationship.

After the miscarriage, she took a week off work, which appeared to have a contrary effect on her wellbeing as it caused the depression to escalate. Duncan was very caring and sympathetic to her vulnerability, but he sometimes felt that he was becoming more of a father figure than a lover.

At Whitsun, Duncan decided to ask Venetia if they ought to consider getting engaged now. He loved her passionately, and he was happy to push for a divorce if Elizabeth would consent and clear the path for them. Venetia was overjoyed, and threw her arms round him, saying yes. He would arrange to go home this coming weekend and sort it out one way or another whether with or without Elizabeth's approval. He would also call at the estate agents to see if there was any news on the sale of the bungalow and also visit his friend Karel.

Fortunately, he was able to book a day's holiday at short notice, so on the Friday morning he took Venetia to work and then set off on the long drive to Kirkcaldy. He arrived at his former home just as Alexander was about to go out for the evening.

Alexander said, "Hi, dad. I didn't know you were home this weekend. Before you go in, can we have a word, in private?"

Alexander then brought him up to date with all the news of Sylvia's suicide and Elizabeth's accident.

He explained, "Whatever you do, don't give her a hard time. She's in a very bad place right now. She's like a zombie. Her face is devoid of any feeling and her eyes just stare into nothing. I'm worried about her. I dread to think of what she'll be like at the funeral. It's next week on Tuesday."

Duncan couldn't believe it. He had known Sylvia well, and was very sad to hear of her passing. He was worried for his wife as he was aware of the effect it would have on her, and he knew that this would not be the time to talk about a divorce. He cursed himself for not phoning beforehand, as he knew that it had been a wasted journey.

His apprehension was confirmed when he saw Elizabeth a few minutes later. He was shocked to see the extent of her malaise. She was wearing some old tattered gardening clothes and her hair was a bedraggled mess. He knew then that his son was not exaggerating.

He said softly, "Hello, Elizabeth. I've come home to see how you are. I've heard about Sylvia. I'm so sorry for you."

Elizabeth looked up with expressionless eyes and said nothing, then moments later she muttered quietly, "You ought to be sorry. It's all your fault. Get out, and don't come back."

Duncan should have known better, but he continued, "But, Elizabeth. We have lots to talk about. We have something that needs to be sorted out one way or another."

Elizabeth's eyes were filled with hate as she rose from the chair, "*Get out, get out of my house, it's your fault.*" She screamed hysterically as she looked round for something to use as a weapon.

At this point Alexander came into the lounge and said, "I think you'd better go, dad; mum needs to rest."

Duncan left the house to go and find accommodation and later he was reflecting on the earlier events of the evening. He couldn't understand how Elizabeth was blaming him for Sylvia's suicide. He hoped that she would be more reasonable in the morning, as he would try again tomorrow.

However, Elizabeth's mind was set: it was all his fault. In her opinion, if Duncan had been at home where he belonged, then Sylvia would not have had the opportunity to share a bed with Elizabeth, and their night of drunken shame would not have happened. Elizabeth's distorted mind was convinced that the events of that night contributed enormously to Sylvia's decision to end her life. It was down to him; it was all his fault. There would be no convincing her otherwise.

The next morning Duncan called at the estate agents and was disappointed to hear that although there had been several viewings, there hadn't been any concrete offers for the purchase of the bungalow. Things became considerably worse as Elizabeth refused to let him into the house, and he could only exchange pitiful conversation with her through his daughter who was acting as a go-between. He reluctantly concluded that he would have to seek the services of a solicitor, and when he told Charlotte to "tell her that," Charlotte burst out in tears, crying, "Don't do that, dad. Surely there's a way you can both sort things out properly. Can't it wait until after Sylvia's funeral?"

"I came all this way to sort it out this weekend. Tell her that the next time she sees me will be in the divorce court unless she's reasonable and allows us to talk like adults," he said.

Moments later, a tearful Charlotte came back to the door and shook her head, "Sorry. She's got nothing to say."

Duncan gave his daughter a hug on the doorstep, before setting off back to Nottingham regretting his wasted journey. Seven hours driving gave him a lot of time to reflect on the events of the last two years. He understood and sympathized with how Elizabeth was feeling, especially with the loss of her best friend, but he couldn't accept that it was his fault, and concluded that Elizabeth was becoming deranged. However, he still had strong feelings for her, and he was very distressed to see the deterioration in her wellbeing.

Venetia was delighted he returned a day earlier than planned. She told him that she had received another letter from the prison also containing the same exaggerated claptrap as her ex boyfriend's first letter, and she concluded he was pulling out all the stops to convince the prison authorities of his reformed character, but nevertheless, she would ignore it.

Unfortunately, it was on the next Monday evening that something happened she could not ignore, nor was she likely to forget. She walked to the supermarket to get some milk, and as she left the store, she was followed by two men who stopped her when she was nearly back at the flat.

One of the men said menacingly, "He's heard that you've got a new bloke staying with you. He doesn't want anything to hinder his chances of parole, so you'd better get rid of him, now, *or else!*"

"Or else what?" She replied, visibly shaking.

"Just get rid. I'll leave it to your imagination if you don't," he said threateningly.

Venetia was ghostly white as she arrived back at the flat and explained to Duncan what had just happened,

He said reassuringly, "There's nothing to be afraid of. Bullies like him don't scare me. There's nothing he can do while he's still in prison. If he does get parole, we'll cross that bridge when we come to it. Anyway, when I get the money from Jack's estate, we can move somewhere else and get a place of our own instead of paying rent on this flat. There's something else I've decided. I'm going to inform Elizabeth that I will stop having my salary paid into the joint bank account with her. I will then pay a reasonable amount as my support towards the children's welfare. It's her fault if she can't be bothered to discuss it like proper adults."

Duncan decided not to tell Elizabeth until after Sylvia's funeral. At the burial, Elizabeth was heartbroken to see such a pitiful number of mourners, and she was reminded of her own father's sparsely attended service. Her friends Colette and Bobby and a few neighbours had also made the effort, but the woeful number of attendees added to Elizabeth's misery. Later that evening, Elizabeth was looking at old photographs of when she and Sylvia were students, and the tears were cascading down her cheeks and dripping off her chin onto her lap. She remembered those days as among the happiest of her life.

The following evening, as Elizabeth was still embroiled in her throes of misery, Duncan phoned her after work to inform her that he was cancelling his salary from being paid into their joint account. Henceforth, his salary would be paid into his own individual account, but he would then pay sixty pounds a week into the joint account towards the welfare of the children.

Elizabeth was devastated, she screamed, *"That's not enough. How are we going to live on that measly amount?"*

He replied, "I tried to be reasonable with you, but last weekend you wouldn't even speak to me. I've given you the house, I've said you can have what's left in both bank accounts, but now I've got to start thinking of my own future, and Venetia and I are hoping to get a place of our own. I think I have been very generous as it is by giving you the house and our money."

"How long do you think the money will last? In six months we'll have nothing left. How could you? What are we going to live on then? Do you want me out on the streets selling myself?"

"It needn't come to that. Look for another job, and try not to lose it next time," said Duncan, before instantly regretting his choice of words.

"You horrible swine, I hate you." Elizabeth slammed the receiver down and went straight to the drinks cabinet to find solace in the gin. She told Charlotte and Alexander all about their father's wicked meanness as they were eating dinner. It was a surreptitious attempt to turn them against him, and it left them confused as he had always been very reasonable with them, and ultimately he would not see them suffer or go short.

Later that day, Charlotte privately whispered to Alexander, "That doesn't sound like dad. It looks like we can forget about them ever getting back together now."

On the Friday morning, Elizabeth rallied herself to leave the house and walk into the town, just to get some fresh air and look for any bargains that were on sale. She was not looking for anything in particular, and there was nothing that was needed desperately; she just wanted to get out of the house.

She never understood why it happened, she couldn't even remember how, and it certainly wasn't planned. But when she arrived back at home later in the afternoon, she opened her handbag to find that she had concealed a plethora of stolen items. Namely a bottle of eau-de-cologne, three eyebrow pencils, a tube of lipstick, a wand of mascara and a pallet of eye make-up. She was totally perplexed. She looked at the spoils as they were spread out on her bed and realized that she had inadvertently put them in her bag without paying for them. Horrified, she pulled out a suitcase from under the bed before concealing the stolen items in the suitcase and returning it back under the bed. She sat down on the bed wondering how and why it had happened and what to do next. The lipstick wasn't even her usual favourite colour, but she suddenly mustered a slight smile for the first time in many months, and she felt a warm glow of contentment. That night she managed to go to sleep without soaking her pillow with tears, and she would visit the department store on four more occasions over the following days with a similar result.

She was beginning to amass quite a horde of stolen items, many that she neither wanted nor even needed, until the inevitable occurred. She was apprehended after leaving the store without paying for a quantity of make-up items and underwear, and she was subsequently arrested. Ironically, it was the same two police officers who had arrested Maud, and they couldn't understand why Elizabeth was smiling when she was arrested. She didn't deny the accusations of theft or show any concern whatsoever. Later they were talking to the desk sergeant and said that it was almost as if she had been happy to be arrested, without a care in the World.

Alexander and Charlotte were horrified when their mother casually told them that she had been charged with shoplifting and would be appearing in court. They were due to start taking their exams shortly, and they didn't need the worry of their mother going to court.

On the Friday evening, Charlotte was very concerned what to do over the weekend. She had previously arranged to see Campbell on the Saturday morning as he had planned to come to Kirkcaldy to meet her family and take her out for the day. She was desperate to see him, but she didn't want him to know about her mother's disgrace. He phoned her on the Friday evening to confirm the following day, and after a difficult conversation, she eventually relented and told him everything about her mother and father splitting up, her mother losing her job, then her friend's suicide and her mother's arrest. Campbell told her he would speak to his father for advice and still see her in the morning anyway as *she* had nothing to be ashamed of. Charlotte was unaware that Campbell's father was a Queen's Counsellor. When Campbell arrived on the Saturday morning, he spoke privately to Charlotte outside in his car.

"My father says that it sounds like your mother is likely to be experiencing a very traumatic, unsettling period in her life that may have temporary affected her stability of mind. He said that he has seen this type of scenario before, and it is usually a desperate cry for help, a way of gaining attention when the whole world seems against you. He will write a statement on your mother's behalf to hand to the court and hopefully she will be treated leniently and with compassion."

Charlotte smothered him with kisses, thanking him and his father for their genuine concern.

After Charlotte had introduced Campbell to Elizabeth, she told her mother that Campbell's father would assist her by writing a letter to the court, but Elizabeth just shrugged her shoulders in a meaningless gesture of apathy.

Campbell was shocked by her indifference and explained it to his father the following day.

He said, "According to Charlotte, she's totally changed in the last few months. She's got hollow eyes that just stare into space as if there's no feeling. She needs help in my opinion."

As Campbell's father was a highly respected QC, his letter to the Justice of the Peace Court carried a lot of influence, and the case was concluded with Elizabeth receiving an absolute discharge, as a prosecution was not in the public interest. She was advised to seek meaningful professional help, and as Charlotte had returned all the stolen property, the matter was closed.

Unfortunately, an overeager reporter from the local evening newspaper had access to the court's findings, and the proceedings were reported on the inside pages of the evening newspaper the day before Charlotte and Alexander were due to take their first exam. It was unnecessary and irresponsible in Charlotte's eyes, as she was to find out the next morning when she arrived at school. She was in the school playground talking with Rebecca when several other boys and girls surrounded her and started saying nasty things about her mother.

One spiteful boy said sneeringly, "What's it like having a thieving bitch for a mother?"

All the other children were laughing with many poking fun at Charlotte until Alexander suddenly appeared out of nowhere and grabbed the boy by the scruff of his neck. He spun him round and delivered a mighty blow which dislocated the boy's jaw and knocked out three teeth, spreadeagling him on the floor. It had the effect of silencing the crowd immediately. It was a foolish mistake. Ten minutes later, as the ambulance arrived to take the stricken boy to hospital, Alexander was escorted by his class teacher Mr Whare to the head's office where Mr Hart told him to sit and wait outside until after the school assembly.

He said, "Baker, wait there and reflect on the futility of your own stupidity. I will deal with you after the assembly."

Alexander had an awful feeling that he knew what was coming. Thirty minutes later, he was standing facing a tearful Mr Hart as the verdict was declared: "Alexander, you leave me with no other option. Despite all your hard work over the last two terms, I'm afraid that you will be sent home immediately, and very likely permanently excluded from this school. It is a crying shame that someone as intelligent and hard-working as yourself can throw it all away with an act of senseless violence. There is no excuse. I feel that as your headmaster I have failed you in my duties of care and diligence for all pupils. We must both share the burden of your failure."

Alexander had expected to hear the same verdict and it came as no surprise.

He said to Mister Hart, "If it's any consolation, sir, I don't want you to feel as though any of this is down to you or the school. It doesn't matter who it is; if I hear anyone calling my mother after all she's been through, I'll do exactly the same again."

Alexander picked up his satchel and walked out of the school never to return. His permanent exclusion was confirmed by letter a week later. When he arrived home from school, he was shocked to find his mother already drinking gin and tonic very early in the morning. He explained that he had been sent home for fighting, but didn't tell her it was because someone was haranguing Charlotte and calling her mother wicked names.

Elizabeth was staring at her gin tumbler; she spoke casually with no feeling or sentiment in her voice, "Ah well, put the kettle on and make yourself some breakfast. There's plenty of toast."

RESOLUTION

In Beeston, Venetia's predicament was deteriorating as the weeks in July elapsed. First, an envelope containing extremely violent threats was pushed through her letterbox with a vivid description of how much damage a razor-sharp knife can do to a man's face. She received another letter from her ex-boyfriend stating that his parole had been confirmed, and he would be released on Monday August 3rd. She was mortified. How could he take it for granted she would want him back? She knew he was using her as a pawn in his campaign for an early release, or was he? Would he leave her alone once he was out of prison and let her get on with her life? She couldn't be sure either way, so she came up with an idea that she hoped would solve her dilemma. As she loved Duncan passionately, she didn't want any harm to come to him, but she thought it would be safer if he wasn't in the flat for a while until after the release date. If her ex-boyfriend showed no interest in her when he was released, then the path was clear for Duncan to return. He didn't like it one bit, but succumbed to Venetia's wishes and moved back into the B&B.

As July ended, Charlotte had completed her exams and broken up from school for the summer holiday. She spent much of her free time with Campbell, and although she was very wary of how her previous relationship with Fraser had ultimately soured, she felt comfortable and safe in Campbell's presence. He felt the same way about Charlotte. He couldn't abide loud brashy self-opiniated girls and Charlotte was the exact opposite. He took her to meet his family on the first weekend in August, and his parents were delighted that their son had met such an amiable and polite young lady. When Campbell took Charlotte back home, he was kissing her goodnight and Charlotte felt happier than she had ever felt before. Two years earlier, she had thought she had been in love with Fraser, but she now realized that that was just a teenage crush, and this was completely different.

As she went indoors, she looked at her mother who was sitting half asleep, drunk, sodden with gin, and her brother who was staring blankly at the television and despaired at the state of them. She shook her head before going to her room without speaking.

The following morning, Charlotte berated her mother, telling her it was about time she pulled herself together and stopped feeling sorry for herself, and, although Elizabeth was very embarrassed at being spoken to in that manner, she was immensely proud of her daughter's maturity. After two hours of heart-searching conversation, Charlotte acknowledged that her mother was distraught because she hadn't taken her father back when she had the opportunity, and the ensuing events compounded the misery, especially the suicide of her dearest friend. One thing Charlotte knew for certain was although her mother wanted Duncan back desperately, she was finding it hard to swallow her pride and forgive him.

Charlotte was also very concerned for her brother. Since his expulsion from school, he would spend most of his time in his bedroom playing a violent video game. Otherwise he would sit silently and watch the television before shuffling off to bed without speaking. She tried in vain to speak to him on the Sunday morning, but he completely ignored her and continued shooting monsters in his video game.

On Monday August 3rd Venetia came home from work to find her unwanted ex-boyfriend stood waiting at the door, carrying a cheap bunch of flowers obviously bought from a local garage as a last-minute thought. She couldn't believe his nerve that he thought he could just turn up and walk straight back into her life. When she told him that she had already sent him a letter years ago explaining she wanted to get on with her life without him, he denied that he ever received it. He went into a pre-rehearsed monologue telling her in detail how he had changed his ways and how he accepted that his previous way of life was wrong and how he was thankful that the authorities had given him another opportunity to atone for his sins. Finally, he gently lowered his voice to a whisper as he swore his eternal love and gratitude for her, especially for patiently waiting for him. She suspected it was all a sham. She knew that his parole would very likely be monitored and he probably wanted to give the impression of being in a stable relationship. Reluctantly, she invited him into the flat as she didn't want to continue the conversation in the doorway.

Once inside she said, "That letter I sent you; how do you expect me to believe that you didn't get it, and what about the threats telling me to get rid of my new fella?"

"I don't know anything about a letter. Perhaps the warders read it and kept it from me. There's a lot of suicide in the pokey when men find out their girlfriends have left them, particularly if there is another man involved. I don't know anything about threats. How could I when I've been locked up? That's nothing to do with me," he replied.

"You must think I'm stupid. I'm sorry, but I think it's better if we go our separate ways."

"Venetia, please give me another chance. I'll make it up to you. Let's go out for a meal tomorrow night, anywhere you want. We can have a long chat and see how you feel then."

"Okay, just this once. I'll book a table for seven thirty at the Italian restaurant on the High Street. Meet me outside, and now I'd like you to leave please."

Venetia met Duncan in the company canteen on the Tuesday and told him what was happening and that she was hoping to have her ex out of her life completely by the weekend.

Later that evening, Duncan went out of the B&B down to the river and casually strolled down to Beeston Weir enjoying the sunshine and watching the barges going through the locks. He went into the riverside bar for a drink, and upon leaving, he became aware of three men who appeared to be following the same route. He was unaware they were stalking him. When he was walking back through the nature reserve, he was suddenly attacked and dragged into the undergrowth by the three men, who punched and kicked him into unconsciousness before leaving him hidden under a pile of shrubbery.

It was almost dark before a dog walker heard his pitiful groans and raised the alarm. He was taken to hospital and the police were informed of the attack. He had a scan in the morning that thankfully didn't show any permanent damage to his brain or skull but his aching body was a mass of cuts and bruises, and he was in severe pain with morphine being administered to ease his suffering.

He remained in hospital under observation for two more days. Venetia was completely unaware of the assault when she looked for him on the Wednesday lunchtime, and she assumed he was working through his lunchbreak, which he had often done previously.

On the Wednesday afternoon, he was interviewed by WPC's Harewood and Black and he informed them of the threats that Venetia had recently received. They spoke to Venetia later that day and told her about the attack and that Duncan was still in hospital, but he was okay and would be discharged tomorrow. Venetia was shocked. She knew straight away why it had happened, and the fact that her ex had a pre-arranged alibi as they were dining together made her feel sick inside. She could imagine him thinking, "if I can't have her, nobody else will have her." She adored Duncan, but she was now beginning to fear for his life. She knew things would get worse and possibly result in his death or permanent disfigurement. She told the officers all about the threats and who she thought instigated the attack, but he had a cast-iron alibi and he was safe from further interrogation. The assault was recorded as a random attack by unknown assailants.

Duncan was discharged on the Thursday afternoon, and as he was totally unfit for work, he decided to drive back to Scotland on the Friday. After taking several breaks to rest his aching body, he didn't arrive in Kirkcaldy until the evening, and he booked into a hotel for the night. The next morning, he phoned his former home and spoke to Charlotte who was expecting a call from Campbell.

"Hello, sweetheart. Tell your mum I'll be over later to see you all. I'm going to the estate agents first to see if there's any progress. I'm looking forward to seeing you all, but be prepared. My face is a bit of a mess, I was attacked and badly beaten up on Tuesday, but I'm okay. See you shortly."

It was good news at the estate agents as they had received a concrete offer from a viewing the previous day. It was slightly under the original asking price, but Duncan said he was happy to accept it.

Ten minutes later, he arrived at his former home before tentatively knocking on the door. In her excitement, Charlotte threw her arms around him as she opened the door, making him recoil in pain. She was horrified at the swelling and bruising on his face which gave him an awful hideous appearance.

"Oh, I'm so sorry, dad. I never thought," she apologized.

"It's okay, sweetheart. Is your mum at home?" he asked with a painful grimace.

"She's in the kitchen. Come in, dad. I'm glad I've seen you because Campbell should be here any minute and we are going out for the day. He's coming all the way from Carnoustie."

Duncan went into the lounge and Charlotte hailed her mother from the kitchen. Elizabeth's first comment when she saw him was, "Sit down you idiot before you fall down."

Duncan was relieved to see Elizabeth was more like her usual self and he was thrilled to see she had not lost her ability to put him down. They talked amiably for half an hour until another knock at the door heralded the arrival of Campbell. Charlotte was keen to introduce him to her father, but what he thought when he saw Duncan's bruised and battered face was anyone's guess. Duncan was very impressed with his daughter's new boyfriend and shook his hand before he and Charlotte went out for the day. Duncan sat down to continue his conversation with Elizabeth, and he felt sure she was looking at him with sorrow in her eyes because of his injuries.

He continued, "He looks a nice boy. He's a big lad, he's very polite and well-mannered and Charlotte seems smitten by him. They'll hopefully make a lovely couple one day." As soon as he said those words, he instantly regretted it, but it was too late.

Elizabeth answered bitterly, "We were a lovely couple once upon a day, until you spoiled it by skulking off with your new whore. I worshipped you, and I had loads of opportunities in the past to go with other men and cheat on you, but because I loved you so much, I was never interested. I would have died for you, but then you ditched me for a younger girl at the first opportunity. You'll never know how much I loved you, how much I still love you, but I hate you at the same time for what you have done to me."

Duncan knew he had made an enormous mistake with his choice of conversation and immediately tried to change the subject. He inquired, "Where's Sandy. Is he at home?"

"He's in his room, probably killing monsters on his computer."

Duncan was allowed to go upstairs and see his son; he was very disappointed to see that Alexander preferred to be alone.

"Hello, Sandy. How are you?"

"How do you think? I lost the only woman I'm ever likely to love, I can't play football again, I'm not able to swim in a straight line, and now I've been expelled from school even before I took any exams, so *you* tell *me* dad, how things are."

"It's no use spending all your time up here sulking, Sandy. You need to get out there and make something out of your life."

"My life's already over, it's not worth a bent penny now. Close the door on your way out."

Duncan went back downstairs deeply saddened at the apathy displayed by his son. When he was talking again with Elizabeth, she said, "Well, what did you expect? Did you think we would put the welcome mat out for you and all of us have a jolly day out? Get real, Duncan, some of us have had our lives ruined."

"I'm so sorry, Elizabeth. I'll go back to the hotel now. Do you mind if I call in tomorrow morning before I drive back to Nottingham?"

Elizabeth nodded assent and Duncan went back to his hotel knowing that his son needed renewed inspiration to get on with his life. He was relieved that Elizabeth was at least talking to him again, although it was hardly in a civil manner. He was very delighted with Charlotte's progress, particularly as Elizabeth had told him about her excellent results and grades. After a quiet evening reading, he went back to see his family in the morning.

Charlotte noticed the car pull up outside and came out to meet him in a rush, she said. "After I came home last night, I had a long talk with my mum. She really regrets wasting the opportunity of letting you come back and she's missing you like crazy. She blames herself for it getting to the stage where it looks like you'll end up getting divorced. It's the last thing she wants, she wants you back, but she doesn't know how to go about it. Don't let on I've said anything though, dad."

Duncan talked to Elizabeth and Charlotte for two hours during which time he hoped that she would instigate talk of the possibility of them patching things up and getting back together. Unbeknown to him, she was thinking exactly the same, waiting for him to make the first move. It was like a game of chess that was drawing to an inevitable stalemate. Before he left, Duncan went upstairs to see Alexander and say his farewells. Alexander was playing his video game again and barely managed to turn his head slightly to mumble goodbye. Duncan was visibly upset when he came downstairs again and made another comment regarding his son's apathy to Elizabeth.

She snapped back at him harshly, "If he had a father that actually cared for him and took him in hand, he wouldn't be like that."

An embarrassed Duncan bade his farewells and kissed his daughter on the cheek before slowly walking to the lounge doorway. He turned round and said, "Goodbye, Elizabeth. I'm so sorry about everything. I still love you, I always will."

As he walked down the footpath, Elizabeth looked out of the window and muttered under her breath, "Yes, and I still love you, God knows why? But I will always love you."

Duncan began his long drive back to Nottingham, as Elizabeth was only two hours away from having her whole world crash down around her feet. As she was eating her lunch, she heard the very loud screeching of brakes so she looked out of the window. Two police cars had pulled up outside the house and half a dozen officers were rushing to the front and back of the house. As she reached the front door there was a loud banging from an over-enthusiastic officer.

"All right, all right. I'm coming. What are you trying to do, knock the door off its hinges?"

"Excuse me, madam. I'm WPC Lydia Crowe. We are looking for Alexander Baker. Is he at home?" We'd like to ask him a few questions.

"Yes, wait there. I'll get him for you," said a worried Elizabeth. She went upstairs and said to Alexander, "The police are here and want to speak to you. Are you in any trouble?"

Alexander quietly put on his trainers and slowly walked to the stairs before repeatedly saying, "Sorry, mum. I'm sorry."

He went downstairs and walked straight out between two waiting officers, and was directed into the back of one of the cars with an officer on either side of him. As the car pulled away, a distraught Elizabeth demanded to know what was happening and the two remaining officers asked her to sit down.

"We want to talk to Alexander to ascertain if he has any connection with the death of Fraser Burley. Fraser's body was found about midnight on Friday night. It appears he had been attacked. We are aware that there is a history of violence and threats between them which resulted in a physical assault two years ago. I think it may be wise for you to contact a solicitor."

"Oh God, how can I call a solicitor on a Sunday. Why didn't you come a few hours ago when his father was here? Why is everything going wrong? Oh God, help me?"

Elizabeth broke down hysterically crying on her knees praying that it was all a dream. One of the constables tried to reassure her. "There will be counsel for Alexander at the station, but you may wish to get your own solicitor tomorrow morning."

While under interrogation, Alexander freely admitted that he alone was responsible for beating Fraser to death. He had knocked him down initially with his fists and then punched and kicked him until he finally stopped moving and twitching. He said, "I'm not sorry at all. That bastard ruined my life and he tried to rape my sister."

Inspector Collier then asked, "Alexander, had you previously planned to attack Fraser, or was it just a spur-of-the-moment assault?"

Alexander admitted. "I'd thought about it before, but I hadn't planned it. I spotted him walking home on his own on Friday night, so I thought, 'What the hell?' Once I started, I couldn't stop."

By the time Elizabeth had regained her composure sufficiently enough to drive to the police station, Alexander had already convinced the officers that he alone was responsible for the attack. She was told that he would certainly not be coming home today and would be facing a very serious charge. Elizabeth broke down again in the police station, and had to be given assistance to get home with her car.

After she had returned, she had the unenviable task of telling Charlotte what had happened, and they both fell into each other's arms crying. Later, at seven o'clock in the evening, the phone rang, and Elizabeth rushed over to answer it, desperately hoping that it was Duncan so she could tell him exactly what had happened. She was shocked to hear the voice of Martin Gemmill on the line.

Martin said, "Elizabeth, are you currently employed? If not, we would love to see you come back to work. We have missed you. We have tried several agency secretaries, but they haven't got a clue, and I end up doing everything myself. I'm due to break up for a two-week holiday next Friday and I can't trust anyone, I didn't realize how indispensable you were. Look, I know we had a bit of a fall-out, but I forgive you, and if you come back, I will give you a big rise. What do you think of that?"

"You *forgive* me...? You *FORGIVE* me!...Are you insane? ... You ask what do I think? ... I think any woman who's daft enough to let a pervert like you grope and drool all over them wants her bloody head examining. You can take your offer and stick it up your arse, although a pervert like you might enjoy that."

Elizabeth slammed down the receiver in anger. Her head was spinning in a whirlwind of confusion, and she went straight to the drinks cabinet. Her thoughts were that at least if she was drunk, things couldn't seem any worse.

The following week was a traumatic hell for Elizabeth as she spiralled further into an abyss of bewilderment and depression. She was informed that Alexander would likely be facing a manslaughter charge, although Fraser's parents were pressing for a murder charge. She appointed a solicitor who was not overly optimistic about Alexander's chances of avoiding a murder charge as he had admitted on his statement that he had previously thought about killing Fraser.

He said, "We will have our work cut out keeping it down to a manslaughter charge, but in his favour, he has admitted his guilt and with the previous history between the two of them it's possible he may be looked upon leniently and get away with a less severe sentence. But I must warn you, Elizabeth: he will receive a severe custodial sentence, of that there is no doubt."

Duncan was back at work on the Monday morning still feeling very sore. The staff in his department were all nudging each other and pointing at him as his badly bruised face became the topic of the day's gossip. He wasn't meant to hear Jack Fairclough say, "Look at him, that's what comes of messing with another man's wife."

Duncan casually walked over and said, "Jack, you are sadly mistaken, this is what happens when you stick your nose in other people's business, I suggest you get on with your work if you don't want to end up looking like this." He knew it was not a nice thing to say, but he felt much better for saying it, and it had the desired effect.

At lunchtime in the works canteen, he met Venetia for the first time in what seemed an eternity, but it was only six days. She told him that her ex was still pleading with her for them to get back together, but it was possible he was gradually coming to terms with the fact that it wouldn't happen. "If we leave it for another few weeks, he will probably have given up by then and we can get back to normal."

"I hope so, I'm as full as a butcher's dog and I can't wait to get to grips with you again," a frustrated Duncan stressed.

"So am I. He's going away this weekend to Skegness with a load of his cronies. You can come round on Saturday, and on Sunday if you can still stand up ," she teased provocatively.

Duncan's workload kept him very busy all week as it was the holiday season, and many of the employees were taking their annual vacations. He was unaware of Alexander's arrest, and Charlotte was frantically trying to get in touch with him to tell him what had happened. She didn't know the name of the company where he was employed or the name of the B&B where he was staying, however after going through one of his coats, she found a receipt for the B&B and asked the landlady to tell her father to call her urgently.

He rang her on the Wednesday evening, and Charlotte told him all about Alexander's arrest.

She said, "There's something else, dad. It's mum. She sits there staring like a zombie. She doesn't talk, she drinks too much, she's miles away. I don't know what to do. I think she needs help, but there's not much I can do."

Duncan promised to come home on Friday evening to see if he could help her. He also promised to phone Charlotte every evening from now on so she could keep him informed of events.

Venetia was not happy when they met on the Thursday in the canteen, when he explained that he was going back to Scotland at the weekend, but she completely understood the reasons why.

Duncan had begun walking to work and back from the B&B as it was just as quick as queueing in the traffic at the gate, and also it was additional exercise. On the Friday after work he walked back to the B&B to collect his car for the trip home. It was then he realized the full extent of the spiteful vendetta being waged against him. All four tyres on the car were flat, they had been slashed. He needed a set of brand new tyres and it was 5.15 pm. He tried everywhere, but he couldn't find a garage to come out at such a short notice. The best offer he had was from a garage that promised to be there in the morning. He was desolate. He phoned Charlotte and told her that he "had serious problems with the car," and he wouldn't be able to make it home. Charlotte was devastated, as it was she that was bearing the brunt of her mother's melancholy malaise.

Duncan went to the police station to report that his tyres had been slashed, but he felt that it was a waste of time because they didn't seem remotely interested and just gave him a crime number so he could call his insurance company.

The following lunchtime as he wrote a cheque for the new tyres and the call-out fee, he was feeling dreadfully homesick, but it was far too late now to think about going home. At least he had the compensation of going to see Venetia again, but he had reached the end of his tether with England.

His temper was stretched beyond the limit on the Sunday morning as he came out of the B&B and looked at his car. Someone had poured paint-stripper all over the roof and the bonnet, probably sometime during the night. The car looked absolutely hideous. He was appalled, especially with the pitiful response he received when reporting the crime at the police station again for the second time

The desk sergeant explained. "With no witnesses and no CCTV there's not a lot we can do. I'm sorry, sir."

Duncan went to Venetia's flat to tell her the news, and she was horrified. She knew her ex was conveniently in Skegness and out of the way of suspicion, but she also knew that it would have been some of his gang members that were the cause of the damage. She went to the kitchen to make Duncan a cup of tea, and while waiting for the kettle to boil, she made a drastic decision. She loved Duncan passionately, but she was becoming increasingly scared for his future. She knew they wouldn't stop, and he was likely to end up dead.

She returned to the lounge, before tearfully saying, "Duncan, this is a nightmare. They won't stop, I know it. I have this terrible feeling that one day they will cripple you or kill you, I would hate anything to happen to you. I've never loved anyone as much as you, but I think it might be better if we finish and you get out of this town and as far away as possible, somewhere where they can't find you. I'm sorry, but I think it's safer for you that way."

Duncan was absolutely dumbstruck; he couldn't take it all in. He was contemplating what to say or what to do, but he couldn't think of anything.

When he regained his composure he said, "Are you sure? Is that what you *really* want?"

"No, it's not what I want, but it's the only answer. I think it's better if you go now. I want my last memory of you to be when we were in bed together yesterday. That was wonderful. I don't want to see you in a wheelchair or a coffin, please go, before it's too late"

Duncan stood up and momentarily moved towards her to give her a kiss goodbye, but he stopped as he understood she was right, it *was* time to go. He walked back to the B&B with tears welling in his misty eyes. He had loved Venetia. She was beautiful and made him feel special. However, now it was over and it was time to go.

He looked through the yellow pages and found a B&B in West Bridgford that had vacancies. He packed his bags and left straight away, pleased that nobody would know where he and his car would be overnight, and that no more vandalism would be done to it, or him.

While sitting in his new bedroom on the Sunday night, Duncan decided he would hand in his notice on the Monday morning and go back to Kirkcaldy to try and rescue what was left of his shattered marriage. He would beg and plead on his knees if that was necessary. He had been cruel and deceitful to his faithful wife, and she deserved better. She also needed help and support, especially now with their son's imminent imprisonment. He would find out in the morning what the minimum notice period would be that he would have to serve before leaving to go home if she would have him. If not, he would sleep in the shed, or even on the doorstep until she relented.

He went straight to see Jospeh Wignall on the Monday morning to tell him of his decision. Jospeh already knew about the severe beating, but he was shocked to hear about the threats, the tyre slashing and the paint stripper.

Duncan continued, "I need to get away before it's too late. I'm afraid they might find my new accommodation. It's a pity because I love this job, it's the best position I've ever had, and I thank you for the opportunity. But I don't think you have to worry about my department, Des Pearce is an able and competent ready-made replacement. He has worked tirelessly as my understudy, and I would have no hesitation in recommending him to take over. I could spend time going through the ropes with him but there's not much he doesn't know already."

"Thank you for your service with the company, Baker. It's a shame it has to end like this. Normally we would expect a month's notice, but in light of recent events, I will clear the path for you to leave on Friday, if that's what you really want."

"Yes sir. Thank you for everything."

" I wish you all the very best in the future, Baker, good luck."

Elizabeth had an appointment with her doctor on the Monday morning, and Dr Birtles prescribed her a course of tranquillisers for her shredded nerves. Charlotte was with her and promised Dr Birtles that she would make sure that her mother stuck to the course. On their way home, Elizabeth complained bitterly that she wouldn't take them and end up turning into an addict.

An official letter was on the doormat when they arrived home, confirming that Alexander was due to appear in court for a preliminary hearing on Monday the 14th of September. The letter had a significant effect on Elizabeth completely overwhelming her with the enormity of Alexander's crime. Charlotte urged her to take her first dose of tablets, but they ended up having a blazing argument, with Elizabeth becoming hysterical. It was during the height of Elizabeth's raging tantrum that the phone rang. The call was for Elizabeth. It was Martin Gemmill.

He said, "Elizabeth, don't hang up. Hear me out, I understand your anger when I called recently, but I want you to reconsider. I should have been in Portugal now, but I can't go as I can't leave the business in anyone else's hands. I have just sent the fifth agency secretary packing as she was useless. Look, I will double my offer of a wage rise and give you another two thousand pounds a year, and give you back-pay for the months you have missed. I can't say fairer than that can I? Please say you'll come back, please, I'm begging you."

"You just don't understand, do you? Nobody will ever abuse me again, nobody! Is that clear? Now leave me alone!"

"But, Elizabeth, we are …."

His words were cut short as Elizabeth threw the phone and receiver against the wall, smashing it beyond repair.

Charlotte was appalled, she said, "Mum, what are you doing? We need a new phone now."

"I don't care. It'll stop that pervert from calling me. Perhaps he'll get the message now."

"Yes, but how can dad call me every evening, or Campbell call me? I'm supposed to be seeing him tomorrow and he was due to call me tonight to make arrangements. I was going to tell dad about the date of the trial tonight as well. Your doctor's right, you need to take something to calm you down, and I don't mean gin either."

Elizabeth shrugged her shoulders with a meaningless gesture of apology. Charlotte stormed upstairs to her bedroom, contemplating that much more of her mother's similar behaviour would leave them both needing tranquillisers.

Later that evening Charlotte went out with a pocketful of change to look for a payphone that hadn't been vandalized. She called Campbell and explained that their phone was broken and they made arrangements for the following day. Then she tried to call her father at the B&B in Beeston, but the landlady explained he had left suddenly the day before with no forwarding address. She was frustrated, as she desperately wanted to speak to him, and, ironically, half an hour later, her father was trying to ring her without success. He also tried ringing through the operator, but she informed him that there was a problem at the other end, and she couldn't help him.

On the Tuesday morning, Charlotte was ready and waiting very elegantly dressed for her day out with Campbell.

Elizabeth inquired in a caustic aggressive tone, "Where the hell are you going?"

"Campbell's picking me up and we're going out for the day. You'll be alright, won't you?"

Another argument ensued with an enraged Elizabeth ranting, "Oh, I see, so you think more of your boyfriend than you do of me. Everyone else has left me so you might as well clear off. I don't need anyone, but be warned: he'll break your heart like your dad broke mine. They're all the same once they get what they want."

"Don't be ridiculous, mother. Campbell's not like that, and I'll tell you something: he's never tried to lay one finger on me yet, not once, but if he did, I wouldn't stop him. I have a life of my own, and I love you with all my heart, but I'm not permanently staying here as your skivvy."

On the way to Edinburgh, Charlotte was excited to hear that Campbell had acquired two tickets for the International Arts Festival held annually every August. She told him about the argument with her furious mother, and she was impressed by his level of compassionate understanding saying she ought not to be so harsh with her mother.

After Campbell had taken Charlotte home later that day, he returned home to Carnoustie overjoyed at his choice of girlfriend. He told his father on the Wednesday morning, "I'm very fond of Charlotte. She's very polite, well-spoken, intelligent and full of personality. I'm taking her out again on Friday for another day at the Arts Festival and I'm thinking of asking her if she wants to get engaged."

"*Engaged?* You've only known her for five minutes," said a stunned parent.

"Yes, father, but I'll be going back to High School in September, and then I'll be studying for my degrees, and what with playing rugby on Saturdays, I won't have much time to see her. I was thinking if we did get engaged then I stand less chance of losing her. She's everything I want in a woman."

"*Woman, woman?* She's only a chit of a girl. She's lovely I admit, but have you given it enough thought? Look at her family! Her father clears off to England and takes up with a woman half his age, her mother gets arrested for shoplifting and is now a gin-sodden neurotic mess and her brother's in prison pending a murder charge. They're hardly the most stable family unit are they?"

"Charlotte has been a pillar of strength for her mother. She might only be sixteen, but she's mature beyond her years. And another thing, she's as pure as driven snow and I love her."

"Well, it's your choice. You're old enough to think for yourself. I hope things turn out well for you both."

On the same Wednesday, Elizabeth received an invoice from her solicitor explaining his astronomical costs to date and she flew into an uncontrollable rage. Yet again, it was Charlotte who bore the brunt of her anger. Elizabeth complained bitterly that the whole world was conspiring against her, and Charlotte tried very hard but was unable to soothe her mother's anguish. They had another argument after lunch, because Elizabeth had not ordered a new phone and Charlotte was desperate to be able to speak to Campbell as often as possible. She was also aware that it was possible her father might be trying to call them, which, of course, he was. He had tried for the last two evenings, and on the Wednesday, he was frustrated yet again. He then thought of sending a letter, but appreciated it wouldn't be worth it, as he would likely be back before it arrived. So, he decided, it was "wait until Friday night and head off home and hope for the best."

On the Thursday, Duncan was in the company canteen eating his lunch. He had not seen Venetia since their split and he was coming to terms with their parting. Halfway through his meal, his attention was broken as Venetia sat down at his table in order to speak to him.

She said, "I'm glad I've caught you, Duncan. Please don't say anything, but I'm leaving tomorrow. Nobody here knows, so please don't tell anyone."

"You're leaving? Where, why, how?" he asked.

"After you left me at the flat last Sunday, I was writing in my diary, and I noticed the date and it reminded me it was my aunt Daphne May's birthday. We've always been close. She has a wicked sense of humour. Anyway I'm glad I rang her as it was her fortieth birthday. Furthermore, I was telling her about how fed up I was losing you, and about that control freak who won't leave me alone, and she said why don't I leave and come and work for her? She is the CEO of a big finance and investment company in London. She has offered me a job in the Accounts Department. When I then asked her about getting accommodation, she said I could stay with her in her flat. She's got a penthouse apartment in St John's Wood, three bedrooms all en-suite. I couldn't believe it. The salary is four thousand a year better than my salary now, and when I asked her about rent, she just said pay me the same as you are paying now. Apparently, it's only about ten minutes travel on the tube train to her office, so I'm leaving tomorrow. Nobody knows, only you. There's a train to London from Beeston station at five minutes past ten in the morning and I've booked a seat, first class."

"Is she married, or has she got any family?" he asked.

"Er no, she's not remotely interested in men, she's more interested in women, but she won't bother me as she knows I'm not like that as you well know. We get along well though. She's funny, and very kind. Although I did hear that she runs the company with a rod of iron. She also told me that there are some quite dishy men who work there "if you like that sort of thing."

Duncan smiled. He was delighted to see that her future would be safe and prosperous away from Beeston, but he was sad it was time to say farewell to her for the last time. She stretched her arms across the table, and they held hands while his dinner went cold. They were the only two people in the canteen when eventually Venetia stood up and said she ought to go back and she leaned over to kiss him goodbye. She said, "It's such a relief to know that creep will be out of my life for good. And another thing: you're twice the man he ever was, either in or out of bed."

Duncan smiled semi-contently as she walked to the exit. He watched her all the way to the door before abandoning his cold meal and going back to work. While walking back to his office, he realized that he hadn't told Venetia he was leaving too.

On the Thursday morning, Elizabeth received another official-looking letter. Horrified, she didn't open it and hurriedly threw it in a drawer in the lounge sideboard. In her anxiety, she hadn't noticed it was addressed to Mr Baker and not Mrs Baker. The letter was from the solicitors dealing with the estate of Jack McKinlay, and it contained a bill of charges and fees and the final account invoice with a cheque made payable to Duncan Baker for £37,802.00.

Elizabeth was in a foul mood and tried to vent her anger on Charlotte after she returned from a local shopping trip in Kirkcaldy.

She screamed, "I see you've been splashing money out on clothes again; I've got bills coming in left right and centre and all you think about is tarting yourself up for your boyfriend."

"That's not fair, mother. I've saved this money since my birthday and I needed a new top. You're horrible sometimes. If I had anywhere else to go, I would pack up and leave. And I'm not joking. You're becoming a dreadful person."

Charlotte stormed out of the room, leaving Elizabeth bitterly regretting her latest outburst and sobbing heavily into a sodden tissue.

Tempers did not improve between them as Charlotte was up early on the Friday morning to get showered and dressed for another day in Edinburgh with Campbell. As Elizabeth came downstairs and saw her daughter attractively dressed up and wearing a touch of make-up, she knew instantly she would be left on her own again.

She inquired, "Where the hell are you off to again? Don't you ever think of me, stuck in this house on my own?"

"I'm going out with Campbell, to the Edinburgh Arts Festival. And for your information, if he wants to book a hotel and he wants to sleep with me, I won't be back."

Charlotte stormed outside to wait for Campbell, leaving Elizabeth agog with shock. Charlotte had never spoken to her in that manner, and it compounded her existing depression. For months she had been spiralling into a dark void of despair, but now she had finally reached the absolute nadir of desolation and sat crying for hours. She was wailing repeatedly, "What has happened to my family? Why has Sylvia left me? What is wrong with me? Am I such a monster that nobody loves me anymore? I can't stand it anymore." Once again she reached for the bottle of gin.

Duncan arrived for the final day of his notice feeling excited about going back home to Scotland after work. It was tinged with a degree of sadness because he had enjoyed his employment with all the trappings and responsibility of senior management, and he was sorry at the thought of never seeing Venetia again. However, at 9.30am he decided, "What the hell. They can't sack me now anyway," so he told Des Pearce to "hold the fort" while he walked down to the train station. He was standing on Platform 2 at 9.50am when Venetia appeared carrying two suitcases. She was surprised yet delighted to see him as she did not expect him to come and see her departure.

They stood hugging each other tightly for five minutes before Duncan said, "I suppose if this was a classic Hollywood love film, I'd get on the train with you, and we would leave together holding hands and live happily ever after. But I know that you are excited about your move to London and coming this far south was a bit too far for me. There's something I didn't tell you yesterday, I should have done. I'm also leaving today; I have been serving my notice this week and I'm going back to Scotland tonight. My daughter, bless her, told me recently that Elizabeth is missing me and is hoping that we get back together. She needs me and I'm going back to try and patch up my marriage. But I'll never forget you; I loved you from the very first moment we ... well, you know what I mean. I will never forget you."

"You talk too much," said Venetia as she turned her head to give him a long passionate kiss. Their lips were glued together with their arms holding each other tight until they could hear the rumble of the train approaching.

"It's here now. Let me carry your bags," said Duncan and he scuttled down the platform to find the first-class carriage and held Venetia's hand as she boarded. He then lifted her suitcases into the carriage. Venetia was standing by the door, and they were blowing each other kisses as the train slowly pulled away. Duncan watched it accelerate into the distance towards Attenborough until it was just a tiny speck on the horizon, and then there was nothing.

Charlotte and Campbell were approaching Edinburgh, excited by the list of artists who were programmed to appear today. Campbell explained that from September he would be studying for the higher level degrees which he needed to pass to go to Veterinary College. He would also be playing rugby on Saturdays through the winter, but he hoped to see her as often as possible. She felt the same way about Campbell and she would also be studying for her exams.

He plucked up the courage and asked her, "I'm glad you feel the same way. Would it be presumptuous if I bought you an eternity ring as a token of our feelings for one another?"

"You can buy me anything you like; I love you and I would marry you today if we could."

"Well then, shall we skip round the eternity ring and get engaged?" Campbell asked as he took a deep gulp.

"Yes, yes. I've never been so happy." Charlotte replied.

The couple spent a wonderful day in Edinburgh at the festival holding hands most of the time when they were not kissing. It was a day Charlotte wanted never to end.

It was completely different for her brother, who was writing a letter to his mother telling her not to worry about him as he was okay, although he was masking the truth. He hadn't anticipated the sheer horror of being in prison on remand at such a young age. The bullying came as a shock, the drug barons were constantly intimidating him to buy their wares, either with sexual favours or hard cash. There were a lot of hard prisoners who wanted to put the young upstart in his place and show him he was nothing. The food was appalling. There was a permanent acrid stench of urine in the air, and the night times were a living Hell with many disturbed men screaming and shouting through the night, making sleep almost impossible. He couldn't tell his mother about any of that. Not that it would have made any difference to her. She was beyond help. She had suffered so much heartache, her spirit was utterly broken and her will to live had disappeared. Even her own daughter had turned against her, and she had nothing left but a miserable life of debt and loneliness. Why should she carry on?

Duncan sat in his office in deep reflection of events of the last two years. Although he had been in love with Venetia, he realized that it was stupid to think that she was worth wrecking his marriage. He adored his wife and children, and was excited to be finally going home. He didn't expect Elizabeth to welcome him back with open arms, but he would do whatever it took to rescue his marriage as Charlotte had already told him that Elizabeth now wanted him back. He finally realized that the grass is not always greener on the other side, and he cursed his own stupidity. He would grovel, plead, beg, or crawl on his knees to be accepted back in the family fold.

He had a surprise as he was tidying his desk when Olive Mackay knocked on his door. She had a very big "Sorry you're leaving" card which all the staff in the department had signed.

She said, "I wish you all the best for the future, although I admit, I had my doubts about you when you first took over. However, you proved me wrong. This department runs like clockwork, which is testimony to your managerial skills. Good luck in your next venture."

One by one, all the departmental staff came in to shake his hand and wish him "bon voyage" and good luck for the future which gave him a great feeling of contentment.

Half an hour later, Duncan set off on the long drive back home to Kirkcaldy. He knew from previous experience it would likely be anywhere between six to eight hours.

In Edinburgh Campbell and Charlotte were making plans for later in the evening. They decided to have a meal in the city centre, and stay at the festival until quite late before going back to Kirkcaldy. Charlotte suggested that Campbell could stay the night at her house as he could sleep in her brother's bedroom. He could then drive home to Carnoustie the next morning. She was looking forward to telling her mother about the engagement, just to see the look of shock on her face. Campbell told her that she ought to be a little more sympathetic with her troubled mother.

It had been yet another torturous day for Elizabeth, and she was sitting at her dining room table with a half-empty bottle of gin, gazing at three old photograph albums through tear-sodden eyes. She was holding a photograph of Sylvia and herself from when they were young students at St Andrews. They both had long black hair and were wearing matching miniskirts, and she remembered those blissful days as among the happiest of her life. Now, she thought bitterly, my family have all left me, Sylvia has left me, there's nothing left to live for. She would take her own life. Perhaps if there was such a thing as an afterlife, she might even meet Sylvia again. She had a full packet of painkillers and the bottle of tranquillisers that she had been prescribed at the doctors. She still had half a bottle of gin to wash them down, but first she would write farewell letters to her husband and her children.

Her hands were trembling as she took the writing pad and three envelopes out of the sideboard. When she started to write the first letter, her tears were saturating the writing paper causing the print to be unreadable, so she screwed up the page and threw it on the floor. She hadn't bothered eating all day as she thought "what's the point" and subsequently she was feeling very feeble as she dried her eyes with tissues. She looked up at the clock on the living room wall to see it was 9.17 pm and steeled herself to start again, and this time to get on with it.

Four minutes earlier, Duncan had been driving just over four hours and had completed 220 miles. He was filling the car with petrol at a service station in Jedburgh, but he still had another 80 miles to go, and he was glad of the short break if only to stretch his legs. After the stop, he set off optimistically hoping to be in Kirkcaldy by 10.45 pm.

Alexander was laying on his bed at 9.32 pm unable to sleep at such an early hour. He could not understand or come to terms with why he never acquired Mandy's telephone number. The fact that she was actually searching for him without success made their parting all the more unbearable and he cursed the chain of events that brought him to this prison. He repeatedly thought, " if only."

From untapped sources of energy, Elizabeth scraped together a modicum of inspiration and started the first letter again to her

284

husband. It wasn't easy as she both loved him and loathed him at the same time. She started the letter by saying how much she loved him and stating she would never have cheated on him and she would have followed him to the ends of the earth. She thanked him for the twenty plus years they had been happy together and for the joy of their two wonderful children that had made her life complete. She continued by berating him for ruining everything. It was *he* that had wrecked their marriage; *he* had left home to work away and found a younger woman. It was *his* fault that Alexander had "gone off the rails." He should have known that his son needed a fatherly figure to guide him through his troubled period of losing his football career, his swimming career and the woman whom he loved passionately. Alexander needed him, and he was never there. It was also Duncan's fault she lost her job, she explained, as when she found out he was with another woman she became very upset and was crying at work causing her boss to console her and get too friendly with her. This led to an over-familiarity that caused her boss to think he could exploit his friendliness with sexual favours. That was the root cause of her losing her job after she hit him when he molested her. This then led to her being suspended from the golf club after a vendetta with her employer's wife, which was down to him, and this led to her depression and heavy drinking and then her shoplifting, which all traced back to him leaving her for another woman. She also blamed him for Sylvia's death, but she couldn't explain exactly why he was to blame. When she finished writing the letter, she put it an envelope and simply wrote Duncan on the front. When she sealed the letter, she inadvertently put three kisses on the seal which had always been her habit. She looked up at the clock and it was 10.26 pm and similarly Duncan was approaching the Forth Road Bridge and he had a quick glance at his watch to see the time.

" I'll be back in twenty-five minutes," he thought.

Charlotte and Campbell were about to leave Edinburgh after a day that Charlotte thought was the happiest day of her life. At the start of the day, she had thought that she was in love with Campbell, but now she knew for certain that she loved him, more than any words could say. As they set off to drive back to Kirkcaldy, she was gazing at him adoringly, hoping that today would last forever.

Elizabeth started to write the last two letters for Alexander and Charlotte. She began by saying how wonderful they both were and how proud she was of them and that she was sure they would have no problems being successful in the future. She loved them both dearly, but her life was now a constant battle of misery, loneliness, debt and depression and she was sorry to leave them to face their future without her. She hoped, for their benefit, that their father would show a great deal more interest in them, as he had done recently with her, because she knew he loved them dearly. It was 10.53 pm and Duncan was on the outskirts of Kirkcaldy as Elizabeth opened the packet of painkillers and swallowed the first tablet.

Alexander and the rest of the inmates on the wing were all struggling to get to sleep owing to a prisoner screaming and shouting at the top of his voice. Alexander's cellmate explained that he was probably being raped, which sent a shiver down the teenager's spine. He wouldn't sleep easily tonight. It was 10.56 pm.

When Duncan arrived in Kirkcaldy, he was approaching the old disused railway bridge that had caused him so much heartache two years earlier when it was daubed with graffiti slandering his daughter's name. Every time he had passed under the bridge, it was his usual custom to look up and see if the graffiti had been removed. Whether it was acute tiredness, carelessness or a combination of both, Duncan didn't notice the unlit scaffold lorry parked underneath the bridge as he was looking up to see if CHARLOT IS A HARLOT was still visible in large white letters.

His car smashed into the back of the lorry, and the impact caused the lorry driver to drop his cigarette. He got out of the cab and ran to the back of his lorry to see the mangled wreckage of the car embedded in the back and underneath the lorry, with scaffold tubing scattered everywhere over the road.

The noise of the impact alerted nearby residents and all three emergency services were called immediately. The first to arrive was two police officers who were on patrol in the town centre when they got the call, and they were there within three minutes. They rang the Emergency Highways Department as a road closure was necessary and they couldn't believe that the workmen were there immediately with cones and detour signs loaded up ready for immediate action.

"Bloody hell, we were going to close this road off tonight anyway," said one of the workmen.

"Why is that?" asked PC Wiggins.

"They're having this bridge cleaned. We're supposed to set up a diversion from midnight until six tomorrow morning."

"Get on with it now, please," ordered PC Wiggins.

The second policeman, PC Bush, could hear very faint gurgling noises coming from the wreckage of the car. He said to his partner, "There's some poor sod still alive in there. Where's the fire brigade?"

On cue, a fire engine and crew arrived a minute later and immediately set about extricating the crushed car from under the back of the lorry. It was a slow, delicate manoeuvre, and the medics were frustrated that it was taking so long.

At 11.06 pm Elizabeth forced another handful of tablets into her mouth with trembling fingers while looking at her favourite photograph of the family, taken in a professional studio when the children were toddlers. Her vision was blurred by a stream of tears as she slowly swallowed the tablets with a mouthful of gin.

Campbell and Charlotte were sitting in a queue of stationary traffic on the approach to the town centre, wondering what the cause of the severe delay was. Campbell noticed a workman in a Hi-Viz vest walking alongside all the vehicles speaking to the drivers. When he reached Campbell's Mini, he told them that the road was closed, and a detour would shortly be in place, but if they knew an alternative route, they should turn the car round and make their own detour. Charlotte told Campbell that if they doubled back and then headed towards the north end of the town, they could then come down the Esplanade eventually leading to Charlotte's home.

At 11.13pm the wreckage of Duncan's car was clear of the back of the lorry. The firemen quickly removed the crushed roof, and It seemed almost impossible that anyone could survive such an accident. Duncan had suffered many catastrophic trauma injuries and he was taken to hospital immediately for emergency treatment by the critical care team.

PC Bush said to his partner, "One thing's for sure, the lorry driver is in for the high jump. Scaffold poles sticking out of the back of the lorry with no lights or warning signs. Health and Safety will have a field day. It looks like being another bloody long night."

Elizabeth was almost halfway through the packet of painkillers as Campbell and Charlotte were passing Ravenscraig Castle and about to enter the Esplanade.

Charlotte said to Campbell, "There's a chip shop here by the quay. Do you mind if we stop and get a bag? I really fancy a chip sandwich with brown sauce when I get in. I can get a bag for mum; she's always been partial to a bag of chips."

Campbell pulled up outside the chip shop and looked at his watch. It was 11.29 pm. Charlotte ran into the chip shop and two minutes later came out with just one small bag of chips. She said, "They only had a few chips left. The man said they should have closed earlier so he gave me these last few chips for nothing. Shall we sit and eat them on that bench over there? There isn't enough to take them home and share them between us with my mum."

Charlotte and Campbell sat eating their bag of chips, enjoying the warm summer evening, talking, and making plans for their next date and their future together.

Charlotte said, "I'm so happy. Whatever happens in the future, I don't think I will ever feel happier than I feel right now. I love you so much, Campbell. I could sit here forever enjoying this moment. Let's stay for a while, there's no rush anyway."

At 11.53 pm the hospital critical care team leader Doctor Clough announced to his team that there was nothing else they could possibly do. After thirty minutes of frantic work by the team, Duncan's appalling injuries were too severe and he was officially pronounced dead at 11.54 pm.

It was almost midnight, and Elizabeth had taken nearly the whole packet of painkillers. She was already having severe convulsions and her heartbeat was becoming very irregular. Her vision had deteriorated and had become blurred as her vital organs were beginning to fail. She looked down at the last four tablets on the table, each one representative of the four family members who were on her favourite photograph, the family that had been a happy, stable unit only two years earlier before Duncan left home to work in England. With her last vestiges of reserve, Elizabeth swallowed the four tablets one by one as the convulsions increased. Her heart was beginning to falter as the darkness descended and her vision disappeared. A new day had already dawned as Elizabeth took her final breath. She slowly slumped forward over the table, still holding the photograph in her hand. She was beyond help... it was too late... there was no going back.

"You're very popular, especially with the girls"   Sam Robertson
"The girls all call you 'Dunk the Hunk'"   Sam Robertson
"You are the best centre forward we ever had"   Stuart Bowyer
"I wish you still played for us now"   Martin Gemmill
"This department runs like clockwork, which is
testimony to you managerial skills"   Olive Mackay
"You're twice the man he ever was"   Venetia

He has it all. Tall, handsome, a beautiful wife, two wonderful children, and a lovely home. He had been a brilliant footballer eleven years earlier but a cruel injury deprived him of a big money move to England. Now in 1985 he has another chance of a big money move to England. Will he accept it? If so, what will be the consequences?

Printed in Great Britain
by Amazon

33647577R00163